Also by Boman Desai

**TRIO: a Novel Biography of t**

A *Kirkus Reviews* BEST BOOK OF 2016!
A riveting dramatization of musical history…. Desai has produced a magisterial work, which is clearly the result of astonishingly thorough research. Although the story revolves tightly around the three main figures, there are also fascinating cameos by such musical luminaries as Richard Wagner, Franz Liszt, and Fréderic Chopin, and he memorably depicts the ego-driven rivalries between them. Each has a unique personality, and the author does a lovely job of dramatizing their quirks.

—*Kirkus Reviews* (starred review)

Boman Desai has dramatized the story of the Schumanns and Brahms in the form of a novel, citing their original correspondence among his sources. He writes so compellingly that it is like discovering the story anew. The great composers of the age make appearances when their lives intersect those of the trio, and I was glad to see that Desai presents them to us, warts and all, with the deepest sympathy and understanding.

Zubin Mehta (Music Director: Los Angeles, Israel, and New York Philharmonic Orchestras)

I finished reading your novel, TRIO, and found it compelling and illuminating. Would that the American (or Canadian) reading public could appreciate such a story as well told. It's a story that Tolstoy might have told in similar terms, and I do hope that it eventually gets the recognition it deserves. It is surely a tour de force.

Vernon A. Howard (Former Co-Director, Philosophy of Education Research Centre, Harvard University)

I loved and admired this book.
> Diana Athill (Author/Editor: *Instead of a Letter, Stet,*
> *Somewhere Towards the End*)

I loved your book. You completely transported me. I read it through at a gallop. The love & feeling you have for the subject comes through—you disappeared & they appeared on the page, in the flesh, & I could *hear* their music. Congratulations!
> Sooni Taraporevala (Screenwriter/Photographer:
> *Salaam Bombay, Mississippi Masala, Parsis, Yeh Bombay*)

In portraying the lives and loves of the Schumanns and Brahms in his novel, TRIO, Boman Desai accomplishes a remarkable feat. Exhaustively researched, charming and readable, I was loath to put the novel down. It is a massive achievement and I recommend TRIO wholeheartedly not only to music lovers but to all those who love to read.
> Bapsi Sidhwa (Author: *The Crow Eaters,*
> *Cracking India, Water*)

Boman Desai approached his sprawling novel, TRIO, a dramatized history of the Schumanns and Brahms, as a biography for people who hate biographies and a novel for people who hate novels. Desai does a wonderful job describing the music. The language of TRIO is so vivid it makes one want to explore the composers' repertoires which get some evocative descriptions. So do the performers themselves: Clara's meticulousness, Liszt's power and bravura, Brahms's perfection at the piano as a cocky young virtuoso and sloppiness as an old man, Mendelssohn's spot-on imitations of Liszt and Chopin. Like the music, the book is meant first and foremost to be enjoyed—and on this account, it does not fail.
> Chris Spec, *Quarter Notes*

**THE MEMORY OF ELEPHANTS: a novel**

A big book with a baroque design. By an interweaving of narrative voices, a brilliant picture is drawn not only of individuals, but of a whole upper-class Indian family.

*Punch*

India comes to life with great vividness and humor. Added to that are rewarding insights into the alien wisdom of exiles. The writing is never dull. The observations are acute; you sense a generosity of spirit in Desai's way of looking at the world and at people.

*Yorkshire Post*

Fantastical though the framework, the book is neither a fantasy nor science fiction, but a vividly realistic presentation of three generations of Parsis. A variety of strikingly life-like characters, drawn with a warm feeling of kinship, yet with much humor, and often with a penetrating satirical observation, give the novel a vibrant sense of reality.

*The Indian Post*

The characterizations are vibrant. The writing has so much drive that, once started, it is almost impossible to leave this book unfinished.

*The Statesman Literary Supplement, India*

**DANCING ABOUT ARCHITECTURE: a Songwriter's Guide to the Lennon-McCartney Catalog**

A close look at the 162 Lennon-McCartney collaborations from "Love Me Do" to "The Long and Winding Road" unearths nuggets yet to be mined from their catalog. Rock music, generally speaking is judged less for its musical value than for its performance, packaging, and delivery—less for the distribution of notes on the page than for their impact on the listener. Matters of taste cannot be questioned (those are personal), but matters of quality not only can be questioned, but must be questioned and objectively asserted. That is the business of music criticism, also the business of *Dancing About Architecture*.

It is widely known that Paul McCartney requested sole credit for just "Yesterday" from Yoko Ono (who holds Lennon's rights to the song). The song had blossomed fullblown one morning after a good night's rest, so complete in its first incarnation that Paul found it necessary to play it for others to assure himself that it was a new song. He had no lyrics and used "Scrambled eggs / Oh, my baby, how I love your legs" to sound out the melody. Yoko denied the request, but for the wrong reason. John's contribution is undeniable (as the book reveals), but Yoko doesn't know what it is, and Sir Paul himself just may be amazed to find this tip of the hat to his longtime, longdead, longlovely friend. Roll over, John Lennon, and tell Paul McCartney the news!

# A GOOGLY IN THE COMPOUND

## (a Novel of the Raj)

### BOMAN DESAI

First published as *Servant, Master, Mistress* in 2005 by IndiaInk, imprint of Roli Books, for distribution only on the Indian subcontinent.

Copyright © 2021 by Boman Desai. All rights reserved.
Library of Congress Control Number: 2021907461
ISBN: 979-8-7162-5662-0 (sc)

All characters and events in this book are fictitious and any resemblance to real characters, living or dead, is coincidental—except for historical characters and events.

Book designed for Amazon KDP by Word-2-Kindle (www.word-2-kindle.com)

for Ronnie

My friends are like the steel in reinforced concrete. They may be invisible, but without them I and my work would be weaker. They know I need solitude for my work, but their continual presence in my hinterland makes everything easier to bear. I have the following to thank for doing so very much without knowing how very much they do—indeed, without giving it a second thought. The Dadabhoys (Porus, Zerin, Grandma, Darius, Dina—& Amir, Cyrus, & Arianna—& Vispi Cooper), the Tata-Colchesters (Shirin, Giles, Farah, & Peter), the Weils (Richard & Zarine), the Limbeck-Siegels (Kevin & Wendy), Robin Blench, the Suerth-Ernsts (Frank & Susanna), the Diller-Ernsts (Lois and Ron), Marilyn Diller, the Coopers (Farobag & Ashees), the Koptaks (Linda & Paul), Tom Gross, Cheryl Dority, the Fachs-Bermans (Val & Sonny), the Kennedietsches (Bill & Jeanne), the Englishes (Jim & Emily), the Franklins (Steve & Suzanne), the Tarapores (Erach & Silloo), the Wisnowski-Profumos (Jim & Ally), the Parrises (Linda & Allen), the Katrak-Karkarias (Kamalrukh & Cyrus), the Ghadialy-Karanjias (Rashna & Rohinton), Hosi Mehta, the Chokseys (Vera & Farhad), the Tatas (Jimmy & Farida), the Godrejes (Pheroza & Jamshyd), Aban Mukherjee, Piloo Tata, the Chibbers (Homi & Maki, Percy & Yasmin, Darius & Ranjana), the Taraporevalas (Kamal

& Kai), the Del Sestos (Xun Mei & Tony), the Zimochs (Hank & Linda), the Lalas (Sharookh & Zenobia), the Mittals (Vijay & Priti), the Mirzas (Parveze, Noshir, & Meher), the Gulyases (Stephen & Norma), Steve Barron (for always coming through), Barry Birnbaum (more than a neighbor, more than a friend), Khorshed Karanjia (for the story of her father who made the perilous journey from wartorn Rangoon to Calcutta in 1942), Soonamai Desai (my grandmother [the model for Dolly] for the story about the shikari), Mom and Dad (of course)—and, as always, Diana Athill, my first editor, without whom …

Googly: in cricket, a ball bowled to catch the batsman off guard; expected to spin in one direction, it takes off in another.

A Governor's daughter shocked the first-class passengers en route from London to Bombay by dancing through most of the ship's fancy-dress ball with a second-class steward she fancied, and cut him dead shortly after leaving his cabin in the morning with the remark: 'In the circle in which I move, sleeping with a woman does not constitute an introduction.'
GEOFFREY MOORHOUSE, *India Britannica*

# A Googly in the Compound

| | |
|---|---|
| DAY OF THE TIGER: 1 ............................................. 1 (September 25, 1945) | |
| Dolly's Story ................................................ 9 Navsari (1913–1915) | |
| DAY OF THE TIGER: 2 ............................................ 87 (September 25, 1945) | |
| Sohrab's Story ............................................ 95 Bombay (1924–1927) | |
| DAY OF THE TIGER: 3 .......................................... 163 (September 25, 1945) | |
| Daisy's Story ............................................. 169 London (1935–1939) | |
| DAY OF THE TIGER: 4 .......................................... 307 (September 25, 1945) | |
| Rustom's Story ........................................... 315 Burma (1940–1942) | |
| DAY OF THE TIGER: 5 .......................................... 381 (September 25, 1945) | |
| Phiroze's Story ........................................... 385 Mesopotamia (1914–1916) | |
| Afterword .............................................. 415 | |
| Glossary ................................................ 419 | |

# HOLIDAY, DALAL, AND SANJANA FAMILY TREES

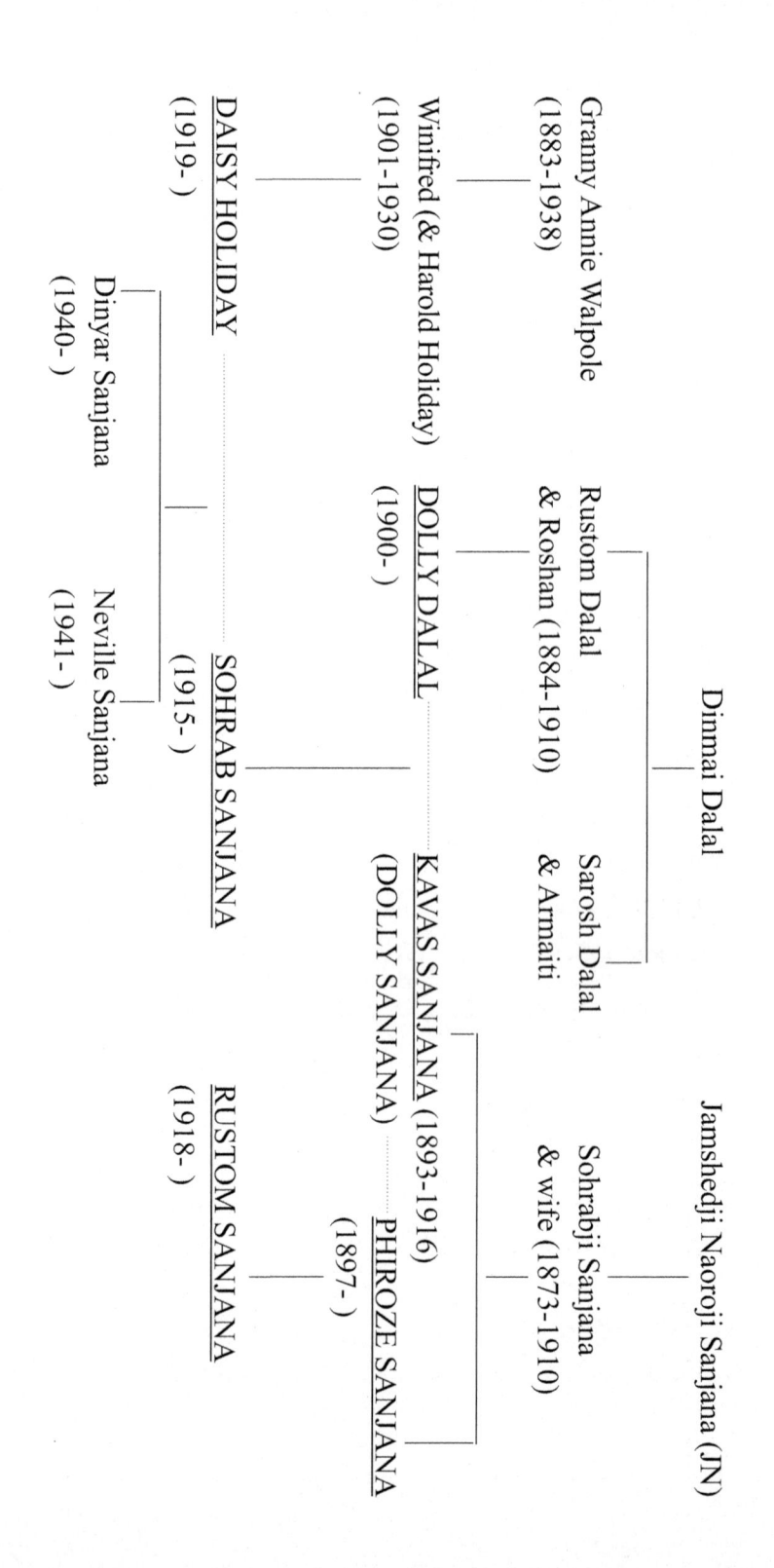

```
Granny Annie Walpole        Dinmai Dalal              Jamshedji Naoroji Sanjana (JN)
(1883-1938)                                            │
 │                                                     │
 │         Rustom Dalal      Sarosh Dalal      Sohrabji Sanjana
 │         & Roshan (1884-1910)  & Armaiti     & wife (1873-1910)
 │          │                    │                   │
Winifred (& Harold Holiday)  DOLLY DALAL      KAVAS SANJANA (1893-1916)
(1901-1930)                  (1900- )         (DOLLY SANJANA) ········ PHIROZE SANJANA
 │                                                                    (1897- )
 │                                                                     │
DAISY HOLIDAY ················ SOHRAB SANJANA                    RUSTOM SANJANA
(1919- )                       (1915- )                          (1918- )
              │
       ┌──────┴──────┐
   Dinyar Sanjana   Neville Sanjana
   (1940- )         (1941- )
```

# DAY OF THE TIGER: 1
## (September 25, 1945)

THE BUNGALOW APPEARED DEPRESSED. It had housed a tragedy for decades and the further the tragedy receded the deeper grew the depression. It was depressed no less for its location beside the high Ashapuri road into the town of Navsari. Low and flat and sprawling, it lay hidden from the road, tucked into a coverlet of foliage (banyan, mango, banana, guava).

Steps embedded in the ground led down the incline to the gate. The gateposts, like giant chesspieces, two castles with crenellated crowns, once whitewashed and clean, were overrun with vines, webs, and bugs. Grillwork arching over the gateposts, no longer bronzed and bright, proclaimed the name of the Sanjana home: TRUTH BUNGALOW. The basin of the fountain ahead was choked with dead leaves. The wand of the pudgy Cupid pointing skyward was dry. The path around the fountain, once crackling with gravel and damp with spray, had vanished under mud, weeds, and twigs.

The height of the road made passers-by seem onstage, but passers-by were few and had been fewer when Dolly Sanjana, then Dolly Dalal, had been just another Navsari girl. The road arrowed through wooded areas harboring among other animals monkeys, wolves, snakes, and pigs. Dolly could hear their chatter, howls, grunts, and screeches by night—and her bed, cozy for its tent of mosquito netting and nest of blankets, became cozier yet for the whistle and chug of steam engines from the railway station on the far side of town.

# A Googly in the Compound

Shortly after she married Kavas Sanjana, Dolly had seen a caravan of camels pass along the high road, goats trotting knee-high to the camels, scoring magical silhouettes against a pink dawn, underscoring how dramatically marriage had changed her life. She had been born and raised in a dark row house in town from which even the dawn looked smoky and grey showcasing silhouettes of squat tenements, clothes on a line, and rows of crows roosting on the roofs.

She had twice become a Sanjana: first, at fourteen, marrying Kavas; and after Kavas's death just three years later, marrying his younger brother, Phiroze. They lived in Bombay, a few hours south of Navsari by train, rarely visiting Truth, but returned every anniversary to solemnize Kavas's death with ritual: organized prayers and sanctified meals to be delivered to relatives and friends. The ritual wasn't meant to continue beyond the first anniversary, but Dolly and Phiroze persevered despite the stories that had mushroomed. Some called it penance, but reaching the twenty-ninth anniversary of the tragedy, penance long paid in full, they continued to observe the ritual.

Kavas's death had marked the beginning of the decline, followed half a dozen years later by the death of his father, Sohrabji Sanjana. Kavas had shown promise as successor to the Sanjana enterprises; Phiroze had shown not even interest, and after losing his right arm in the Great War had seemed to retire from life itself. There was capital enough to sustain generations of nonworking members of the family, but folks liked to speculate that the heart of Sohrabji Sanjana coagulated as he watched the heart of his enterprises shift to cousins and nephews instead of sons, leading to his final thrombosis. The mali had been pensioned, and the compound, once a lacework of manicured hedges and cushions of color, was infiltrated by the roaming fingers of the forest.

A flagstoned verandah spanned the front of the house, harboring an upholstered swing, once pink and plush, now hard and faded, wood showing through the upholstery. The fanlight over the front door portrayed the rising sun in glass red and orange and yellow, an emblem of Zoroastrianism, the religion of the Parsis. Windows were barred to keep out monkeys who stole objects from the bungalow, anything that glinted, anything they could lift, and what they couldn't lift they tipped over. Dolly sometimes strode through the forest shooting to warn them away. The right wing of the house led to an outhouse for servants, the left to a freestanding room with an adjoining bath meant for women during menstruation.

The Sanjanas were modern enough not to put the room to its traditional use, but they had found a use novel even for a modern family, refurbishing it with a hutch, blankets, and toys for Victoria, a tiger cub. The compound walls would have kept her from straying, but she had shown no inclination to stray. Curiosity pulled her into the forest under the watchful eye of Fakhro, the caretaker, but hunger and thirst pulled her as reliably back. She darted after anything that moved, but nothing held her attention long. Fakhro saw in her more than a charge, more than a pet, a child—more precious than his own because his wife Laxmi had borne him no sons, but three daughters: Radha, Rekha, and Rupma. Fakhro lived with his family in a single room in the left wing of the bungalow.

Arriving the night before, the Sanjanas had peeked through Victoria's barred window, but she had been asleep, it had been dark, and they had let her alone, all agreeing with Daisy that she appeared too snug in a hutch she had long outgrown. Daisy was Dolly's English daughter-in-law, married to her older son, Sohrab. When Sandy Corbett, a family friend, had bagged Victoria's mother (eight and a half feet from tip to tail) on a shoot with the Maharajah of Bharatpur, he had returned with three cubs, all promised to a zoo—until Sohrab had requested one for Dinyar and Neville, their sons. Sandy had given them the cub, but Victoria's final destination had never been in doubt: Victoria Gardens (the Bombay zoo), cub and zoo named for the dead queen who had styled herself Empress of India.

The compound in the back, once as much a garden as the front, was now wild with grass. The Sanjanas breakfasted in a circle on wicker furniture in their usual configuration: Dolly to the right of Phiroze (a stronger right arm than the one he had lost); Rustom, her second son, to her right; Daisy to his right; and Sohrab closing the circle. In previous years they had brought Dinyar and Neville, but they were now five and four, without friends in Navsari, and insisted on staying with Jamshed and Jehangir Shroff, their best friends in Bombay.

They had enjoyed Victoria in the dawn of her cubhood in Bombay, but once she had grown too large for the room she shared with Patty and Nancy (the ayahs), not to mention too gamy for the flat, they had brought her to Navsari. Phiroze had wanted to send her to the zoo even then, but some expert had objected: the cub smelled too much of humans to be trusted by other cats who might attack her, and so they had brought her to Navsari to roam the forest, regain a more natural smell, grow a little larger. The plan had always been to enjoy the cub and surrender the adult to the zoo—but, as Dolly liked to say, no plan had been made for the adolescent.

Kavas's tragedy bonded the family every year, but looking at her sons Dolly still felt a weakness in her bones, like the change of weather on a fracture long healed, teeth gnawing at the crack, tongue flicking at the marrow. They were halfbrothers, their fathers had been brothers, and Dolly wondered at the role she had played in fusing the genes of the brothers in the halfbrothers. Sohrab was fair as an Englishman and Rustom dark as an Indian—like their fathers (Kavas fair with green eyes, Phiroze dark with black). Rustom was younger, but bigger, brawnier, and had regained the fifty pounds he had lost in the three years since his return from the war. Sohrab had suffered at Rustom's hands through boyhood even as the older brother. Dolly remained vigilant, after almost thirty years, for the bad gene which had destroyed Kavas, and sat up straighter as her younger son challenged her older. "Sorry, Sohrab, but I have to disagree. Of course, the Americans would have dropped another bomb. Otherwise, what would have been the point of dropping the first two?"

Sohrab grimaced, exasperated to have to explain himself. "Don't be an idiot, Rustom! I'm *not* disagreeing with you. I'm just saying it's not in for a penny, in for a pound. I mean—Hiroshima, Nagasaki, how many hundreds of thousands dead already, women and children—and then what? on top of that another bomb? as if it were a Sunday picnic? Hell, Rustom, you of all people should know better."

He referred to the Burma campaign which Rustom had survived with a fractured finger and a bullet in his brain. For months after his return, shellshocked, he had kept to himself, interested only in news about the war, particularly in Burma, collecting and reading and filing articles and pictures and books, stepping gradually into his former life at the gymkhana, attending concerts and movies and plays, fostering the illusion that he had needed nothing more than time to return to his previous life, but more than anything Dolly was pleased that he planned to study medicine at the University of Edinburgh once the world had regained its feet. Sohrab had insisted the Americans would not have bombed Tokyo, but Rustom spoke quietly, wishing no more discord with his brother than did his mother. "I do know better. That's why I say they would have dropped the bomb. It's not a question of a Sunday picnic. It's just common sense."

Sohrab's sigh seemed to rise from the depth of a well as he shook his head, salting and peppering his acouri. "I swear, Rustom, you never listen. Of *course*, it's common sense. Of *course*, they would have dropped the bomb—foregone conclusion. That's *just* what I'm saying. If the buggers refused to surrender, of *course* they would have dropped the bloody bomb, but it's not something they would have undertaken lightly, not after they had dropped two bombs already."

Rustom shrugged, peppering his own acouri, familiar with Sohrab's debating style. He snatched victory from defeat by reversing himself, fooling only himself, talking to impress himself and impressing only himself—and changing the subject, as he did now, if a new subject suited him better.

"The madness is over, but not for us Indians. We are still mad. Once more we have helped our enemy win the war. Once more we are so bloody hungry for our bloody swaraj we believe everything they bloody well tell us, even after decades of broken promises—and they know it. How else do you think a handful of Englishmen have kept millions of stupid bloody Indians under their thumb for so long? They tell us what we want to hear and do bloody well just what they want. We are Indians, and what do promises matter when they are made to Indians?"

Dolly bustled in her seat as she buttered toast for Phiroze. "Come, now, Sohrab. No need to be so cynical. We don't exactly live hand-to-mouth, you know."

Sohrab frowned. "Mummy, no need to patronize me. If we are stupid enough to fight their battles we have only ourselves to blame. I mean, just look at good old daddy. What more evidence do you need?"

Phiroze, veteran of the Great War, had lost his right arm in Mesopotamia. Dolly flinched at the implication that Phiroze was stupid. Phiroze knew better than to heed Sohrab's careless talk, but not she. He had been the best father to Sohrab, technically his nephew and stepson, but Sohrab clung to this difference between him and his brother—halfcousin and halfbrother, as he liked to emphasize—imagining he elevated himself in the process. Without looking at her son she cut the buttered slices of toast into three strips and placed the plate next to Phiroze's tea. "Sohrab! Apologize at once!"

"Whatever for?"

"You bloody well know whatever for!"

Dolly rarely spoke strongly anymore except in Phiroze's defense. Phiroze never spoke in his own defense—but spoke instead, softly as always, and as she might have expected, in Sohrab's defense. "It's all right, darling. I'm sure Sohrab meant nothing.by it."

Dolly said nothing, but Daisy smiled, smashing bacon into her acouri. "Of course not. Of course, he didn't. He never means anything—and he never stops his needling."

Sohrab turned to Phiroze, adopting the humble tone of a babu and saluting. "Arrererere! Sorrysorry, so sorry, Daddyji! Please forgive. Please forgive."

Dolly said nothing and neither did Daisy though she turned her head from Sohrab.

Sohrab ignored her, returning his attention to Rustom. "To get back to what I was saying: We Indians are so bloody stupid we even pay the bloody English to let us fight for them. We are the biggest bloody volunteer army in the world, two and a half million strong—and what do we do? We fight for the bloody English after they have looted us blind. Such a forgiving lot we are. Bharatmata ki jai! Three cheers! Hip hip hooray! God save the King and all the rest of it."

Sohrab's apparent anglophobia was at odds with his appearance. He looked the perfect Englishman of the 1920s when he had studied in London, cleanshaven, black hair parted down the middle, smooth, shiny, and flat as a cap. He was dressed, like his halfbrother and stepfather, in a white shirt and baggy grey pants. His only concession to Indianness was sandals. His face remained expressionless; his irony was met by silence. He tore his toast into bits over his acouri, mixed the egg and toast with his fork, and heaped his first mouthful.

Daisy shook her head. "What rubbish! You can hardly say that about Gandhi. You can hardly say that about the Nehrus."

Sohrab's lip curled. "The father, the son, and the holy ghost—but the father is dead, and if we are lucky the son and the holy ghost will soon follow."

He spoke as the British sometimes did of the Nehrus (the elder and the younger) and of Gandhi. Daisy grinned. "Spoken like a true Englishman, Sohrab."

Dolly liked Daisy for speaking her mind to Sohrab, almost the only one among them who dared. She never knew what Rustom thought and Phiroze preferred not to challenge his dead brother's son, milking instead the empty sleeve of his shirt like an udder in an effort it seemed to grow back his arm. She herself had grown rigid, a spine of steel, too long the only member of the family to challenge him, but since Daisy's arrival she had happily surrendered the chore. They knew one another well enough not to have to talk much to communicate, but what little needed to be said she would never say—she *could* never say, and neither could Phiroze, though neither could forget what Kavas had done—oh, so very many years ago. Silence was best; there was no telling what they would reveal if they started to talk.

Sohrab shook his head. "I tell you they are fools, without exception they are all fools, the whole jingbang lot of them. Gandhi is an old fool, Nehru is a young fool, and the rest of the bloody Congresswallahs fill up all the spaces in between—all of them bloody fools."

Daisy laughed. "Say what you wish, but there's no fool like a fool who will not see."

Dolly grinned, encouraging Daisy, seeing in Sohrab's frown her own victory. In appearance the two women differed clearly: one had salmon skin, the other sallow; one chestnut hair, the other black streaked with grey; one green eyes dominating the freckled bump of a nose, the other a commanding nose dominating large black eyes; one wore a blue pleated skirt and white sleeveless blouse, the other black slacks and a white shortsleeved blouse; one was small for an Englishwoman, the other big for a Parsi, making them the same size. In temperament they were alike: Dolly rarely confronted her son, but often seconded Daisy when she did. "Sohrab's got it all wrong as usual. He should be the one defending Gandhi, not Daisy."

Sohrab grimaced as if she didn't rate a reply and she wished she'd said nothing, left the teasing to Daisy. She was forty-five, almost twice Daisy's age, hardly old, but the older she grew the more she grew superstitious. She feared another death, progeny of the first, seed of the bad seed, transmitted through her from husbands to sons. She wished they hadn't named their sons Sohrab and Rustom: the Rustom of legend had killed his son, Sohrab, but they had wanted to be traditional, naming their first son after his paternal grandfather, their second after his maternal; and they had wanted to be modern, free of superstition; and they had kept the names despite the legend to prove they were free of the past as much as of superstition, but she realized she would never be free of either.

# DOLLY'S STORY
## NAVSARI (1913-1915)

IMAGINE THE HISTORY OF THE WORLD in hundreds of thousands of millions of rows of dominoes, lined in hundreds of thousands of millions of directions, some parallel, some crossing, some crashing to a close, all dependent, one on the other, as they topple forward, clack-clack-clack-clack, through space and time. The moving finger records births, lives, and deaths galore in the register, repeating stories through centuries, through millennia, but never exactly, and so it was with Dolly Dalal. She met two brothers both of whom vied for her hand, she birthed two sons both of whom vied for the same woman.

Dolly met Phiroze Sanjana on the day she saw her first Englishman. Thirteen years old, attending the annual Navsari tournament with Jhangu Mama, she wasn't disappointed. Her mother had said they were tall and strong and courageous, inhabitants of a cold tiny foggy island venturing far from home, circling the globe on ships once barely seaworthy, conquering the world. Once, they had ruled even America. They were a pale people, paler than Parsis, their numbers tiny, but they were everywhere in spirit, dotting the earth like pale pink ghosts. Edward Allgood attracted more attention at the tournament than the gymnasts and wrestlers, and Dolly saw his face in the sunrise for days after: it was the same color, now milky, now rosy, his hair a nimbus of gold flakes. Named Edward after the last king, son of Victoria, and surnamed Allgood, she imagined he could be nothing but the best of men.

## A Googly in the Compound

Dolly had left Jhangu Mama holding their seats to see Jor Singh, the premier wrestler of the evening, sitting on a bench amid a coterie of admirers, barefoot, leaning forward, elbows on knees, a brown egg of a man, biceps like coconuts, an embroidered shawl resting on his shoulders, a thick belt circling his waist. He wasn't the biggest of the wrestlers, but the quickest, energy stored like a coiled spring in a hard dense body. Dolly had been staring at his bald head when Edward Allgood strolled into view, taller than everyone else by a head.

He was visiting Navsari, the guest of Sohrabji Sanjana, who was also visiting Navsari to see his father, Jamshedji Naoroji Sanjana, the JN of magazines and newspapers, now retired from the business. Edward Allgood wore a pale three-piece suit, a tie of yellow and white stripes, and a sola topi. It was too hot for a suit, but Dolly marveled that he cared about his appearance regardless of comfort. He removed his topi, showing thin blond hair combed straight back, parted in the middle. He wiped his brow with a large white handkerchief, fanned himself with the topi, and put it back on his head. His face was more red than white, but the colors seemed to change with the light, with each turn of his head. The blond handlebar moustache was so pale it was barely perceptible until it glinted in the sun. Most startling were his eyes, blue as a peacock, the first blue eyes she had seen.

Sohrabji Sanjana also wore a suit, tie, and topi, but seemed merely a lesser Mr. Allgood—Mr. Almost Good. She grinned as the joke suggested itself. If not for Mr. Allgood, she knew Sohrabji Sanjana would have worn a bush shirt and baggy trousers like everyone else—but now he smiled, his hand at Mr. Allgood's elbow, ushering him through the crowd toward their seats in the school compound, waving to acquaintances near and far, all too aware of the height to which Mr. Allgood's proximity raised him. The old man, JN, his father, dressed with no less affectation than his son, was no more impressive despite his brown balding head and trowel beard flapping in the wind.

An entourage surrounded them, bobbing like a merry-go-round, including the boys, Kavas and Phiroze, twenty and sixteen. The boys lived with their father in Bombay, visiting their grandfather yearly in Navsari. Kavas was back from studies at London's Inner Temple, soon to return, but it was no secret that Phiroze showed no interest in the family businesses, not even in going to England.

Watching the brothers, Dolly imagined she could guess their ambitions from their appearances. Kavas walked to display himself, slim and straight, blind to everyone and everything; Phiroze slouched and shuffled, looking everywhere except where he was going. Kavas's hair was oiled, sleek, straight, combed back, parted in the middle in the English fashion; Phiroze's thick, curly, uncombed, uncombable. Kavas sported a pencil moustache; Phiroze a hairless upper lip. Kavas had green eyes, Phiroze black. Kavas frowned; Phiroze smiled. Kavas might have passed for Mr. Allgood's darker cousin; Phiroze for any Parsi boy on the street.

Jor Singh smiled as if Mr. Allgood were the celebrity. "Welcome, Misterji!" Mr. Allgood's nod of acknowledgment was barely perceptible, his stare disinterested, as if Jor Singh provided no more than a backdrop for himself—as did his admirers, including Dolly.

Dolly stared intently into the blue eyes, frowning as they gazed as easily through her as through air—but if Mr. Allgood missed her frown Phiroze Sanjana did not. He said nothing, but his eyebrows rose an inch. Dolly turned abruptly to Jor Singh. "Arre, Jor Singhji, give us an autograph, no?"

Jor Singh had also begun to frown, but smiled turning his attention to Dolly. "Show your book, no? Where is your book? Where is your pencil?"

They spoke Gujarati, a language Mr. Allgood wouldn't understand, but she would stand out in his memory. "Arre, Jor Singhji. I do not have my book with me—but you can sign this, no?" She plucked a newspaper from a chair, ripped off a corner, and held the curling triangular wedge of paper in his face.

Jor Singh frowned again, pushing her hand aside. "What are you thinking? I am some ghati that I am going to sign any filthy piece of paper you are picking up?"

A Googly in the Compound

Dolly felt the eyes of the party swarm over her, including Mr. Allgood's. Someone chuckled and she held the paper again in Jor Singh's face. "Arre, Jor Singhji, you think I would want you to sign if you were a ghati? The paper is not filthy. Look, no? It is clean. It is a newspaper. It is the *Jam-e-Jamshed*. Sign, no, please?"

Jor Singh's frown deepened as he pushed her hand aside again. "What kind of young people we are having nowadays? No manners they are having, no respect."

"Arre, Jor Singhji, I said Please, no? I said Ji, no? What more manners you want?"

Jor Singh turned his head. "Come back tomorrow. Bring your book. Then I will sign. Otherwise, no. Now go."

Someone held a pad and pencil by Dolly's side. It was Phiroze Sanjana, grinning. "Take, take. Get his autograph."

"Thank you." Dolly smiled for Phiroze, wishing he might have been his brother, and held the pad and pencil in Jor Singh's face. "Jor Singhji, look, no? I have got a pad and a pencil!"

Jor Singh wouldn't look at her. "Too late. I know how it is now. Come back tomorrow—with your own book."

"Arre, Jor Singhji, what you are saying? Please, no? Sign, no? This is a pad, no?"

"Bring your own book. Come back tomorrow."

"Arre, Jor Singhji! You think I have got nothing better to do or what? You think I am only interested in seeing wrestling everyday or what?"

"Who is asking you to come? Who do you think you are? If you want the autograph, bring your book. Otherwise, stay home. What do I care? I am Jor Singh!"

Dolly smiled. Mr. Allgood and his hosts had moved on, but she had made her point. "Attchha, Jor Singhji. I will come tomorrow. Thank you very much, Jor Singhji. Thank you very much."

Dolly found the Sanjana party easily and approached Phiroze in his seat to return the pad and pencil. "Thank you so much. Very considerate of you."

## DOLLY'S STORY

Mr. Allgood paid no attention, focusing on the performers entering the clearing before them, but Phiroze couldn't stop grinning. "Arre, my pleasure—but you did not have to bring it back. We have got many pads and pencils."

"But I had to bring it back, no? Take it, no, now that I have taken the trouble?"

"All right, but it was my pleasure. It was too funny, I tell you, when you were holding the piece of paper in his face—a little chit of a girl like you and the big bad wrestler, like David and Goliath. You gave us all a good laugh, I can tell you."

In the clearing the gymnasts, sporting tunics and ribbons of red, blue, yellow, and green, sprang into a pyramid, shot upward like a beanstalk, and twanged into a bouquet of giant flowers.

Someone shouted from behind: "Sit down, no! We cannot see!"

"We have not paid for these seats so we have to stand up!"

Dolly had nothing to say, but was enjoying herself too hugely to walk away.

"ARRE, SIT DOWN, NO!"

"IT IS YOUR FATHER'S COMPOUND OR WHAT!"

A voice like a hiss slithered toward them from the same row. *"Phiroze! Either shut up or get out! Remember who you are. What kind of example is this to set?"*

Though he had addressed Phiroze, Kavas stared at Dolly, eyes narrowing to green slits, mesmerizing her with his attention. He seemed more handsome, more English, in that moment than she had thought possible for a Parsi. Even the lip twisted in scorn seemed just right. No man had enveloped her before in so tight a focus, but he seemed in that moment to hate her. Her temples throbbed, the color of her face deepened, but she remained frozen in the prison of his gaze until released by Phiroze who rose from his seat, no less reluctant to conclude the conversation. "Let us get out of the way."

*"Don't be bloody stupid, Phiroze! The show has begun! Just shut up and sit down!"*

## A Googly in the Compound

Phiroze excused himself, nodding to his brother, pushing Dolly ahead of him out of the row.

Kavas muttered under his breath. "Stupid bloody fool!"

Dolly whispered, frowning. "What he is eating? Chillies? Why he is getting so mad?"

Phiroze chuckled. "Nono, he is just an excitable chap. That is all."

"Arre, if he is so excited about something like this, how will he get when there is really something to be excited about?"

Phiroze chuckled again, but said nothing.

"Sorry if I got you in trouble. I only wanted to return the pencil and pad."

"Don't worry. Take my word for it. He is always like that."

"Always eating chillies?"

He grinned. "Yes, always eating chillies. What is your name?"

"Dolly Dalal."

"I am Phiroze Sanjana."

"I know."

"How do you know?"

"Arre, why you are surprised? Everybody in Navsari is knowing."

Phiroze nodded. "All right, listen. Kavas is leaving for London next week. He is studying Law. We are having a party for him on Saturday. Many people are coming. Come if you can."

Dolly chucked her head toward the crowd. "He will not mind, your chillies-eating brother?"

Phiroze grinned. "Who cares? *I* want you to come. That is enough."

She grinned back. "Where?"

"At our place—Truth Bungalow—on the Ashapuri Road. We have ordered a private bus to pick up everybody from the Tata High School at four o'clock. We have ordered it especially for those who cannot otherwise come. You can bring your mamma and pappa if you like."

Dolly lost her grin. "I do not have."

"What? No mamma and no pappa also?"

"No."

"I am so sorry. You know, I do not have a mamma either."

His mother had been dead for six years of a heart attack. "I know."

He smiled. "Everybody in Navsari is knowing?"

She nodded, grinning again. "I live with my Jhangu Mama. He lets me do what I want, but he does not like parties."

"But you will come?"

Dolly still grinned. "Maybe."

Phiroze also grinned. "Just maybe?"

Dolly giggled. "Just maybe is a lot."

That evening she clapped more loudly for Jor Singh than for anyone else, but her mind was no longer on the tournament, too happy with her adventure and Jhangu Mama's amazement that she had been invited to a party at Truth Bungalow by Phiroze Sanjana himself.

THE ECONOMY OF NAVSARI was driven by farmers, weavers, carpenters, fruit growers, toddy planters, also by a diamond cutting, polishing, and processing plant. The population, primarily Gujarati, had been a stronghold of Parsis since the 12th century, and they managed their wadis and mohollahs like townlets within the town. The Mughals had rewarded the Parsis for their service with large tracts of land, making them collectors in a largely agricultural district, accounting for their hegemony. The houses in Navsari, fronted by verandahs, stood shoulder to shoulder like ramparts, two storeys tall, flats burrowing deep into the bellies of lightless buildings. Town squares had been designed to be blocked, one from the other, by doors wide as barns, making fortresses of the mohollahs, and battlefields of roofs and terraces for feuding families, but feuds had long been part of the past.

Accustomed as she was to traveling distances in bullock carts, Dolly enjoyed immensely the bus ride to Truth Bungalow with about thirty other guests, but she kept to herself, the sole solo traveler. They were met by a servant on the Ashapuri Road, led down the incline, along the gravel path past the Cupid fountain, up the verandah steps stamped for the event with auspicious patterns in chalk of stars and

## A Googly in the Compound

fish, and through the sitting-room to the compound in the back. Eyes widened and jaws dropped at the size of the house, tables with marble tops, porcelain figurines behind glass, a German cuckoo clock, the thickness of carpets, splendor of chandeliers, profusion of photographs, abundance of electric light.

The compound had been laid with a large red carpet, and banana leaves on the carpet laden with samosas, sweets, and iced water in metal tumblers. Edward Allgood and the Sanjanas were seated in wicker chairs at a table with friends engaged in conversation. Sohrabji Sanjana rose to welcome them, inviting them to seat themselves at the meals on the carpet, after which there would be ice cream and games and prizes. Phiroze smiled at Dolly and she smiled back waiting for him to say something, glad no longer to be alone, but Kavas spoke first nudging his brother. "Look, Swolter. Your Ilsabeth is here."

He sported a red tila on his forehead, rice grains plastered to the tila, coconut for luck on the table, garland of marigolds around his neck. Some in the party chuckled, but Dolly didn't understand. Old JN looked the other way, lifting his trowel beard in the air. Kavas's gaze made her flush as it had the week before, as if she had made an exhibition of herself with her best dress, newly polished black buckled shoes, red and blue ribbons in her pigtail. Phiroze continued smiling, ignoring his brother. "Hullo, Dolly."

"Hullo."

She wondered if they expected her to join the company or the other guests on the carpet. She wished Phiroze would give some indication, but again Kavas spoke first, twisting his lip. "Go, eat first, Ilsabeth. Swolter will still be here when you are finished. Then you can talk."

There were chuckles again from the company. He might have been dismissing a servant. She said nothing, glaring at him, sitting at one of the banana leaf settings on the carpet, her back to her hosts, listening to their conversation, tasting nothing she ate. One of the bor trees was shaken and guests invited to pick the dislodged fruit, but she held back. She took part in a game of musical chairs, but gave up a chair she might easily have secured. One event followed another, but

Phiroze remained too busy to notice her, too busy even to look at her. Finally, Mr. Allgood asked riddles and Phiroze forwarded two trolleys laden with prizes for the winners: tops, toys, books, ribbons, coconuts, envelopes with sums of money, prizes enough for everyone whether or not they won any of the games.

"What is it that is lost when it is named?"

She marveled again at his three-piece suit; Sohrabji Sanjana also wore a suit, but he had loosened his tie, removed his jacket, appearing again a diminished Englishman, Mr. Almost Good. His father, old JN, sitting aloof from the rest, holding his beard in the air as before, was little better. Blue eyes pierced her momentarily, focusing again at some point behind her, and she shivered. It was a trait she was beginning to associate with the English. They neither looked at you nor talked to you, but blessed you with their presence. They barely opened their mouths when they spoke, but everyone stopped talking to listen, nodding and smiling even when they understood nothing. She envied his ability (a birthright it seemed of the English) of drawing others in by holding himself back.

Phiroze repeated the question in Gujarati for those who did not understand English or could not follow Mr. Allgood's accent. "What is the thing that is lost when the thing is named—meaning: if you say what it is, then it is gone."

Dolly frowned. He had said nothing to her all evening, and when he spoke he only echoed the silence she had felt all evening. She spoke almost to herself. "Silence. The thing is silence."

Mr. Allgood cast a bland look over her head. "Congratulations! The little girl is correct."

"Shabash!" Phiroze clapped, smiling, finally looking at her, but she refused to look at him.

Kavas twisted his lip again. "So clever, our Ilsabeth."

Dolly stared again into the green eyes, bewildered again, blood coagulating in her head, unable to understand why he called her Ilsabeth.

Phiroze pushed forward the prize trolleys. "Take a prize, won't you?"

She turned her head from him. "I do not want a prize."

"But you have won it. You have solved the riddle."

She kept her head turned. "I do not care. I do not want. I only want to go home."

"I say, Phiroze, I rather believe you have made your Ilsabeth angry. What a shame!"

Phiroze ignored his brother. "Dolly, we are having ice cream later, Kolah's ice cream. Stay, no?"

"I do not want ice cream."

"What do you want? Tell me."

"I told you. I want to go home."

"But why? Are you not feeling well? Is something wrong?"

"Nothing is wrong. I only want to go home." She walked toward the house, heavy with the weight of everyone's gaze. Old JN beckoned Phiroze with his finger. "Go after her. See what is wrong."

Phiroze caught up with her in the sitting-room. Two grandfather clocks tolled seven times together, counterpointed by the chirrups of the cuckoo clock. "Dolly, wait. You cannot go home now. It is too far, and we cannot send the bus with only you."

"I will walk. I know the way."

"Don't be silly. It is an hour's walk at least."

"What rubbish you are talking. It is only twenty minutes."

"Dolly, wait. If you want to go I will take you myself on my bicycle. Will you wait?"

She was astonished that he had his own bicycle, but shook her head. "Why you want to trouble yourself? I will be all right. I am not a little girl—like *he* says." She tossed her head in the direction of Mr. Allgood, her ribboned pigtail swinging violently over her shoulder.

Phiroze frowned. "Dolly, don't be silly! Just wait for me while I tell Pappa. I will be right back."

She raised her chin. "Do not tell me I am a silly. I am not a silly."

She stared, no smile on her face, nor in her glance. His large black eyes were anxious. He seemed no less puzzled than she had been all evening. "I'm very sorry if I have upset you. I didn't mean to. Will you wait for me? I've been wanting to talk with you all evening."

"Then why you didn't?"

"I was waiting for the right time."

"How long you were going to wait?"

"Please, I'm sorry. Will you wait?"

She turned her head to one side. "All right."

He turned the switch for the chandelier, leaving the room in sudden brightness. He felt the gaze of the guests burn him as he reentered the compound, but Mr. Allgood distracted them with another riddle as he approached his father. "Pappa, she is not feeling well. I have said I will take her home on my bicycle. I will be back in a jiffy."

Sohrabji Sanjana frowned, but Kavas spoke first. "Why do you have to take her home? Does she think she's a maharani? She didn't seem unwell to me, just jiddi."

Phiroze looked at his brother. "Kavas, granted she is jiddi, but she is also not feeling well." He turned to his father. "She is our guest and it is getting late. We cannot let her walk home by herself."

Kavas's green eyes blazed. "No need for her to go walking. The bus will take her in thirty minutes. She can lie on the sofa if she is not feeling well. Give her some chai if she is not feeling well."

"But she is jiddi, Kavas, just like you said. If she has made up her mind to go, she will go. Nothing we can do to stop her."

Phiroze spoke too mildly to betray irony, but Kavas's eyes narrowed. Sohrabji Sanjana glanced warily at his older son. It had been a while since his last outburst, but he remained prone to fits of rage which evaporated as suddenly as they condensed, leaving him for moments unpredictable—manic, his friend, Dr. Dadabhoy, had said, who had studied psychoanalysis in Vienna, met the great Freud himself, discussed mania and melancholia with Emil Kraepelin (the final authority on the subject since the 1899 publication of *Psychiatrie: in Lehrbuch fur Studirende und Arzte*). "Kavas is right. Tell her she should wait for the bus. She can lie down on the sofa if she wants."

"But Pappa, she will not wait. She did not even want to wait for me to come and tell you. She may be walking home as we talk. It will take me ten minutes to take her and ten minutes to come back. That would be the best thing, I think, the least fuss."

"How the least fuss? Pappa, everyone will see them go. What will they say when they get home?"

"They will say she was not feeling well and I took her home—but what will they say if we let her go by herself? What will they say if something happens?"

"Nothing is going to happen. This is Navsari, not the Belgian Congo."

JN cleared his throat. "It doesn't matter if nothing happens. She can't go by herself. It would be best if Phiroze took her." He looked at Phiroze. "Go before it gets too dark."

It was rare that Phiroze got his way against Kavas. He wanted to laugh, embrace his grandfather, vault over his chair, bound to his bicycle, but concerned for Kawas as they all were he allowed himself barely a smile. "Pappa, I really think that would be the best thing."

Sohrabji Sanjana nodded. "I think, after all, you may be right."

Kavas dismissed Phiroze with a wave of his hand. "Go, go, do what you want. I don't care." He rolled his eyes, focusing again on the party, and Phiroze went to the carriage house for his bicycle.


**BY THE TIME** Phiroze wheeled his bicycle to the front of the house, Dolly had left the sitting-room for the swing in the verandah feeling too visible under the bright chandelier, but with the disappointment of the evening receding she found herself glowing no less brightly. A gecko appeared on the wall from behind a portrait of George V; frogs croaked from the fountain against the sound of spray, splashing as they jumped off lily pads in the basin. She pushed the floor with her feet, raising the swing to its crest, before straightening her legs and lifting them off the floor. She closed her eyes, reveling in her solitude, the dip and lift of the swing, expanse of the verandah, pitter-patter of the fountain, duet of frogs and crickets, gossip of breeze and branches, opening her eyes again almost in disappointment to the crackle of gravel and the ring of Phiroze's bicycle bell as he stopped at the base of the steps. "Come on. Let us go. Are you ready?"

She stopped the swing, stretched her arms, yawning to hide a smile. "I do not know. I am feeling very nice."

Phiroze raised his eyebrows. "You are well? You want to stay?"

"No, I am just feeling very nice all by myself over here. Such a luxury to be alone like this. I am never alone like this. Always there is someone—in the next room, in the wadi, everywhere."

"So, do you want to stay or go?"

Dolly got up. "Let us go."

"Okay. Good. Sit." He held out the bicycle so she could perch on the bar.

She shook her head. "It is such a nice night. I want to walk."

Phiroze frowned, looking at the bicycle. "But it is late. You are a girl. It is too far to walk alone."

Dolly said nothing, but turned her head to hide another smile.

"Also, it will be too dark to see where you are going. My bicycle has a lamp."

"All right. You can walk with me if you like—with the bicycle."

"All right. Let us go."

They walked past the fountain, Phiroze wheeling the bicycle, Dolly walking alongside, up the incline to the Ashapuri Road, neither speaking, neither looking at the other, Dolly finally breaking the silence. "So, what you told them?"

"I told them you were sick and I was taking you home."

"You told them I was sick?"

"What else could I say?"

Dolly turned her head again to hide yet another smile. "Nothing—but you lied for me?"

"Lie is such a strong word. I improvised."

"Improvised? Is not the same as lying?"

"You want me to lie for you?"

"Lying carries more risk, no?"

"You want me to risk for you?"

"No."

"Then why do you care?"

"For no reason." Dolly shrugged. Parentless, she had more freedom than her peers. She could walk alone with a boy into the evening as they could not. Jhangu Mama let her do what she wanted, but most parents were mindful of what people said—the newspaper class, spreading tales about everyone. "What is wrong with Kavas? I do not know half the time what he was saying."

"Arre, Dolly. He is going to England in a few days. I do not think he likes it very much. I think he is lonely. Do not let him bother you."

Dolly frowned. "But what did he mean? Why was he saying Ilsabeth-Ilsabeth all the time?"

"He was having a little joke. That is all."

"What little joke? Ilsabeth who?"

"He was talking about the Queen of England, Elisabeth."

"He was calling me a queen?"

"No, no! He was just having fun. Sir Walter Raleigh put his coat down for her to walk on the puddle, no? And I gave you a pad, no? Kavas was just having fun—also with me! He called me Swolter, no?"

Dolly knew nothing of the Queen and Sir Walter's gallantry, but asked nothing about it. "You think he was funny?"

"No." He grinned. "If you want my honest opinion, I think he is jealous."

"Jealous? Of what?"

"You can see how different we are, no? When he was born he had light brown hair—and, even later, when it turned black, our mamma called it dark brown—insisted, even on his passport."

Dolly knew how it was, some even said it out loud: light was English, dark was Indian; and if the Parsis couldn't be English they liked to think they were at least not Indian. Kavas was darker than Mr. Allgood, but fairer than Phiroze. "His eyes also are green."

"See? You also noticed. Everyone notices. Our mamma used to say they were emerald—but mine are black, like everyone in India."

"So what? Mine are also black!"

Phiroze kept his eyes on the handlebars. "I know—very pretty."

Dolly faced him, her smile triumphant. "What?"

He grinned. "What do you think? They are almost as pretty as mine." He batted his lashes at her.

She laughed, slapping his arm. "Now who is being the silly?" He tried to slap her arm, but she dodged and walked out of his reach. "You are trying to hit me?"

"Only because you hit me."

"A girl is allowed to hit a boy."

"Oh, yes? and a boy is not allowed to defend himself?"

"No! He is not!" She grinned, slapping his arm again. "So tell me, no? Why is Kavas jealous?"

"Arre, who can say? He is the older brother. He got everything he wanted, and I got everything he got after he was finished with it. Our mamma could never say No to him—and Pappa is the same."

"Arre, but if he is always getting everything he wants then why is he still jealous? Jealous of what?"

"Maybe because he is going back to England and I am walking here—with you."

Dolly smiled. "You do not want to go to England?"

"Sometime, yes, to see the country, but not to study. I am sixteen years, lots of time to think about what I want to do, but if I go to England I have to think about what I want to study, and the only thing to study in England is Law, and I do not want to study Law. It is such an unnatural thing!"

"Unnatural? How?"

"It is not about anything real. It is about laws that are made up by men—but I am interested only in the laws of nature, gravity, astronomy—that the moon goes around the earth, planets go around the sun, whole solar system maybe goes around something else. That is what has meaning for me."

Dolly laughed. "Arre, but what is the point of all that? If you study Law you can at least help people in the court—but what can you do with the sun and the moon and all that?"

His face fell. "Why are you laughing? What do you know about it? What does it matter what happens in a law court? More important to know what happens afterward. More important to know what holds us together than what tears us apart. More important to know how we are all the same than how we are different. More important to know who we really are. Law does not tell us that."

His barrage of recriminations made her defensive. "And the sun tells us?"

"The sun tells me more than Law."

She found herself jealous of his interest. "What the sun tells you?"

Phiroze stopped walking, taking a deep breath. "I think I should light the lamp. It is getting dark."

"So light, no?" She watched while he lit the enclosed wick of the lamp mounted on the handlebars. "So tell, no, what the sun tells you?"

He closed the lamp and spoke in a level voice. "Do you know about Tycho Brahe?"

"Who?"

"Tycho Brahe. He was a Danish astronomer in the sixteenth century."

Dolly rolled her eyes. "Arre? How I am going to know about him?"

Phiroze smiled. "On eleven November of 1552 he saw a supernova –"

"What?"

"A supernova, the birth of a star—only it was actually the death, but he thought it was a birth."

"Stars are born—like cats and dogs?"

"Yes. Exactly. Like cats and dogs."

Dolly remained silent, barely comprehending what he said.

"He tracked all the changes in the sky until March of 1554 when all traces of the star disappeared. Think, Dolly, just think! With his naked eye he saw all that—with his naked eye! Telescopes were not invented until 1609, in the next century, but this star was outside the solar system—*outside! And he saw it with his naked eye!* Can you imagine! In those days they had not yet discovered Uranus and

Neptune, but this star was beyond even Neptune—*and he saw it with his naked eye!*"

"How he could see so far? How he could see without telescopes?"

"Because the star was so big—*huge* it was!"

"But if they could not see Uranus and Neptune, how he could see the star?"

"Because it was bigger than Uranus and Neptune, bigger than Jupiter—bigger than all three of them put together!"

"*So* big!"

"Bigger! Think like this. Our whole earth can fit into Jupiter more than thirteen hundred times!"

"Really? *So* big!"

He held up a finger for patience. "Bigger! Much bigger! The supernova was *so* big *the whole orbit of Jupiter would have fit into the star—not just Jupiter, but the whole orbit of Jupiter around the sun!* Imagine if you can how *huge* that is."

"Bigger than the *or*bit of Jupiter!"

"Exactly! Just think! What is the significance of law courts in a universe so big? When the universe is our university what does it matter if you go to England or to America or to the moon?" He laughed. "In a universe so big we are all relatively in the same place. It is only our vanity that says I have been to England and I have been to Europe and all the rest of it."

"Arre, you are talking like a madman! We are in Navsari. We sometimes go to Bombay. Your brother is going to England. Some people are going to America. Others are going to Australia. How are we all in the same place? Maybe your star thinks we are all in the same place—but *we* know we are not in the same place."

Phiroze's eyes lost their shine. "It doesn't matter. You are like everyone else. My pappa, my brother, my bapavaji, all of them are the same—even my mamma was the same. No one understands what I am saying—but after all what does it matter what anyone thinks? What matters is what *is*. Everyone is free to believe what he wants."

His voice became a monotone and she wished she had been less dismissive. "But you are right. What do I know? I am just a little girl—how you said? a little chit of a girl?"

He laughed unexpectedly, looking up. "If it wasn't so cloudy I could have shown you the north star—Polaris. It is about twenty degrees above the horizon."

"That is the star which is guiding all of the ships in the sea, no?"

"Yes, but not all of the ships—only in the northern hemisphere. In the southern hemisphere the earth itself gets in the way."

Dolly smiled, walking closer to him. A sliver of moon was barely visible through the clouds, the stars even less, without the lamp they would have been in blackness. The path narrowed, flanked on both sides by forest, before entering the town. A jackal screamed in the distance, setting the trees chattering around them. Dolly's eyes widened. A monkey scurried across the path before them and she walked closer yet, goosepimples on her arms, the back of her neck damp.

Phiroze smiled. "We are being watched, you know?"

She became aware of the constellations of monkey eyes on either side of them and above, but looking straight ahead she said nothing.

"Are you afraid?"

"I am not such a little girl as to be afraid of monkeys."

"Still, shall we go the rest of the way on the bicycle?"

There was a short stretch ahead through the forest. "You will not drop me?"

"Have no fear."

She smiled. "Then maybe better if we did."

He held the bicycle while she slid onto the bar, clutching the handlebars, gazing ahead as they rode, snug within the circle of his arms, conscious of the warmth of his body, his breath on her ear and neck. He was no less conscious of the smell of soap in her hair, the occasional jump of her pigtail when they negotiated a bump, of his heart thudding from his exertion as much as her proximity. He spoke to distract her from the beating of his heart. "For a little girl you are quite heavy."

"I am not a little girl!"

He laughed.

Each was relieved by the sight of people again, but sorry the evening was drawing to a close, unsure what would happen next between them. When they made the last turn Dolly spoke almost under her breath, so quickly he could barely follow her. "Phiroze, thank you so very much for bringing me home. I had such a very good time. Really!"

Phiroze dismounted carefully, silent because the words in his head and his heart couldn't find their way to his mouth. She had called him by his name for the first time.

His silence spurred a greater flurry of words from her. "The food was also very good—especially the samosas, but everything was very good—really."

Still he remained silent.

"I also want to learn about stars and everything. I think you are so clever that I feel like a little girl when you are talking—but I am *not* a little girl."

In the continuing silence her face seemed to lose its contours, flatten to paper, giving him courage finally for words. "Dolly, it was my pleasure, entirely the pleasure was all mine—but you will simply have to come back."

"For what?"

"You left something behind."

"What?"

"Your prize—for solving the riddle."

She smiled. "You pick a prize for me."

"But what would you like?"

"You pick. I will like anything you pick."

"You will have to come soon to get it. We are leaving in two days."

"When I should come?"

"Maybe better if I came here—on my bicycle, maybe tomorrow, in the evening, about seven o'clock—and we will go for a long ride. Will that be all right?"

The glow returned to her face, her sallow face which otherwise invited no light; her pigtail seemed to hop by itself on her back. "Seven o'clock? Why so late?"

"I was thinking if it got dark and if the sky was clear I could show you Polaris—maybe even the Great Bear."

"Yes, all right. I think that is a good idea—but maybe better if we met outside the town—on the Ashapuri Road, just outside?"

"Yes, that is a good idea."

He rang his bell mounting his bicycle, scattering two goats, grinning all the way home, wind whistling through the hedge of his hair, dismounting shortly before reaching the bungalow, letting air out of his back tire to excuse his late return.

NAVSARI WAS A SMALL ENOUGH TOWN for everyone to know about Dolly's parents, but no one said anything to her about them and she said nothing herself. She had been ten, returning from the home of her grandmother, Dinmai, when her life had poured into a hole. Dinmai had never learned to read and write and dictated letters to Dolly on Saturday afternoons. After sealing the letters, she entertained her granddaughter with sodas and snacks and stories about exploits from her girlhood, of lives saved thanks to hidden trapdoors, false ceilings, and narrow passageways behind walls built into the Navsari buildings during the time of the feuds.

Dolly looked forward to the visits, but not since Dinmai had begun to shout. She was a pingpong ball of a woman, but anger puffed her into a full moon. Her fat round face got fatter and rounder and her head bobbed with her words as if to spring off her shoulders. Her mother said Dinmai was getting old, losing her hearing, but Dinmai had lost more than hearing. Losing hearing, she talked loudly, but losing her younger son, her Rustom, Dolly's father, she shouted at everyone, most loudly in her letters, the same letter to dozens of residents, many of whom she hardly knew. *One photograph it was, because of one photograph they took away my son. What kind of people take away a son from a mother. Swines and rascals, all of them. Bloody swines and bloody rascals.*

Her older son, Sarosh, had done well with the family business, Dalal Textiles, went to Surat and Bombay every month on business, but there had been something wrong with her Rustom from birth. She hated to admit it, particularly since Hindus and Muslims liked to say that generations of inbreeding had debilitated Parsis, cousins marrying cousins through centuries until everyone was almost a sibling. Many resented Parsis because they wielded influence incommensurate with their numbers, maybe a hundred thousand in a country of more than three hundred million—and while many had been knighted, many also, like her Rustom, fueled the myth of Parsi lunacy.

She had worried about finding him a wife—but Roshan Tumboli, widowed at seventeen, had diminished prospects herself. The famous Parsi nose had found its apotheosis on her face, handicapping her further—and Rustom, if nothing else, was a handsome man. Together they had triumphed, but Dinmai still regarded Rustom her failure. It was traditional for the wife to move into the husband's home, but she had sent him to live with the Tumbolis, arguing she had done everything she could, he needed a change, and she needed room for her other son, Sarosh, and his wife, Armaiti, and their children when they came—but Sarosh was away on business much of the time, Armaiti never became pregnant, and her stupid Rustom and his Roshan with her brinjal nose had given her Dolly.

Dinmai said giving up Rustom was the best thing she could have done, but the guilt of his absence had followed the guilt of his presence. If she had let him stay he might have been with them still, but after the neighbors had taken the photograph the proof against him had become irrefutable. They had planned everything, called a crack photographer from Bombay to take the photograph, and waited for their chance to get evidence against a poor harmless innocent ignorant fellow. Not even the Gaekwad of Baroda could refute the authority of a photograph; not even Lord Hardinge, the new Viceroy.

## A Googly in the Compound

Dolly had almost reached their wadi when someone dashed around the corner, hurtling toward her like a cannonball, dropping to the ground just as he might have knocked her down, genuflecting at her feet. "Dollybaby, pleaseforgive, pleasepleasepleaseforgive! Forgive your old Jagat! He did not mean it! On his dead mother's soul, he swears he did not mean it!"

The words poured like a waterfall, drenching her though she heard nothing. Jagat was their chaprasi, and no sooner had he thumped his head on her shoes than her Jhangu Mama erupted around the corner, swinging a cricket bat. "Behnchot! Madarchot! Salo harami! Bloody swine!"

Dolly froze. She had never seen Jhangu Mama in such a purple rage, a mild man, her mother's brother, with whom they lived, a weaver too shy to marry—but now he was a stranger, swearing like a sinner, swinging the bat for momentum even before he reached them, so intent on destruction that he kicked and struck Jagat simultaneously, diluting both kick and strike, minimizing the damage he might otherwise have inflicted.

Jagat curled like a worm on his side, hands outstretched to protect himself, screaming for mercy. "Ayiiee-ayiiee! RamRam, seth! My bone is broken! Arre, seth! You are Himalayas, I am mud, I am shit. Arre, seth, mercy, no, please?"

Dolly broke out of her paralysis, eating the ground with her feet as she scurried home, burst into the bedroom she shared with her mother, wrenched open the cupboard, and pulled out the photograph. It was black and white, six inches by four, a naked man peeing out of a window, the thin dark line of his pee so faint it might have been penciled in, but it was enough. The nakedness was enough. The neighbors had been scandalized and their mercy succumbed to their moralism. She ripped the photograph in halves and quarters and more. It wasn't until the photograph was in shreds that she saw the disarray in the room, the overturned chair, scattered notes and coins, rupees, annas, pice—and her mother on the floor beyond the far side of the bed, a pillow over her face.

The facts were revealed at the trial: the Dalals had planned to visit Bombay the next day; her mother had withdrawn money from the bank for the trip; Jagat had entered the room as she napped, been caught with the money when she woke unexpectedly, and thrust the pillow in her face in a panic to drown her screams—drowning her instead in cotton (as Jhangu Mama was to say later), filling her lungs with cotton.

Dolly's cheeks burned with tears. The bedroom was awash in color and light. She stared at her mother as people flooded the room, converging on her, attempting to shield her from the sight, but she refused to leave her mother's side, and when they forced her she screamed until she lost consciousness.

**WHEN PHIROZE ARRIVED AT THE PREARRANGED SPOT** on his bicycle, Dolly was playing gili-danda on the shoulder of the Ashapuri Road. She placed the wedged stick on the ground, hit the narrow edge of the stick with another stick sending the first spinning into the air, and whacked it hard at its center, sending it twirling in a long arc. He marveled at her agility, unable to hit the stick himself except peripherally, providing no more than a hiccup to its trajectory—marveling also at the difference between her and the girls in Bombay who jumped rope and played with dolls. The Bombay girls were closer in age, fastidious of speech and manner, his social and scholastic peers—the very reason they intimidated him. Some were English, cause enough alone for intimidation. Dolly was less conventional, which might have been greater cause for intimidation, but also three years younger, spoke bad English, village girl to his city boy. Her ignorance was her charm, the welcome mat on which he stood so comfortably. He dismounted as she picked up her stick. "Hullo, Dolly!"

Her smile threatened to slice her face in two, enlarging the mat beneath his feet. "Hullo!"

He waved one hand at the sky as he dismounted. "Nice day."

"Very nice! Where should we go?"

"Just for a walk. What time are you expected back?"

"No time! Anytime! Jhangu Mama and his friends are playing cards. I have got nothing to do."

"Don't you have friends?"

"Not so much anymore."

"Why not?"

She didn't want to admit her father was in the asylum. "Because I have no mamma and pappa they think there is something wrong with me." She raised her chin. "I do not like to talk about it."

"All right. Tell me what you like to do."

"I like to read. I like to play gili-danda. I like to play with tops. Sometimes I play cards with Jhangu Mama and his friends. I like his friends—so much more mature they are than the girls in my school. I like to study. I am getting the best marks now in school."

He was defensive about his own marks. "It is not so easy in Bombay. Standards are higher. We have to compete with English boys. They have the advantage because it is their language."

"You go to an English-medium school?"

"Yes."

"There are also girls?"

"Not in the school—it is a boys' school—but in my building, where I live, there are English girls—but I do not like them very much."

"Why not?"

He grinned. "They are not like you."

"How they are not like me?"

"In many ways. They do not play gili-danda. They do not play with tops." He hesitated for a moment. "They also do not like to play with Indians."

"Why not?"

He was surprised at the ease with which he spoke, but most of all he was surprised how much he was enjoying himself. "Fiona Tavistock says it is because we are dirty."

"How she can say such things? Who does she think she is that she can say such things?"

"Just the daughter of a friend of my pappa. She lives in our building. She didn't mean me—we are Parsis, not Indians. I do not see her so much now, but when we were younger we used to play together."

"What about Kavas? He did not play with you?"

"He was too old—he was always too old. I think he was jealous because there were no English girls his age in our building. I think that's why he was jealous last night also. I didn't tell him I was coming to see you or he would have made a fuss. I just told them I was going to look at the stars. They think I am half-cracked, you know—arre!" He slapped his forehead. "Here we are walking and talking so merrily I forgot to give you your prize."

Her mouth dropped. He had remembered. "What you brought?"

He leaned the bicycle against a peepul tree and rummaged in a bag clamped over the rear wheel. "It is not one of the prizes from the trolleys last night. I brought you a book of my own instead I would like you to have."

"A book of your own?"

"About Astronomy. Look."

She took the book from him, *Stargazing* by Archibald McKnight, made more dear by an inscription with a date, *September 1913*, on the frontispiece: *Dear Dolly, We are all stars! Sincerely, Phiroze*. She was suddenly too shy to look at him, shutting the book, opening it again, putting it down, picking it up again. "Arrerere, Phiroze, thank you so veryvery much. I will always treasure. Cover to cover, I will read it. Promise. I will get a dictionary. If I do not understand a word I will look it up."

"You will understand it easily." He wanted to add that she could ask him if she had difficulties, but he was returning to Bombay the next day and would not be in Navsari again for a year. He was pleased to see her caress the book as if it were a living thing. Both were silent for a moment as the mood changed. "Dolly, something else I want to tell you. You know, we really are stars. Iron in our blood, iodine in our thyroid, gold and mercury in our teeth—all are manufactured from dying stars. I am not talking metaphorically, Dolly. I am talking literally. We are literally stardust."

Afraid to say the wrong thing, she said nothing.

"It is also in Shakespeare. We were studying *Romeo and Juliet* in school last year."

"*Romeo and Juliet* is a love story, no?"

"Yes. Do you know the story?"

"No, but everybody is knowing about Shakespeare. I would like to read the story."

"It is a very romantic story, but so sad—but let me quote you about the stars."

No one had quoted anything to her, let alone Shakespeare. Her face wizened into seriousness, her eyes grew larger, blacker. "Please, quote, no?"

"Juliet is calling Romeo." He looked into the distance as if he were reading words in the sky: "*Come night, come Romeo, come thou day in night, for thou wilt lie upon the wings of night, whiter than new snow upon a raven's back.*"

"Arre, oh, that is so beautiful—poetry!"

Phiroze held up his hand. "There is more."

"Sorry. Please, go on quoting, no?"

Phiroze looked again into the distance: "*Come gentle night, come loving black-browed night, give me my Romeo*"—Phiroze looked at Dolly to emphasize the significance of what followed—"*and when he shall die take him and cut him out in little stars, and he will make the face of heaven so fine that all the world will be in love with night and pay no worship to the garish sun.*"

He looked at her again, but she remained silent until she was sure he had finished quoting. "Arre, Phiroze, that is so beautiful—just so beautiful."

"Very romantic—the whole play is like that—but also very sad."

"Both die, no? That much I know. Can you tell me the whole story?"

"If you like."

They found a copse among the trees and nestled among the roots and vines of a giant banyan. Her eyes remained wide as he related the story, growing blacker as her pupils expanded with the advent of twilight, glistening as he concluded. "Such a romantic story it is, no? Are all English so romantic?"

"Romeo and Juliet weren't English. They were Italian."

"Of course, but Shakespeare was English, no?"

"Shakespeare was English, no?"

"Go, now you are making fun of me. That is not nice. It is not my fault if I am not going to an English-medium school."

"Sorry. I could not resist, but I am sorry."

"If you are sorry then it is all right. I forgive you. Tell me more about Shakespeare, no?"

"Shakespeare was everything—all things to all men. He was the English Kalidasa, Valmiki, and Vyasa all rolled into one—also their Firdausi and their Tagore, everything."

"He must have been a great man, but such a sad story it was, no? Why it had to be so sad? Why they had to go through all that when they only wanted love?"

His voice turned bitter. "Why, indeed? People never learn! That is why!"

"Arre, what do you mean?"

"Everywhere people are the same, families are the same. They will never stop telling me: *Go to England. Study Law. Study anything, but go. You are a Sanjana. You owe it to yourself.* Arre, so much nonsense, Dolly, you never heard."

Dolly didn't understand Phiroze's antipathy for England; she would scarcely have believed her luck had the chance been hers; not even her dreams could have matched such a reality; but wishing not to be disagreeable she said nothing.

"Tomorrow we will be back in Bombay. After that, Kavas will be leaving and everyone else will say again and again: *Arre, but why won't you go? Don't you see what a fine example your brother is setting? Why not follow in his footsteps?*"

"What you will tell them?"

"What I have always told them. I want to make my own footsteps."

"What footsteps you want to make?"

"That is what I want to find out—but they are all in such a hurry. Afterward you will have time. Now you must study. Law! But afterward it may be too late to do what I want."

"But what you want to do, no?"

"I don't know!"

Dolly said nothing.

"Worst of all is when they bring my mamma into it. *Your mamma wanted you to go. It was her dying wish. How can you let your dear and departed mamma down? How can you be so shameless?*" He stared at Dolly. "What I want to know is how *they* can be so shameless as to bring my mamma into it."

"That is not right. They should not bring your mamma into it. They are the ones who are shameless." She couldn't look at him anymore. She still thought too much about her own mother.

"Let us not think about it. Let us only think happy thoughts."

Dolly shook her head as if shaking off her melancholy. "Yes! Only happy thoughts!"

A mango fell to the ground ten yards from where they sat, a monkey swooped down to collect it, another following on its tail, their trajectory tracing a diamond in the air. "We should be getting back to the road. It is getting dark."

He lit the bicycle lamp again and Dolly walked alongside holding her book tightly. "So when you will come back to Navsari now?"

"After a year."

She nodded, saying nothing. They walked silently, looking toward the road, until he heard her breath coming in short shallow gasps and turned to see her cheeks glistening.

"Arre, Dolly, what is the matter?"

She shook her head, still saying nothing, staring at the road, letting her tears flow unchecked. She knew she was thinking again about her mother, but it was more than that: her mother, the astronomy book, the deepening night, Romeo and Juliet, but worst of all Phiroze disappearing gradually even as they walked toward the road, their time together growing shorter by the second, their time apart looming like infinite space without stars! She could hardly explain what she hardly understood herself. Phiroze, like her, was without a mother—but he had no sooner appeared than he would disappear, and infinite space seemed to hold no terror for him.

"Dolly, what is the matter? Tell me."

She shook her head, eyes still on the road. "I do not know."

"But you must know. Why don't you tell me? I am your friend."

It was what she wanted to hear, but it wasn't enough. She shook her head again. "I do not feel like such a big girl after all. I feel like a little girl who does not want to hear that it is time to go to bed."

"Arre, Dolly, no need to be so dramatic. It makes me quite happy actually to see you like this."

"Happy? Why?"

"Because it means that maybe you are feeling the same thing that I am feeling."

She stared. "You think I am happy?"

"No, but you have made me understand something about Romeo and Juliet I never understood before."

She could not believe he was thinking about Romeo and Juliet in the face of her distress. "What?"

"What he said to her before he left her on the balcony." Phiroze stared again as if he were reading the sky: "*Parting is such sweet sorrow that I shall say goodnight till it be morrow.*"

He appeared blurry through her damp lashes, and distant, interested only in what he was saying, not in her—but she didn't blame him. In his eyes, his world, she could be only a little girl. He had already shown her more kindness than she might ever have expected. "Yes, very nice. Poetry."

"No, Dolly, you do not understand. Before they were just words—but now I am beginning to understand how he must have felt. Something that is just sweet is for children—but sweet sorrow, such as a parting brings, is more deep, more grown-up. I am going to miss you, Dolly. You must write to me. Will you promise?"

A geyser climbed her throat erupting in a series of gasps. "Promise! Promise, Phiroze! I promise!"

"Good, that is very good." He grinned. "What this means is that we can be happy if we are sad about the same thing."

She didn't stop laughing then until she snorted and stopped out of embarrassment. "You do all the talking now. Say what you want—say anything you want. I am feeling too good to talk."

He grinned, pointing to stars in the sky, naming them as he led from one to the other, and she followed, paying scant attention until he indicated the last star. "And look, over there, we are in luck, that is Polaris, the north star."

"The star which is guiding all of the ships in the sea?"

His grin was so wide he might have discovered the star. "Yes! Also the star about which lovers talk when they talk about being constant as the northern star."

Reaching the road she perched again on the bar of his bicycle, happy again in the circle of his arms as they approached the town. Content with the sound of his voice she no longer heard what he said, thinking of the letters they would exchange, the book he had given her, and the pounding of his heart like a hammer on her back.

"WHY YOU ARE NOT WRITING? What you are thinking?"

Dolly stared at the pencil in her hand. "Nothing."

"What you mean nothing? Got to be something. Or why you are not writing?"

Dolly said nothing. Dinmai's words scolded, but her tone was gentle and Dolly knew what it meant: something was expected, but she didn't know what. Phiroze had written to say Kavas had been called to the bar and enrolled in the High Court. He had been back in Bombay for a couple of months, and they would be returning to Navsari for two weeks in September. It would be almost a year since they had met. Dinmai knew of the correspondence, everyone in Navsari knew, and though Dolly didn't mind she wished she knew what was expected.

She was fourteen, but girls younger than herself had been married off, dropping out of school as their lives turned—and though she knew her turn loomed, and sometimes envisioned herself mistress of the Sanjana household, the path in between remained murky.

"Arre, Dolly, what you are thinking? Tell me, no? What is there to be afraid?"

Dolly looked at Dinmai who was smiling as she had never seen her, not quite shy, not quite sly, unaccustomed to entreaty. She had treated her differently since she had known of the correspondence, at once relieved and happy for her granddaughter and in awe of her connection. "I am not afraid."

"Then tell, no? It is about that Phiroze Sanjana, no?"

"If it is about him, then it is still nothing about him. If it is about him, I still do not know what I am thinking about him."

"Arre, Dolly, what is there to be thinking? It is your destiny. When you were born the astrologer said, no, that there were houses and motors and suchlike in your future? Your name is Daulat for what? In Gujarati it means wealth. In English it sounds like dollars. What is there to think? Whatever will happen will happen. You have only got to be there when it happens."

"But I do not know what to do about it. I do not know what I am supposed to do."

"I said, no? Nothing! You have got to do nothing! Just be clean and keep your mouth shut—and smile when he says something. That is all any girl has to do. Leave all talking to men. He has written letters to you, no? Everybody in Navsari is knowing about it, no? If he has got any respect he has got to marry you, no?"

"But why has he got to marry me? They are only letters he is writing, no? Why has he got to marry me because he has written letters?"

Dinmai snorted. "Because everybody in the post office is a newspaper. Everybody is knowing about it. Or what will people say? He was only enjoying himself. He is not a serious boy. Already he has got such a reputation. Does not want to do this, does not want to do that, does not want to do anything, does not even want to go to England, only wants to live on the family money—but he has also got his own good name to think about, no? not the Sanjana name, but his own personal good name, no?" She paused, frowning, struck by a thought. "He *has* written you letters, no? Manymany letters, no?"

"He has written some."

"How many?"

"I do not know exactly."

"About how many?"

"About ten-fifteen."

Dinmai sighed. "Arre, bawa, ten-fifteen is enough. In just one year ten-fifteen is more than enough. Ten-fifteen means he is thinking about you seriously."

Dolly said nothing. Phiroze had arranged for them to meet where they had met last, but she was afraid to see him again, afraid to disappoint him, no less afraid to be disappointed herself.

Dinmai watched her closely. "About what he writes?"

"Nothing."

"Arre, Dolly, why are you always playing the goat? Why are you always so jiddi? Ten-fifteen letters he has written—and he has written nothing? Tell me what he has written."

Dolly rolled her eyes. "He writes about stars."

"What stars?"

"In the sky—stars in the sky."

"What about stars. One star is like another. What is there to write?"

"There is lots to write. Every star is different—according to him. Every star has got its own name. He knows them all. He knows how far they are. He knows what they are made out of. He knows everything about stars." She pursed her mouth, her tone turned bitter. "But nothing about anything else."

"And this is what he writes about?"

"Yes."

"Nothing else he writes about?"

"He also sometimes corrects my English."

"Your English? What is wrong with your English? They do not teach you properly in school?"

"They teach, but for us it is a second language. In Bombay he goes to an English-medium school with English boys. His teachers are all English. Everything they are learning in English—maths, history, geography. Of course, he is going to know English better than me."

"Arre, Dollybaby, you are looking at this all from the wrong side. If you look at the sun during eclipse you will say the sun is dark—but that is not so. If he is correcting your English, it means what? Only that he is interested. If he is not interested you think he would correct your English? If he is not interested you think he would write at all? This means only one thing. He is interested."

Dolly had taken the corrections as rebukes, evidence that he thought he was better than her, and less sure of herself had allowed her end of the correspondence to flounder, writing once for every two or three of his letters. She had read the book he had given her, using dictionaries and other reference books from the library to understand what she read, but the library wasn't always helpful, and what she understood hardly filled her with Phiroze's fervor. She found herself more in sympathy with his family, even with Kavas. She repeated the words to herself that Phiroze had written: *Kavas has been called to the bar and enrolled in the High Court*—in London, in England! An Indian, a Parsi, someone she knew, had been recognized in England as one of their own! "But Dinmai, he does not want to do anything, only look at stars. What kind of man only wants to look at stars?" Her eyes flashed. "He quoted for me once from *Romeo and Juliet*, but only about stars. With him everything is about stars."

"From *Romeo and Juliet* he quoted? From your English Shakespeare? He could say nothing about Rustom and Tehmina? or Rama and Sita, or Krishna and Radha, or Arjuna and Draupadi?"

"Maybe there is nothing about stars in those stories. If there is something about stars I am sure he would have quoted. He is not interested in Shakespeare because he is English. He is not that much interested in the English. He is interested only in stars—even in Shakespeare only because of stars."

"So what? He is interested in stars. So what? That is better than drinking and gambling, no? Nothing wrong with stars. Stars are fine—shining and bright and all."

"But he should do something, no? A man should do something. If a man doesn't do something, then he is nothing, no?"

"Arre, Dolly, what you want him to do?"

"Something! Anything! It does not matter what, but he should do something. His brother has studied Law—in London. Now he will be a solicitor. He can help people. That is something. But Phiroze does not want to do anything, only to look at stars. He does not even want to go to London."

Dinmai watched Dolly closely again. "You want him to study law? in London? like his brother?"

"I do not care what he does—as long he does *some*thing."

"You like his brother better?"

"I like Phiroze better—but I think I admire Kavas more."

"Kavas? You know him also?"

"Only his name. I think he hates me. He says to me only bad things."

"What bad things?"

"Ilsabeth, he called me—and he called Phiroze Swolter." Dolly explained.

"And what you did for him to say such things?"

"Nothing. I did nothing. I never even spoke to him. But he is always angry with me."

Dinmai smiled, nodding. "Arre, if he is angry with you it means what? What have you done that he is so angry with you."

"Nothing! I have done nothing!"

"That is what I am saying. You have done nothing and he is angry with you. If you had done something he would not be angry. He is angry because you have done nothing—because he thinks he is nothing to you."

Dolly frowned, absorbing what Dinmai had said.

"Arre, Dolly, it is simple. If he is angry with you it means he is thinking about you, but you are not thinking about him. Or why is he angry? Why should you mean anything to him? If you are thinking about him, then you must talk to him. Or why should he not be angry?"

"But, Dinmai, you only said just now, no? to keep my mouth shut? to leave all talking to men?"

Dinmai frowned. "Do not tell me what I have said. I know what I have said. You must keep your mouth shut, but if you want gold then you have to dig, no? Or why should you get?"

Dolly said nothing.

"Arre, listen, Dolly. Both brothers have got money, but the older brother has also got ambition—and ambition is better than money. A rich man can lose his money, but an ambitious man will make it back. If you are liking Kavas you must tell him."

"But I do not like him. I admire him—but with me he is always angry."

"Arre, like, admire, what is the difference? If you admire him now you will like him later."

"But will I love him later?"

"Arre, what you are talking now about love! What you are thinking? You are English? You are American? You want a love-marriage? What you are thinking? You are Romeo and Juliet or what? What you think, love is coming full speed like an engine train breathing fire and smoke and going so loudly khut-khut-khut-khut? Nono, love is like a tree. First you have got to plant the seed, then you have got to water the ground. Then, after some years, there will be a tree. That is how love is coming."

"But if it does not come then I will be trapped, no? I will have a tree with no leaves and no fruit."

Dinmai snapped. "If you water the seed, the tree will grow! It is the law of nature!"


**DOLLY REACHED THE PREARRANGED SPOT** before Phiroze, but heard his bell accompanied by whistling almost right away. Her lungs shrank, her windpipe narrowed, orange and yellow spots orbited her head, her heart hammered to break its cage, her knees turned to custard. She shut her eyes, ran a hand over her neck and chest, took a deep breath, and waited clinging to the vine of a banyan.

Phiroze dismounted to fanfare from his bell. "Hullo, Dolly."

He was taller, but otherwise the same. He smiled as if they had met the day before and she responded no less nonchalantly. "Hullo."

"Good to see you again."

She clung to the vine, wondering if he was angry she hadn't written more often. "Thank you. Good to see you also."

Her uncertainty fed his own and he stood, rigid with his bicycle, less than ten feet away, wondering if his letters had led her to expect too much. "Shall we go for a walk?"

"Okay."

They were careful not to walk close. "We are having a party for Kavas on Saturday."

"Another party?"

"We have a party every year in Navsari. You know that."

"Yesyes."

"We don't need an excuse, but it is better to have one. This year it is again for Kavas—for being enrolled in the High Court. I wrote to you about that, didn't I?"

"Yesyes."

"He asked especially for you to come."

"*He* said? *Ka*vas said?"

"If he had not asked I would have asked myself—but why are you surprised?"

"He does not even know me."

Phiroze grinned at last. "I told you he was jealous!"

"Yesyes, but I did not believe you—I *still* do not believe you. *Al*ways he seemed so angry with me—not only one or two times, but *all* of the time—*re*ally!" When Phiroze remained silent she looked at him. "Sorry, I know he is your brother and all—but *re*ally, I am not fooling."

Phiroze nodded. "Dolly, I am going to trust you with a confidence. Can I count on you to say nothing about it to anyone?"

Dolly stared. He spoke with such gravity. "Confidence? Like a secret? About Kavas?"

"Yes. Can I trust you?"

"Of course! Who I am going to tell?"

"Not even your Jhangu Mama or your Dinmai must know. You must swear."

"I swear—on the memory of my dead mother, I swear I will tell nobody, not even Jhangu Mama or Dinmai."

"All right." Phiroze chose words with care. "Kavas has had a psychological condition since his birth—nothing serious, but he is a very moody fellow."

"Arre, everybody has moods. What does that signify?"

"Not like Kavas. In him they are exaggerated, everything is exaggerated—but it is not serious, nothing unusual. This kind of thing has been going on for centuries. The Greeks called it Melancholia, meaning he has an excess of black bile, that is when his mood is depressed. The other mood, which the Greeks called Mania, meaning he has an excess of yellow bile, is when his mood is elated. One minute he is sad, next minute he is laughing. One minute he is angry, next minute he is numb. Just like that, for no reason."

Dolly spoke in hushed tones as seemed to befit the revelation. "Psychological! Attchha! I see!"

"When Mamma died it got worse –"

"Of course! Poor fellow! Nothing can be done?"

"Actually, he is much better already. Pappa took him to the best doctors—to Vienna, Pappa took him. They have the best psychologists. Everybody said the same thing. Behave as if everything is normal. Don't get him too excited. Don't get upset if he gets upset. Around him, whatever happens, you must behave as if everything is normal—always, whatever happens! That is the best way."

"Arre, poor fellow! And all this time I thought he was such a badtempered fellow. I am so sorry. Thank you for telling me."

They walked in silence before Phiroze turned to her again. "So, will you come to the party?"

"There will be a bus again?"

"Yes, just like last year—then if you want, I will take you home on the bicycle."

"They will not stop you?"

"Where there's a will, there's a way."

Dolly grinned. "England hath a Will, but Anne Hathaway."

"What?"

"A little joke I read about Shakespeare. I was reading about him in the library after you told me the Romeo and Juliet story."

"Oh, good one." Phiroze looked sideways as they walked, almost shy. "So, will you come?"

"Yes. I will come."

"Good." They walked silently again before Phiroze spoke again. "Just in time he made it, you know. Kavas made it just in time."

"Made what? Just in time for what?"

"I mean because of the war. It had started before his steamer reached Bombay."

"Really?"

"Such amazing things are happening in Europe, Dolly, I tell you."

She nodded, more comfortable talking about the war. "Did Kavas see any fighting?"

Phiroze laughed. "No, thank God, by then he was already on the steamer—and thank God also that he arrived before the trouble began with the *Emden*. Pappa was worried enough before, but after the news about the *Emden* he would have been impossible. Now not even the seas are safe."

"Jhangu Mama told me about the *Emden*. They bombed Madras, no?"

"Not, actually, Madras—but almost. The rules of engagement prevent them from bombarding undefended towns."

Dolly nodded, repeating the phrase with respect. "Rules of engagement—thank God for that." The *Emden*, a light German cruiser, had sailed from Tsingtao, the only German port in China, to capture thirteen ships in the Bay of Bengal within a fortnight. Sailing south to

Ceylon, the cruiser had bombarded oiltanks near Madras setting them on fire, destroying 500,000 gallons of oil.

"Every country is fighting every other country, and every country says it is only defending itself."

"But every country *must* defend itself, no?"

"Yes, but that is just the ruse! Germany has been building its might and main for a long time, ever since the Franco-Prussian War of 1870, even collecting colonies in Africa and everywhere as the so-called great powers are supposed to do—but they needed a ruse to show their supremacy. England has been the dominant power in Europe since the defeat of Napoleon and they do not want to give up their supremacy—and when the Germans went through Belgium to get to France they got it. They don't care about Belgium, but if Germany looks too strong then they will look too weak. It has been like dominoes. One after the other, all of the countries declared war. First, Germany on Russia because they refused to stop mobilizing. On the same day France began mobilization. Then Germany declared war on France—but, because French troops were lined up along the border, the Germans planned to circle around them by attacking through Belgium. But England had guaranteed Belgium's neutrality, and when Germany refused to withdraw from Belgium, England declared war on Germany—and when England declared war the whole empire declared war, including India."

"Omigod! Nothing can be done?"

"Nothing now, and nothing for a long time past. There were alliances between Germany and Austria and Italy, and between Russia and France and England."

"So six countries are at war: Germany, Austria, Italy, Russia, France, and England? Only six countries?"

"Actually, more." He laughed. "But how bloodthirsty you are, Dolly. Six countries are not enough for you?"

She grinned, comfortable enough now to slap his arm. "That is not what I meant. But how do you know so much? Why do you care?"

"Why do I care? Arre, the question is more correctly why do you *not* care? It is in all the newspapers. Nobody talks about anything else. How can anyone *not* care? The so-called greatest countries in the world are all fighting like animals—including our own glorious conqueror, our own wonderful England. The only thing more stupid than Europeans fighting one another is their colonies are also fighting—Africans and Indians and Australians and everyone, all are fighting a European war. It is like the Capulets and Montagues again, the royal families of England and Germany are all close relatives. I was actually thinking about going to Australia myself, but Pappa thinks it is not such a good idea now, and maybe he's right—but I am still thinking of going."

A screw turned infinitesimally in Dolly's head. "Australia? Why?"

"To see the southern sky by night—actually, anywhere in the southern hemisphere would be all right, but Pappa has connections in Australia, and that would be helpful."

Dolly frowned. "What is there in the southern sky? You can see it in the book, no? It is in the *Stargazing* book you gave me, no? Why go all the way to Australia just to see stars? Indian stars are not good enough? I mean, what is the point? You are only sightseeing."

"I am not only sightseeing. I want to study things—and to study them, I have to see them first."

"Study and do what?"

"Study so I can understand."

"Understand and do what?"

"Understand so I will know more about the world, the meaning of things."

"Arre, bawa, this is the *same* question I am asking. Know and do what? What will you do with what you know? What? Tell, no? What are your plans?"

Phiroze's mouth shrank. They stared at each other, Dolly no less surprised than Phiroze at her outburst. Phiroze lowered his tone, compensating it seemed for hers which had risen steadily. "I don't have any plans. I don't have to have plans. That is my fortune being a Sanjana. That is the beauty of money. It lets you do what you want. We already have more than we need. What is the point of making money for the sake of making money. Sheer selfishness that would be. Money should be a byproduct of doing something we love."

"Yesyes, very nice. My Jhangu Mama likes to play cards. What you are saying? He should be given money for playing cards?"

Phiroze's eyebrows rose in a pagoda. "Arre, Dolly, why are you getting so excited? I am only making a philosophical point. If we do not have money we must work, but if we have money what is the point of working? No need to get personal about this. I was only making a philosophical point."

He had underscored the big difference between them: poor people did not have the luxury of making philosophical points. "Sorry, sorry. Of course, only a philosophical point—nothing to get excited about. I thought you were making a point about something *real*. Sorry I got so excited about nothing."

She was pleased to see his jaw drop, his mouth crumble, his eyes blink rapidly.

DOLLY APPROACHED HER SECOND VISIT to Truth with the same trepidation as her first, her rationale turned back to front. From hating every minute Phiroze had ignored her, she no longer cared. Lacking a plan for his life, he had set a hurdle in the plan for her own. The evening started as it had the year before, decorations and program the same, but Dolly's quarry was Kavas, not Phiroze, and it was evident from the start. Phiroze approached as she descended the steps. "Good to see you, Dolly. I was afraid you might not come."

"Afraid? Why?"

He had hoped their differences might have been forgotten in the interim, but Dolly held her chin high, her shoulders back, appearing taller. In one of her letters she had said her height made her slouch because a girl should be smaller than a boy, but he had reassured her saying he preferred tall girls and now her unconcern about height made her seem more bold. "No reason—but, you know, anything could happen."

She looked beyond him at the red carpet bearing foodstuffs, the trees wired with lights, the family and Mr. Allgood gathered as before on wicker chairs in a circle to one side, until she found Kavas, decked as before with tila, rice grains, coconuts, and marigolds. She made sure she was close enough and loud enough for Kavas to hear before speaking. "Why should anything happen? I wanted to congratulate Kavas in person. I may never get such another chance again, no?"

Her strategy had the desired effect. Kavas looked up from his group, the wings of a smile hovering around his mouth. "Hullo, hullo, hullo, hullo, Dolly Dalal. Very good to see you again."

"I came to give you my very best congratulations, Kavas. Such a very difficult thing you have done. I came to wish you my best, my absolutely best wishes."

The focus of the group shifted as if a giant face had turned toward her, but she was aware only of Kavas's eyes boring through a green tunnel into her own. The most aggressive act of her young life had succeeded admirably. "Thank you, Dolly. Come, sit with us, won't you?" He made room between his chair and the next.

"Thank you very much." She walked into the group as everyone spread to make a wider circle. Someone set a chair for her on Kavas's left. JN sat on his right, then Mr. Allgood, Sohrabji Sanjana, Phiroze, and others. Kavas introduced her to others in the company, each of whom she acknowledged with a nod, smile, "Hullo": JN's widowed sister Zarine, Sohrabji Sanjana's sister Banu, her husband Minoo Kharegat, their son Faredoon, other Sanjanas, Kharegats, and inlaws. Dolly noticed the Kharegats smiled more than they spoke, spoke mainly when addressed by Sanjanas, and always with deference as if Sanjanas were as English as Mr. Allgood. Finally, Kavas turned to her exclusively. "So, Dolly, tell us. What is your news?"

Her grin was almost as wide as his own. "Nothing much—nothing like your news."

"No, no, do not be modest. I understand that you and my brother have been burning up the post office with your correspondence?"

## DOLLY'S STORY

Dolly sensed Phiroze glowering five chairs away. She felt the blood rush to her own face, her smile twitch, but forced herself to speak. "We have written some letters—but mainly he has been correcting my English, which made me only want to stop writing."

Kavas's laugh was loud and sudden, rattling like a machinegun, eliciting a smile of triumph from Dolly. "Of course, of course! What else? When a professor finds himself out of his depth, he tries to raise everyone to the shallows. When Phiroze is afraid he pontificates."

A silence fell on the circle. Phiroze's smile was unconvincing. He would normally have ignored Kavas's remarks, but more seemed at stake than he had imagined. "Very lawyerly statement, big brother. It seems, you have not been enrolled in the High Court for nothing."

Dolly spoke immediately, looking at Kavas. "Actually, I was thinking more poetic than lawyerly, no? Very poetic, no?"

Sohrabji Sanjana looked at Dolly. Kavas looked at Phiroze, his smile twisting as he spoke. "No, not poetic, never poetic. Poetry is Phiroze's domain, isn't that right—little brother?"

The focus of the group swung between the brothers like a pendulum. Phiroze's smile remained unconvincing. "Poet, artist, scientist—in the end it is all the same thing. The greatest scientists are all artists at heart, and lesser artists are all scientists."

"Yes, yes, Phiroze always knows the politic thing to say—but it is always just talk. The point is first to do something, then to talk about it—but to voice fine sentiments and never to do anything is a form of cowardice. Put up or shut up is what I say. Otherwise, you can talk forever and die before you do anything at all."

The circle held a collective breath, as if air had become precious. Dolly might have bounced in her chair recognizing the very point she had made to Phiroze, but her limbs froze. Sohrabji Sanjana spoke quietly. "All right, boys, enough. A good debate is the best way to clear the air, but not if you are going to get personal. Sometimes a stiff upper lip says more than a wagging chin."

The company laughed. Air seemed plentiful again. Sohrabji Sanjana leaned back in his chair ignoring the laughter, picking up the thread of their conversation before Dolly's arrival. "I say, Teddy, to get back to the subject, make no mistake, I am with you one hundred percent, as are all Indians—except, you know, the fringe element. The war will be the best thing for Indians and English alike. It will cleanse the blood. Show them something of life."

Mr. Allgood tilted his head so slightly it was impossible to say if he was in agreement or not. "Righto, Sohrabji! War builds character and good fellowship. By Christmas it will all be over—and then I daresay you will find England not ungrateful."

"Goes without saying! We expect nothing less. The English are nothing if not fair. That is why I say the fringe element cannot survive. It is simply not cricket to say that England's necessity is India's opportunity. Only cowards take advantage of an adversary's weakness."

"That too goes without saying, my dear Sohrabji, but it does the heart of an Englishman good to hear it said. We are *all*, after all, fighting the good fight, England *and* India—to preserve the right of *all* nations to determine their destinies. What could be more sacrosanct than that, I ask you?"

Kavas slapped his knee. "Nothing! Even an extremist like that Tilak has finally realized it. He has even encouraged our youngsters to enlist."

Mr. Allgood nodded without looking at Kavas. "That comes in something of the nature of a relief to all Englishmen, I can tell you. There were some of us who weren't quite sure of the empire, but of course there was nothing we could say—but in the wake of the *Emden* there is simply no more doubt in anyone's mind how the Indians feel."

Kavas laughed. "I say, Teddy Uncle, good one, bloody good—'in the wake of the *Emden*.' Hah! Yes! We all know now what's what."

Mr. Allgood smiled. "No pun intended, I'm sure, Kavas."

The pun was lost on Dolly, as was some of the conversation, but she was thrilled to be part of a circle conversing in English, including not only the Sanjanas but an Englishman. After the episode of the

*Emden*, Jhangu Mama had said that England no longer doubted India's loyalty, but India now doubted England's ability to protect her—but she said nothing.

JN stroked his trowel beard to a point, swaying gently as he spoke. "If there is ever any doubt of loyalty, Teddy, you must always see how much money secures the doubt. That is the acid test."

Mr. Allgood laughed. "Of course! But that is only now becoming clear. We had no way of knowing when the war broke."

Dolly had once more lost the thread of the conversation, but Kavas smiled. "One hundred million pounds, Dolly! India has given England one hundred million pounds for the war effort!"

Dolly gasped. "*So* much!"

Kavas still smiled, still nodded, enjoying her consternation. "Pounds, Dolly, pounds—not rupees! Do you have any idea how much that is?"

"Lakhs and lakhs?"

Kavas laughed. "Much more—much, much more!"

"Arre, of course!" She cupped her face in her hands. "A million is ten lakhs already, no? Crores and crores of rupees?"

"That's more like it."

"I did not know there was so much money in the world."

Kavas laughed again. Sohrabji Sanjana smiled. JN lifted his beard in the air. Phiroze was frowning, but when he spoke his brow was clear. "Most of the money came from the maharajahs, of course—who have always been pally with the English. They have so much money it means nothing to them—and they don't even work to earn it."

Kavas nudged Dolly. "Just like Phiroze."

Phiroze smiled. "Touche, brother—but I am hardly in their league."

"Granted, brother, but if a pauper has enough for his needs you might say he is living like a prince—or like a maharajah."

"And if a prince—or a maharajah—has *not* enough for his needs you might say he is living like a pauper. What is your point?"

"Only that you do not have to live like a maharajah to be in the same league. You only need some of his attributes, and neither you nor the maharajahs"—his laugh rang again like a machinegun—"choose to earn your living."

Phiroze pursed his lips. "Point well taken, but –"

Sohrabji Sanjana frowned. "Boys! Please! I have told you already how I feel about this debate! Enough now!"

"But, Pappa –"

"Phiroze, I said: E*nough!*"

Kavas's grin could not have been more smug as he turned to Mr. Allgood, resuming the earlier conversation. "I say, Teddy Uncle, I hear the Indians are to be sent to Mesopotamia. Do you know anything about it?"

Dolly noticed that Kavas's voice became more anglicized when he addressed Mr. Allgood, owing to his stay in England everyone would have said—but Mr. Allgood's voice never seemed Indianized though he was surrounded by Indians. An Englishman, Dolly would have said, was impermeable, but permeated everyone around him. "Mesopotamia, Africa, France. They will go where they are needed. They will go where they are told to go. That is what soldiers do and they are soldiers—or God help us all!"

"Of course! They are soldiers!"

Phiroze grinned at Dolly. "Hear, hear!"

She understood he mocked the soldiers and turned her head—but she was thrilled again when a servant brought plates of food to the circle, delighting in her rise from the banana-leaf settings on the ground to the upper circle of which she was now a part. Everyone in Navsari would know the next day that she had been seated next to Kavas Sanjana.

**RETURNING FROM A BATHROOM VISIT**, Dolly found Phiroze waiting in the hallway, eyebrows again in a pagoda. "The bus will be going soon, but you can stay if you want. I can take you on the bicycle later."

"Not to worry. I will go in the bus like I came. No need to trouble."

"It isn't any trouble. Just let me know when you are ready to leave."

"But I said, no, I will take the bus? Let me just take the bus."

Phiroze's eyebrows steepled higher. "Dolly, what is the matter?"

She narrowed her eyes. His plans for Australia had dashed her own and his question implied he was not to blame. The disappointment had fanned her anger to a flame. He would do what he wished—but he was running like a rabbit, hiding behind the stars, showing his back by pretending to face her, and she refused to bless his decision, refused to gloss his cowardice with her approval, refused to accept the burden of explaining her refusal to him. She would then be in his debt, he would always say he had given it up for her. She wanted him instead to give it up for himself, make his own choice and accept the responsibility of his choice. If he didn't know how she felt already she would only devalue her feelings further by telling him, and if he didn't value her feelings she would have to value them more highly herself. "Nothing. Why?"

"Why won't you let me take you home?"

"But why should you trouble when there is a bus?"

"But it is no trouble. I would like to do it. For me it will be the best part of the evening."

He had hoped for a smile, but again she turned her head. "I am telling you, no? There is no need. Really, now, I should be getting back, or people will be wondering what has happened."

The hallway was dark and getting darker as the evening deepened. She took a step, but he stood in her way. "Dolly, something is wrong . You are angry about something. Please tell me what it is."

She tried to step around him. "I am not angry. I only want to go back. Please let me go."

He touched her shoulder. "Dolly, please!"

She sighed. "All right. I am not angry, but if you think I am angry then you should tell me why you think I am angry."

"Dolly, I am not a mind-reader."

"I am not saying to read my mind. I am saying to tell me why *you* think I am angry." He hesitated, no less willing than herself to put words to thoughts and feelings, until she grew impatient with the silence. "Arre, I am telling you I am not angry—but you are making me angry by not believing me."

He took a deep breath. "Dolly, I do not know what to say."

"Then say nothing. If you do not know what to say then say nothing. Now let me go."

"Dolly, have you got absolutely nothing to say to me?"

"Arre, tch-tch-tch-tch! What are you saying, making mountain out of a hill—but I will ask a question if it makes you feel better."

"Ask!"

"Why you said nothing just now about the ruses you were telling me?"

"What ruses?"

"About the ruses you were saying, no, the other day, that England and Germany used for the war, both countries wanting to show their superiority?"

"Why should I say anything about that now?"

"Arre, everybody was saying, no, that the war is being fought for the rights of all nations to determine their destiny and all that?"

"That's rubbish! Sheer unadulterated rubbish! Rank hypocrisy! England has determined India's destiny too long already! How can they talk like that?"

"Then it is cowardice, no, to say nothing—if you are disagreeing with them?"

"Is that what this is about? You think I am a coward?"

"Just say, no?"

Phiroze shrugged. "It would have been rude, that's all—in front of Teddy Uncle, I mean. He is our guest, and he is an Englishman. How can I say such things?"

"Ah!"

"Is that what this is about?"

"No."

"Then shall I get my bicycle?"

"No!"

Kavas entered from the compound before he could say anything. "Oh, there you are, Dolly! We thought we had lost you, but I see

Phiroze has monopolized you instead. Listen, I say, can we offer you a ride home?"

Dolly smiled. "Thank you, but too late! You are too late! I just told Phiroze I was going in the bus—but thank you so very much, so very thoughtful of you."

Kavas frowned. "I daresay Phiroze got what he deserved—but I daresay also that your logic is not irrefutable. It does not follow, as night follows day, that if one turns down one brother one must then turn down the other. In fact, in some things one can accept only one."

She was surprised. Kavas's frown was darker than she might have expected, as if she had wounded him personally. "Yesyes, I dessay, like you say, in some things, yes, one can accept only one—but not in this, no?"

He accepted her logic with a nod. "No, not necessarily in this. I suppose you're right."

She was glad he had allowed himself to be persuaded by her. "But maybe another time?"

His frown departed as suddenly as it had arrived. "Well, all right, as long as you promise there will be another time."

"Of course! I have had a such a very good time!"

Kavas smiled. "Well, then, would you be interested in seeing the Maha Yogi on Friday? I understand he's to walk on water—that is, if all the posters mean anything. It should be quite a show."

Phiroze couldn't keep his voice from sounding sour. "I thought only Englishmen could walk on water."

Dolly frowned, but Kavas grinned. "It seems my brother has lurched into the truth. He is right to say Englishmen can walk on water—and so can the England-returned."

Dolly laughed. "But everybody is saying he is a fake, no? He cannot be real!"

"Well, of course not, but one runs out of options for entertainment rather quickly in Navsari. Besides, it might be fun."

"Who all are going?"

"I don't know. I only just thought of it. Everyone's welcome, I'm sure—though perhaps we should keep the number small. Phiroze is welcome, though I wager he thinks himself too good for such an entertainment."

"Why too good?"

"Well, it's not Shakespeare, it's not Shaw."

Phiroze shook his head. "If I'm not too good for wrestling and gymnastics I'm certainly not too good for the Maha Yogi—but why not just go for a walk, or a ride on our bicycles?"

"Because, dear brother, we can do that at anytime—but on special occasions one should try to do something special, don't you think?"

"How is this a special occasion?"

"It will be—if Dolly joins us."

Dolly smiled. "It will be fun, no, Phiroze? You will come?"

"I don't think so."

"Why not?"

"I would rather go for a walk."

"But we can go for a walk anytime, no, like Kavas said?"

"Actually, we cannot. We're going back to Bombay next week, and a walk would give us a chance to talk."

"But we can talk, no, when we see the Maha Yogi?"

"But not properly, not without interruptions, not without distractions."

Kavas laughed. "Of course not, not seriously, and sedately, about poetry and astronomy and other such im*por*tant things. Come on, Dolly. We mustn't make a mountain out of a hill." Phiroze stared at Kavas wondering how long he had been eavesdropping, but Kavas just grinned. "Phiroze has his invitation. He will do what he wants. The question is whether or not *you* will join us. Will you?"

Dolly didn't look at Phiroze. "Oh, yes! Thank you! Thank you veryvery much!"

"Good. I'll send someone with a chit to your place, shall I, after I've worked out the bundobast?"

"What?"

"The bundobast—the arrangements."

She had misunderstood because he sounded too English to be using Parsi words, but her grin widened. "Yesyes! Of course, yes! You shall! Very kind of you! Yes! Thank you!"

THE CHIT WITH THE BUNDOBAST came the next day. Dinmai's faith in her astrologer soared. "What I told you, Dolly? Just like he said, no, it is happening? He said, no, you will have houses and motors? What I told you?" She gave Dolly a new cake of Pear's soap. "On Friday you must take a bath three times. You heard or what? Three times! All whitewhite you must be, smelling like English. Also wear your best clothes, but clean them first two times."

The Maha Yogi was to walk across the Ganga Talao lying in the hinterland of the Ganga Mandir. The body of water had been constructed like a Roman bath, twenty feet by thirty, descending step by step from either end to a depth of ten feet in the middle, but it had been in disuse for so long the water was murky. The mandir grounds were enclosed by a shallow brick wall, eroded by weather, defaced by graffiti, cracked by cricket balls, splattered with scarlet expectorations of paan. Kavas guessed rightly that the grounds would be too crowded for comfort even if they sent a servant early to reserve space for them at the talao's edge. Instead he asked Dolly to meet him at Harmony, one of the Sanjana homes, where the Kharegats lived, across the street from the mandir. The Kharegat terrace offered greater comfort and a clearer view than anywhere on the grounds.

Dolly arrived fifteen minutes late to ensure that Kavas would precede her. The door was opened by Faredoon holding two pairs of binoculars. He attended the Madresa Boys High School, one standard below Dolly's. "Hullo, Dolly. Good to see you."

He might have spoken in Gujarati like everyone else in Navsari, but Kavas's influence, the influence of the Sanjanas, was strong even in their absence. "Arre, good to see *you*, Freddie—sorry I am late.

# A Googly in the Compound

Like a fool I took a wrong turn at the Mota Bajar—and then you cannot believe how the crowd is for the Maha Yogi!"

"I know, I know! All day we have been talking about nothing else. Everywhere-everywhere people—like cockroaches."

Dolly laughed. "So where is everybody?"

"On the terrace. Everybody is on the terrace."

"Kavas also—and Phiroze?"

"Phiroze did not come—not feeling well—but Kavas is here, only just came, ten minutes ago."

She was relieved Phiroze wasn't coming. His presence would have made her own ambiguous, but his absence gave her a sign. "Not feeling well? What is the matter?"

"Stomach trouble—something he ate." Faredoon grinned. "You know how these Bombay stomachs are—sissies. Everything has got to be boiled and baked and stewed four and five times before they can eat anything."

Dolly laughed again. "Yesyes, of course! But he is all right?"

"Of course! Temporary inconvenience is all. Come, no, this way? All are waiting for you. Everything has been set on the terrace."

Harmony was a freestanding house, like Truth Bungalow, but its rooms were neither as large nor as plentiful, stacked one atop the other into three storeys, but the Kharegats, like the Sanjanas, lived better than anyone Dolly knew. She followed Faredoon in silence up the stairs, admiring paintings of ballerinas and lilies and swans on the walls, envious of photographs of family and friends, thinking once more of the photograph of her father and the distance she had bridged from her home to the Kharegats and Sanjanas, marveling at the fate prophesied by Dinmai's astrologer. The planets were lining up in her favor and she was determined to seize her advantage, seize her fate with both hands.

Faredoon led her through an upstairs bedroom, past four-poster beds shrouded with mosquito nets, to a terrace sporting a picnic table around which the company had gathered. Minoo Kharegat was first to greet her, getting up, holding out his hand. "Hullohullo, Dolly! There you are! Good to see you!"

Dolly congratulated herself on her modernity, shaking his hand. Jhangu Mama would have joined his hands in a traditional namaste. "Hullo, Uncle! Good to be here! How are you?"

"Fine, just fine!"

Banu Kharegat, a Sanjana before marriage, smiled, not bothering to leave her seat or shake hands. "Sit, sit. We have got lots of time yet."

Kavas waved from his seat. "Dolly, glad you could make it."

She waved back seating herself between Kavas and Minoo Kharegat. "Me too."

Banu Kharegat wore a skirt and blouse, unlike most women in Navsari her age who couldn't have imagined not wearing a sari after they married. "We are going to be very informal today, Dolly. Just bhel we are having for dinner, from our own special bhelwallah—but first what will you have to drink?"

"Just water will be fine, Aunty."

"Arre, Dolly, water you can have anywhere. Have a naryal pani, no? Or a nimbu pani? Or if you want you can have a tea or a coffee?"

Kavas held a coconut in his hand, the top sliced open, straw inserted. "Have a naryal. It is perfect with bhel, and one can have the flesh later for dessert—a perfect sandwich of sweet and spice and sweet."

Dolly nodded to Banu. "All right, thank you, I will have a naryal."

Banu nodded approval. "Much better! Bhindu, ek naryal laojo, please?"

The servant disappeared from the terrace and Dolly turned to Kavas. "Freddie told me about Phiroze. Nothing serious, I hope?"

"No, no, of course not! Just his excuse, you can be sure."

Faredoon sat next to Kavas. "His excuse? Do you mean it was not his sissy Bombay stomach?"

"You may call it that if you want, but I have been eating the same things with my sissy London stomach and I am all right—and if a sissy London stomach can stomach the viccissitudes of a Navsari repast I am sure I do not understand why a sissy Bombay stomach cannot."

## A Googly in the Compound

Minoo Kharegat applauded as he chuckled. "Hear, hear! Well put, Kavas! Well put, indeed! Good for you that you left your sissy London stomach in London."

Dolly raised her eyebrows. "You think it was something else?" Kavas held her in his green gaze, saying nothing, implying she knew the answer to her own question, pressing her to babble on. "You mean, that the Maha Yogi is not Shakespeare?"

"Yes, of course—that! Did you think it might be jealousy?"

Blood flooded her head. She laughed with the others as if it were a joke, gratefully accepting the coconut Bhindu brought, hurriedly taking a sip. "You were right, Kavas—so cool and sweet it is."

Kavas grinned. "I am always right. Ask anyone."

Minoo Kharegat laughed. "Yes, yes! You have it on the best authority! Kavas is always right!"

It was a silly joke, but the company was in a silly mood, and Dolly joined everyone in the laugh that followed, until Banu got up. "Okay, everybody, I do not know what time the Maha Yogi has scheduled to make a fool of himself, but I am going to see to the bhel. Then whatever happens our evening will not be spoiled. Dolly, anything you want, just please ask. Freddie, give her the binocs, no? Let her get a feel for them."

Faredoon gave her a pair of binoculars. "We have got three. All are equally good. Try them all, no? See which you prefer."

Minoo Kharegat nudged Kavas. "Go, go, Kavas, show Dolly how to work the binocs."

Kavas and Dolly went to the railing, each with a pair of binoculars. People had gathered as well on adjacent terraces with binoculars. "Arre, my God! They are like a sea of people. Even the roar is like the roar of the sea."

Faredoon joined them with the third pair of binoculars. "Can you see him, Dolly?"

Dolly adjusted the focus. "Very clearly I can see him, very thin fellow, sitting very straight by the talao, legs crossed, eyes closed—must be meditating still."

# DOLLY'S STORY

Kavas snickered. "He had better have done with his meditating by now. How anyone can meditate with all this garbar I cannot understand."

Dolly's eyes never left the binoculars. "These binocs are terrific! Such a skinny-minny he is I can see his ribs."

Kavas's lip curled. "What the bloody fool hopes to accomplish I cannot understand. It's not as if he's charging admission."

Minoo Kharegat grinned. "If he was charging admission how many people would come? What he is doing is building a rep. Why do you think he invited the newspapers? After today people will be coming to him for the rest of his life, bringing food, money, clothes, whatever he wants, just to see him."

"But first he has to walk on water, no?"

"Come on, Dolly! We all know he is not going to walk on water. The question is if we can figure out his trick."

Banu and Bhindu set the table behind them with bowls of sev and mamra among the various seeds, cereals, and spices that went into bhel. At one end of the table they placed leaves. "Come, come, everybody! Self-service! Make your own as you like! Sweet or spicy is up to you!"

They were soon eating the flaming crackling bhel with their hands from the leaf cones, sucking air, swirling coconut water with their tongues to cool their mouths. Dolly interspersed mouthfuls with sips from her coconut. "Right you were, Kavas. The naryal is absolutely perfect with the bhel."

"What did I tell you? I am always right."

Dolly laughed. "Yesyes, now I know—but bas now, enough, Mr. Always Right."

The others laughed, Kavas grinned. When an Englishwoman mocked him he felt affronted, his dignity at stake, unsure whether she was being affectionate or rude, but with a Parsi there was never any doubt. Among the English, even with Teddy Uncle, he was on his guard, unsure where to draw the line between a joke and an insult while his face remained a mask of interest, his spine a bar of steel.

## A Googly in the Compound

The roar of the crowd turned to a caution, sssssshhhhhhhhhHHHHH!!!!!!, and Dolly's eyes turned round with excitement. "Omigod! They must be starting!" She wiped her hands, heading for the railing, raising the binoculars slung around her neck to her eyes. "He's getting up! He's getting up!"

Banu put down her coconut. "Why don't we take our chairs to the railing?"

They moved their chairs to the railing, but Dolly remained standing, eyes glued to the binoculars, the crowd straining no less expectantly, children raised to the shoulders of adults, people perched in trees. Faredoon stood motionless by her side, eyes no less glued to his binoculars. "Look! He is walking to the talao! Maha Yogi is walking to the talao!"

The yogi walked slowly to the brink of the talao, palms joined, eyes closed, hands raised as if he were about to dive, and held the pose, still as an obelisk before letting his foot sink into the first step of the talao.

Dolly stared without blinking. "So far at least it is not working. The water is up to his ankles. I cannot see his feet anymore, so dirty the water is."

Faredoon stared intently. "Someone has put a red dye in the talao. For the effect, must be, for the dramatic effect."

The yogi stood on the first step, going through the same motions, joining his hands, raising them, joining them again before taking a second step. This time his foot didn't sink into the water. He remained standing, one foot in front of the other, as if he were walking a tightrope, before stepping forward again—again without sinking though wobbling a little as if he were balancing himself on the surface of the water. A collective gasp cushioned the air. The yogi was walking on water, ankle-deep—but walking on water!

Kavas frowned. "How do you suppose he is doing it?" Minoo Kharegat took the binoculars from Faredoon, but Banu wrenched them from him almost at once holding onto them when Faredoon tried to get them from her. "He is doing it! He is doing it! Maha Yogi is walking on water!"

The yogi had walked a third of the length. Already members of his audience were prostrating themselves on the ground, wailing and keening with awe. He might have walked the remaining two-thirds as easily if not for an interruption, but a monkey swooped from the banyan behind him, bounced off the water, and caromed from the yogi's shoulders back into the banyan.

The yogi fell heavily into the talao. Monkeys began shrieking and whooping and jumping in the trees as if the branches were on fire. The crowd swerved forward past the flimsy cordon of rope, some unable to stop before their momentum propelled them into the talao as well.

"Arre, what is happening?"

"He at least walked to the middle of the talao, no, before the monkey knocked him down?"

"If not for the monkey he would have done it, no?"

Minoo Kharegat was the first to understand what had happened and couldn't stop laughing. "The monkey also could walk on water! Didn't you see? The monkey even jumped on the water! Now we have a holy man—*and* a holy monkey: Maha Yogi and Maha Monkey!"

Banu slapped her husband's arm. "Arre, stop laughing like a madman and tell us what happened."

Kavas, looking through the binoculars, understood as well what had happened, and joined in the laughter. "Minoo Uncle is right. We seem to have a little Hanuman on our hands."

Dolly, still staring through her binoculars, finally understood as well. The crowd was climbing onto what might have been a plank under the surface of the water, balanced across the talao on the steps at either end. It was not an easy trick, but easy enough with practice. Thus were legends born. She grinned. "The monkey has made a monkey out of Maha Yogi."

Kavas put a hand on Dolly's shoulder from behind. "Yes—and just think, the monkey was only monkeying around."

Dolly shrank with surprise from the touch, but no one seemed to care that Kavas's hand was on her shoulder. Bhindu had carved the flesh from the coconuts and left it in the shells for their dessert. Minoo Kharegat carried his chair away from the railing. "Monkey see, monkey do." She leaned into the hand, joining in the general laughter.

**THE ANGER OF THE CROWD** soon turned to merriment, but the yogi was taken into custody for his safety. The Kharegats served toddy, retiring to the sitting-room downstairs as it got dark. Kavas stayed by Dolly's side and no one, not even Dolly, found it strange. The toddy made him seem an old friend and when he touched her hand she was neither uncomfortable nor surprised. "I came on my bicycle. I will take you home when you are ready. Just say the word and we will be off."

She slid closer to Kavas. "Ready when you are."

They said goodbye, Kavas wheeling his bicycle, she walking alongside as she had walked alongside Phiroze wheeling his bicycle. The path was dusty, no longer as crowded but hardly clear. Kavas was taller than Phiroze and not just because he was four years older. He walked briskly, rarely looking around, but fidgeted with the brake and rang the bell for no reason. She wondered if she had made him cross, but said nothing though she felt pressure to say something as she hadn't all evening.

"So how you find India after coming back from England?"

"Well, it's home, but it's still a servant country. It is not England. The only thing that makes it the least bit bearable is knowing I can leave whenever I wish."

"Really? But what is the difference?"

"One fine day I will take you to England. You will see for yourself."

Dolly stared at him, but he kept his gaze on the hyperbola of light flashed on the path ahead by his lamp. She chose to be no less nonchalant herself, ignoring his astounding invitation. "But you cannot tell me anything? Nothing at all you can tell me?"

"I can tell you one thing."

"What?"

"The girls are very different."

"How are they different?"

"They will let you kiss them."

He had narrowed his eyes, underscoring the challenge of his words, but she refused to be intimidated, arching her shoulders, flinging her answer with a toss of her head. "What do you think? Indian girls do not kiss?"

He raised his eyebrows. "Do you?"

It was the most impudent question anyone had asked her, but she laughed. "What do you think? I am so stupid I am going to tell you?"

"Why not?"

She shrugged.

"Did you ever kiss Phiroze?"

Again she said nothing, pursing her lips.

"Did he ever try to kiss you?"

She stared ahead. "One thing I will tell you. Phiroze would never ask such questions."

Kavas was silent. She was afraid she had offended him, but when he spoke he was calm. "I am sorry. You're right about that, but here's the main difference between us. He wants to marry you, but he doesn't know it. I want to marry you—and I know it."

Her head turned momentarily numb and she spoke in a flurry of words. "Arre, what you are saying? He wants to go to Australia to see the southern sky in the night. He is not even thinking about marriage."

"That's what I'm telling you. He wants to marry you, but he's not willing to admit it—and I am."

"Arre, please, what you are saying? You are not even knowing me. What you are saying?"

"Phiroze wants to marry you, but he's not going to."

"No? Why not?"

"Because I am."

"Really? How you can be so sure?"

"Because Phiroze is a coward and I'm not. He doesn't really want to go to Australia, but it's easier than asking you to marry him—and perhaps by the time he comes back you'll already be married and he won't have to ask you. He can blame you then for not waiting for him—much easier than actually asking you from the start."

It was as she had thought, Phiroze was a coward. She would have been happy to go to Australia with him, but he had never asked, apparently never thought of asking—but more likely he was waiting for her to make the suggestion.

"There's also another reason why Phiroze will not marry you. He is welcome to study the moon and the stars and write poetry and quote Shakespeare and do whatever he wishes, but first things first, and the first thing is that he should support a wife and family—but that does not count a jot in his calculations. He's a dreamer—and whatever dreamers do, they do not make good husbands and fathers."

Dolly nodded. "That is something I have got to think about."

"With Law I can help people. With Law I can provide a service to people who need it. I can be useful. Phiroze doesn't think like that. He goes with the flow—where the wind blows, Phiroze will go." He laughed. "You know, like Ariel."

"Ariel?"

"From Shakespeare's *Tempest*. Phiroze said you liked Shakespeare."

"What I know I like, but I know very little. What is Ariel?"

"He's a spirit, flitting about just like Phiroze, merrily, merrily."

"Merrily, merrily—just like in row-row-row-your-boat?"

Kavas laughed. "Not quite. Would you like to hear it?"

"Shakespeare? Yesyes, very much."

Kavas nodded, gazed into the distance, not unlike Phiroze when he quoted Shakespeare: "*Where the bee sucks, there suck I. In a cowslip's bell I lie. There I couch when owls do cry. On a bat's back I do fly after summer merrily. Merrily, merrily shall I live now under the blossom that hangs on the bough.*"

Dolly didn't understand everything he said, but her eyes were wide and bright when he finished, entranced by the images. "Lovely, so lovely. I love Shakespeare."

Kavas's grin was wide, but ironic. "That's Phiroze for you, frittering away his time like a fairy."

Dolly didn't disagree, but neither did she want to talk about Phiroze behind his back. "And what will you do? Help rich people make more money from poor people?"

To her surprise Kavas laughed. "Of course! What else? Arre, Dollybehn, think about it like this. If I get poor clients I cannot make money—and if I do not make money I cannot help poor clients. What would be the point?"

She laughed, surprising herself, and said nothing, but couldn't help smiling.

"You do not have to say Yes, Dolly. Just do not say No."

"No to what?"

"To marrying me."

"Arre, bawa, I am not saying anything like that about anything. You are not even knowing me and what-all you are talking."

"What is there to know? How well did your mother and father know each other before they were married? How well did mine? The key is to put your best foot forward. The man should support his wife, the woman should nurture her husband. It's that simple."

Dolly stared ahead.

He rang the bell to get her attention. "What are you thinking?"

"I am trying to think what you are doing."

"I would have thought it was plain. I'm asking you to marry me. That's what I'm doing. There, now you have it. What do you say?"

"Arre, just like that? What about love?"

Kavas grimaced. "It's been my experience that people who know the least about love talk about it the most—and vice versa. People don't fall in love to get married; they get married to fall in love."

"But then it does not matter, no, who they marry? Then anybody can marry anybody and they will also fall in love, no?"

"My God, Dolly, I must say you sound nothing at all like a Navsari girl. An English girl might want to fall in love, maybe even a Bombay girl, but not a Navsari girl. Where did you get such a notion?"

"In *Romeo and Juliet* they fell in love first, no?"

"Romeo and Juliet! Well, yes, of course, but you know what happened to them—and to Tristan and Isolde, and Paris and Helen, and to our own Rustom and Tehmina—all ended in tragedy. Love comes from doing one's duty. If a man supports his family and a woman nurtures her family, then there is love—if not, there is no love. Again, it is as simple as that."

"Everything is so simple?"

"It is! That's precisely my point—but most of us simply cannot leave well enough alone. We have to complicate things with talk of love—I mean, here we are, two perfectly good people, a man and a woman, both healthy, both young, both in our prime, both able to make good lives for ourselves—and what are we doing? We are cluttering the simplicity of the situation with talk about love—a subject with which the greatest minds of the world have struggled in vain."

She couldn't deny the way she had felt with Phiroze, the tears when they had parted a year ago, her heart hammering to break out of its cage when they had met again—but no more could she refute Kavas's logic, so rooted in the ground, unlike Phiroze's, so rootless among the stars. "But why me? What about all the English girls you have kissed and all? You could have an English girl, no, if you wanted?"

"But I do not want an English girl. Why should I want a girl who will let other boys kiss her? That's not what I want. My experience with English girls has taught me one thing, that one is better off with one's own kind. There is less chance of misunderstanding. With English girls one is always left guessing whether or not they will sooner or later go back to their own kind."

"But there must be Parsi girls, even in Bombay, no, who would be better for you—for a Sanjana, instead of myself, only a Navsari Dalal?"

# DOLLY'S STORY

"Don't sell yourself short, Dolly Dalal. Of course, there are Parsi girls in Bombay, but they know I am a Sanjana, and that is the main source of their interest. You, on the other hand, stand no chance with a Sanjana. You became our friend almost by accident. That's why I trust you. When we get married it will be because *I* wish it, not you."

Dolly frowned. "What you are saying? I should not wish? Only you should wish?"

"Now don't go putting words in my mouth, Dolly. You know what I mean. As a Sanjana I have to be more careful because ... I have more ... daulat than most people."

He grinned, pleased with the pun on her name, but her frown remained. "You say you are trusting me, but what about me? Should I not also be trusting you? You say you are different from Phiroze, but you are really the same."

"How are we the same?"

"He is not thinking about me, and you are also not thinking about me. You are both thinking only about what you want. He wants to go to Australia and you want to get married. Nobody is asking what I want, only telling what they want. Why should I care what anyone wants? What is it to do with me?"

"But I thought that was understood. If you marry me I will give you what you want—as any husband would for his wife. I have more than enough daulat for my Daulat."

He grinned again, but she grimaced. "Arre, you think you are so clever, but I do not want your daulat. I am already my own Daulat. You do not even know what I want!"

"Well, then, the remedy is simple. You have only to tell me what you want and it will be yours."

"What I want is to trust you also, like you say you trust me. I want to also trust you."

"Well, then, tell me how I am to prove myself. Tell me how I am to win your trust."

"Just like that, jut-phut?"

"Well, yes, exactly, just like that. I'm not the one without trust. You are. I trust you already—jut-phut, as you put it."

"Maybe you can tell me something about yourself?"

"What sort of thing do you mean?"

"Something you would not tell other people."

"And what would that prove?"

"That you trust me, no?"

"I see. Well, do you mean some sort of indiscretion or something? I mean, that wouldn't exactly be cricket, would it?"

"Just something about yourself that nobody is knowing."

He looked at her sharply. "I say, what has Phiroze told you?"

"About what?"

"About me."

Dolly was surprised. "Nothing—just the usual things. He said you were the older brother and you always got everything—but you also wanted his things. He said you were jealous of him."

"Jealous of Phiroze! I say, if that isn't the pot calling the kettle black! What else did he tell you?"

"What does it matter what he told me? I am asking you to tell me something about yourself, and you are asking me to tell you what he told me. You are answering my question with another question. You are not telling me anything. If you only tell me what I already know—then where is the trust?"

Kavas was silent, apparently in thought. "He has told you about my … affliction, has he not?"

She did not know the word. "I do not know. I am asking you to tell me."

"Well, it's true, but it's not as bad as it sounds. It's entirely under control. It could have happened to anyone. Did he tell you how it came about?"

She began to understand. "He did not say very much."

"I did not think he would—just enough to better his own chances, I suppose." The wadis were getting more deserted. The soft tramp of their feet was magnified in the silence that followed, as were other

## DOLLY'S STORY

sounds blotted until then by the startling conversation, crows cawing, pigs grunting, verandahs humming with evening discourses. "Did Phiroze tell you it started with our mother's death?"

His voice had softened and she spoke more gently herself. "No."

Again he was silent, preparing what he wanted to say, walking more slowly. "It's really very simple, but I don't like talking about it. The heart of the matter is that I was the only one with my mother when she died. Pappa was away on business. I was saying goodnight. Phiroze was already in bed."

He seemed to be dragging the words out of his throat and came to an abrupt stop, standing still with the bicycle. Dolly stopped with him, spoke more softly yet, afraid she had asked too much. "It is all right—no need to say more."

He shook his head. "No, I might as well get it over with now that I have started. You must know sooner or later—and better sooner than later. It was a heart attack—nothing to do with me, just an ugly coincidence—but I was kissing her goodnight when it happened. They say the problem started because I blamed myself for what happened and wanted to separate myself from the incident."

"Phiroze said you had it from birth!"

Kavas raised his voice, eyes like green arrows, his entire body puffed into a balloon. "It was *greatly exa*cerbated by my mother's death! That is God's truth! What you choose to believe is up to you!"

"I believe! I believe whatever you say! I just wanted to know—that is all."

Kavas deflated immediately, looking down at the handlebars, slumped in reverie, whiter in the dim light of a lamp strung across a wire overhead—white as an Englishman.

On an impulse she touched his arm. "I am sorry. I should not have asked."

He shook his head, ignoring her hand, wheeling the bicycle ahead again. "Not at all. I am glad you did. It means you are thinking seriously about my proposal." He looked at her again. "Is that the sort of thing you wanted? Do you trust me now?"

"Kavas, I am really very sorry. I did not know. I did not mean to pull it all out of you like that."

"Well, it's true for all that. Now do you trust me?"

"Yes!"

"Just like that—jut-phut?"

He was mocking her, but she did not mind. "Kavas, my mamma also died, you know. She was murdered. I am understanding a little bit about how you must be feeling."

"I know about your mother."

"You know?"

"Of course. Pappa inquired about your family when he learned you and Phiroze were corresponding. I know about your father as well."

She said nothing, but frowned, feeling he had taken something from her without permission, losing her sympathy.

"Don't look so shocked, Dolly. Sanjanas have to be more careful than other people, but don't take it personally. Pappa would have done it no matter who I married—and so would your Dinmai and Jhangu Mama, wouldn't they? What kind of people would they be if they let their children marry strangers?"

Dolly nodded, melting again a little. "So now what will happen?"

"That will depend on you."

"On me? How on me?"

"Well, unless you are entirely averse to the idea, someone from my family will pay a visit to someone from your family, women will talk to women, men will talk to men, and that will be that."

"Just like that?"

"Dolly, I tell you. Everything is really just that simple. I don't understand why we unnecessarily complicate matters."

"I do not know what to say."

"Don't say anything. You don't have to say Yes—but, please, just don't say No."

She liked him for saying Please. "Okay."

"So what do you say?"

She smiled. "I do not say No."

**S**HE REALIZED AFTERWARD she might as well have said Yes. She remembered what Dinmai had said: love was not like an engine-train coming at you khut-khut-khut-khut, but a tree; you planted the seed, you watered the ground, and after some years you had a tree—but her marriage loomed like a locomotive, and she felt railroaded into receiving its rattling wheels and belching smoke. The Sanjanas spoke with the Dalals, men with men, women with women, and the course was set. Dolly left the Tata Girls High School, left Navsari, moved to a lavish flat in Bombay, the entire top storey of Sanjana House, a four storeyed building in the Fort area, where she and Kavas were to live after they married, and had daily lessons in English and etiquette with a tutor, Miss Fuller-Sessions. Various Sanjanas visited to make her acquaintance and help with plans for the wedding to be held in Bombay with a reception in Navsari. Dinmai stayed with her in Bombay, so did Jhangu Mama for a week during a leave from the textile factory. Dinmai was more ecstatic with the luxury of the Bombay flat than Dolly. She could look over the tallest trees in the Cooperage Maidan to the sea from her balconies, wave at crows and kites as they flew by, laugh at people below tiny as ants. Jhangu Mama regarded Dolly with new respect, amazed no less than Dinmai with the regiment of servants, the world reduced to toys in the panorama of her windows, cricketers in the maidan, motors on the road. Other relatives from Navsari and Bombay were no less impressed, all smiles and praise; no less were her schoolfriends, suddenly numerous, solicitous, and congratulatory before she left.

Not saying No was the same as saying Yes. She was sure Kavas had known, but she didn't mind. The attention was a drug and she found herself perpetually gay. Kavas was tall, fair, rich, handsome, England-returned, almost-English himself, and it was easy to imagine she was in love. Her life was out of her hands, but again she didn't mind. The one person in whose hands she had wished to put her life appeared to have washed his hands of her. Phiroze's was the only dissenting voice, but not dissenting enough to change her mind. If anything, he emboldened her to continue her great enterprise. "Dolly, are you quite sure this is what you want?"

Had he offered an alternative, had he not presumed to know what she wanted better than herself, she might have reconsidered, but his presumption only sharpened her will. "Arre, Phiroze, what are you thinking? I am doing this to spite you only?"

"Yes, I do!"

They were in her sitting-room, she in a rosy loveseat, he in a rosy clubchair. He would not look at her as he spoke, his face fractured with dignity, reminding her of the Kavas of old—but Kavas was now jolly enough for both brothers, reminding her of the Phiroze of old. She smiled. "Arre, do not be such a silly-billy. You are only jealous. That is all—because you are now wearing the other shoe."

"What?"

"Miss Fuller-Sessions is teaching me proverbs. It means tables are turning."

"I know what it means, but you said it incorrectly. What you meant to say was that the shoe was on the other foot."

"That is what I said, no? You are now wearing the other shoe. What is the difference?"

"If you do not say a proverb correctly it becomes nonsense. You might as well have said the shoe was on your head for all the sense you made of it. You have to say it correctly."

"Attchha, anyway, have it your way, so that is what I am saying. You are jealous because the shoe is now on the other foot. Now you are happy?"

"My happiness has nothing to do with it. You simply had it wrong. That is all."

"Arre, Phiroze, comecome now, no? This is not about feet and shoes and all that. We must not argue now about smallsmall things. We are going to be brother and sister."

"If I had wanted a sister I would have asked my mother to give me one, but you are right about one thing. It is not about feet and shoes.

It is about something else—but if you do not know what, it is not up to me to tell you."

"Then what? It is up to me? I have to read your mind?"

"You *know* what it is. Why should I have to tell you what you already know?"

"Because some things a man should say. He should not assume everybody knows what he thinks they know—and even if they know he should at least say it one time himself. Or what kind of a man he must be, no?"

"Are you saying I am a coward? You say that a lot, you know—without using the actual words. You imply it all the time."

"Maybe you *are* a coward. I do not know—but that is not what I am saying. What I am saying is that you are now being not only jealous, but also jiddi—stubborn, like a mule. Did I say that also *in*correctly? You see, Miss Fuller-Sessions is also teaching me similes."

He got up to leave. "I see, yes. I see I was wrong after all. I am sorry to have wasted your precious time with my foolishness, but I see now where I stand. Let me just wish you the heartiest congratulations on your marriage and we will leave it at that."

Her voice rose. "Arre, go, then, go, no? Go! Run! Run away like a bailo—like you are always running away. Why should I care if you do not care?"

He stopped at the arched doorway leading to the hall. "*I* not care!" Dinmai, sitting at the dining table across the hall, pretending to be engrossed in a game of patience, looked up from her cards and smiled, thrilled with the drama Dolly had brought into her life. She would get the details later. Phiroze, stung by the unfairness of her remark, rolled his eyes to the ceiling and back to Dolly. If not for him, if not for his *care*, she would never have risen to the heights of a Sanjana, never have been more than little Dolly Dalal of Navsari, married finally to some mouse of a man who would never question her bidding, with whom she would live in a little wadi in little Navsari for the rest of her little life. "*I* not *care!* My God! How dense does one have to be not to see what is in front of one's eyes?"

"Yesyes, very easy to call me stupid. Blame me if it makes things easier for you—but do not fool yourself that I do not understand. Some things need to be said, and if you are not the man to say them … then that is not my fault."

He took a deep breath. "You *know* in your heart—what is in my mind, what is in my heart—but you insist on the vulgarity of bending my will to yours. Perhaps I was wrong about you after all."

"Yesyes, again so many words to tell me why you are not telling me what you could tell me in so few words—and on top of that you are calling me vulgar. Bas, enough. If you are going to go, then go. Maybe I was also wrong about you. Go, no? Why are you standing there like a puppet?"

He took another deep breath, still staring, but she turned away. Dinmai still smiled from the other side, drawing a card from her pack. He left without another word, slamming the door behind him.

**TWO WEEKS LATER** Kavas surprised her, arriving one morning without warning, his face as animated as a shoebox. The servant let him into the dining-room where Dolly and Dinmai were playing cards, snacking on pastries, drinking tea. He remained somber, but they were too immersed in their new lives to notice. They greeted him with smiles as he joined them at the table, holding out a brown paper package to Dolly. "For you."

Her black eyes glittered. "A present?"

His face remained a shoebox. "Yes."

"What is it?"

"Open it and see."

Dolly tore open the package to find three books: *Pride and Prejudice*, *A Tale of Two Cities*, and *Jane Eyre*. "Arre, Kavas, but this is too good of you! So much you are doing for me! What I did to deserve this new present?"

Kavas frowned. "What *have I done* to deserve this."

"What I said?"

"What *did* I say?"

"All right, I understand. You are correcting my English, no?"

"You are correcting my English, *aren't you*? Yes, I'm correcting your English. You must learn to speak properly, Dolly. One is judged constantly by the way one speaks, eats, dresses—everything. You are becoming a Sanjana and you must grow into the part—as I have no doubt you can, and will."

"I am trying, Kavas! Really, I am trying! I am learning something from Miss Fuller-Sessions everyday. Really!"

"I know—and I'm proud of you. That is why I have brought you the books. The best literature is the best education for a mind."

"Goodgood. So, tell me, no –"

"Tell me, won't you?"

"Sorrysorry! *Tell* me, *won't* you? What should I read first?"

"*Which* should I read first—because you are choosing among three books."

"*Which* should I read first! *Which* should I read first! *Which* should I read first! I will remember."

"Good. It's not so difficult once you get the hang of it. You have to start thinking in English instead of translating Gujarati thoughts into English in your head. It's the best way to get rid of your fractured syntax. Reading to yourself in English will help you to think in English. You'll see I'm right."

She grinned. "Of course! How could I forget? You are always right!"

He almost smiled, but couldn't quite cast the shoebox from his face. "Of course! What have I always said?"

"All right, all right, so *tell* me—*won't* you? *Which* should I read first?"

"I suggest *Pride and Prejudice*. It was the earliest of the three to be written—but I think you might like it best for another reason as well. It says something about our respective situations."

"Really? Jane Austen is writing about us?"

"Just read the first sentence."

She opened the book and read slowly, tracing the words with her finger. "*It is a truth universally acknowledged, that a single man in possession of a good fortune must be in want of a wife.*" She looked up, black eyes again aglitter. "Arre, oh, Kavas, again you are right. That fits you to a T, no?"

He raised his eyebrows.

"I mean: doesn't it?"

"It is what I have been trying to tell you all along. Love will come if all other things are considered first. You will see."

Dinmai, unable to understand the conversation, had been munching a Napoleon, but finally nudged Dolly. "Ask why he is looking like that. Somebody has died or what?" Her mouth was smeared with cream from the Napoleon and Dolly wiped her lips with a serviette holding her face. She was still just fourteen, but their roles had been reversed, Dinmai now the child, grimacing and squirming.

Kavas nodded, understanding Gujarati though he spoke it only when necessary. "Dinmai is right. I have some news that I'm afraid might upset you."

"What?"

"It is about Phiroze."

Dolly dropped the serviette and her hands flew to her mouth. "What?"

"We received a letter from him. He didn't want to be at the wedding, so he's gone away."

"To Australia?"

Kavas shook his head. "He has joined the army."

"Arrerere! Omigod! He has joined the army?"

"No one had an inkling of what was on his mind. He was careful not to let his plans slip until it was too late—and to post his letter just before his ship sailed. He is bound as we speak for Mesopotamia."

"Mesopotamia! Arre baap re! Can't we get him back, no? Arre, but we must get him back, no?"

The more she was upset the more she fractured her syntax, but Kavas no longer corrected her. "It's too late. Pappa tried to reach him as soon as he knew—but it was already too late. Phiroze timed everything perfectly. He's been too clever for us, but I hope he hasn't been too clever for himself. I'm afraid there's nothing we can do about it now."

"Arre, but he is not a hero or anything. He will only get himself killed. Omigod! Omigod! Now he will be dead soon. OmigodmiGod!"

Kavas pursed his lips. "Dolly, please, try to control yourself. That is very unlikely. Everyone says the war will be over by Christmas. For all we know he might be shipped back before the wedding—before he has even seen any fighting. A fine fool he'll feel then, I am sure."

The hammer of her heart was crashing at her ribcage. She crossed her hands over her chest to keep it still. "But it is *my* fault! He has joined because I called him a coward. He has only joined to prove how brave he is. Omigod! What have I done?"

"I didn't know you had called him a coward."

"I did not, not really—but he thought I did—but I did not!"

"In any case, there's nothing to be done now."

Dinmai nodded, vaguely comprehending, picking up key words from the conversation, brushing her mouth delicately with the serviette she had picked from the floor. "Praying we can do. Now we must do praying. For all of us, we must do praying."

Dolly got up suddenly, her world blurred by tears, her mind a white fog, and dashed from the room, locking herself in her bedroom, ignoring Kavas's and Dinmai's pleas from the door, hugging a pillow to her chest to still the hammer threatening to shatter her from within.

**It was early September.** The last of the monsoon rains fell in sheets, lashing the side of the old house. The high narrow verandah swayed, drenching Dolly as she balanced herself in her advance against the wind upon an uneven mosaic floor, shouting for her husband. "Kavas! Where are you? Answer me, please, my darling! Where are you?"

The Sanjanas inhabited the large rooms in the front of Sanjana House overlooking the Cooperage Maidan, the sea beyond. The

# A Googly in the Compound

smaller rooms in the wings behind, overlooking the courtyard in the back, linked by narrow inner verandahs, open to the weather on the sides, comprised godowns and servant quarters. During the monsoon, with the wind heaving rain in waves onto the verandahs, not even an umbrella, raincoat, and gumboots could keep visitors dry. An iron spiral staircase, rickety from its base, used only by servants, resembling a giant black ant, climbed one corner of the house.

Dolly shared the top storey with Kavas after they were married; various Sanjanas inhabited the second and third storeys; an English family rented the first; the ground was leased to anywhere from four to six firms at different times, among them two Sanjana enterprises, the rest mostly English. Phiroze's enlistment had stripped the wedding of joy, but she had borne it stoically, no less it seemed than Kavas though this became clear only later. He had acceded to all her requests, a small wedding in respect of the war and Phiroze's predicament, and shown a concern and affection that convinced her she had made the right choice after all—but it seemed to have been a supreme effort, exhausting him for subsequent efforts.

They had married in January, he couldn't have been in higher spirits during their honeymoon in the Nilgiris, the decline was gradual enough for her not to notice at once, but in time she realized he was withdrawing, not only from her but the world. Occasionally, he appeared to be missing, only to be found in the oddest places, sitting on the toilet, in a backroom searching for the watch on his wrist, once under their bed with a pad and crayons drawing the pictures of childhood, stick animals and families in box houses. He had been searching, he said, for his mother, emerging from his hideout only after she had said she would be his mother. When she had relayed her concern to JN, visiting from Navsari, the patriarch had urged her to be sure Kavas took his medicine and to reassure him of her affection at every opportunity—but that, she assured JN, she did already.

"Kavas, my darling!" She had reached the last of the rooms in the back, aware of the servants peering from their barred windows, pitying the poor memsahib, seven months pregnant, with the pagul husband. The wooden verandah rail was splintering, ready to mulch, and she preferred to keep her balance against the wall. She was ready to turn back, frightened by the tilt of the verandah, the weakness of the rail, the continued lash of the rain, the floor slippery with water under her slippered feet, imagining she might easily lose her balance to a wind vicious enough to sweep her over the rail but without power to cradle her fall, when she was arrested by an unexpected sight. Kavas stood perched on top of the iron spiral staircase, swaying more than the verandah. "Kavas! Omigod, Kavas! What are you doing? Come into the verandah!"

Kavas gripped the rail with both hands, but the spiral staircase was without cover and he bore the brunt of the deluge on his head and shoulders, drenched no less by water dislodged in a flood from the roof. He said nothing, but shook his head. She could see he was petrified, afraid to lose his balance should he lose his grip on the rail, but afraid no less to retain his precarious perch on the swaying staircase. The fixtures had been loosened by long neglect, exposure to the elements, left unmaintained because they were rarely used even by the servants. Her first task after the monsoon would be to repair the fixtures.

The stairs led directly onto the verandah, but the rail was low and Kavas was afraid to let go, hands and feet glued to rail and stair. Dolly shucked her slippers—and, gripping the bars of the closest window with her left hand, extended her right. "Kavas, take one hand off the rail and take my hand. One step at a time and we will do it. We will do it together. Come on now, my darling."

Kavas stared a moment apparently without comprehension, but with a sudden movement lifted both hands at once, grabbed wildly at her hand, and stepped onto the verandah almost dragging her down. His hands, slippery with rain and sweat, slid from hers—but his step saved him, allowing him to lunge forward and grab her swollen belly. She held onto the bars of the window with both hands to keep her balance, he trembling on his knees, arms around her hips. Slowly she got him to rise and stand safely beside her. They still had the long narrow verandah to negotiate before they were back in the flat proper, but the worst was behind them.

He said nothing and neither did she until they were in their bedroom, towels in hand, removing his clothes, drying him off, drying herself next. "Kavas, my darling, what is the matter? What were you doing on the backstairs like that? Tell me, please."

He sat on the bed in a white dressing-gown, hands and eyes in his lap, the picture of the penitent, but said nothing.

"Kavas, please, talk to me. I can't go on like this. I love you, my darling, I want to help you, but you have to tell me what is wrong. Otherwise, what can I do?"

He nodded, still with his hands and eyes in his lap.

Dolly whispered. "So, tell me, my darling. What is the matter?"

Kavas echoed her whisper. "It's my fault. It's all my fault. I alone have done it."

"What, my darling? What have you done?"

"About Phiroze."

"What about Phiroze?"

"If not for me he would have married you, he wouldn't now be God knows where doing God knows what. He's not a soldier. He will die, my brother will die, because of …"

His breath gave way, his head sank lower, but she understood easily what he was saying. It was a dilemma she had battled continually herself, but she had been selfish, too thoughtless to recognize he might equally blame himself, with as much if not greater cause. She had felt responsible for one brother, now for two. She stood beside him, holding his head to her breasts. "Oh, my darling, is that what this is all about? Is that all?"

His arms circled her hips, his face nuzzled her breasts. "All because of me, Dolly. First, mamma … and now…. All because of me. I am no good. You should leave me before … something else happens. I should go away … somewhere."

Somehow she managed to smile. "Don't be a complete idiot, my darling. I'm never going to leave you. Of course, I liked Phiroze, and during the time we were writing letters, yes, of course, I thought we might marry—but when we finally met again, when he said he was off to Australia, I just changed my mind. I didn't think he would go to Australia and leave me behind, not if he loved me. That was when I realized I had been looking at the wrong brother all the time."

Kavas remained motionless in her arms.

"Even Dinmai said you were the ambitious brother, you were the one who mattered. Phiroze was the gate, you were the house. You never changed my mind. I changed my own mind, and you fortunately were in agreement. That is what happened. I would not have married Phiroze. I didn't think he loved me, but you talked to me like someone who had thought the whole thing out. Even if you didn't say right away you loved me, your actions showed it. How you could think otherwise, I don't know."

Kavas nuzzled her breasts again. "I did … I did love you, but it was too soon to say. It would have been cheap to say anything so soon."

"No, my darling. I knew it then, and I know it now. It was just right."

JN had been correct. The right mixture of medicine, affection, and reassurance worked wonders with Kavas. His demeanor was restored to what it had been at the time of the wedding … until the day Phiroze returned from Mesopotamia a year later.

# DAY OF THE TIGER: 2
## (September 25, 1945)

R ADHA STEPPED BAREFOOT into the compound carrying a bowl of sliced and sugared papaya, holding it in both hands the better not to drop it, and walked toward the Sanjanas at breakfast. She was nine, Fakhro's oldest daughter, a skinny girl with a round face, wearing a clean tattered dress, black hair in a long pigtail sporting two ribbons, one red, one blue. She went to school, played with her friends, and helped her mother and father and sisters with the upkeep of Truth Bungalow—but when the Sanjanas visited all her activities became secondary to theirs. Being the oldest she had boiled water for tea, sliced bread for toast, set the table for breakfast, and helped her mother cook acouri. She worked quietly, not least because she was afraid of Sohrab sahib who was an angry sahib, and an angry sahib needed little provocation to vent his anger. He had been angry all through breakfast, but she had made it so far without drawing attention to herself, and hoped the rest of the meal would prove as uneventful. She had barely started across the compound when he began to shout.

"What are you doing? Why are you bringing the papaya already? Bring more acouri first! Bring more toast! Bring the papaya *af*ter we have finished the rest of the breakfast—not be*fore*! What have you got? Porridge for brains?"

She knew from the start he was addressing her, even before he mentioned the papaya. Otherwise, he would not have spoken in

Gujarati. Her head filled with ice as she imagined everyone's eyes upon her.

"Go on! Why are you standing there like a statue?"

She turned, almost tripping as she scurried back to the bungalow, up the stairs, across the hallway, into the kitchen to her mother. Fakhro, standing by one of the open windows in case he was needed, disappeared behind her. They could hear him shouting at his daughter from the compound.

Daisy looked at Dolly. "Why is *he* shouting at her? Bad enough she has our Sohrab to put up with without *him* lashing at her as well."

Sohrab spoke without looking at his wife. "You don't know what you're saying. We have got to train these people properly from the start. Otherwise, they get into all sorts of bad habits. They develop all sorts of fancy ideas about themselves. Fakhro is quite right to shout at her. She has got to learn—and she is lucky to be learning from us rather than from some babu who wouldn't be half as understanding."

Daisy had been six years in India, but the more she learned about her adopted country the more she wanted to learn. She had no qualms about violating customs if she disagreed with them, but preferred to violate them knowing what she was doing than out of ignorance. In such matters she found Dolly her best guide and looked to her for confirmation.

Dolly nodded, accepting her role with pleasure. "There is something to what Sohrab says. The servants expect you to be firm with them"—she turned to her older son—"but there's no need to shout at them. They're not deaf."

Sohrab didn't look up. "If one doesn't shout at them one doesn't get any work out of them."

Dolly shook her head for Daisy's benefit. "If you shout at them you can be sure they'll get back at you behind your back. They respect a firm hand, but not a tyrant's hand. They have a grapevine, and if you lose the respect of one you will lose the respect of all of them."

Sohrab brushed her aside with a wave of his hand. "Come on, Mummy! That may be true in Bombay, but not here in Navsari—*surely* not!" He looked at Daisy. "You know how the servants are in Bombay, thick as thieves. They meet all the time—in the school, in the bageecha, at the children's parties. How could they *not* know about everyone else? But here the network is not even a web, just a piece of string at best—and a rather short piece of string considering how isolated we are in Navsari."

Dolly shook her head. "Less isolated by the year. Navsari is expanding by leaps and bounds. When I was a girl it took an hour to walk from Truth to the town. Now it takes fifteen minutes. I should know. Your daddy and I did a lot of walking." Phiroze said nothing, casting his eyes down, but Daisy saw the corners of his mouth rise—resembling the corners of Dolly's own mouth as she continued. "And we are hardly ever in Navsari, which gives the servants a lot of time on their hands, and time will make a gossip out of a saint. Besides, Sarosh and Armaiti are here on weekends, also their friends and neighbors, and God alone knows what they say about us behind our backs."

Sohrab frowned. "Why should they say anything? And in any case, what is there to say?"

Dolly smiled. "Arre, Sohrab, what have *you* got? Porridge for brains? It is human nature. Grass is always greener on the other side. People always bite the hand that feeds them. Besides, it really wasn't necessary for you to shout at the poor girl like that. You should have let her bring the papaya. It's not as if it was going to get cold or anything—and she tries so hard, the poor thing, without having to put up with your bullying."

"Sticks and stones …"

Daisy grinned. "It seems someone didn't get enough sticks and stones when he was growing up."

Sohrab glowered. "Very funny—but of course you English are known for your sense of humor."

"Of course! It's our finest export!" Daisy's grin expanded and for a moment the entire group joined her, but the brief silence amplified the drama in the kitchen until Daisy spoke again. "But why *is* Fakhro shouting at her? Why is he *still* shouting at her?"

# A Googly in the Compound

Rustom was buttering toast. "For our benefit, you can be sure—not hers."

"How would it be for our benefit?"

Sohrab shook his head. "Now who has porridge for brains?" He stared into his plate making a morsel of acouri, toast, and bacon. "He wants to ally himself with his masters—with the high and the mighty, the rich and the powerful—much easier than standing up for a little girl even if she happens to be his daughter."

Dolly nodded agreement. "Launching a preemptive strike."

"But how very cowardly of him."

Dolly shook her head. "Not really. He doesn't know any better."

"But how could he *not*?"

"It's a matter of breeding. It's been going on for generations. I remember when he was born, when Fakhro was born, his father came to us saying *not* 'I have a son,' but 'your sons have a servant,' meaning of course Sohrab and Rustom though neither of them had been born yet. He was telling me that his son had been born to be the servant of mine even before my sons were born."

Daisy rolled her eyes.

Sohrab kept his eyes on his plate. "Of course, only a workingclass Englishwoman would be surprised to hear that."

Daisy had revealed little to the Sanjanas about her life before she had come to India, saying it didn't help to talk about something you wished to escape, and was composed enough not to rise to Sohrab's bait. Sohrab opened his mouth to elaborate on his theme, but Radha appeared again on the steps with a rack of toast in one hand, a dish of acouri in the other, and Daisy cast him a warning glance. "Now just you hush up, Sohrab. Don't you dare scare the poor girl again."

Radha avoided the shortest approach to the table, between Sohrab and Daisy, approaching instead between Daisy and Rustom. Daisy gave her a broad smile. "Thank you very much, Radha."

Radha appeared not to hear, keeping her eyes on her hands as she placed toast and acouri on the table and hurrying back to the bungalow.

Sohrab reached for the toast. "If you ask me, you just bloody well embarrassed her more than I did by about a hundred percent. They expect you to yell at them, that's the master-servant relationship for you, and they understand it—but they have absolutely no idea what to do if you suddenly become courteous: please this, and thank you very much that."

Daisy didn't look at him. "Well, no one asked you."

Dolly passed the acouri to Rustom after spooning some into Phiroze's plate and pushing the plate within reach of his left hand. Phiroze thanked her as he always did for the least favor, speaking softly as always, before turning to Daisy. "You know, I am reminded of something."

"Yes, Dad? What is it?"

Sohrab grunted. He knew she liked his stepfather, but imagined she called him Dad no less to annoy him. "Yes, Daddyji, what is it?"

He had adopted his babu tone again, mocking both Phiroze and Daisy. Phiroze's smile never wavered, but Daisy caught his involuntary wince. "Don't you mind what he says, Dad. You know he doesn't mean it."

Sohrab grimaced. "I must say I'm getting rather sick and tired of everyone telling me what I mean and what I don't mean when I've just told them in plain English exactly what I *do* mean."

Daisy appeared not to have heard him and so did Phiroze, sparing Sohrab not even a glance as he spoke. "What we were discussing earlier, about Fakhro making a preemptive strike—scolding Radha."

Dolly slid more toast, buttered and cut diagonally, into his plate. "Yes, my love?"

Daisy found the affection between Dolly and Phiroze endearing—never overt, never in doubt. Phiroze spoke again, still softly. "It's not just human nature, it's also in animals. When a pack of jackals is cornered by a tiger it turns on the weakest jackal—and offers it to the tiger. It's a survival mechanism."

Daisy took a deep breath. "Fascinating!"

## A Googly in the Compound

Phiroze nodded. "Indeed, and we Indians are the same when we are with the English. If one of us makes the smallest mistake it's as good as a signal for the rest of us to gang up on him." He laughed. "We also want to be allied with the high and the mighty."

Dolly smiled. "And Sohrab maybe most of all."

Sohrab grimaced again. "As I said, sticks and stones—OUCHH!"

Everyone turned to Sohrab. Daisy spoke first. "What did you do now?"

Sohrab had cut his thumb cutting his toast. He whipped it in the air before sucking on it. "Bloody hell! Why we don't have the bloody toast sliced and buttered before it's brought to us I'll never bloody understand!"

Dolly shouted toward the kitchen. "Laxmi! Come at once!" She turned to Sohrab. "You know exactly why we don't do that. If the toast is buttered it gets smashed because the butter is too hard. If it is cut diagonally, you want strips. If it is cut in strips, you want it cut diagonally. It's simply impossible to please everyone. Better to let everyone cut and butter their own toast as they please."

Sohrab continued to suck his thumb. "I still don't see what is so very difficult about leaving the butter out overnight so it spreads easily in the morning—and then cutting some of the toast diagonally and some in strips. I simply don't see what's so very difficult about that!"

"Sohrab, I re*fuse* to have this argument again. If you are unable to cut a piece of toast without cutting yourself maybe you should just stop eating toast." Laxmi came running down the steps and across the courtyard. "Laxmi, seth has cut his thumb. Bring the lal dava from the bathroom, also cotton wool."

"Arrerere! Yes, bai! I will bring at once!"

Sohrab shook his head. "No, leave it alone. It's just a scratch—nothing to worry about."

"Arre, Sohrab, don't be silly now. A dab of mercurochrome is all it needs."

"It's nothing. Mercurochrome will only make it look worse than it is. Why they have a red medicine to cover something that bleeds I'll never understand." He continued to suck his thumb, waving Laxmi away. "Go! Go! No need to bring anything. Bai is making a fuss about nothing. It is only a small cut. If you bring it you will only have to take it back."

Laxmi looked at Dolly who sighed. "Let it go, Laxmi. If seth will not listen, he will not listen."

Sohrab said nothing, but glared at his mother, still sucking his thumb.

# SOHRAB'S STORY
## Bombay (1924–1927)

**I**F YOU CHECKED THE ANNALS of myth and history for the names of Rustom and Sohrab, the earliest entry of note would reveal a father and son locked in mortal combat, champions of opposing armies, not knowing the other's identity, father killing son knowing not what he had done until it was too late. Trace the rows of dominoes clacking and crisscrossing their paths through space and time and you will find Sohrab and Rustom, brother and brother, descended from Kavas and Phiroze, brother and brother. Trace another row clacking toward them from London and you will find a pretty girl in the form of ten-year-old Gillian Collins.

She stood to display herself in the doorway of her brother's room, wearing a white pleated low-waisted dress with a Peter Pan collar. A maroon beret set off her reddish blond head to perfection—and she knew it. She had gathered the flood of her hair in two loose braids behind and secured each with a satin maroon bow for the same reason. She wore white socks, black buckled shoes, and spoke with a plush white hand on her hip, knee turned inward, voice breathless. "Dear Tums, it's just too divine that you will be spending three whole weeks with us—but, of course, it's just too awful about Rabs."

The Collinses lived in Sanjana House, one floor below the Sanjanas, in an otherwise identical flat. Gillian was too old for her four-year-old brother, and Terry too focused on the Humpty Dumpty Circus he was assembling with Rustom to care—but Rustom looked up. Just six, he was flattered by the attention of an older child, a pale English girl—and eager to embrace his new name. No one else called him Tums; no one else called Sohrab Rabs; and though it was, as Gillian said, just too awful about Rabs, it was a new life for him. Sohrab, older by three years, had succumbed to chicken pox, a disease that sounded to Rustom like a game, but it had quarantined him in his room and deposited Rustom in the flat below with the Collinses for the duration. The room he shared with Terry was the same as his own, one floor above.

Terry concentrated on balancing a tightrope walker on a highwire, but Rustom set aside the row of elephants emerging from the tent, looking up to see dimpled white knees in the doorway. It had taken him a while to organize the elephants so each held the tail of the preceding elephant in its jointed trunk, but live English girls were more exotic than the host of toys and games littered outside the perimeter of the circus paraphernalia. He stared, wondering what to say, feeling something was expected, when she spoke again.

"Do you know how to escape from a locked room?"

He shook his head.

"Would you like me to show you?"

Terry looked up suddenly. Gillian had taken scissors and safety pins to his new sailor suit to fit one of her dolls. Their father had laughed and their mother had promised him a new suit, but Gillian had shown no remorse, never acknowledged wrongdoing, never apologized. It was an hour to bedtime and he didn't want to lose his playmate. "No!"

Gillian turned pale blue eyes on her brother, apparently seeing him for the first time. "You mustn't be selfish, Terry. You've had Tums to yourself all day."

Terry held her gaze. "Where's Georgina?"

Georgina was Gillian's best friend. "She went home. She wasn't feeling well."

Terry returned to the tightrope walker as if the matter were settled. Rustom looked from Gillian to Terry and back to Gillian for direction.

Gillian smiled. "Come on, Tums. You can play with Terry tomorrow."

Rustom followed Gillian to her room, slightly larger, the same as Sohrab's upstairs, and littered no less with games and toys though dolls, books, stuffed animals, a Plasticine set, and a toy piano took the place of Terry's wagons, dirigibles, airplanes, automobiles, and circus. There were stills of Chaplin, Garbo, and Douglas Fairbanks on the walls, and magazines on the table (*Queen & Princess*, *Girls Digest*, *Screen Stars*).

Gillian picked a large iron key from her dresser and bounced on her toes with anticipation. "Oh, Tums, I can hardly wait. You're going to laugh when you see how easy it is." She inserted the key from outside, but left the door unlocked, the key still in the lock, when she shut the two of them off in her room.

Rustom pointed to the latch. "You didn't lock it."

She nodded, smiling patiently. "I know—but if I locked it I would be outside and you would be inside—and I wouldn't be able to show you how to get out."

Rustom frowned. "The key is in the door. If someone locked us in he would take away the key."

Gillian shook her head. "No, he wouldn't. You see, if he took away the key you would be able to see through the keyhole, and he wouldn't want you to do that, would he? He wouldn't want you to know what he was doing—but if he left the key in the door you wouldn't be able to see out, would you?"

Rustom still frowned, but nodded.

Gillian smiled again. "Now, watch! This is how you get out of a locked room. It's really quite the simplest thing in the world."

Rustom watched closely, still frowning, as she slid three-quarters of a magazine through the crack under the door below the keyhole. She unbent a hairpin into a straight wire, knelt before the keyhole, and jiggled the wire in the keyhole until the key fell on the magazine.

His frown turned to a smile as she pulled the magazine back, drawing the key with it, and held the key upright between her thumb and forefinger. "Abra kadabra!"

Rustom nodded. "Can I try?"

She locked him in. He was careless the first time, and the key fell on the floor beyond the magazine. The second time, jiggling the key more carefully, he was successful. He let himself out four times before he was satisfied, grinning as widely as Gillian. He would have tried it again, but she hugged him as he reached for the key—"You're so cute! Little boys are just so cute!"—and kissed his lips.

Rustom pulled back. Her kiss was wet like that of a dog. "I am big. Mummy says I am a big boy."

"You *are!* For your age you're a *big* boy, *big*ger than Rabs—for your age."

"That's what Mummy says. She says I will be bigger than Sohrab."

"You *will* be! You're bigger than him already—for your age." She grinned. "We all know the story, of course, of Sohrab and Rustom."

Rustom frowned. "About me and Sohrab there is a story?"

"No, Tums, you big silly, not about *you* and Sohrab. I mean the *leg*end of Sohrab and Rustom. I would have thought that with your name, and a brother named Sohrab, that would have been the first story you would have learned."

"Oh, *that* story." Rustom shook his head. Dinmai had once begun to tell them the story, but their mother had called her from the room and the story had never been resumed. He never forgot Dinmai's face when she returned, ballooning with rage, eyes unblinking and fixed on air, lips trembling as she warned them from asking for the story again, succeeding only in arousing their curiosity. "Mummy doesn't want us to know the story. She said it's a bad story."

"Oh, but what a *fright*ful thing to say. It's a *beau*tiful story—it's a sad story, but it's *beau*tiful. Would you like to hear it?"

He shook his head again. "Mummy doesn't want us to hear it."

"Oh, but how silly! How will you know if it's good or bad if you never hear it?"

"But Mummy doesn't *want* us to hear it."

"You don't have to tell her, do you? I always think it's best to make up your own mind about what's good and what's bad—about everything—don't you?"

Rustom remained silent, frowns creasing his brow, but he nodded.

"I just happen to have the book. Shall I read it to you? Would you like that?"

Rustom remained silent, but nodded again.

Gillian pulled the book from her shelf and read the story of the ongoing battle between Persia and Turan, Rustom, the hero of the Persian Empire, pitted through the connivance of his enemies in single combat against his son, Sohrab, whom he had never seen. The Emperor of Turan had calculated well: if Rustom won he would be weakened knowing he had killed his son; and if Sohrab won Turan would celebrate the death of their greatest enemy. Father and son suspect each other's identity, but the Emperor's aides swear to Sohrab that this is not Rustom whom they know from the battlefield, and Rustom knows only that his son is fourteen and his opponent appears much older.

On the first day of combat father and son fight to a draw. On the second day, Sohrab has Rustom at his mercy, but spares him when the older man says it is their custom to kill only at the second chance. On the third day, Rustom deals a mortal blow, giving Sohrab no second chance, only to be warned by the dying Sohrab that his father, Rustom, will avenge his death—but by then it is too late for them both.

Gillian shut the book, her smile beatific, her pale face reddening, her tone suitably choked. "Isn't that the most beautiful story you ever heard?"

Rustom had listened spellbound. "Rustom killed Sohrab?"

"Yes, but he didn't know what he was doing. That's what makes it so sad."

"But he *killed* him? Rustom *killed* Sohrab?"

"Yes, he did. Rustom killed Sohrab. He killed his only son."

Rustom shook his head, repeating the words in wonder. "Rustom killed Sohrab?"

## A Googly in the Compound

Unable to contain herself, Gillian grabbed him, held him tight, and kissed his mouth again, flicking her tongue over his lips.

Rustom was overwhelmed, but not uncomfortable. Unsure what was expected he remained limp, registering a taste of toothpaste, a smell of powder, and the texture of her arms plush and smooth as satin.

When he struggled she loosened her grip, but kept her arms around his waist, her grin blazing with mischief. "You know, you really are the cutest boy!

SOHRAB ARRANGED THE WOODEN COINS on the carom board, black and white men around a red queen, lining the whites so they would shoot straight into a pocket. Each coin carried a point, except the queen which carried five, but the queen needed to be covered by either a black or a white coin or back it came to the center of the board.

They sat around the board on a chatai on the floor of his bedroom in Sanjana House, Sohrab partnered with his best friend, Berzin Shroff, Rustom with Alphonse. The queen with her cover would decide the game. Rustom was good with close shots, but not coordinated enough at six to pose a threat, making for a fair game because Alphonse, at eleven, was the oldest and strongest, and Sohrab and Berzin, both nine, were equally matched.

Alphonse called Sohrab by his first name, played with them as an equal, learned English from Jesuits in Goa, but he was still the son of Sohrab's ayah, Gracie, ate in the kitchen with the other servants, and slept on a sheet on the floor of the godown among suitcases, old newspapers, and dirty clothes. Gracie sat crosslegged on the floor to one side, sewing buttons on Sohrab's school uniform. Rustom's ayah, Janie, washed dishes in the kitchen.

They had dined early, six o'clock, roast lamb with potatoes and stewed apples, just Sohrab, Berzin, and Rustom, because Dolly and Phiroze were preparing for a dinner party at the Collinses downstairs.

# SOHRAB'S STORY

Sohrab placed the flat white striker in home position. His tongue crept out of his mouth as he aimed—but, trembling with strain, sticky with heat despite the ceiling fan, his forefinger slid past his thumb hitting the striker at an odd angle, setting it briefly aloft, barely cracking the cluster of coins in the middle. He almost jumped to his feet. "It slipped! I get to go again!"

Alphonse shook his head. "Arre, Sohrab, no! If the striker hits the coins—even touches just a little bit—you cannot go again. It is against the rules. Look if you do not believe."

"I don't care! It slipped! Aphoos, you *saw* it slipped! The rules do not apply if your finger slips!"

They called him Aphoos, the Gujarati name for Alphonse mangoes, a name he detested but was powerless to protest. He spoke softly, eyes on the board. "Yes, they apply. Why they do not apply?"

"What do you know, you stupid blackie? You *know* it slipped! You *saw* it yourself!"

Alphonse's response was predictable—a glare, a growl, a grimace—wanting to frighten the son of the house, knowing he could never touch him in anger. The abuse was never easy to bear, especially not from someone two years younger, but Sohrab returned his glare secure in the protection of Alphonse's own mother. Alphonse was the handsomest boy he knew, his features sharp as an actor's, skin smooth as a girl's, and in his insecurity, particularly since the chicken pox had permanently pocked his face, most prominently one eyebrow, his upper lip, and the bridge of his nose, Sohrab never let him forget his color, who was the master, who the servant. Alphonse might have said nothing, but instead he grinned, catching Rustom's eye. "Doesn't matter, Rustom. We will still win. Remember, Rustom killed Sohrab."

Rustom nodded, returning his grin, aiming a finger pistol at Sohrab. "Bang! You're dead! Rustom killed Sohrab!"

Sohrab's intake of breath was as sharp as it was involuntary, a hissing of air between bared teeth as his eyes grew to saucers. "Stop *say*ing that, you *bloo*dy *fool*."

Berzin's grin was ironic. "He's right, you know. Rustom did kill Sohrab."

Sohrab scowled. "What? You also? What is the *mat*ter with everyone? Has *ev*eryone gone mad?"

Berzin retreated before Sohrab's fury, hands open in appeal. "Arre, Sohrab, why are you getting upset? It's just a story. Don't you know the story?"

Sohrab's mouth shrank, suddenly gummy and toothless, his voice hushed with fear. "It's a bad story. Mummy said we were not to hear it."

Berzin frowned. "Well, I don't know how bad it is, but it's a sad story—and Rustom is right. Rustom killed Sohrab—in the story, I mean, of course."

In the silence that followed Alphonse turned his eyes back to the board. "It is not in the rules. If it is not in the rules, it is not allowed."

Berzin's grin was ironic. "Arre, Aphoos, so what? So what if it is not in the rules? Whose board is it? Whoever owns the board makes up the rules. You don't know that still?"

Sohrab raised his voice again. "Berzin, you just shut up! No one is asking for your opinion!"

"Arre! Since when do I have to ask permission for my opinion?"

Gracie snapped the thread of the button she was sewing with her teeth. "Baba, for what you are making so much noise? Talk quietly, no? What is the matter?"

"Aphoos is saying I am cheating! That is what is the matter!"

Gracie made peace the only way she could between her son and the son of her master, scolding the child over whom she had greater jurisdiction. "Alphonse! Be good. Say sorry."

"Why should I say sorry? I never said, Mummy! I never said he was cheating!"

Sohrab shouted. "Might as well have said! Might as well is the same as actually saying!"

Berzin laughed. "Righto! And might as well shouting is the same as actually shouting! And might as well playing the game is the same as actually playing the game! And might as well going to school is the same as actually going to school! And might as well –"

"You shut up, I said—you Berzinwerzin Bumblebee!"

"Stick and stones may break my bones, but names can never hurt me."

"Alphonse, say sorry, no? Be good boy, no?"

"But I *ne*ver said, Mummy! I *ne*ver said he was cheating!"

"Just say, no? Just say sorry—for your old mummy?"

Alphonse took a deep breath. "I am sorry. Okay, now? Satisfy?"

Sohrab's grin was ugly with triumph, so was the mockery in his voice, mimicking Alphonse's mistake. "Satis*fy*—yes, I am very satis*fy*."

There was a moment of silence while Berzin powdered the board. Sohrab stared Alphonse down before threatening Rustom with his gaze, nodding as if there were a lesson in it for him as well. Rustom grinned, holding his brother's gaze, aiming his pistol again. "Bang! You're dead!"

Sohrab threw himself at Rustom, pinning him to the floor with his knees, but swinging his arms so wildly that he landed only glancing blows. The others got out of the way, anticipating a good fight since Rustom was almost Sohrab's size. Gracie rose to separate them, but Rustom raised his legs, knotted them at the ankles under Sohrab's chin, and pulled him off. The brothers were on their feet at once, ready to engage, but Sohrab called it off, saying he was still recuperating. He pleaded recuperation to get out of fights, but it didn't stop him from starting them. It was true he was weak from the pox, but also newly aware of Rustom's strength, afraid to be beaten by his younger brother.

He arranged the coins on the board, breathing heavily, glaring at everyone, and shot with more strength than before, but not enough to sink any of his whites in the pockets. Instead he exploded the center so that both whites and blacks crowded the pockets allowing Alphonse, who shot next, to sink three blacks. Next he sank the queen, but couldn't cover her, and returned her to the center of the board.

## A Googly in the Compound

Sohrab clapped his hands. "Berzin, take the queen. It is a sure thing. You have got so many covers. Take the queen."

"Arre, I have got the covers, but I haven't got the queen—smackdab in the middle she is, and so many pieces in the way."

"Just take the queen. Then worry about the rest."

"Arre, Sohrab, I might as well take the covers while I can. If I miss the queen I will miss the chance for the easy shots."

"Berzin, take the queen! If you take the queen we have as good as won. If you don't take the queen it will not matter how many easy shots you miss."

"Okay, okay. Take it easy. I swear, Sohrab, so excited you get over just a game!"

"Just play!"

Berzin concentrated, sinking the queen.

"Good shot!" Sohrab clenched both fists in the air in a victory salute. "First class! Now get the cover!"

For the cover Berzin chose an easy inner shot; a slight touch of his thumb to the striker would have tipped the coin into the pocket; but he was careless with the easier shot and accidentally covered the queen with one of the black coins, giving the five points to Rustom and Alphonse.

Alphonse grinned, clenching fists in the air as Sohrab had done. "Good shot! First class!"

"Berzin, you fool! You bloody fool! What have you done? What is the *mat*ter with you?"

"Arre, Sohrab, take it easy, man! I'm sorry. What can I say? My thumb slipped. In any case, old chap, we haven't lost yet."

"As *good* as! We have as *good* as lost!"

Alphonse placed the striker in the home position for Rustom. "Rustom, do what I say, and we will win! I give you my top guaranty!"

"Your top bloody guaranty is no bloody good!" Sohrab swept his hand across the board, sending the coins flying. "That's for your bloody guaranty! That's what you get for being a bloody cheater! Cheaters never prosper!"

Rustom grinned, waving both hands in the air like pistols. "Bang! You're dead!" Gracie stood by, her face a big teardrop. Alphonse glowered, picking up the pieces, speaking in an undertone. "Nobody was cheating."

Sohrab ignored him. The game was over and so was the evening. It was just half past seven, but Berzin was tired and ready to go home. He lived in Wellesley House, two buildings away on the same road. "Tell your mum and dad thanks for the dinner. It was delicious."

"Tell them yourself. They will be ready in a minute. Their party isn't until eight."

"Arre, Sohrab, no one ever goes to these things on time. You know that."

Sohrab nodded, eyes blinking and glistening. "Berz, I'm sorry I lost my temper. Why not stay anyway? We have time for another game."

Berzin had anticipated the apology. It was why he remained Sohrab's friend. "Not today. I really am really tired for some reason."

Sohrab nodded, walking his friend to the door. "Really, I'm sorry, Berz. Something just happens to me when I see people cheating—and I really don't know what's the matter with Rustom. I've told him to stop saying that, I don't know how many times. I swear I'm going to give him the bloody pasting of his life if he keeps it up, but I'm really sorry."

"It's all right, really. I had a good time."

Sohrab allowed himself a small smile. "Me too, really."

"Well, then, nothing to be mad about."

"Righto."

"Well, then, bye-bye, old chap."

"Cheerio, old Berz."

It didn't occur to Sohrab to apologize to Alphonse. If he thought about it at all it was to satisfy himself that Alphonse would think twice before crossing him again. When he got back to his bedroom he found Rustom, Alphonse, and Gracie joined by Janie who had finished washing dishes. Rustom was arranging the coins again in the center of the board for a new game. "Sohrab, you want to play?"

"No."

"Mind if we use your board?"

"No, but take it to your room. I want to read. I need peace and quiet."

"All right." Rustom began putting the coins back in the box.

Alphonse picked up the board, Gracie the chatai and powder. Sohrab didn't want to play, but resented their quick exit. "Janie, before you start, I want some chips. Make me some chips first."

Janie was surprised. "Chips, baba? But I have just cleaned up the kitchen for the day, no?"

"So what? I want some chips! Just cut up three big potatoes and fry them. That's all you have to do—and don't forget to put in the salt *while* they are frying, not afterward."

"But, baba, why not I will heat up some of the lamb dinner? It is not all finished still. You will like that, no, your lamb dinner?"

"No, I will not like! I said I wanted some chips!"

"But, baba, too late now for chips, no? Tomorrow I will make you chips for lunch and dinner if you like, all right?"

Sohrab began to shout again. "I don't know if you're *deaf* or just plain *stu*pid! I *said* I *wan*ted some *chips!*"

Gracie got up hurriedly. "I will make you chips, baba. Not to shout. I will make you chips."

"Thank you very much!"

Gracie went to the kitchen, Alphonse in her wake. Rustom went with Janie to his own bedroom, taking the board, coins, and chatai. Sohrab changed into pajamas and got into bed with a Billy Bunter, but finding himself unable to focus went to Dolly and Phiroze's bedroom.

IT WAS ALMOST EIGHT O'CLOCK, but Dolly's gold handpainted sari remained spread on the bed, Phiroze lying beside it in his sadra and white cotton drawers, fresh and warm from his bath, evening clothes laid beside him in readiness. Dolly stood in a silver petticoat and gold blouse before the full-length mirror of her cupboard, selecting earrings for the evening from the safe. Phiroze enjoyed watching her dress. After all they had been through she was still just twenty-four, fourteen marrying Kavas, seventeen marrying him, and only now blossoming to womanhood, skinny limbs turning plush, bony torso turning sleek. She had bobbed her hair in the American fashion—and even, very faintly, applied lipstick. He might have said the same for himself, seventeen in Mesopotamia, nineteen returning limbless, twenty marrying Dolly, and happier at the ripe age of twenty-seven than he could remember. Dolly looked up as Sohrab entered. "What? pajamas already? Did Berzin leave?"

"Yes."

"Why so early?"

"He said he was tired."

"Really? What were you doing that made him so tired?" She looked at him, brow wrinkling. "You're still recovering, you know. You're not supposed to be exerting yourself."

"I didn't. We were just playing carom. He was just tired."

Her face remained concerned though she turned back to her mirror to insert earrings. "Did you have a fight? I thought I heard shouting. Was that you?"

Sohrab wanted to say Rustom had started the fight, but there were too many witnesses to the contrary. "Yes, but it wasn't a fight. Aphoos said I was cheating—and he made me mad. That's all."

"Alphonse said that? He said you were cheating?"

"He as *good* as said it." Sohrab explained what had happened.

Dolly listened in silence, winding the sari around her waist. "I wish you wouldn't lose your temper so easily, Sohrab. It is such a small thing—a game of carom, for heaven's sake. What will you do when someone gives you a *real* reason—explode, I suppose, like a bomb or something."

She spoke lightly, not wishing to alarm her son, but concerned about the similarities between Sohrab and his father, thinking about Kavas's great self-destruction. She discussed her fears only with Phiroze who was aware of the similarities more even than Dolly, having known Kavas since boyhood. "But Mummy, a game is like playing at life. You said it yourself. What happens in games happens in life—and how we deal with it in games affects how we deal with it in life. You said it yourself."

Phiroze was aware of Sohrab's resentment, however muted, an uncle usurping the place of a father. He left Sohrab to Dolly, intervening occasionally only to encourage or defend him—and spoil him, Dolly said, though she tarred herself with the same brush. Both gave him the benefit of the doubt, largely for the similarities he bore his biological father. Phiroze smiled. "The boy is right, Mummy. You said it yourself. The child is the father of the man, and our games are the fathers of our lives."

"Yes, yes, very poetic you can be, we all know that—but I am not denying what I said. I am only suggesting that he should make the punishment fit the crime. You see, I can also be poetic."

Sohrab frowned. "But, Mummy, there was no crime. What crime are you talking about?"

"I *said* I was being poetic. If a small crime deserves a small punishment, then a small action deserves a small reaction, no? No point getting so upset over something so small—not to mention upsetting Berzin and Rustom and the servants as well. Doesn't that make sense?"

Sohrab's frown became more thoughtful. "I guess so." The grandfather clock in the hallway struck eight. "You're going to be late, Mummy."

"Nobody is ever on time for these things, Sohrab. If we were on time that would be rude. The Collinses wouldn't know what to do with us."

Sohrab nodded. "Is Gillian going to be there?"

Dolly smiled. "I suppose she will at least make an appearance. Why do you ask?"

"She's very pretty."

Dolly and Phiroze looked at each other. Dolly turned again to Sohrab. "Do you think so?"

"Yes, I do. She has very white skin, like moonlight—like silver in moonlight."

Dolly raised her eyebrows. "It seems everyone is a poet tonight."

"But it *is!* It's like silver—like silver in moonlight!"

"Yes, it's very white. We all know."

"Because she's English—not Spanish or Italian, who are not so white."

Dolly smiled. "Yes, of course, Sohrab—but what a thing to say!"

"*You* said it, Mummy. *You* said it first. *You* said Parsis could pass for Spanish or Italian, but not for English or German or Swedish."

"Yes, I suppose I did—but what a thing to remember."

Phiroze pursed his lips. Parsis took pride in the paleness of their skin, all too often paying less attention to what lay underneath. In that they were not unlike other races, but it would be refreshing to hear someone say that Parsis could pass for north Indians but not for south, or for Europeans but not for Africans, as if the darker color were the more desirable. He might sometime find a good fit for the remark himself, perhaps in the context of a larger conversation, but the irony would more than likely pass unnoticed. He interrupted the conversation quietly. "Do you like to play with Gillian?"

Sohrab smiled like a cat recalling cream. "Yes, I do—very much! She showed Rustom how to get out of a locked room."

"Did she really?"

"Yes!"

"And did he show you?"

"Yes, but"—he frowned again—"I don't know what's the matter with Rustom these days."

"What do you mean?"

"He keeps shooting me and saying Rustom killed Sohrab. At first, I didn't mind—but he does it all the time. It's *re*ally getting an*noy*ing now."

Dolly looked at Phiroze, her face hardening to stone. "I think we should have a talk with him."

Phiroze nodded. "I will. Tomorrow."

Dolly shook her head. "No! Now! Sohrab, bring your brother here—no, don't shout for him. I said to bring him here."

# A Googly in the Compound

Phiroze was first to speak after Sohrab left. "He knows. It was inevitable."

Dolly frowned. "Of course, he knows. The question is what are we going to do about it."

Phiroze spoke calmly. "Darling, it's really not a serious problem. Let me talk to him."

Dolly said nothing, but nodded, grim as she swung the sash of her sari over her shoulder. A small action deserved a small reaction, but it was more difficult taking advice than dishing it out, particularly her own. They should either have named her sons less provocatively—or, having named them, ignored the legend altogether. She had imagined herself strong enough, as Phiroze had proven himself, but she had been wrong. He could let the past remain the past, but not she.

Phiroze began to dress as they waited. It had taken him a while to adjust, but he could do most things almost as well with one hand as with two. He had begun to wear his shirt when Sohrab returned, smiling, herding his brother into the bedroom, imagining Rustom would be scolded, but frowning when he saw Dolly had surrendered the talk to Phiroze. He pushed Rustom forward as if he were a prisoner to be interrogated. "Here he is."

Rustom remained silent, on his guard against Sohrab's sudden gaiety.

Phiroze's tone was mild as always. "Rustom, I am going to ask you a question, and I expect you to tell me the truth. Do you understand?"

Rustom looked away.

Phiroze's tone remained mild. "Look at me, Rustom. Do you understand?"

Rustom looked at his father buttoning his shirt. "Yes."

"All right, then. Do you know the story of Rustom and Sohrab?"

Rustom pursed his mouth, not wishing to betray Gillian. "No!"

Phiroze paused before talking again. "All right, then. I have another question. Sohrab says you keep shooting at him and saying 'Rustom killed Sohrab.' Is this true?"

"No!"

Sohrab shouted. "He *did!* He's *ly*ing! I can *prove* it! Ask Berzin! Ask Aphoos! They *both* heard."

Dolly took a deep breath. "Sohrab, really! We've had enough shouting for one day."

"But he's *ly*ing!"

Dolly raised her voice. "Leave it to your father!"

Phiroze's voice remained measured as he slipped into his trousers. "Rustom, is Sohrab right? Would Berzin back him up if I called him on the telephone?"

Sohrab spoke earnestly. "Also Aphoos. He also heard him."

"Is this true, Rustom? Is Sohrab telling the truth? Both of you cannot be telling the truth—and what have I told you about lying?"

Rustom spoke by rote. "It is better to confess than to be found out."

"All right. So, now, do you know the story of Rustom and Sohrab?"

Rustom replied in a tiny voice. "Yes."

"And did you shoot at your brother saying 'Rustom killed Sohrab'?"

"Yes."

"Why did you do it?"

Rustom shrugged. "I don't know."

"Was that a nice thing to do?"

"No."

"Will you do it again?"

"No."

Sohrab watched with satisfaction until he was struck by an ugly thought. "I say, did Gillian tell you the story?"

Rustom resumed his dumb stance, looking past everyone and everything. Phiroze turned to Sohrab. "What makes you ask that?"

Sohrab kept his focus on Rustom. "I've seen the book on her shelf."

Phiroze broke the impasse. "It doesn't matter how you found out. The important thing is that as brothers you should defend each other—not shoot each other."

Rustom nodded. "Can I go? I was playing carom with Janie."

Dolly was fastening Phiroze's cufflink, the one chore he couldn't manage alone. "Yes, of course."

Sohrab sprawled on the bed after Rustom left. "I bet it was Gillian who told him the story. I just bet it was."

Phiroze stood before his mirror with his comb. "It doesn't matter who it was. I'll tell you the story myself tomorrow if you want."

"No, I'll ask Gillian. She's a good storyteller."

Dolly smiled, exchanging glances again with Phiroze. "She is very precocious, that I will grant you. Our Gillian is precocious."

Gracie spoke from outside the room. "Bai?"

"Yes, Gracie? What is it?"

"Baba's chips ready."

"Chips? Sohrab, did you ask for chips?"

"Yes, Mummy."

"Why? Didn't you have enough dinner?"

"I just felt like it."

"But did you finish the lamb?"

"No, I just wanted some chips."

"Sohrab, you really mustn't give the servants more trouble than necessary. If you were hungry you should have finished the lamb. Didn't you like it?"

"Yes, Mummy—but I just wanted some chips."

"Let him be, Mummy. He won't do it again—will you, Sohrab?"

Sohrab ignored Phiroze. "I only wanted some chips. What's wrong with that? I only wanted some chips."

"All right. All right. Go on, then. Go and eat your chips before they get cold—but I really do wish you would be a little more considerate, Sohrab."

"I just wanted some chips!"

"I think we all know that now. Go on and eat your chips."

Sohrab left, not unconscious he had displeased his mother. After his parents left and after he had finished the chips, lying in bed, ready to sleep, he called Gracie to sing him the lullaby she had sung when he had been much younger, an old Konkani song from her home state, the Portuguese colony of Goa, the first European stronghold in India, and the only non-English European stronghold left.

Gracie expanded before his eyes, her face shining like the moon. There was something the matter with her young master, her baba, her surrogate child, her lovely white boy, whom she had known since his birth, but she never doubted his affection, not through all his antics. He had said often that he was now too old for lullabies, but he had called her at this moment when he knew he had hurt her feelings to sing to him. It was his way of making things right again. She pulled the covers to his chin as she had done when he had been younger, turned out the light, and sat by his bedside stroking his arm.

| | |
|---|---|
| Ek, doan, teen, char | One, two, three, four |
| Moag yamcho tor par | My mood is so sore |
| Potta jatta gadda guddu | Belly going pitta-patta |
| Tu mujha mogga cho ladu ladu ladu | You are the sweet of my hatta-hatta-hatta |
| Tu mujha mogga cho ladu ladu ladu | You are the sweet of my hatta-hatta-hatta |

**IT WAS ALMOST NINE O'CLOCK** when Dolly and Phiroze descended in the lift to the Collinses' floor, she shimmering in the gold sari, diamond earrings and necklace, he in a white doublebreasted dinner jacket and black bowtie. She took his arm, providing support for legs brittle from war injuries, while appearing to be supported by him; he was less social than her, but attended such functions knowing how much she enjoyed them—indeed, he encouraged her to attend, deriving pleasure from her pleasure. Otherwise, he continued to enlarge his knowledge of astronomy, anthropology, oceanography, paleontology, and other esoteric subjects which had never appealed to her though she took pride in his knowledge. She poised her finger over the bellpush. "Ready?" He smiled and nodded. Muted sounds reached them through the door: voices raised in debate, waltz music from the gramophone. She squeezed his arm, ringing the bell.

A Googly in the Compound

The door was opened by Peter, the Collinses' Goan bearer, wearing his dinner uniform, a white captain suit with brass buttons and chappals, a dark stocky man with a handsome head of hair who bowed, greeting them with Good Evenings, leading them through the foyer (over which presided a huge buffalo head) into a sitting-room dim with smoke. Guy Collins, in a pale lounge suit, hailed them the moment they entered. "Dolly! Phiroze! Over here!"

The flat was furnished as opulently as their own, with an emphasis on wildlife. A tiger skin flew up one wall; an ibex head glared down another. "Wine, Woman, and Song" blared from the gramophone combined with a wireless in a vast cherrywood showcase. About thirty guests (English, Indian, and Anglo), all in evening attire, comprised five or six fluid groups. Dolly raised a cupped hand, fluttering fingers at familiar faces as they crossed the room nodding and smiling.

Guy Collins was bald, redfaced, barrelchested, six-two, and forty-four years, but lean as a man in his twenties. He shook Phiroze's hand and kissed Dolly's cheek, gripping her arm before introducing them to the group. "My neighbors, ladies and gentlemen, who live upstairs—and are always the last to arrive."

There were no strangers among the group, but it wasn't unusual for Guy to provide such introductions. In fact, Phiroze rose to his cue without hesitation, patting the empty sleeve tucked into his pocket. "My arm, ladies and gentlemen. It takes forever to dress."

Guy put his arm around Phiroze's shoulders during the ensuing laughter and pulled up a chair for Dolly. "I'm sure Dorrie and Kavita won't mind squeezing you in between them—will you, girls?"

Phiroze looked around. "That's all right. I can stand."

Doris Gibson inhaled a cigarette before inching to one side of her seat, patting the space between her and Kavita Bannerjee. "Rubbish, Phiroze! There's room enough for two of you. You're no Tarzan of the Apes, you know." Her hair was blond and bobbed, her skirt rode high to reveal thick red knees.

Kavita's long black hair hung loosely behind her; a slender brown torso showed between the waist of her sari and the rim of her choli; silver bangles adorned both wrists. She nodded, scooting to the other side, slapping the middle of the seat. "Of course, Phiroze—plenty of room, plenty! Sit, no? Without your arm you only need half the space."

There was more laughter as Phiroze took the seat. "Thank you, ladies."

Guy clapped his hands as much for attention as to show how well he was enjoying himself. "By the way, do you know the one about the viceroy and the priest?"

Doris shook her head. "No, but something tells me we're about to find out."

Guy clapped his hands again. "Well the priest asked the viceroy if he was interested in lepers ... and the viceroy answered: 'Oh, yes, I shoot them by the dozen.'"

No one laughed louder than Guy at his own joke. Dolly smiled. "I daresay that's a joke I would appreciate better with a drink in hand."

Guy slapped his bald head. "Oh, forgive me! How remiss!" He raised his hand and snapped his fingers. "PETER!"

Dolly looked around. Bowls of nuts and chips stood on the side-tables, dishes of samosas and triangles of tomato and cucumber sandwiches, just large enough for mouthfuls.

"PETER!"

Peter was making his way through the dining-room, chappals slapping the mosaic, carrying a tray of drinks to be dispensed among the guests before approaching Guy's group. "Just coming, sahib!"

Guy turned his attention again to the newcomers. "I've got everything. Whatever you want, I've got it: whiskey, beer, punch. Phiroze? The usual for you?"

"Yes, please."

"And you, Dolly?"

"A gimlet, please."

Guy turned to Peter. "One whiskey for Sanjana sahib—a burra-peg, mind you—and one gimlet for memsahib."

"Yes, sahib. One burra-peg whiskey for Sanjana sahib, one gimlet for memsahib."

"And jaldi! Jaldi!"

"Yes, sahib!"

Peter almost ran from the room. Doris shook her head, sipping her drink, grinning. "Really, Guy, you big bully. It's not as if the poor fellow has nothing to do without you yelling jaldi-jaldi after him like a burra-sahib."

Guy gulped his whiskey. "Just playing the part, my dear—unlike you. A trueblue dyed-in-the-wool burra-mem couldn't have sent enough jaldis after the poor fellow."

"Well, I'm *not* one of *them*, thank God—and thank you very much for pointing it out."

Guy grinned. "I say, while we're on the subject, does anyone know the difference between a burra-mem and a chhota-mem?"

He grinned with anticipation, until Kavita finally tossed her hair. "Well, tell us, no? What is it? Can't you see we are just dying to know."

"It needs a set-up. You know the difference, of course, between a burra-peg and a chhota-peg?"

Kavita waved her hand impatiently. "Of course! Three fingers for a burra, two for a chhota."

Phiroze interjected: "And one and a half for a Parsi peg."

Guy laughed loudest of all again: it was so like Phiroze to mock himself with the Parsi reputation for parsimony, and so quietly you almost missed what he said. "That's almost better than my own joke—the way Phiroze tells it."

Kavita waved both hands, bangles jangling. "Just tell it, Guy! Get on with it!"

Guy grinned. "Actually, Kavita hit the nail right on the head: a burra-mem is one into whom you can slip three fingers, and a chhota-mem two." He grinned, staring at Dolly. "I'll leave it up to you to figure out what that says about a Parsi mem."

Doris laughed out loud. "I should have known it would be something naughty. You really should be ashamed, Guy."

Guy only laughed more loudly. Kavita shook her head in disbelief. Phiroze and Ashok had smiles glued to their faces. Dolly, too, was shaking her head. "So dirty already—and the night still so young."

Peter returned with Phiroze's whiskey and Dolly's gimlet.

Doris continued shaking her head at Peter's retreating back. "I simply don't understand why you didn't hire more help."

"We did. They're helping Lavvie set up dinner."

"You should have hired someone to help poor Peter. Where's Kalpana?"

"The poor dear's having a lie-down in the godown. She's got a bit of a fever."

"Nothing serious, I hope."

Guy shook his head. "Doc Warren said she just needs to sleep it off."

"YOUR ATTENTION, PLEASE!" Gillian appeared under the arch of the doorway leading to the hall, clasping her hands and silhouetted in the light from the dining-room. "Dinner is served. Everyone, please come and help yourselves. Thank you very much."

Smiling at the announcement the guests began slowly to move toward the dining-room. Gillian's translucent skin reminded Dolly and Phiroze of the moonlight with which Sohrab had poetized her. Her pink satin dress left one shoulder bare, pink ribbons adorned her hair. She walked to her father's side, greeting guests along the way. Reaching Guy's group she held out her hand to Phiroze. "Hullo, Mr. Sanjana. You're looking very well tonight."

Smiles brightened the group. Phiroze shook her hand, amused and touched again that she had very considerately extended her left hand. "You're looking very glamorous yourself, my dear."

"Do you like this dress, really? Daddy picked it out—but I do love it so well myself too."

Dolly, aware of Gillian's infatuation for Phiroze, much to do with his missing arm, rendering him among the more romantic lights in her experience, held out her hand. "It's a lovely dress, Gillian, but you haven't said Hullo to me yet tonight."

"Oh, I'm so very sorry, Mrs. Sanjana. I've been so very busy." Gillian shook her hand. "*How* do you do?"

"I'm very well, thank you. We were just talking about you before we left. Sohrab is very fond of you, you know. Do you like playing with him?"

"Oh, yes! I love Rabs! He always does everything I say!"

Gillian smiled as the group convulsed with laughter. Dolly could barely recover herself. "You really must tell me your secret, my dear. I have such a hard time getting him to do anything at all. You must visit more often. I am sure I could learn a thing or two from you."

"Thank you, Mrs. Sanjana, but I would rather he visited me because I have everything I need down here. If I visited him then I would have to take my things upstairs, and that would be such a lot of needless trouble."

"Well, I suppose it doesn't really matter—as long as you have fun together."

"Oh, we do. He's coming to see me on Sunday morning at half-past nine."

"That's funny. He didn't say anything about it to me."

"It really doesn't matter. I *told* him to come. He *will* come!" Gillian's smile broadened as laughter mushroomed again.

Dolly looked around. "Where is your brother? Don't tell me he's sleeping through all this."

"He's spending the night with a friend." Gillian took her father's hand. "Isn't anyone going to have any dinner?"

Kavita smiled. "In a minute, my dear, in a minute. After the line has shortened a bit. No point in rushing. I am sure your mummy has prepared enough food for everyone."

**LAVINIA COLLINS WAS ANNOYED** with her husband, hardly a rare occurrence. He hadn't changed much in twelve years of marriage, still with an eye for a pretty woman, but for the longest time she had been that pretty woman, the only pretty woman for him in Manchester, and he a junior engineer in her father's firm: STREAMLINED AERONAUTICALS. They had come to India to represent the firm, but his interests, professional and personal, had changed. He had started JILLY'S EMPORIUM, dealing with Indian exports (textiles, paintings, brassware, woodwork, mirrorwork, papiermache, tiger skins, elephant feet, ivory), and she seemed to have become the only woman who didn't have his eye: having less need of her father he seemed to have less need of her.

If not for his baldness he even looked much the same, but she couldn't say the same for herself. Her skin had lost none of its gloss, her eyes their startling blue, her thick blond hair its sheen brighter yet in the Bombay sun—but she had long lost the quality of novelty. STREAMLINED AERONAUTICALS no longer held the stick of redundancy over Guy and the years had taken their toll. She was no longer the streamlined girl he had married. Corsets and stays had countered the pounds of her mother's generation, but the war had changed all that. Shortages of sugar and butter had trimmed women's figures from hourglasses to posts (with fashions to match), not to mention the newly fashionable sports of tennis and hockey. A slim trim boy of a girl had supplanted the pudding of a woman of former days. Short hair provided economies of toilet as short skirts did of material. Women had commandeered jobs vacated by men doing their bit, and worn clothes commensurate with the work. You didn't get dressed to work in a farm or factory. Besides, corsets hampered movement, men didn't dance with women in stays (only staid women stayed in stays), and the pretty woman Guy had married had lost herself in her poundage.

The merry-go-round of guests around the table, in one doorway to the dining-room and out another, concluded with Guy. He winked at Meena Chudasama serving herself the jhinga curry. "At your peril, Meena. Lav's forays into Indian cookery usually send her guests to the lav!"

Guy's comment, uncharitable though it was, might have passed with a chuckle or two of acknowledgment, but his tone was caustic, inviting dissension. The hubbub in the air became less dense—like clockwork winding down. Gillian shrank, wishing she were invisible, skin turning from translucent to transparent. Lavinia's smile never wavered; it was hardly the first time she had heard the joke; but a frost covered her eyes as she turned to her husband. "Guy, how many pegs have you had?"

Mary Hartley, standing next to Lavinia, wavered no less with her smile. "It's the same silly joke, Lavvie—just Guy's way of guying you. Don't give him the satisfaction."

Her joke was greeted with muted chuckles around the room where none such had greeted Guy's. Rhonda Mehta spoke firmly. "He's talking rot, Lavvie, and he knows it. The jhinga curry is exquisite. Don't listen to a word he says. It's just like Mary said, it's his little joke."

She stared defiantly at Guy, but he ignored her, staring instead at his wife, speaking in the same dismissive tone. "It's a joke all right, darling, but it's a joke you can hang squarely where it belongs—on her daddy's door." He looked around the room. "He played it twice, you know—just in case you didn't get the joke the first time around."

Some of the guests knew what he meant. Lavinia's younger sister was Louise, Loo to her friends. The clockwork of the conversation broke completely. The air seemed brittle, the guests carefully frozen in a tableau as if the least movement might break something, no less carefully averting their eyes from Gillian who stared across the room between her parents as if she were alone. Phiroze coughed discreetly, smiling as if nothing were the matter. "Actually, Guy, you might say her father was paying her a compliment with the name."

Guy raised his eyebrows. "How's that again?"

"Well, correct me if I am wrong, but I understand it is the middle classes that call it a loo. To the upper classes it's a lav, isn't it? You might say her father meant Lavvie's name to be higher among the classes than Louie's."

Dolly marveled at Phiroze's ability to find an appropriate fit for what might easily have been an inappropriate observation, and smiled to see the room filling again with smiles, Gillian's brighter than the rest—and laughs, Guy's the loudest.

"PHIROZE, may I have a word with you."

Guy spoke with more seriousness than he had all evening though he held yet another burra-peg in one hand, pipe in the other. Phiroze had finished his ice and was back in the sitting-room with a cup of coffee. "Yes, of course, Guy."

"Let's go to the den, shall we? We'll have more privacy."

Phiroze followed Guy out of the sitting-room, down the hallway to the den, notable chiefly for its leopardskin upholstery, and the antlered head of a sambhar on the wall surrounded by photographs of hunts and kills against the wainscoting. Guy closed the door behind them. "I won't draw this out, Phiroze. It's really very simple. Jilly's, I'm glad to say, has been doing rather well—truth be told, rather better than I'd expected. I'm thinking of expanding the business, getting into imports, a shop right here in Bombay, maybe another in Calcutta depending on how it goes, maybe Madras. What I want is a partner—not a full partner to begin, of course, but certainly with the possibility down the road—preferably an Indian partner, someone who could communicate with the natives on their own terms. It would mean a bit of travel across the country, surveying merchandise, establishing contacts, that sort of thing. What do you think?"

Phiroze sipped his coffee. "If that is what you want to do, then that is what you should do."

Guy frowned, confused. Phiroze had spoken sensibly, straightforwardly, but seemed entirely disinterested—but in the next moment he laughed, understanding the disinterest. "I say, I *am* sorry! I *am* a bit muddled, it seems, after all. I'm offering *you* the partnership. I'd like *you* to consider the offer."

Phiroze's eyebrows rose. "Me? You mean for Jilly's?"

"Yes, precisely!"

Phiroze laughed, understanding Guy's confusion. "But I have no experience."

"It's not a matter of experience." He held his pipe in his mouth and placed a hand on Phiroze's shoulder. "It's mainly a matter of honesty and an ability to organize—which I think you have in spades."

Phiroze wouldn't look at Guy. "Guy, I'm flattered, but –"

"Don't say a word just yet. I know you're a man of leisure, and this may not be your cup of tea, but I'd like you to consider it. If it doesn't suit you—well, you can always withdraw, and no bad feelings, eh? I don't need an answer right this minute, but I'd like you to give it some thought."

Unsteady strains of "Alexander's Ragtime Band" wafted from the sitting-room, Mary Hartley at the piano. Phiroze said nothing, but appeared to be thinking.

Guy laughed again. "I didn't mean right now, old chap—take a week, take a fortnight. I'd like you to be comfortable about your decision."

Phiroze shook his head. "It's not that, but here is a thought I would like *you* to consider."

"What ho? Already?"

"Yes, would you consider Dolly for your partner?" He smiled. "I think she would be a better man for the job than myself. She's much better at hobnobbing with the locals, the common touch, that sort of thing—part of her upbringing, you know."

"Dolly?"

"Yes."

"I must say I never thought of it … but it makes sense. Certainly! Why the hell not? Do you think she'd be interested?"

"I don't know, but the boys are growing up, and she has talked occasionally of finding something to do with her time. I think she would at least consider it."

"Well, then, absolutely! Top-hole, old chap. Tell her also that I'd like her to pop down a moment to look at the books sometime before she makes up her mind."

"I will."

"You're sure you're not interested yourself?"

Phiroze smiled. "If Dolly is interested, I shall be just a little more interested myself."

"Well, then, yes, by all means, old man! Count her in, and let's shake on it!"

It was twenty minutes to ten o'clock on Sunday morning when the Sanjanas descended to the Collinses' flat, Sohrab ringing the bell insistently because he had already kept Gillian waiting ten minutes against his will. Dolly grinned. "Take it easy, Rabs. Gillian is not going to run away."

Sohrab scowled over his shoulder. "Mummy! Only *she* can call me that!"

"Yes, yes, of course, only she. She who must be obeyed!"

Phiroze stroked her arm warningly. Sohrab had lingered longer over his toilet, insisted on his velvet shorts, incessantly brushed his jacket and Oxfords, and examined his mirror closely with brush and comb. Rustom stood among them, almost as tall as his older brother though younger by three years. Sohrab bent his head listening to the door. "Sssshhh! Someone is coming! Quiet!"

Dolly said nothing, but couldn't stop grinning as Kalpana opened the door. "Good marning, bai-seth. Good marning, baba-log."

Sohrab ignored Kalpana, rushing past her. Rustom gazed, surprised, after his vanishing brother. Phiroze returned her greeting. Dolly asked if she had recovered since the evening of the party.

Kalpana nodded, smiling. "Arl right, bai. Veryvery arl right, thank you veryvery much." She looked well, juicy bronze torso amply revealed between choli and her sari as she led them into the foyer, all except Sohrab who was already in the sitting-room.

"Good. I'm glad it wasn't serious, whatever it was."

Kalpana switched on a ceiling fan. "Nothing serious, bai. Nothing serious. Please to sit down, bai-seth. I will tell seth you have come."

"Isn't bai home?"

"Bai garn sharping."

"Shopping? So early? On a Sunday? But nothing will be open."

Kalpana seemed not to hear. "Bai garn sharping. I will tell seth."

The Sanjanas sat down to wait, all except Sohrab who had disappeared into the flat before the rest of them had reached the sitting-room. Dolly sat comfortably in a morris chair. "I wonder where Lavvie's got to. She can't possibly have gone shopping so early, not on a Sunday!"

Phiroze shrugged. "None of our business."

He appeared to know more than he let on, but Dolly didn't question him because Gillian appeared in the doorway. "Hullo, Gillian."

She wore a lilac jumper, white ballet slippers, and her maroon beret over hair long and loose with bows perched like butterflies. "Good morning, Mrs. Sanjana, Mr. Sanjana. Hullo, Tums."

She nodded with each greeting and settled her gaze on Phiroze, but Dolly spoke first. "Did you see Sohrab? He dashed off like a bat out of hell. I have never seen him move so fast in my life."

Gillian smiled. "He's in my room. I thought it would only be polite to say Hullo."

"Of course. I do hope you will do a better job of teaching Sohrab some manners than I have."

Gillian turned coy. "It's a matter of finding out what he wants—and then *not* giving it to him."

Dolly's eyebrows rose. "Really! Then you must know what he wants."

Gillian lost her smile. "It's always the same thing." She turned to Phiroze before Dolly could recover her composure. "Daddy will be here soon."

Phiroze nodded. "Of course. We are in no hurry."

Dolly's eyebrows descended into a frown. Gillian seemed upset about something. "Kalpana says your mummy went shopping."

Gillian's face shriveled to a point of anger. "What does *she* know? She knows *nothing*. She's the *stu*pidest woman in the *world*."

Dolly was shocked by the suddenness of her transformation. "Oh, my dear, I am so sorry. I didn't know you felt quite so strongly about her."

"I *don't!* I *don't* feel *any*thing about her at *all!* She's too *stu*pid to even *think* about."

Gillian smiled again, her transformation no less sudden as her father appeared, beaming at everyone. "Morning, all! Sorry to have kept you waiting."

Dolly turned her attention to Guy. "Not at all. We only just got here—but don't get all insulted if I don't get up. It's much too hot and I'm much too comfortable."

Phiroze got up to take Guy's hand. "We can hardly complain when the hostess is so charming."

Guy shook Rustom's hand next. "I say, where's Sohrab got to?"

Dolly looked at Gillian. "He could hardly wait to get here. He's already in Gillian's room."

Guy laughed. "Weeeell! Hmmm! And where's Terry?"

"He's in his room."

"Well, then, Jilly, why don't the four of you get together for a nice game of Monopoly or something? I have work to discuss with Mr. and Mrs. Sanjana."

"Terry and Tums are too young for Monopoly."

"Well, then, do whatever it is you do, but get on with it."

Gillian turned to Phiroze. "Would you like something to drink, Mr. Sanjana?"

Phiroze nodded. "Yes, thank you, Gillian. I think a nimbu-pani would just hit the spot."

Guy shook his head. "Shamed by my own daughter. What about you, Dolly?"

"The same. I hate this hot weather. It makes me perspire like a pig. I could drink a hundred nimbu-panis and they would all turn to perspiration in a minute."

Gillian turned again to Dolly. "Mummy says one way for a lady to keep from perspiring is to hold an iced drink against the inside of her wrist."

"Really? And that keeps one from perspiring?"

"It keeps the cooler blood circulating throughout the body."

"Now why didn't I know that? There is always a scientific explanation for all the old wives tales, isn't there? Thank you, Gillian. I will remember that. A lady is never supposed to perspire, is she?"

"Okay, Jilly, dear, now run along—and tell Kalpana to send us three nimbu-panis."

"*KALPANA, COME* HERE AT *ONCE!*" Gillian startled them with her shout. "*You* tell her, Daddy. I don't want to be bothered. I'm with friends. Come along, Tums."

Guy stared in consternation as Rustom followed her out of the sitting-room. "They grow up so quickly, don't they? or, at least, they think they do."

They could hear Kalpana from within. "Baby, you carled?"

"Yes. Go to Daddy."

Kalpana stood outside the sitting-room. "Sahib, Jilly baby say you carled?"

"Yes, I did. Three nimbu-panis, please, Kalpana—and bring them to the den, will you?"

Kalpana smiled. "Yes, sahib. Three nimbu-pani."

**DOLLY BEGAN TO UNDERSTAND** Gillian's moodiness. Kalpana walked so fluidly she might have been walking on air. Phiroze appeared benignly and blissfully unaware, but he had said it was none of their business, and for Phiroze that was enough. She would have said nothing, but Guy noted her thoughtfulness and winked. "An eyeful, isn't she, our Kalpana? Brown Venus right out of a frieze from one of those temples at Khajuraho, wouldn't you say?"

The question was directed toward Phiroze who merely smiled, but Dolly was quick to reply. "Not for me she isn't."

"Well, I should hope not—for Phiroze's sake, if nothing else. In Mozart's time, you know, such goings-on were taken for granted."

Dolly found Guy's nonchalance inappropriate, his smile insolent. "What do you mean? What goings-on?"

"Oh, you know, servants and masters, that kind of thing."

Dolly looked at Phiroze, who continued to smile noncommittally. "In Mozart's *Marriage of Figaro*, the Count chooses to exercise what might be called feudal or seigneurial rights over a peasant woman, Suzanna, who is to marry his valet, Figaro. In those days such undertakings were accepted as a matter of course more than choice."

Dolly took a deep breath. "Well, thank God, we have come a long way since Mozart's time."

"Not musically, we haven't."

"I'm not talking about music."

"Neither am I, not in the strictest sense—but, you might say, about a different kind of music, the music that transcends music—one might say, the music for which music was composed."

Dolly laughed. "Well, all I can say then is that this is certainly *not* a debate that transcends debates—from the sublime to the ridiculous."

Guy sighed, not without regret. "Of course, but then again I'm no elitist. Why should one reach for the sublime when the ridiculous is quite satisfactory enough?"

"Because if the ridiculous is satisfactory enough, then ridiculous is what one remains."

"Touché, my dear Dolly! You're a woman after my own heart."

Dolly couldn't tell if he was being facetious, but felt she needed to draw a line. "Guy, sometimes I must say I do not know what you are talking about, but this much I can promise you. Should I ever wish to reach for the ridiculous, I promise you I shall happily consent to be a woman after your own heart."

Guy laughed out loud. "There may be something in that. That may be one of my liabilities." He stopped laughing as suddenly as he had started. "I suppose it's true in life as in business, we all come packed with our own personal assets and liabilities. That may just be one of mine."

"What exactly?"

"Not asking for more—being satisfied with … with the ridiculous."

"That is such a lot of rot, Guy! If one is dissatisfied with oneself, one can always make a change. One simply needs to be dissatisfied enough."

Guy laughed again. "Well, I suppose we should just get on with it. There's not that much to know. As I said to Phiroze, I'm looking for someone who's honest and organized."

"Yes, yes. Phiroze is honest, and I can organize. What else?"

Dolly looked at Guy, expecting a laugh, at least a smile, but he gazed into the distance, appearing thoughtful, even sad, as he pulled a ledger from a shelf. "Well, shall we get down to business?"

GILLIAN STRODE SO QUICKLY from the sitting-room holding Rustom's hand that she almost dragged him into the flat, forcing him to take two steps for each of hers until they reached her brother's room. "Terry?"

Terry was on the floor, face screwed with concentration guiding a red enameled model Roadster along a narrow path he had constructed with blocks, seemingly unaware of his visitors.

"Terry!"

Still he didn't look up. "What?"

Gillian didn't shout, but the exclamation in her tone was unmistakable. "You have a guest!"

Terry wore blue shorts and a white shirt, one of his kneesocks down to his ankles, one of his shoes unlaced, not unlike Rustom though not as immaculate. He remained on the floor, toys scattered around him: another model car, cowboys and Indians, toy soldiers, a bugle, a drum with a broken skin, a model aeroplane suspended from the ceiling, an airman suspended from a parachute. He said nothing, his attention remaining on the roadster. Rustom twisted his arm out of Gillian's grip, but held her eyes with his own. "I want to play with you."

Gillian drew a sigh, shaking her head in exasperation, hands flying to her hips. "Then, who, pray tell, will play with Terry?"

Rustom said nothing, holding Gillian's stare, but confused by her tone. He pursed his lips, picked up the second model car, and followed Terry's lead through the avenue.

Gillian left, closing the door behind her, returning to her room where Sohrab was sitting on her bed looking at the bookshelf alongside. She had tidied her room, put away her magazines and games, seated her golliwog at the toy piano, hands on the keys, and leaned her princess doll in her skirt of gauze against the piano as if she were listening. The bedcover was pink and white, a pattern of butterflies, toads, and fairies with dragonfly wings against a landscape of ponds, mushrooms, and toadstools. Sohrab turned as she came in. "I say, Gillian, I have got almost the same books as you—almost *exact*ly the same!" He was smiling, happy to have found a point in common though one he had taken pains to cultivate, badgering his mother to get him the books he had seen in her room.

He had found *Sohrab and Rustom* and was about to draw it off the shelf when Gillian sat beside him on the bed and sighed. "Oh, Rabs, what's the use of books after one has read them all? I mean, what's the bloody use?"

His eyebrows rose. "You have read *all* your books?"

Her voice droned. "Yes, and I've played *all* my games—*ov*er and *ov*er and *ov*er and *ov*er." One hand flew to her temple simulating a headache. "I'm bored, Rabs. I'm so bored I could die. Life is so boring, isn't it?"

Sohrab lost his smile, wishing still to please, unsure what to say. "Yes, it bloody well is, isn't it?"

"Is it boring for you, too, Rabs, dear?"

Sohrab had not only lost his smile but affected an ennui no less bottomless than Gillian's. "Yes, it is. It is so boring. I have also read all my books. I have also played all my games. I don't even like to play games anymore because someone is always cheating—especially at carom. I am very good at carom, but I cannot win when somebody cheats. I hate cheaters. Cheaters never prosper."

Gillian sighed again. "Sometimes they do."

Sohrab echoed Gillian's sigh. "Yes, of course, *some*times they do—if you put it like that."

"I *do* put it like that, Rabs, but I also agree with you. It's a pity when they do. It's *al*ways a pity when cheaters prosper."

"That is what I meant. When they prosper it is really a pity, and when they don't prosper it is also a pity. What I mean is it is *al*ways a pity about cheaters."

Gillian smiled a broad smile. "Dear Rabs, you *do* understand."

Sohrab wisely remained silent.

"Sometimes I think you are the *on*ly person who understands me, Rabs."

"I think it may be because we are both so very much the same."

Gillian frowned, crossing her arms. "How are we the same?"

Sohrab spoke quickly. "I mean, because we both live in Bombay, we both have the same books and games and things and all that—and our parents are friends—and in another year I will be the same age as you are now—and we both hate cheaters—and we are both so very very bored."

"Yes, of course. I never thought of it like that." Suddenly she was smiling, her voice breathless. "Rabs, have you discovered the secrets of keyholes?"

Sohrab returned her smile. "Yes. Tums showed me. That was very clever of you."

"Oh, yes, but I didn't mean that. I mean keyholes reveal so much, don't they?"

Sohrab's head bobbed on a spring, eager as he was to agree. "They do! They do!"

"I mean, one can solve so many mysteries."

"Yes, one can do that with keyholes because they are so small—and so mysterious."

"They *are* small, but they're *not* mysterious. They *solve* mysteries. They reveal solutions."

"That is what I meant! That is e*xact*ly what I meant!"

"Oh, Rabs, you *do* understand! What have they revealed to you?"

Sohrab waited a moment, hoping to be guided by her, but she remained silent though still speaking volumes with her unfathomable smile. "I don't know."

She sniffed, rolling her eyes. "You don't know?"

His voice shrank and fell. "No."

She seemed to consider what he said before smiling again. "It's all right, Rabs. If you don't know I can show you."

He said nothing, smiling again, at once more attentive and tentative.

"Rabs, I am going to ask you a question and you must promise to tell the truth."

"I promise!"

"I don't want to force you to say anything you don't mean, so if you don't want to tell me the truth you mustn't say anything at all. Do you understand?"

Sohrab nodded.

"But if you say anything at all it must be the truth. Is that fair?"

Gillian's eyes pierced him with an excitement to rival Christmas. "It's fair! It's very fair."

"Well, then, tell me: Do you fancy me?"

The question was bold, requiring a bold answer, but Sohrab's courage was slow to rise. Someone was pounding for release within his chest. He opened his mouth to speak, but shut it saying nothing.

Gillian's stare was no less fixed than her smile, eyebrows arched in expectation. After a long silence she spoke again. "Well, that's fair enough. If you have nothing to say, I know what you mean—at least, you're being truthful."

Sohrab suddenly found his voice though squeakier than he had found it in a while. "But I *do* fancy you!"

"Do you really? You mustn't say it if you don't mean it."

"I *do* mean it. I was telling Mummy and Daddy just the other day how your skin is like moonlight, all silver and shining and all."

"Really? You said that to your mum and dad?"

"Yes! Really! You can ask them."

Gillian's eyebrows dropped, her stare grew softer, her smile relaxed. Her mouth opened in what might have been a laugh, but she spoke triumphantly instead, though not unkindly. "I knew it! I was sure you fancied me! That makes it all right, but we must be careful. There are keyholes everywhere."

Sohrab didn't understand, but was happy with her happiness, watching as she locked the door with the iron key, leaving the key in the door, and pirouetted to face him again, flaring her dress as she turned, revealing dimpled knees.

"Rabs, do you know what I'm wearing under my dress?"

Her boldness was infectious. "Knickers!"

"Would you like to see?"

He nodded.

She kicked off her slippers, fell on her back on the bed, and raised her knees. Her dress slipped back revealing plush thighs, smooth as marble, and white cotton knickers.

He might have turned to stone for his fixed gaze and brittle expression.

"Would you like to touch?"

He nodded, but remained where he stood at the foot of the bed.

She grazed the surface of her knickers with the flat of her hand. "You'll have to come closer."

He came closer, lifted one knee to the side of the bed, and gingerly touched the fabric.

"Do you like it?"

He nodded again.

"You don't have to be afraid. You can rub it if you want."

He rubbed with the flat of his hand as she had done.

She closed her eyes, grabbing his hand, holding it like a brush, scouring herself. Soft moans tripped from her tongue, escaping in tiny breaths. She rubbed herself so hard that his hand turned lifeless until she opened her eyes, letting go his hand. He renewed the effort then on his own, afraid she might otherwise conclude the encounter, relieved when she voiced her approval. "Would you like to see more?"

He nodded vigorously, speeding the motion of his hand, keeping his gaze on her knickers until she leaned forward to pull them down and lay on her back again, legs apart, bent at the knees, shackled at her ankles by the knickers. "You may touch me if you like."

Sohrab was speechless, motionless. Her pale secret flesh resembled nothing as much as the core of an apple sliced in half, perhaps the apple Eve had offered Adam. The skin was as white, veined with traces of red and blue, like the vines of lotuses showing under the still silver surface of the Lunsi Kui talao in Navsari.

"It's all right, Rabs. It's what your mummy and daddy do when they're alone. You would know that if you knew about keyholes."

Afraid to move, but no less afraid to lose his astonishing new privilege, Sohrab dredged indignation from the swamp in his stomach. "He's not my daddy! He's my uncle!"

"What?"

"I said he's not my daddy! He's my uncle."

"I know, Rabs. Everybody knows—but he's also your stepdaddy."

"My real daddy was a hunter. He hunted tigers. He had two arms."

Gillian shut her eyes. "I think I like your daddy better with just one arm. He's so brave and romantic—like Lord Nelson."

"Well, of course, when you put it like that—like Lord Nelson."

"I *do* put it like that. I put it *just* like that. It means something's happened to him. I like you better because of the pockmarks on your face. It means something's happened to you. It's the same thing. It makes you so romantic. Your daddy's been through the war, you've been through the chicken pox."

Sohrab was buying time, defrosting his brain, finding refuge in indignation, but found he had moved from cul-de-sac to cul-de-sac. He had never considered his pockmarks romantic and wondered if she were mocking him.

"Well, are you going to touch me or aren't you?"

Her tone was impatient, imperious. Sohrab forwarded a stiff nosy finger, prodding the core of her apple, curious and bewildered. She arched her back as before, pushing against his finger. He held his finger

# A Googly in the Compound

in place, riding her gyrations until she rubbed herself harder with his finger, bouncing on her back. The golliwog fell from the piano, legs raised and bifurcated, the princess fell in between. Sohrab tried to speak, but could manage no more than a whisper. "I didn't know girls liked this stuff."

"I wouldn't like it if you didn't fancy me. Do you like it?"

He smiled, surer of himself. "It's all right. I never –"

A loud knock on the door cut him short. "Baby, why you have lark dar? Open dar, no?"

Gillian sat up, swung her legs to the floor, almost knocking Sohrab off the bed. "GO A*WAY*, YOU STUPID AYAH! CAN'T YOU SEE WE DON'T WANT TO BE DISTURBED?"

Sohrab was surprised by the sudden and violent change in her expression, holding his finger in the air in readiness for her return.

"Sanjana bai-seth go home, baby! You warnt say bye-bye, no?"

"LET THEM GO! WE'RE *BU*SY! TELL THEM EVERYTHING IS IN ORDER. RABS WILL COME WHEN HE'S READY!"

"Everything in ardor! Very good, baby! I will tell. Everything in ardor!"

THE CLUNK OF THE IRON KEY falling to the floor could not have been louder. Gillian and Sohrab looked up from their ministrations in bed, her skirt raised, his trousers lowered. Not only had he continued to stroke her since their first time—but, when she had asked, he had let her stroke him. He had not wished it, preferring to leave his soo-soo hidden, dark sheltering the dark (white as he was, she was whiter), but it had seemed only fair, tit for tat, one good turn deserving another, and he had pulled down pants, pulled down underpants, without resistance, without question, for her inspection. He understood nothing, why a pure pink plush powdered prepubescent English bud had led him down a primrose path, but he imagined she took pleasure as he did in the secrecy of their play as much as in the play itself, and sniffed continually the forbidden bathroom smell on his fortunate forefinger. Their idyll lasted barely days, the sweetest days of Sohrab's young life, before the world intruded.

He was brave behind the locked door, the blinded keyhole, but without the key in the door the keyhole had an eye. He felt doubly naked and still with shame and fear, unable to retrieve his trousers from the floor, whispering as he looked to Gillian for guidance. "Is it Kalpana, do you think?"

To his surprise, Gillian was smiling, eyes fast on the keyhole. "Don't be silly. It's Tums. He's jealous. Do you think we should let him in?"

"No! He's too young. He would spoil everything."

She shook her head, still smiling, eyes still fast on the keyhole. "He's almost as big as you. I think we should let him in."

"No! I *don't* think it would be a good idea." He no longer whispered, but Gillian no longer listened, hopping off the bed, heading for the door. He moved quickly, hopping off the bed himself and into his trousers, not managing all the buttons, but making himself presentable more quickly than ever.

Gillian's knickers lay on the floor, but she was otherwise dressed, and the room otherwise pristine. She giggled, picking them up, draping them on the doorknob, covering the keyhole, before picking up the key and opening the door. "Tums, would you like to join us?"

If Rustom heard he gave no heed, but zoomed past like a greyhound from its box. She almost fell as he pounced on his brother, bore him to the floor, and sat on him landing punches without end. Surprisingly, Sohrab took the punches without resistance, without even a whimper. She smiled at first, imagining they were fighting over her, but wondered why Sohrab remained so wooden. It took only a few seconds for her to pull Rustom from his brother, realizing what had happened, but the damage had been done. He was still because he had hit his head on the bedpost as he had fallen and blood spilled in a pool on the floor around his head.

Gillian ran screaming from the room, but could not have been more self-possessed relating the story later, recalling the sound of Sohrab's head hitting the post, a coconut being slammed on the ground.

## A Googly in the Compound

So fell the last domino in Gillian's row for her part in the story though it continued elsewhere with a shipboard romance, and more such in London as she sought more revelations through keyholes, and so fell the dominoes for the other Collinses, three rows in three directions, occasionally intersecting. They no longer concern the story, clack-clack-clacking away elsewhere in space and time, but not without repercussions still for the Sanjanas, evident first in Rustom's new recalcitrance. Phiroze stood over his son. "Rustom, you must say you are sorry."

The scene played out in their bedroom in Sanjana House, Dolly standing by, Rustom standing before them defiant as they had never seen him. "But I'm not! I'm not sorry!"

Phiroze brushed his hair back, bewildered but calm. "Why are you not sorry, Rustom? Don't you see how you have hurt Sohrab?"

"He deserved it."

"How did he deserve it?"

Rustom remained silent.

"What did he do to deserve it?"

Rustom remained silent.

Dolly could not forget Gillian, brimming with triumph for the mayhem she had caused, as unable to suppress what she said as the pleasure with which she said it, that the brothers had been fighting over her. "Were you fighting over Gillian?"

The answer wasn't clear even to Rustom. If they were fighting over Gillian he didn't know what he had won with his victory. He didn't know what he had been fighting for. He didn't want to implicate Gillian, but she had implicated herself. He didn't know what Sohrab had done, but he had done something. His best response remained silence, but it wasn't good enough for Phiroze.

"Rustom, tell me. What did Sohrab do to deserve it?"

Rustom stared at the ground. "I don't know."

Phiroze pursed his lips. Sohrab had lain unconscious in a hospital bed for almost a day. The magnitude of the injury may have been accidental, but not the attack—and not the attacks either after Sohrab's return, ranging from a punch to the arm to a cricket bat to the leg, to an arbitrary kick or shove, all of which may have been explained easily on the playground, but not in the flat, not in the bedroom. Punishment seemed appropriate, a spanking, toys confiscated, face to the corner, particularly since Rustom showed no more remorse for the subsequent attacks, but he accepted punishments as part of the process of beating Sohrab, answering all questions with "I don't know."

Considering the family history they took no chances, they consulted Dr. Dadabhoy, son of the Dadabhoy who had treated Kavas, who said there were new methods available, but not in Bombay. He had colleagues in Vienna who could help and provided the introduction to Dr. Xerxes Mistry.

"R**USTOM! WALK, DON'T RUN!** Remember where you are."

"Yes, Daddy!" Rustom reined his dash to a stride toward the swing doors of the cafe, its glass panels engraved with its name: Franz Josef Cafe-Konditorei. He was grinning, proud in his first pair of long trousers and dark overcoat against the cold, his imagination swimming with expectation. Vienna held many wonders, not least the giant Ferris wheel in the Prater, but none so fine as the coffee house, and he had worked his way systematically through its many delights. It was difficult to keep himself from running to see what new delicacies would be on display.

A tram trundled on the tracks lining the darkening cobbled street outside. It was early in the evening, but winter days were short. Phiroze smiled, exchanging glances with Dr. Xerxes Mistry, a man much devoted to dining himself from his appearance, as they passed through the swing doors behind Rustom. "This has been the best thing for Rustom. I cannot remember when I have seen him so happy. I think the change alone was enough."

Xerxes grunted, not looking at his guest who had proven to be just another unsophisticated Indian. "Of course, he is happy. Look how you are feeding him, but how long do you think it will last?"

## A Googly in the Compound

They entered a long hallway at the end of which stood an enormous mahogany buffet. Rustom gazed at the sea of cakes and canapes spread before him, towers of plates, mountains of chocolates, pyramids of pastries. Seeing him wideeyed and smiling, Phiroze was comfortable with his decision. The new methods comprised, among other things, electroshock and hydrotherapy. There was no telling how it worked, but work it did, so said Xerxes—but not always, and Phiroze had balked. The therapy seemed counter-intuitive. He had written his impressions to Dolly, and his reservations regarding the treatment, and to his relief she had agreed, making a trunk call to say the Collinses had left, and she was sure everything would be well again if they came back, bringing to an end their month-long visit.

To their right was a large room, marbletopped tables standing close enough for companionship and far enough for privacy, wooden chairs with cane seats. A wicker frame held newspapers, some of which were being read by customers at their tables. Mirrors adorned the walls alongside sconces and plasterwork and, among other paintings, a large canvas of the young Franz Josef in a white uniform, brass buttons, red trousers, a sash and medals. Boys in white aprons reaching the ground bussed the tables. Waitresses in black and white uniforms bustled from the buffet to the tables, one of whom approached Phiroze and Xerxes at the buffet. "Will the gentlemen be having their usual?"

Xerxes nodded. "But not the child."

The waitress smiled. "And what will little Tumerl have today?"

Rustom pointed to five separate plates in succession. "And I want canary's milk on everything."

Phiroze smiled. "Canary's milk separate, please. Thank you."

The waitress nodded. "As the gentleman says."

Rustom found their table and seated himself, swinging his legs. Phiroze and Xerxes joined him, and the waitress appeared with a tray bearing two cups of coffee and three glasses of water, holding up her finger at Rustom for patience. She was soon back with the rest of their order, naming each item as she set it down. "And a separate jug of canary's milk. Would the gentlemen like anything else?"

Phiroze thanked her, assuring her they had more than they needed. Rustom helped himself, pouring canary's milk over everything. He loved vanilla sauce, but called canary's milk it assumed a zest beyond its appeal to his taste buds.

So IT IS ALL YOURS NOW? The whole jingbang lot of it, kit and caboodle, all of it is yours?"

Aspi Palia was short, stout, and balding though barely thirty. Dolly was amused and annoyed by his incredulity. Her mother and Aspy's father had been cousins. As a child she had enjoyed visiting her Bombay relatives with her mother, but after her mother's death the visits had stopped. She had not seen Aspy and the others until her return to the city as Kavas's fiancee. She had once been the country mouse visiting her city cousins, but was now not only a city mouse, but as a Sanjana a city cat, and for the past year as a businesswoman a city tiger. She smiled cordially. "Yes, yes, Aspi, just like you put it, the whole kit and caboodle—not something I expected, mind you—but ..." She shrugged.

Aspi's eyebrows rose skeptically. "Arre, it is amazing! Just amazing! My best congratulations! Goes without saying."

His wife, Aloo, a sparer version of himself, long black hair braided behind, echoed his sentiment. "Of course, of course, best congratulations—and best of luck! Have more sev-ghantia, no? Have more jalebi, no, Phiroze? Aspi, pass him the plate."

Aspi passed the jalebi plate to Phiroze who broke off a couple more twigs for himself, while Dolly helped herself to the sev-ghantia. "Thank you."

Aloo looked at her husband. "What about the children? Shall I call them or should we just send them a plate?"

"Arre, no need to bother them. Children do not like to be bothered when they are playing."

"Arre, what rubbish, Aspi! Children love to be interrupted from anything for food."

"Then send them a plate, no, since you know so much? Send them a plate. But no point in disturbing our own conversations on their account."

"I suppose you are right." The Palia sitting-room was about a quarter the size of the Sanjana, the furnishings more functional than decorative, in need of refurbishment. Aloo shouted through the doorway. "Samson, take a plate of pendas and burfi and everything for the children. Take it to baby's room."

A voice came from the kitchen. "Already took, bai. Dinaz baby said to bring."

Aloo turned smiling to Dolly. "There! I should have known. Too bad about Rustom. He likes jalebis so much."

"Yes, but he has his own friends now and they were going on a picnic. I'm sure he will get all the jalebis he wants."

Aloo's brow furrowed telegraphing her solicitude. "He is all right now? Everything is okay?"

Dolly nodded, returning Aloo's smile. "Quite all right. Nothing wrong. Thanks for asking."

Aloo shrugged. "I never understood, you know, why you had to go to Vienna. Boys will be boys, no? He needed a good pasting. Spare the rod and spoil the child, no?"

Dolly nodded again, sympathizing with the implication that psychiatry was a luxury. She was no longer sure it was helpful herself. "We wanted to be sure—you know how it was with our poor Kavas. Didn't want to take a chance."

"Quite right, and shouldn't take a chance, but Rustom is Phiroze's son, no? not Kavas's."

"Yes, but brothers are brothers, common blood all around, sons or nephews makes no difference."

They had been hectic weeks, with Phiroze and Rustom in Vienna, the Collins marriage on its last legs, Guy absconding to parts unknown, and Dolly suddenly the sole proprietor of JILLY'S EMPORIUM. She had wished Phiroze might have been with her, and with Lavinia's departure for her father's home in Manchester, Gillian and Terry in tow, she had felt comfortable calling husband and son back. By all accounts she had done the right thing. She could not have said whether it was the doctors, the exit of the Collinses, the change from Bombay to Vienna, or merely time away from the epicenter, but Rustom had returned a changed boy, more Phiroze's son than before, beginning to show an interest in the esoterica beloved by his father, the whys and wherefores of the natural world, blossoming as a boy of imagination—and, more to Dolly's gratification, no longer bothering his brother, possibly for the treat of Vienna withheld from Sohrab. If she would have preferred them to be close she said nothing, grateful as she was for the smallest favors.

Aloo grinned. "So big he came back, no? Those Viennese pastries were not wasted on him. As big as Sohrab he is now, no?"

Dolly smiled, glad to have circumvented the subject. "He was always big for his age, but right you are. He is going to be bigger than Sohrab."

Aspi lifted his glass of nimbu-pani. "Arre, kids will be kids. They like to eat, Viennese pastries or our own Indian mithai. What to expect? Let them enjoy. You are only young once. Right, Dolly? Remember how we ate when you came?"

Dolly smiled, nodding agreement. "Arre, how I looked forward to our visits. Your mamma could never feed us enough." She began to feel again the pressure of the past. Their relations had remained cordial, but without the intimacy of childhood, and beneath the dead grey skin of courtesy gleamed the bright green veins of envy. They occasionally visited on Sunday mornings, as they were visiting Aspy and Aloo that Sunday, but Dolly had never invited them to a dinner party, the kind where she might have invited the Collinses and others like them. The Palias would not have complemented such company, though they would have liked very much to have joined it. Dolly was embarrassed during her visits to their Grant Road flat, sensing their resentment, but Phiroze insisted. In any interaction, the party with the greater blessings was obliged to make the greater effort, unless the party with the lesser blessings proved ungrateful. Dolly would have preferred not to pay social calls, to visit only when necessary, a death or a birthday party, but if they visited only for deaths and birthday parties, so Phiroze said, their presence meant nothing at all, and Dolly knew he was right.

Aspi grinned. "Mamma was so surprised to hear the news. Our little Dolly, she said—our little Dolly has got her own business?"

Dolly grinned. "Arre, your mamma was surprised? What about me? You have no idea—especially after being in the business such a short time."

"But what happened? You bought him out? He just left, just like that?"

"Pretty much, that is what happened—but it was *his* idea. He *wan*ted us to buy him out. He wanted to travel—work it all through is how he put it."

"But what happened, e*xact*ly what happened? Tell us, no? You were partners first, I understand, no, all three of you?"

Phiroze shook his head. "No, not really, not me. I was never a part of it—always it was Dolly and Guy. I was there only for moral support, nothing else."

"And now I need moral support more than ever—and every other kind in the bargain."

"But what happened? Tell us, no? What happened? Some woman he got mixed up with, I heard?"

Dolly looked at Phiroze who nodded. "More or less, that was it—or something like it. Better not to ask too many questions about such things, I always say. Not our business."

"But *some*thing you must know, no? With his servant, I heard, it was?"

"Could be. Some say there was more than one woman involved—but who knows, who knows for sure what happens in these cases? No one knows what goes on in other people's marriages. These are not things about which we can ask questions—not cricket, you know."

Aspi's brow furrowed. He was being shut out again, he was not in their inner circle, but he accepted Phiroze's reticence philosophically.

"Of course, of course, you are right. Not gentlemanly, not cricket and all that. No need to say more. These English are all the same. One has only to look at their kings and queens to see how they are. It is in their history, in their very blood. After all, they invented divorce, no, with their Henry VIII? I mean to say, what is a Protestant? A Catholic who has married three or four times or more." He laughed. "Better yet, a Protestant is a Catholic who has slept in the marital bed without benefit of clergy."

Aloo smiled in spite of herself. "What a thing to say! What about our Victoria and Albert? What about our George V?"

"What do you mean, *our* George V? Not *my* bloody George V, thank you very much—and not my George the First or Second or Third or Fourth either—no, and not even the plague of Georges still to come." He saw Dolly smiling as she eyed pictures on the wall of Victoria and Albert among other English royalty. "Dolly, you know what that is, no? Aloo's convent school education—thoroughly brainwashed, she was." Dolly nodded, still smiling: Aspi would rail against Aloo's convent school education as he railed against Dinaz's convent school education, never for a moment wishing anything different. Aspi turned to Phiroze. "Phiroze, what do you say? Women talk, but men know what's what. Not so or what? The English are all the same. Not so or what?"

"It is part of their history, certainly."

"Of course, part of their history—and what is history? History is blood! What you study from childhood is what you believe—it is what you become. For every Victoria and Albert there are one hundred and one Dukes of York. Right or not? You know the story, no—from Georgian England, England of the Georges, first, second, and third, that mad fellow?"

"Aspi, now please shut up, no? Everyone knows that story. You have only told it one hundred and one times."

Aspi ignored his wife, winked at Phiroze. "You know about that Kitty Fisher, no?"

"Yes, of course."

"Sir Joshua Reynolds painted her, you know—many times, even though she was only twenty-six when she died."

"Yes, I know."

It was a story of which Aspi never tired. Kitty Fisher, a prostitute, a lady of pleasure as he liked to say, charged a hundred guineas for a single night. When the Duke of York, brother to one of the Georges, probably the mad one as Aspi also liked to say, left on her dresser one morning a bank note of fifty pounds, all he had on his person, she instructed her servants, within his hearing, to say she was not at home should he call again, after which she sandwiched the fifty pound note between two slices of bread and butter and ate it for breakfast. "What a woman she must have been! What pizzazz she must have had! I tell you, Phiroze, such a woman is one in a million."

Aloo shook her head. "I swear, Aspi, sometimes you talk such rubbish! She was a prostitute! People must really be wondering about you that you find such an unsavory subject so fascinating."

"Arre, rubbish yourself! No need to be so insecure. She has been dead, lo these many years. Why are you getting so upset."

Phiroze nodded. "Aspi is right. Better to talk about it than to do it. If someone talks about it enough you can be sure he is not doing it. It is the quiet ones you have to worry about. Our Aspi is as clear as a summer day and pure as the driven snow."

Aloo turned her attention to Phiroze. "Very nice, Phiroze, very nice, but in Bombay we do not have summer, and we also do not have snow—so I have no idea what you are talking about."

The laughter was interrupted by a loud cry from Dinaz within the flat, followed by a wail that rose and fell in a glissando. Aloo and Dolly exchanged looks. Aloo got up, shaking her head, heading for Dinaz's room as the wail continued to issue like a siren. Dolly followed her down the dark hallway, past an ironing board, a cupboard of old books, and travel bags stored against the wall.

A rocking horse stood in one corner of the room next to an iron cupboard. A bright blue desk stood in another corner with a bright blue chair on the back of which Dick Whittington sat on a milestone on Highgate Hill with his cat listening to the bells calling him back to London. Pendas, burfi, and other mithai were scattered on the floor. Dinaz, the same age as Sohrab, sat on the bed wailing though she seemed unhurt. Sohrab stood almost at attention, staring as if at a pantomime.

Aloo sat by her daughter on the bed, stroking her hair. "What is it, baby? What is the matter, sweetie? Why are you crying?"

Dolly kneeled before them, wiping Dinaz's tears with her handkerchief. "What happened? Why are you crying?"

The tears subsided, but Dinaz remained untalkative, taking deep breaths. Samson, on his haunches, picked mithai from the floor, put them back in the plate. Aloo continued to stroke Dinaz's hair. "Arre, baby! Arrerere! There, there. Take your time. You can tell us what happened when you are ready. Take it easy. Take it easy."

Dolly looked at Sohrab, still at attention. "Sohrab, what happened? Did you do something?"

Sohrab took a deep breath, eyebrows rising in bewilderment, shaking his head. "I don't know."

Dinaz spoke suddenly, without looking at Sohrab. "He tried to pull down my chaddi!"

Sohrab responded as suddenly. "She said she fancied me!"

"He asked me if I fancied him, and I said yes, and then he tried to pull down my chaddi."

Aloo cuddled her daughter. Dolly looked at Sohrab. "Sohrab, is this true?"

"She *said* she fancied me, she *did*! She *said* it! She just *told* you! You *heard* her!"

"Arre, but so what if she said it? That does not mean you can pull down her chaddi. Who told you such a thing? What were you thinking?"

It had been almost a year since Mrs. Collins had returned to England taking Gillian with her, and in the long months since he had received but a single postcard, a short note, she had enjoyed the voyage, there had been many boys and girls on board, some of whom would be in London with her. He had replied to the postcard, but hearing nothing since had imagined a Jack for his Jill, a chalky Jack for his moonlit Jill, a pasty Jack for his silver Jill, so much more appropriate for each other, even tumbling down a hill with a bucket of water, than a grey Sohrab and his pink Gillian.

Dolly's brow furrowed with concern. "Just tell us what happened, Sohrab. What were you thinking? Just tell us the truth and it will be all right, but you must tell us the truth."

He wanted to tell them about Gillian, but the postcard and secret were all he had left. He was jealous of the postcard, felt violated if someone looked at it, as if he were sharing more than just the postcard, but sharing the secret would have meant sharing a lung or a liver or a heart—worse, it would have meant a betrayal of Gillian, of himself, of something sunk deeper in him than any vital organ, like inviting hyenas and jackals to drink from a grail. Gillian's departure had taken from him more than just Gillian, but a finer definition of his dilemma proved elusive as air. In giving him something he had wanted she had taken something without his knowledge, leaving Eve's apple wedged in his throat, Newton's apple knocking him senseless. "I told you, Mummy! I thought if someone fancied you it was all right—and she said she fancied me!"

"Where did you learn such a thing? Where did you learn that if someone fancied you it was all right to pull down her chaddi?"

A framed picture of Chaplin's tramp peering from the wall inspired Sohrab. "I think it was at the cinema!"

Dolly and Aloo looked at each other, Aloo the first to speak. "You know, it is very possible. Such a bad influence the cinema is having, especially on children, just jerking pictures without talking to explain what is going on. God only knows what all they pick up."

Dolly turned back to Sohrab. "Sohrab, I do not care what you thought or where you learned it. It was wrong. What you did was wrong. Say you are sorry."

"I am sorry."

"Not to me. Say to Dinaz."

He faced Dinaz. "I am sorry, Dinaz."

"Say you will never do it again."

"I will never do it again."

Sohrab and Dinaz stared silently at each other until Aloo spoke. "It is all right now, Dinaz, baby. It is all right again. Now you are friends again. Do a kissee-koatie, no? Let bygones be bygones."

Dinaz held Sohrab in a clumsy embrace, planting a dry kiss on his cheek to Aloo's smile and Dolly's wrinkled brow. With a lesser relative Aloo would have been less forgiving, but Dolly was a Sanjana, and Aloo liked to foster the illusion that their children were practically siblings.

Women and children returned to the sitting-room. Phiroze was silent hearing what had happened. Dolly knew he shared her fears, but Aspi laughed, winking at Phiroze. "Quick study your little chap—learning all the English ways already."

SANJANA HOUSE OVERLOOKED A BANDSTAND, and across the road to the north of the bandstand lay a vast green sward, the Oval Maidan, large enough to hold a dozen games of cricket at once. Sohrab and Rustom had separate groups of friends which sometimes came together, despite differences in age, for the numbers—but always against Sohrab's will because Rustom was always picked before him. The captains were careful to choose Sohrab immediately after, but he felt the pinch—and found himself, most of the time, on the opposing team.

By the time Rustom was nine he was taller than Sohrab by an inch, and the older brother slouched in the presence of the younger, leaned against walls, sat when he might have stood, and moved around when he might have stood still, all to hide the difference in their heights, all in vain—and since his return from Vienna Rustom had ignored Sohrab except when called to make up a number for cricket.

Rustom could hardly articulate what he hardly understood, but sensed a change in his brother. Sohrab appeared to have shrunk,

## A Googly in the Compound

smaller in size, and smaller yet for his resentment, but it mattered little. Rustom had his own room, his own friends, and retreated further still into books, in particular a *History of Vienna* by Franz von Erlach, his interest kindled by glossy photographs of places he had visited. They had attended an all-Mozart concert—and, returning to Bombay, Rustom had requested piano lessons. Dolly and Phiroze could not have been more relieved, imagining the piano would distract him from his former preoccupation with Sohrab—as, indeed, it appeared to have done.

Sohrab jeered at first, calling him "Piano Boy," equating music lessons with skipping rope, but following reprimands from Dolly and facing a rapidly-growing Rustom he had desisted—and considering Rustom's prowess on the cricket field "Piano Boy" had lost its punch. Adding to Sohrab's frustration, Rustom had scored his first sixer against Julian Ballinger, their best bowler, that very day. He gazed, dispirited, as Rustom thwocked yet another ball into the blue, and both teams erupted with excitement, Rustom's for the chance to score a medley of runs, Sohrab's for the chance to catch him out.

Sohrab shook his head in disgust, watching the trajectory of the ball. That fool, Berzin, was jumping up and down when he should have been eating the ground with his feet like a cheetah to catch the ball on the fly. By the time Berzin caught the ball it was rolling on the ground. He scooped it up and flung it whistling back to the wicket. The screams of the players arrowed toward Sohrab as he found himself at the confluence of the descending arc of the ball and Rustom's mad rush back to the wickets.

Rustom had too much momentum to avoid dashing into Sohrab, but Sohrab had time enough to avoid Rustom's rush—*and* strike him out if he caught the ball. Instead, as time shrank, he seized the temptation of a surer way. Stepping out of Rustom's path, he positioned himself to catch the ball—and Rustom found himself suddenly airborne, tumbling wildly as he hit the ground. Meanwhile, Sohrab had caught the ball and struck Rustom out, yelling all the while: "*Out!* Rustom is *Out!*"

Rustom lay stunned for a moment before catching Sohrab's eye. "You *tripped* me!"

Alphonse turned wide eyes on Sohrab. "Cheating! Yes! I saw how you put your foot!"

Sohrab wondered about Alphonse's idiocy, they were on the same team, but he looked away continuing to yell, surprised and pleased with his dexterity, successfully tripping Rustom *and* fielding the ball. "*Out! Out!* Rustom is *Out!*"

Rustom leaped to his feet and charged his brother. Sohrab tried to run, but Rustom caught him easily and twisted his arm behind so Sohrab was forced up on his toes to keep his arm from breaking. "Admit you tripped me!"

"OW! It was an accident, I say! *OW!*"

The others had gathered around chanting: "FIGHT! FIGHT! FIGHT! FIGHT!"

Alphonse chanted louder than the others, "*FIGHT! FIGHT! FIGHT! FIGHT!*" grinning more widely than anyone.

It wasn't much of a fight. Rustom had the advantage and kept it without difficulty, twisting Sohrab's arm further, whispering fiercely. "It was on purpose! Admit it! You tripped me on purpose!"

Sohrab's face paled. His eyes turned inward so only the whites showed. "I say, you're breaking my arm! Let us go, I say!"

"Admit! Admit, and I'll let you go!"

"*Ow!* It was an *ac*cident—an *ac*cident!"

"Admit! Admit what you did!"

"*Ow!* I ad*mit!* I ad*mit!* Let us *gooo!*"

"Louder! No one can hear you! Louder!"

"I ad*mit*! I *trip*ped Rustom! Let us go! *Please!*"

Rustom released Sohrab, but not before he had ratcheted the twist up a notch—and so violently that Sohrab almost flew through the air, dancing on tiptoe, limbs flailing, before crumpling to his knees and falling on his face, one arm incapacitated, the other too weak for support. He lay unmoving, face to the ground, his arm limp, still twisted behind him.

# A Googly in the Compound

Rustom panicked, kneeling by his brother, understanding something had changed irrevocably, but unable to understand what. Something had been broken beyond skin and bone, something intangible of the flesh, a bond more than a bone. Sohrab was cold to touch, seemed not even to breathe. He tried to turn him on his back, but Julian shouted from behind. "Don't move him! You might make it worse!"

**Days later,** two o'clock on a Sunday afternoon, the household napping, Sohrab was propped against the headboard of his bed, a *Boy's Own Annual* propped against upraised knees, one arm swathed in bandages, a plate of freshly fried chips on the bedside table and a bowl of tomato sauce. The door to his bedroom was open, but Rustom knocked. "Sohrab, may I come in?"

Sohrab didn't look up. "No!"

Rustom had the long face of a bearded priest at a funeral service. "Sohrab, please. I just want to say something."

Sohrab still didn't look up. "Say from where you are."

"Sohrab, I'm sorry. I'm so sorry. I cannot tell you how much. I didn't mean it, you know."

He had never been so contrite, but Sohrab still didn't look up. "You dislocated my shoulder. How could you do that without meaning it?"

"I *di*dn't mean it. I swear to God I didn't mean it."

"You never said sorry before. Why should I believe you now?"

Rustom didn't understand the difference himself: time may have blunted his edge; he may have punished Sohrab enough; Gillian was as lost to Sohrab as to himself; he may have felt a new sympathy for his older brother, smaller and weaker than himself—he simply didn't know. "I didn't mean it before. I mean it now."

Sohrab still didn't look up. "I don't care. I wish you were going to boarding school."

Dolly and Phiroze had discussed the possibility, afraid as ever of what might happen between their boys, but neither wanted to send Rustom away, and unlike before Rustom's remorse had been wider than the horizon. Boarding school would have been no punishment, Rustom would have found absolution in expulsion. "I didn't mean it, Sohrab. I swear by God I didn't. I got caught up in the moment. I was angry because you tripped me."

Sohrab was scornful, but still wouldn't look up. "I never tripped you. You attacked me from behind when I wasn't looking—like a cowardy custard!"

Rustom had no wish to defend himself. "Sohrab, I only want to say one thing."

"What?"

"From now on, anything you want, it's yours. I will never fight you for anything. I will never contradict you in anything. You will always be right."

Sohrab's eyes remained in his annual. "You are a liar. Why should I believe anything you say? It would just be another big fat lie."

"Sohrab, how can I prove it to you? Just tell me what to do and I'll do it. Just tell me, no?"

Sohrab looked up finally. "Tell the truth. I didn't trip you. If you're so sorry, the least you can do is admit it."

Rustom took a deep breath, but said nothing.

"Just as I thought. You don't have the guts. You're a liar and a coward."

Rustom's lips trembled. "Okay. I admit it. You didn't trip me. I attacked you from behind."

"Like a cowardy custard!"

"Like a cowardy custard."

Sohrab returned his attention to his annual, his smile triumphant. "Good! Now get out!"

I**T WAS DRIZZLING** when Sohrab exited the gatehouse of Lincoln's Inn into Chancery Lane—but, accustomed to the Bombay monsoon, he never found a London drizzle less than picturesque. The world became a watercolor. A Bombay monsoon would have swallowed Lincoln's Inn Fields, rendered it a swamp, but a London rain made a fairyland.

Strangely, Londoners seemed loathe to leave home without umbrellas, but no less loathe to use them, preferring to run to the closest doorways and awnings for shelter than to undo a perfectly furled umbrella—even to walk, chins in the sky, through a drizzle imagining the sun still bright on their faces, as fond of rain it seemed as of the midday sun. Umbrellas were for twirling, walking, and otherwise drawing attention (he had seen a passenger in a top hat on a bus poke the conductor with his umbrella to remind him his stop was approaching)—but, much as it flattered him to be mistaken for an Englishman, Sohrab had unfurled his umbrella to keep his hair from being furled by the rain. The meeting with Edwina Carbury was too important not to look his best; he might have hurried to keep her from waiting too long in the rain, but was careful avoiding puddles along the way. He had spent fifteen minutes before the mirror, patting his hair, cutting it, wetting it, drying it, flattening it, and the less the rain interfered the greater his confidence. He had taken no less care of his suit, wearing his trousers at the very last minute to keep their crease, losing count of the number of times he had changed his tie. Finally he had chosen a cream suit, with a deep yellow tie striped diagonally with thin black lines. At least he had the advantage of fellows like Deepak Shanmugam who was black as coal, or Anil Desai who was a vegetarian. He also knew Bach, Beethoven, and Brahms, not to mention Irving Berlin and Cole Porter—also Shakespeare, Shaw, Sargent, Wells, Keats, and Constable among others. When asked why he was not like other Indians he said, not without pride, that he was a Parsi with a bloodline dating back to Persia of the seventh century, untainted by India.

He was flanked by bookshops, wineshops, and the shops of tailors specializing in clothing for lawyers. As he approached Temple Bar, where the Strand turned into Fleet Street, the ranks around him swelled, mainly with inhabitants of the Inns and Temples, constantly wigged and gowned since they were prone to summons at all times without warning, and he regretted as always leaving the sequestered squares and gardens of the Inn for the warren of courts and alleys ahead, the warren of the world.

Reaching Fleet Street he turned left though not without a thought for Middle Temple Lane behind him. Queen Elizabeth had attended the first performance of *Twelfth Night* in Middle Temple Hall, Shakespeare himself among the players, but Sohrab remembered the Hall better for a reprise of the play with Enid Fitton, sister of a fellow-student, Lloyd Fitton, in the role of Viola. He was trying to forget Enid, and with Edwina's help he would. She was not a girl to be easily won, but merely to be tolerated by such a girl was a mark of favor and she had consented to meet him for a drink on rather short notice.

Unlike Rustom, who would have been in his element, he cared little for Shakespeare, little for literature, but in London such affectation was necessary, literature was all around: the very grounds of The Temple had once been the preserve of the Knights Templar from *Ivanhoe*, Lincoln's Inn Fields their tilting grounds; Dickens had opened *Bleak House* in the Old Hall of Lincoln's Inn; Congreve, Fielding, Sheridan, and Thackeray among others had lived in his neighborhood. To his credit, Sohrab had not changed: smug with contempt he had remained smug with affectation. He patted the poem in his pocket, his talisman, his insurance should Edwina prove impervious to his prose.

The dome of St. Paul's hovered on the horizon, a mirage in the drizzle, and appearing with its spire ironically like the Kaiser's helmet, a joke he made repeatedly though it was never well received. The drizzle thinned, and catching his face in a window he touched his hair again, admiring himself once more, sleek black hair to slick black wingtips. He regretted the pockmarks on his upper lip and the bridge of his nose, but they gave him character. His nose, like his mother's, was commanding, his face narrow, in keeping with his torso and long limbs, giving him the look of a young sage. There were fewer shops catering to lawyers as he reached the journalist end of Fleet Street, and finally turned left into Wine Office Court for Ye Old Cheshire Cheese. He saw Edwina at once huddled in a doorway, umbrella furled by her side.

## A Googly in the Compound

She looked, as always, like a painting, single strand of pearls around her neck, white satin blouse, tartan skirt, white cloche hat, single sprig of auburn hair escaped from her hat setting off her pale cheek. He marveled no less that she had consented to meet him at a pub, showing her disdain for what was expected of a woman, and presented his widest smile. "Edwina! You came!"

"Of course, I came. I said I would, didn't I?"

"Yes, of course, but it's nice that you came anyway."

She rolled her eyes, but smiled. "Do you mean to say you didn't believe me?"

"No, of course not. What I meant was not many girls would stand waiting for a man outside a pub at the drop of a hat."

She laughed. "Oh, that—well, that would depend on what century they were living in, wouldn't it? I must say I felt quite dashing—though you are being most exasperating, Sohrab—not at all the gentleman. It's very naughty of you, you know."

He smiled. "Sorry, I'm late."

"You're not late. I was early."

He looked at the ground. "Well, shall we go in? We're only getting wet." He held up his umbrella for her to cross the narrow path to the pub, and opening the door stepped aside to let her precede him.

She looked at him as he shut the umbrella in the hallway, eyes narrowing as he continued to avoid her gaze. "I must say I don't understand at all, Sohrab, why you simply couldn't tell me what you wanted on the telephone. You're a close little devil, you are."

"It's too important, what I have to say, to have said it on the telephone."

She shook her head. "Curioser and curioser—and exasperatinger and expasperatinger."

He kept the mysterious smile, twirling his umbrella, creating a penumbra of raindrops, guiding her into the room to their right, across from the Chop Room. "All will be revealed in the fullness of time."

"I'm afraid I don't have the fullness of time. I told you I was on my way to an engagement."

He nodded, giving her his umbrella. "I haven't forgotten. Why don't you get that table by the window—and I'll get the drinks. What will you have?"

"Sherry, please."

She sat at the table, back to the window, depositing their umbrellas on the floor by her feet, while he engaged the barman and joined her moments later with a sherry and pint of bitter, taking the seat across from her. "Well, here we are."

"Indeed, as you say, here we are—and dare I ask: What next?"

His smile remained. He raised his glass. "Cheers. To us."

She clinked his glass. "To us."

He looked at her finally as they set their glasses down, smile still in place. "I say, I *am* sorry I was late, you know. It's awfully good of you to meet me like this. I do appreciate it."

She shook her head. "I just told you. You weren't late. I was early. And do sit still. I'm getting quite nervy just looking at you."

"Sorry." He continued to grin as if her scolding were a compliment, a good chaffing at worst, indicating she felt comfortable enough to speak her mind.

"Well, what is it? I *am* in a hurry."

"Can't you guess?"

"I'd rather not."

"You know, Edwina, I always imagined you could read me like a book."

"A very mysterious book, if so. What did you have to tell me that simply couldn't wait? Why couldn't you tell me on the telephone? Why are you stalling even now? Just say what you have to say, Sohrab. I'm all on toast."

"All in good time. What's the hurry?"

"I think I made it clear when we talked that I *was* in a hurry, and I think I've made it no less clear since you've arrived—but perhaps you're not listening. I'm meeting Nigel for dinner, and I would rather not keep him waiting."

He felt a loosening in his face of the springs that kept his grin in place. "Nigel Nicolson?"

"Yes, of course! Why, what's the matter?"

"Nothing."

"I should never have agreed to meet you had it not been on the way. I did say I didn't have much time. I didn't think it was necessary to say more."

"No, it wasn't—of course, it wasn't."

"Well, then?"

"You have been straight with me, Edwina. It is I who have been less than straight with you."

"Well?"

"I ..."

"Yes?"

"I had rather thought you might have dinner with me."

"But why in heaven's name would you think such a thing—especially after I made it abundantly clear that I was in a hurry?"

He shrugged. "Hope springs eternally."

"What nonsense! In any case, it wasn't a hope I encouraged—surely you don't believe it was a hope I encouraged!"

"No, it's as I said. You have always been straight with me."

"Well, then, be straight with me. What was it you wanted to say?"

It had not come to pass as he had wished, as he had planned, but he comforted himself. After he had spoken she would understand—after he had read the poem she would be twice as understanding. "It is actually quite simple. I was thinking just the other day that—I mean, what with all that's wrong with the world, that the solution is really quite simple."

Her eyebrows arched. "What do you mean? What's wrong with the world?"

"I mean the Depression and all that. I mean with Hitler reintroducing conscription, and Mussolini in Abyssinia—not to mention Franco and Stalin stirring pots of trouble in their regions of the world—and, I mean, right here in London, with the blackshirts and all that. That's what I mean. That's what's wrong with the world."

Her eyebrows arched higher. "Do you mean to say that you have found a solution to the problems of the world?"

He grinned again, genuinely for the first time since she had mentioned Nigel Nicolson. "Yes."

She grinned as well, but skeptically. "I cannot wait to hear it."

"It is the oldest solution in the world, reaching back to Biblical times—even before, back to Zoroastrian times." His grin remained steady, strengthened by his attempt at humor.

"Really? If it is so very old why has it not worked yet?"

"It has worked for everyone who has applied it."

"And who, pray, might that be?"

"Everyone who has ever been in love."

"In love?"

"Exactly! A lover is immune to slings and arrows."

"Only because he's too bloody potty to know what's going on—or to care."

"But maybe he's not potty. Maybe he only ap*pears* potty. To himself, and to his sweetheart, he is anything but potty."

"Oh, my dear Sohrab, I haven't a clue where this is leading."

"I should have thought you would have had more than a clue by now. I should have thought you would have had at least a blueprint."

She shook her head. "You're getting much too mysterious altogether, Sohrab—and I must say it is not altogether pleasant. I beg you, please, to speak plain English—the plainer the better."

"Very well, then. Has it ever occurred to you, Edwina, my dear, that I might fancy you?"

Edwina smiled, but lowered her head so it was lost on Sohrab. If only the poor boy understood how presumptuous he was she might have found him interesting, but he seemed oblivious even of his presumption. "Fancy me? That you might? Well, which is it? Do you or do you not?"

"I do."

"Fancy me?"

"That's right."

"Oh, my dear!"

Whether she meant Oh, my dear Sohrab, or Oh, my goodness, he couldn't tell. "Have you never thought that I might?"

"Oh, my dear! Oh, my goodness gracious!"

"Have you never thought it? Have you never fancied me?"

"Oh, my dear boy, I haven't the foggiest notion what you can mean. What are you trying to say?"

"Why, that I think I love you, that is all."

"Love! Oh, love! And that you *think* you love! Don't you *know*?"

"Well, then, I *do!* I *do* love you! There, now I've said it."

"Oh, my goodness gracious!"

"I've *said* it!"

"Indeed, you have."

"And?"

Edwina pursed her lips. Sohrab always seemed too pleased with himself, even admitting his love as if it were to his credit more than hers. She granted he meant well, but his were the good intentions that paved the road to hell. "And it seems to me that you are prouder of having said it than of anything else."

"I *am* proud. It was not an easy thing to say."

"But have I given you reason? Have I ever given you reason to think I might care?"

"I do not need a reason. Your presence is enough. It shows you care, and it shows me what I want. It is enough for now that I know what I want. When you know it as well as I, you will want it too."

"And if I don't?"

"But you will—if not now, you will in time. I do not expect anything for the present—except that you consider what I have said."

"But I *have* considered it."

"Already?"

"Yes."

"And?"

"And you have yet to give me the reason I asked. It is not enough that you know, and that I will know in time. I wish to know what it is about me that makes you so sure that you know."

He could hardly tell her what he hardly understood himself. He had transferred the vitality, the virility, of Viola from *Twelfth Night* to Enid Carbury when he had seen her onstage, still seeking Gillian perhaps in a series of substitutes, and having missed Gillian in Enid was making of Edwina yet another substitute. He pulled the poem from his pocket. "Maybe this will explain it better."

"What is it?"

"It's a poem."

"A poem! Do you mean one that you wrote?"

He blinked. Believing all fair in love and war he had selected the poem which best expressed his sentiments from a chapbook he had found in a secondhand bookstore, *Love Poems*, by Robert Bowman, and edited it to suit himself. "Yes!"

"Well, how very strange. Do you mean to read it to me?"

"Yes, absolutely! I wrote it about a month ago, taking off from an image you inspired coming in once from the rain. Your hair was full of water, like clouds—but I took the image a step further. The first line goes: *You did cause all the ponds to run dry when you did soak them into your hair.* The rest followed from that one line."

She smiled, not unimpressed, giving him courage. He gazed between her and his page, reading in a breathless tone.

> You did cause all the ponds to run dry when you did soak them into your hair.
> When the sun caught your eyes you did take his fire away.
> If I had you I would need no forests to walk in,
> > no meadows to play in,
> > no grottoes to lie in.
> But without you my food is ash,
> > my water petrol,
> > my rest a bed of nails.
> Let me be thine.
> Be mine.

"That's it." He passed the poem across the table. "It's yours."

She smiled, looking over the lines. "It's not bad—quite modern, actually—no rhymes."

"Except for the couplet at the end." The couplet was entirely his own inspiration, the only part of the poem owing no debt to Robert Bowman.

"Oh, yes, but that's the part I like least."

"Do you like the rest of it?"

"I like the first lines best—quite topping, actually—but then it flags—almost as if it were written by two people. Did you really write this yourself?"

His eyes clouded momentarily. The first two were the only lines he had left untouched, but the other lines had not suited his needs as Robert Bowman had written them. "Of course!"

"Well, I must say I'm flattered—but it still doesn't answer my question."

"What question is that?"

"Why *me*? What is it about *me*?"

"Because it *was* you. Don't you see? That's the ticket—that it *was* you, and no one else."

"I'm afraid I just can't see it that way. I'm sorry, Sohrab, but I just can't."

"But it's true! The sentiments are all true! You don't suppose I made them up, do you?"

"That's just it. I'm not even sure what the sentiments are, and how they might not apply to—oh, I don't know, to that girl who just came in the door. Look, her hair is wet from the drizzle. Would that be enough for you? Would you say she's soaked the sky into her hair?"

"You're mocking me now, but I meant every word I wrote."

"I am *not* mocking you. I am sure you meant every word, but I am not so sure that you know what you meant. I am trying to make you see things as I do—and you are making it very difficult for me."

"How am I making it difficult?"

"By listening only to what you wish to hear."

"That is quite simply not so. There is nothing that I wish to hear more than what you have to say."

Edwina grimaced, turning away, seeming suddenly thoughtful. "You know, Sohrab, now that I think about it, it is rather strange that you should say anything to me at all."

"Strange? Why?"

"Because I recall now something Enid said to me last year."

He shut his eyes. "Oh, God, no, not Enid Fitton. Do not tell me that you have talked with *her!*"

"Yes, of course, Enid Fitton. Why shouldn't I talk with *her*?"

"She had no right to talk about me—not to you, nor to anyone."

"She had every right. We were all concerned. All you did was mope around the grounds, loping like a wolf who had forgotten how to come down on the fold. We had every right to talk about you."

He had never been as lonely as after Enid had thanked him for his declaration of love, saying she had never been so flattered, unable (or unwilling) to recognize the vulnerability he had risked in her behalf. Unable to face her subsequently he had found himself avoiding her, peering around corners to assure himself she was not in the vicinity before presenting himself, even turning midstep if he saw her too late. He had rescued himself finally by focusing on his examinations, wrenching victory from defeat, but a victory gained at great cost, not one he would willingly revisit. Staring at his glass, he felt a similar dejection descend like a shroud. "What did she say?"

"She said a very queer thing."

He remained silent.

"She said you told her that you were in love with her—or that you thought you were in love."

"That was ... a year ago. You make it sound as if I choose a different girl every term."

"I do not. I am simply speaking my mind—and I must say I think it seems rather queer."

"I don't see why it seems queer. You and she are the only girls to whom I have said such things. What is queer is that you have confided in each other. That is perhaps just my bad luck, but I swear to you my intentions were strictly honorable—and they still are. You must believe me."

"I cannot help what I believe—and I will not make excuses for it."

"I only ask that you reserve your answer for later, that you consider what I have said. In the fullness of time it will appear in a different light."

"Again, the fullness of time … but that I cannot do. I would feel as if I were encouraging you."

"I promise I will not imagine that you were encouraging me. I promise to abide by your decision if you will only take a fortnight to consider what I have said."

"Sohrab, I *am* sorry, but I simply cannot do that. I do like you, *aw*fully, but not in that way, not at *all* in that way—and I am afraid we had best leave it at that."

"Will you give me no hope?"

"I cannot—in all fairness to yourself."

He turned his face from her, looking down at his glass on the table which had remained full while she had emptied hers.

"I am sorry, Sohrab, to be so blunt—but in these matters I do find it best for all concerned. I feel so sorry for you, and I hate to leave you like this—truly, I do—but I'm afraid I simply *must* be off. In the fullness of time, as you put it, I know you will understand—but for now, cheerio."

Her white thighs, visible under the short bright tartan of her skirt, failed to draw his gaze as she got up from the table. Unable to say goodbye he nodded, gazing again it seemed into the blackness of the shroud.

# DAY OF THE TIGER: 3
## (September 25, 1945)

LAXMI RETURNED TO THE KITCHEN. Alphonse Fernandes appeared at the window Fakhro had just vacated. Where Daisy had once seen a black Clark Gable—hair as slick, moustache as slim, smile as sexy—she now saw Machiavelli. Sohrab grinned, still sucking his thumb as he spoke. "There's Daisy's boyfriend. For someone who wanted to breathe the fresh country air he's certainly taken his time getting out of bed."

Daisy stiffened, but said nothing, refusing to look at Alphonse. Alphonse's mother, Gracie, had been pensioned and retired to Goa since Sohrab's twelfth birthday, and dead now for three years—which was also the last time they had seen Alphonse who had come at their request to collect more old clothes and a generous bonus for Gracie's years of service.

Rustom, noting Daisy's discomfort, changed the subject. "Was anyone else bothered by the monkeys last night? I could hardly sleep for all their thumping and scampering on the roof."

Dolly nodded. "I heard. I'll tell Fakhro. A few wellplaced shots will make all the difference."

The monkeys got bold during their absence and needed to be reminded everytime the Sanjanas returned that the bungalow was no longer empty, but Daisy shook her head. "No, don't let's tell Fakhro. He has work to do. Let's tell Alphonse. He needs something to do. It's as Dolly said: an idle mind will make a gossip out of a saint."

Dolly nodded and clapped her hands. "Alphonse!"

"Yes, bai?" Alphonse shifted his gaze from Daisy to Dolly, surprised to hear himself called.

"Come here. I don't want to shout across the compound."

Alphonse came down the steps toward them. "Yes, bai?"

"Alphonse, the monkeys are bothering us. I want you to take the gun and shoot at them, but *not* to kill them. Do you understand? I only want you to scare them so they will stay away from the house. Just shoot the branches around where they are sitting—nothing else. Do you understand?"

Alphonse narrowed his eyes, gazing at her in silence. Dolly guessed she had offended him. He had requested permission to join them supposedly for his health, even as a guest, as a last token of their regard for Gracie, but now he was being put to work like a servant—like the servant he was, she would have said, but waited patiently for silence to wear him down. "Yes, bai."

"Good. Ask Fakhro for the gun. He will show you how to work it."

Alphonse's voice remained flat. "I know. I have shot monkeys before in Goa."

"We have a semi-automatic. I do not know if you have experience with automatics. Let Fakhro show you."

Alphonse spoke with scorn. "I have shot automatics. They are the easiest."

Daisy spoke without looking at him. "The gun's a bit wonky. You will have to shoot a bit to the right to hit your target. Do you think you can do that?"

"I can do it! I am a good shot! If the gun is wonky I will aim directly at their heads—and that will make me miss, no?"

Alphonse's question was as ironic as the smile that accompanied it, which surprised Dolly. Daisy was a good shot. Dolly had taught her and would have said she was as good as herself—but she didn't understand the antipathy between Daisy and Alphonse. He had known Daisy before any of them: she had sailed from England searching for a friend in Bombay who had sailed ahead without leaving a forwarding address; Alphonse, her steward on board, had directed her to the Sanjanas. "They know everybody, English and Indian." The Sanjanas had found her friend, recently married to one of their own friends, after which Daisy had married Sohrab almost immediately.

When Daisy remained mute Dolly spoke. "Do *not* shoot at their heads, Alphonse—or it will be upon *your* head. You must miss them com*plete*ly. Do you understand me? Com*plete*ly! I do not want you even to nick their tails. Do you understand, Alphonse?"

Alphonse replied, tightlipped, still looking at Daisy who continued to ignore him. "Yes, bai."

Noting her annoyance Sohrab seemed no less annoyed, as if the annoyance between Daisy and Alphonse amounted to familiarity, an affront to himself. "Yes, yes, Aphoos. Now take the big banduk and go. Shoot the big bandar, or don't shoot them, do as you please—but just go."

"Yes, Sohrab."

Sohrab glared at Alphonse for this further familiarity, addressing him as if they were still boyhood friends, not master and servant. "Get out, Aphoos! Go on! Just get out! Go!"

"Yes, sahib."

The ironic tone wasn't lost on the company as he walked back to the bungalow, but no one said a word, concentrating instead again on their breakfast. No one said a word a few moments later either when he emerged again from the bungalow with the gun and walked out of the compound. It wasn't until he was out of sight that Sohrab spoke again. "You see, Daise, what I mean about servants? Show them a little kindness and they take advantage of it. Give them an inch and they'll take a yard. It's just their nature and we have to guard against it. Spare the rod and spoil the servant."

He grinned, turning to Daisy, but she sipped her tea, refusing again to look at him as she spoke. "You're right, of course—as always, about everything."

Dolly grimaced: it was what she had often said to Kavas.

Sohrab lost his grin. "Daisy, don't be like that."

"Like what? I don't know what you mean. I am as I have always been."

She was right. Her reserve was her shield. At first he had passed it off as Englishness, the stiff upper lip, and in the first blush of marriage her mere presence had compensated for her shortcomings, but the blush had long passed and so had the honeymoon, an idyllic month on a houseboat, *Shangri-La,* on Dal Lake, in Srinagar. He hated to think Rustom was right, that he had married her for her Englishness, hated even to admit the possibility, but a wise man had said that all hate was spearheaded by fear, and he had been afraid from the first hurried agreement between them that she had married him for the wrong reasons herself, that he had never cared about the reasons as long as she married him. He spoke with a smaller voice, brittle with regret. "I know. I wish I might have changed you—just a little bit."

She looked at him then, not without surprise, softened by his admission. "I daresay you have."

She didn't smile, but her admission gladdened him enormously though he said nothing. In the eyes of the world they had a successful marriage, but such success had less to do with love than a willingness to do what the world wanted, whatever you may have wanted yourself. Such marriage was a matter of commerce masquerading as a matter of the heart. If you were rich you married someone who was rich, but if you were rich and somehow handicapped (either embittered or enfeebled or stupid or old) you married someone less rich—and less embittered, enfeebled, stupid, or old. The continuums ran from rich to poor, healthy to sick, young to old, smart to stupid, fairskinned to dark, beautiful to ugly, vivacious to dull, powerful to powerless, educated to uneducated, upper class to lower—and English to Indian. You defined yourself by the person you married. His parents exemplified the principle: Dolly loud, unworldly, poor; Phiroze quiet, worldly, rich. That they also loved each other he found incidental, blind to the Gordian knot of affection between them. It seemed disloyal to the memory of his true father who had died in a shooting accident—so he had been told. Had he been told more he might have found it easier to accept the death, but all his questions were met with frowns, blank stares, or admonitions to let the dead rest in peace, and he carried his resentment like a cross.

When Dinyar had been born the great fuss had been about the color of his eyes, green, like Daisy's—but also, as Sohrab liked to say, the eyes of his father, Kavas Sanjana, Dinyar's grandfather. Less was said about his complexion, darker than most Parsis—like Dolly's, as Sohrab also liked to say (though Dinyar was darker than Dolly), to nip further speculation in the bud. Neville, on the other hand, born a year later, was fairer, but with black Indian eyes and hair.

There was, not surprisingly, another side to the coin: mothers of wealthy Indian boys worried that their sons, students in strange lands, would become lambs to the slaughter for the daughters of their landladies, for teashop waitresses and dancehall hostesses—not that love might not develop between them, but that it shouldn't. That they might become lambs for duchesses or princesses wasn't a matter even for consideration. Sohrab's face twisted as he sucked the cut on his thumb again, still tasting blood. The cut was deeper than he had imagined. The damned bloody beautiful Brits: even when they were denigrated, they were worthy of denigration: to denigrate an Indian you simply ignored him. The notion of English superiority had been nurtured in him since childhood, since the womb, bred in his bones—but however much an Indian emulated an Englishman, he could never be English, never more than a watery imitation; hence, perhaps, the notion of Indian inferiority. The matter was never acknowledged, let alone discussed, but hovered like a wraith over the country, poisoning the body politic.

Daisy didn't elaborate in the wake of her admission that Sohrab may have changed her just a little bit, and the smile she offered satisfied him enough not to ask for more. There was the sound only of cutlery against crockery as the Sanjanas continued their breakfast, and as Daisy, thick with secrets, grew sicker in her solitude.

# DAISY'S STORY
## London (1935-1939)

**Monday, 6 May, 1935, Jubilee Day,** was bright and hot, hotter for the crush of the crowd, not a cloud in sight. Daisy would have been surprised if the seventy-five degrees registered by the weather bureau had not in fact tottered up to eighty in the thick of the throng where she stood, perhaps even higher. Half a million, so it was said, had descended on London for the event, not only from the suburbs, not only from other parts of England, but from Scotland and Ireland, even the Continent and America. She wished she were taller: for all she could see the King's carriage might have been passing at that very moment. The crowd, like a sea of people, swayed like waves, but aside from an occasional eddy of laughter remained deceptively quiet for its numbers. She could hear the birds in Green Park behind her, the peal of bells from a nearby abbey, the tramp of marching feet following an indistinct command, but the crowd itself was quiet as only an English crowd could be whatever the occasion. Wedged from all sides she was getting increasingly uncomfortable and nudged the girl beside her, pointing to people perched on roofs along Piccadilly. "That's where we should have gone. That's where we should be. Can you see anything at all?"

Cilla Flatly was twenty-two, six years older, and six inches taller. They had shared rooms for less than a year—and, since each was an only child, felt like siblings. Their clothes reinforced the image of sisters: sleek blue dresses, short sleeves puffed at the shoulders, Cilla in a pink hat with a red band and flowers, Daisy in a blue with a black band and wider brim. "I can see all right—sort of. Can't you?"

"No, not at all. Shall we go? I'm turning into a puddle just standing here."

"Oh, don't be silly, Daise. It's taken us hours to get here! It'll take us at least as long to find a better place—and in the meantime the King will have come and gone, and we'll have shown him our backsides. Better half a loaf is what I say."

"Well, that's all right for those of us who *have* half a loaf."

"Oh, Daise, you *know* I didn't mean it like that! It's just that it's the same everywhere. If we leave now we'll never get a place even as good as this."

"Fat lotter good that's gonner do me!"

Moments of anxiety caused Daisy to regress. Cilla's face wizened. "Oh, Daise!"

"Oh, all right! A fat lot of good that's going to do me! Is that better?"

Cilla grinned, not wishing to appear above herself in the crowd. "What do you think?"

Daisy would have told her what she thought with pleasure, but their attention was diverted by a loud voice on their left. "COMING THROUGH! COMING THROUGH! MAKE WAY PLEASE!"

Daisy and Cilla looked in the direction of the voice, Daisy jumping again on her toes to see two police helmets cutting a swath through the crowd toward them. "Now what? What's going on? Cilla, can you see anything?"

Cilla was on her toes again. "Someone's fainted, a woman. It looks like they're carrying her off."

"I'm not surprised. I feel like I could burst myself."

"*MAKE WAY PLEASE! COMING THROUGH! PLEASE MAKE WAY!*"

Daisy rolled her eyes. "There's not a way to be made! If there were a way to be made, we'd make it—but there's not!"

The closer policeman grinned. "If you'll just squeeze up against the gentleman behind you, miss, I'm sure he won't mind."

Daisy had been conscious of a large man behind her, but too preoccupied to pay more attention. Turning now she saw a man with dark hair, brown eyes, and a neatly groomed moustache barely curled at the tips, peering down from the sky, or so it seemed. He was smiling and spoke in a soft voice. "I can't say I'd mind if you did."

Daisy liked the look of the man and smiled. "I don't mind if I do myself."

She made way for the policemen, thrilled with her daring, leaning back against the man who held her steady by her waist as the policemen passed. Only special occasions allowed Londoners to behave casually in public. Granny Annie had told her about the night of Mafeking when she had met her husband-to-be: the West End had locked arms with the East; ladies had danced on tabletops showing their legs; strangers had met and mated in parks and alleys; Londoners had revealed themselves Parisians under the skin. It had been no different for her own mother and father on the night of the Armistice. It was not the kind of behavior that could be tolerated regularly, and Granny Annie's marriage had been successful no more than her mother's, but every generation seemed to experience such a time before donning again the straitjacket of respectability.

She continued to lean against the man, liking the feel of his hands still on her waist, but easing herself slowly away, sneaking a peek out of the corner of her eyes, noting his pale suit, yellow tie, and white homburg. He was still staring down, seeming to have eyes for no one and nothing else. "Lovely day, isn't it?"

His voice was as soft as before, turning her to water. "Oo, I don't know. It's too 'ot—*hot!* It's too hot for me. They say the temperature's seventy-five degrees."

She was glad they had listened to the wireless. Her mention of temperature made her feel scientific and mature. "Right, but imagine how awful it would have been had it rained instead."

"Well, of course, I shouldn't want it to rain—but oo, I say, it might as well. It's so hot I feel like I'm turning all to water."

The man nodded, still smiling. "Well, one's body is composed eighty percent of water, so that's no surprise."

"Oo, eighty percent! You're an Einstein, you are." Daisy raised her eyebrows, pleased again with her reference. The man seemed older even than Cilla, perhaps almost thirty, not to say the biggest man she had known, six feet if he were an inch, and planted as firmly as a tree. She turned to Cilla. "See, I'm eighty percent water—and so are you."

Cilla laughed.

"I don't know what you're laughing at, Cilla Flatly. That's exactly how I feel." She turned back to the man. "Actually, I feel like I could just sort of melt … or turn into a flower."

"A flower! How very unusual! What kind of flower?"

"Oh, a daisy! Most definitely a daisy!"

"Why a daisy?"

"Well, now, that's for some to know and some to not, isn't it?"

The man laughed. "Well, I'd wager your name's Daisy, isn't it?"

"How did you know? Have you been spying on us?"

"I've only been standing behind you for fifteen minutes. That's all."

"Oh, he's an eavesdropper!"

The man's tone turned penitent. "I'm afraid so. Sorry."

"It's all right. You couldn't help it now, could you? But you didn't tell us your name yet."

"It's Basil Ballard."

Daisy's mouth opened, but she said nothing recalling the alliterative names of her parents, Winifred Walpole and Harold Holiday, who had met on a holiday not unlike the Jubilee. "Oo, what a lovely name!"

"Daise, it's almost time! I can see the horse guards! The King's going to be here any minute!"

"Blimey! What *am* I going to do? I can't see a bloody thing! We really should have moved when we had the chance, Cilla."

Basil tapped Daisy's shoulder from behind. "Would you like a lift?"

"A lift? Whatever for? I'm not going anywhere."

"I meant up. I could lift you up—if you like—if that would be all right with you."

Daisy imagined him lifting her from behind by the armpits like a baby. "But what about you, Mr. Ballard? You wouldn't be able to see a thing yourself then."

"I wouldn't worry about me. I'll manage."

"All right, then! I would love a lift!"

Cilla was on her toes. "Here they come! Here they come!"

Daisy waited for Basil's hands under her arms, but he got on his haunches instead behind her patting his shoulder. "Go on, then. Sit down, but mind my hat—and hold on to your own."

Daisy looked over her shoulder. "Oh, I say, this isn't what I thought you meant at all!"

Bells pealed from the Abbey, the crowd roared, Union Jacks fluttered. She could hardly hear Cilla gushing "Oh, my God! Oh, my God!" though she stood right next to her. She could see the helmets of the horse guards without even standing on her toes, but she would never otherwise see the King and Queen in their carriage. Basil remained on his haunches, looking up, patting his shoulder. "Come on, then! Sit yourself down! You'll be all right! You'll see!"

She sat as he commanded on his left shoulder holding her hat with one hand, his with the other.

"Ready?"

"Ready."

"Then it's ups-a-Daisy!"

She gasped as he stood finding herself suddenly floating above the crowd, feeling like royalty herself. The horse guards had almost passed, regal in uniform, long plumed helmets like the long maned heads of their horses, stern as justice, sturdy as statues. They were followed by a series of open carriages, first of the Prince of Wales, first in line to the throne, still a bachelor, handsome as an actor, every girl in England imagining she might be his bride. She and Cilla had two pictures themselves, framed and prominently displayed in their tiny Fulham flat, while the rest of the royals merited just one. He was followed by the tiny princess Elizabeth and the tinier princess Margaret. Daisy lost count of the carriages in the sway of pomp that followed, but there was no mistaking the carriage of the King, gilded, drawn by a team of six greys, with the insignia of the Royal Arms on the door, the King bright with medals in the sun, wearing a tall hat with a plume, the Queen in a feathered hat and plush white cape that settled like snow around her shoulders.

Daisy felt she lived in three worlds: in London; in the presence of the King; and on the shoulders of a strange man who bore her as easily as if she were a child. The procession moved slowly, but seemed over in an instant. Raised above the crowd she had imagined the King waved for her alone. The rest of the carriages blurred as she continued to trail the King's. Her perch made her newly aware of the decorations: paper chains the length of Piccadilly; colored masts reminiscent of a medieval tournament; bunting and balloons and fluttering flags enough to make a fairyland of good old, lovely old, marvelous old London.

She descended slowly from her reverie. Her legs were in the grasp of a stranger, naked calves on display to the world, but Basil Ballard had hoisted and held her so happily she felt ungrateful asking for release. She patted his shoulder. "You can let me down now, Mr. Ballard, thank you very much. You must be all fagged out."

"Not at all—reinvigorated, if anything. I could carry you all the way to St. Paul's if you'd like."

The King's procession was on its way to St. Paul's to attend a service which was to be broadcast on the streets. Daisy was afraid he meant what he said. "Oh, no, I don't think that would be necessary. There's really nothing to see now the procession's gone."

"Very well." He got on his haunches again and Daisy hopped lightly to her feet. He was still grinning when they faced each other. "Were you able to see well enough?"

"Oh, yes, Mr. Ballard! I had the best seat in the house!"

# DAISY'S STORY

Cilla was smiling at Basil. "I wish I weren't so tall. Maybe then I could have sat on your other shoulder, Mr. Ballard."

"You could anyway, Miss Flatly."

"No, she couldn't! She's got her own fellow's shoulder to sit on, and she mustn't be such a greedy Gus!"

Basil looked at Cilla. "Oh, where is he?"

"He's sick, Mr. Ballard!"

"He was feeling queer yesterday, Mr. Ballard—and I was going to stay home and nurse him—but he insisted I was not to be deprived of the day on his account. My Bert—he's a good cove, he is."

"That's right, he is—and he would gladly have given you the best seat in the house as well if he could only have been here. He's a picnic, isn't he, Cilla?"

Cilla smiled, thinking of her Bert. "That he is—but if you ask me the whole world's a picnic today. Don't you think so, Mr. Ballard?"

"It's a holiday, all right—a regular holiday!"

Daisy shook her head. "No, it's not, Mr. Ballard! It's a picnic, not a holiday!"

Cilla wondered if Basil would take the bait Daisy had set. "If you say so, but why not a holiday?"

"Because *I'm* the holiday. My full name's Daisy Holiday."

Basil laughed. "So you're no picnic, I presume."

Daisy's grin couldn't have been fuller, her dimples deeper. "Lord, if I had tuppence for every time someone said that to me...."

Cilla took a deep breath. "Well, now, that's done. What next?"

Both girls looked for direction to Basil. "Why don't we walk to St. Paul's. We could hear the service. We could see the King when he comes out. After that we could have sandwiches and tea somewhere—and, after that, well, we can just wait and see, can't we? What do you think?"

He had assumed command as easily and happily as they had given it to him. "Oh, that sounds divine, Mr. Ballard—just too too divine!"

"That is, if we're not keeping you from anything else, Mr. Ballard?"

"Not at all! Well, then, it's settled. Shall we walk?"

"Oh, yes! Do let's!"

"Yes, indeed! Let's!"

It seemed all of London had entertained the same happy notion as they set off down St. James Street, flower beds aflame with tulips and irises, red and white May trees perfuming the air. Basil walked between the girls, Daisy almost straining to keep from taking his arm as they walked. "Mr. Ballard, do you like the King?"

Basil raised his eyebrows. "Oh, I think he's all right—as kings go. In fact, I think he's a jolly good egg—as kings go."

"Oh, I'm so glad you think so, Mr. Ballard! I think so too! I think he's a bit of all right. I think he's a lovely king—he *must* be if the East End is in agreement with the West End!"

Cilla was surprised to find herself competing for Basil's admiration, but it was fun, the day demanded abandon, and Daisy's vivacity was infectious. She raised an eyebrow. "But, Mr. Ballard, why do you say 'as kings go.' Don't you like kings in general?"

"Kings are like everything else, Miss Flatly. There are good kings and there are bad kings just as there are good people and bad people—or good horses and bad horses."

Daisy raised an eyebrow at Cilla. "And good questions and bad questions, Miss Flatly."

Basil raised both eyebrows. "Oh, but Miss Holiday, I thought it was a very good question."

Cilla ignored Daisy. "Ah, but the *real* question, Mr. Ballard, is: Did you think it was a good question—or just a good question as questions go?"

Daisy stared at Cilla. "What's the difference?"

"Well, Mr. Ballard didn't really answer your question. If kings are good or bad as kings go, and if people are good or bad as people go, and if horses are good or bad as horses go, then nothing is good or bad in and of itself, is it? It's only good or bad as it goes." She looked again at Basil. "Mr. Ballard, do you believe that's true?"

"Well, what I do believe is that it *is* different with kings because they have more power than normal people—or than horses. They affect other people's lives, for good or ill, more than normal people." He laughed. "Certainly more than horses."

Daisy hopped and skipped as she walked. "Mr. Ballard, you mustn't mind what Cilla says. She thinks she can ask the rudest questions just because she works in a solicitor's office."

Basil grinned, enjoying their attention as much as they seemed to enjoy squandering it. "You must find it very interesting, Miss Flatly, to work in a solicitor's office."

"Oh, I do, Mr. Ballard—even if I am just a secretary. It makes one *think* so."

Daisy almost jumped as she spoke. "I'm a typist, Mr. Ballard—in a bank."

Basil's eyebrows rose. "Indeed, a typist! And how do you find it, Miss Holiday?"

Cilla grinned. "They love her at the bank, Mr. Ballard. She's a bank Holiday everyday."

Daisy glared at her friend for stealing her joke. "It's all right, Mr. Ballard. I don't much care to talk about it."

"You still didn't answer Daisy's question, Mr. Ballard. Do you think the King is a good king in himself—or simply as kings go?"

"Ah, if you put it like that, I should have to say he's a good king as kings go."

"Then would it be fair to say you don't care for kings in general?"

Basil grinned. "It would be logical, but it wouldn't be fair."

"Why wouldn't it be fair—if it were true?"

"Because anything I might say about kings in general would be related to this king in particular, and this king has never been so very popular as he is today. It would be most unfair, don't you think, Miss Flatly, to ask anyone what he thinks of so very popular a king? I would be forced to put kings, even in general, in a good light, because otherwise I would put myself in rather a bad light, wouldn't I?"

"My goodness, Mr. Ballard, but I must say you talk an awful lot like a solicitor yourself."

"Thank you. I shall take that as a compliment."

"It was meant as one. Are you?"

"No, Miss Flatly, I'm afraid not."

"There! Do you see what I mean? Cilla's just being nosy. It's no business of hers what you do, Mr. Ballard, and you have my permission to say nothing at all."

"Oh, I don't mind saying. It's not that I do much at all—a bit of this, a bit of that. That's all."

Daisy clasped her hands to her chest. "Oo, that sounds lovely, Mr. Ballard—to make a living doing just this and that!"

They gazed at him, smiles flying off their faces, but he seemed suddenly distracted. Following his gaze the girls saw a man wearing a sandwich board being led gently but firmly away by a policeman. The board on his back was painted in large red letters on white:

I KNOW 3 TRADES
SPEAK 3 LANGUAGES
FOUGHT FOR 3 YEARS
HAVE 3 CHILDREN
AND NO WORK FOR
3 MONTHS
BUT I ONLY WANT
<u>ONE</u> JOB!

Daisy spoke indignantly. "Can you believe it! The nerve of some people!"

"Really! Today of all days!"

"He should be grateful there's a dole for people like him!"

"It's a good thing they caught him before he got to the King!"

Basil smiled. "Don't you think he has more to fear from the King than the King from him?"

"Why, Mr. Ballard, you are not suggesting, surely, that the King means him harm?"

"No, of course not—not intentionally. It's what we were talking about before, isn't it? Kings affect ordinary lives even when they remain unaware of the lives they affect."

"Well, then, Mr. Ballard, what do you think should be done with such people?"

Basil hesitated, but spoke finally still gazing after the man with the placard, now almost out of sight. "Why do you think anything should be done with them, Miss Holiday?"

"Well, what I mean to say is it ... it seems so unpatriotic, doesn't it?"

"Do you mean to say, then, that it is unpatriotic to want to work?"

"No, of *course* not! But to show himself like that to everyone!"

"But doesn't he have as much right to be seen as the King?"

"Oh, Mr. Ballard, of *course*, he does—but to*day* of all days?"

"The best day of all, Miss Holiday, from his point of view—when he would be seen by the most people, perhaps even by the King."

"Oh, dear, Mr. Ballard, if you are not a solicitor, you really must consider it!"

The man was no longer in sight and Basil was smiling again, looking at Daisy. "Thank you very much for the suggestion, Miss Holiday. I shall keep it in mind should the necessity arise."

Cilla stared, her brow furrowed. "You were just having us on, weren't you, Mr. Ballard?"

Basil included her in his big smile. "That's for some to know and some to not, isn't it? I believe that's how Miss Holiday phrased it?"

Daisy slapped his arm. "Go on with you, Mr. Ballard! You are a caution. I know when I'm being had." She turned to Cilla. "Go on, Cilla. You can slap his arm if you wish. You have my permission."

Basil grinned at her proprietary tone. "And do I not have a say, Miss Holiday, in who is to slap my arm and who is not?"

Daisy slapped his arm again. "No, Mr. Ballard, you do not!"

**They followed their unstructured course** until it was time for the service to be broadcast. The Royal Courts of Justice loomed ahead, an imposing facade of gothic arches, spires, towers, and turrets. With the conclusion of the service they walked into Fleet Street, but came to a full stop, laughing and bewildered, when the mass of people proved too overwhelming for progress. The King and his entourage passed them again on the return from St. Paul's and Daisy hopped on Basil's shoulder as if she had been to the perch born, liking the height, the gallantry, his hands on her knees, her hand on his other shoulder while minding his hatted head, convinced the King would remember her as the girl poised on a man's shoulder, particularly since he had seen her twice. Later, Basil bought roast beef and tomato sandwiches and lemonade from a stall, followed by chocolate ices.

It was late in the afternoon when Cilla whispered to Daisy that she wanted to share part of the day with Bert, inviting Daisy along if she wished, but adding she could hardly blame her if she stayed (she could have eaten Basil herself with a spoon). Daisy grinned, whispering back that she would stay. Basil expressed regret that Cilla had to leave, also the hope that he might see her again, and sent regards to Bert who was a lucky fellow indeed for her to leave so festive a day on his account. Cilla cautioned him with a smile not to lose Daisy, to which he said he would take the best care of her that he knew how, adding color to Daisy's face, conjoining all her freckles though she pretended not to hear.

After Cilla's departure they grew quieter. Basil tucked Daisy's hand in the crook of his arm with a smile. "You must not think I am being fresh, Miss Holiday, but Miss Flatly said quite expressly that I was not to lose you."

Daisy clutched his arm with both hands. "Don't worry, Mr. Ballard. I have no intention of getting lost. In any case, you couldn't possibly get fresher than a daisy now, could you?"

Basil laughed. The formal address was already a charade between them, a means of maintaining normalcy. She couldn't say when exactly, but sometime since he had first hoisted her on his shoulder formality itself had become a formality. In her mind he was Basil, and when he tucked her hand in his arm she knew she was Daisy in his. The need for conversation abated as they walked, still aimlessly, though now as one. It mattered less that they had nowhere to go than that they were together. Picture palaces, packed just the day before, were deserted, but there was a circus now in the street that glistened more brightly than any silver screen. They headed finally to the Palace to see the King yet again with his family, answering incessant calls of "We Want George!" from the balcony.

They had been on their feet all day. As shadows lengthened they retired to St. James Park and rented two deckchairs to park among the picnicking multitude. Families from the suburbs, all parts of England's compass, and many parts beyond, sat in parties, wellshod, welldressed, wellbehaved, minding their own business. A teenage girl braided her friend's long blond tresses as if they were alone, a young man asked Basil for the time as if they were at a bus station, a child played with a toy car as if he were in his pen at home, but not a flower was broken in its bed. The only license taken was a disregard of the signs saying KEEP OFF THE GRASS.

Daisy leaned back in her chair, hat in her lap, red hair framing her freckled face, and sighed. "Everything's so lovely I feel like I'm dreaming—but I don't want to shut my eyes! I'm afraid everything will change if I fall asleep."

"I'll still be here."

"Will you?"

"Unless you don't want me to be."

"Oh, but I do! You *must* be here, Mr. Ballard! You are an es*sen*tial part of the dream!"

Basil leaned back himself, smiling, nodding, keeping his eyes on her. "You have the rosiest face—that hair, those freckles. Did anyone ever call you Red?"

"My mum, sometimes, for a joke—but that was a long time ago."

"A long time ago! And you barely of age, I'd wager."

"Well, it seems years. I was eleven when my mum died—and I'm sixteen now!"

"Oh, I say, I *am* sorry to hear that. I didn't mean to pry."

"You weren't prying, Mr. Ballard. I wanted to tell you." She turned her head. Her voice trembled. "She was lovely, she was, me mum." She took two short sharp breaths, and pursed her lips for control. "I still miss her. I'll always miss her. She was very beautiful."

"What about your dad?"

Daisy turned her head away again, saying nothing.

"I'm sorry. I suppose I really am prying now, but you don't have to say a thing."

She faced him again. "It's not that, Mr. Ballard. I want to tell you, but there's no nice way to say it. My dad …" She took a deep breath. "My dad is a bloody bastard is what he is! I'm sorry to be so rude, Mr. Ballard, but there it is—and that's being kind, it is. It was because of him me Mum died—it was an accident, but he did it—as sure as we're sitting here, he did it, he killed her—and he never even told me. He pretended it was something else. I found out from the newspapers later, what really happened. I found out from the boys at school when they made fun of what happened." She turned away. "I shouldn't be talking like this. I hardly know you. I'm sorry I brought it up."

"Don't be sorry. You don't have to stop on my account. If you don't mind I'd like to hear whatever you want to tell me."

"I don't mind. I would like to tell you."

"Then I would like to hear it."

**RETURNING FROM SCHOOL,** she had found her father in the kitchen, the backroom of their flat, a newspaper spread before him, elbows on the table, a cup of tea. He was a small man, but wide in the shoulders, thick in the arms, and in the dim light, hunched over the newspaper in his blue brassbuttoned uniform, appeared like a fortress, a huge rocklike egg to the dome of his head, almost bald though he remained a year short of thirty. His helmet lay on the table, his truncheon in its belt slung to the back of a chair. Neither acknowledged the presence of the other until Daisy switched on the light. He remained still, his

# DAISY'S STORY

face turned to the newspaper, seeming to speak from his head more than his mouth. "Turn it orf!"

"How can you read?"

"Never you mind! Turn it orf!"

"Awright! I'll turn it orff!"

His eyes still bored into the newspaper. His daughter had learned to mock his speech from his wife who made no secret of the fact that her husband had married well, implying that she herself had not. In the first blush of courtship, when her family had chosen to ostracize her, their differences had added the luster of modernity, even virtue, though she had done no more than her mother before her, both of them gentlewomen marrying proles, the mother a fireman, the daughter a policeman. They were the same: mother and daughter, highminded enough to marry low, only to mock the men they married—and the granddaughter was no different: speaking King's English with her mother, mocking him with his own accents. "You watch how you talk to yer dad—or I'll warm yer backside, I will."

Daisy saw he had brewed the tea in the kettle, not the pot, as her mother would have done; saw also no sign of dinner. "Where's Mum?"

That was what he wanted to know, where was the girl he had married, though he had long realized she had existed only in his imagination, or perhaps for just the days of their courtship. They had met, Winifred Walpole and Harold Holiday, seeing portents in everything, including the alliterations of their names, on the first night of the Armistice, when all Londoners had turned seemingly into foreigners, and class differences into a relic of the past along with the years of darkness behind. There had been dancing in the streets, sex among strangers in parks and alleys; a woman had paraded in the Cornmarket waving a flag, skirts hitched above her waist, naked from the waist down, to universal cheers; but the constabulary had orders not to interfere unless lives were at stake. The King and Queen, no less, had blessed the night with continual appearances on the Palace balcony.

"Dad! Where's Mum?"

Whether they had been blind on the night of the Armistice, or blind ever since, he couldn't have said. Things had changed almost immediately, but neither had taken a step back, and too soon it had been too late. He was her lord and master whatever their stations before they were married, though he soon understood that she would never have married a perfect yobbo like himself had the night not been special—but done was done, they had taken vows, and if she chose to flout them he was within his rights to enforce them. "Yer mum's gone."

"Where's she gone?"

"Gone's gone an' good riddance."

"When's she coming home?"

"She's not. Gone's gone an' good riddance, I'm tellin' yer. She's not comin' 'ome."

"I don't believe you."

"You believe what you want. It's a free country."

"But where is she?"

"If you mus' know, she's in 'orspital. She's 'urt somethin' bad. She's not comin' 'ome."

"But what's happened?"

"Yer mum's barmy, she is. You know she is. That's what's 'appened."

"She's not!"

"Oh, yuss, she is! If she come out o' 'orspital she'll be needin' to be somewheres she can't 'arm decent folk, she will—another kind o' 'orspital, maybe." He tapped his temple. "Potty, yer mum is."

"She's not! You're lyin'!"

"Oh, yuss? Whaddaya call it then, when she starts throwin' salt at people in the street? Yuss, an' parks 'erself right by the Palace gate, mind you. Whaddaya call that if not barmy?"

Hearing Daisy speak you would know she was her mother's daughter, but when her voice got too large for her head, her skin too prickly for her body, she became her father's. Far from mocking her father as he imagined she was providing the sincerest form of flattery. "That's 'cause she's a sufferjet. She jus' wants the vote like what you got, like what all the men got, an' you don't want 'er to 'ave it, an' now she can't get it."

"Daft as yer mum, you be. She got the bleedin' vote years ago, right after the bleedin' war."

Women had won the vote after the war, but only women over thirty, younger women too greatly outnumbering younger men for the comfort of the older. Ten years later they had full suffrage, but Winnie remained unsatisfied needing the cause of suffrage more than suffrage itself: without a cause she was nothing herself. He had begun to understand this slowly having once been her cause himself: son of a tenant-farmer, arrived in London from Hertfordshire; and she no more than the daughter of a fireman, but the granddaughter from her mother's side of a man who had made money in the India trade.

Harry had heard it was easier to rise in the ranks of the force than the army, that the force preferred country brawn to city brain, only to learn it was country brain that was preferred, an empty vessel being easier to fill than one which would first have to be emptied. Content nevertheless with his pay and pension he had settled in Clerkenwell for reasons both economic and sentimental: Sir Hugh Myddelton, a wealthy seventeenth century goldsmith, had brought water to Clerkenwell from the springs of his native Hertfordshire via a combination of open channels and underground pipes, a distance of no more than forty miles but no mean feat for his century, for which he had been honored with a baronetcy from King James, not to mention streets, schools, and squares in his name—and a statue at Islington Green. The same sentiment had enrolled Daisy in the Hugh Myddelton School—but sentiment was the bread and poetry of those who could afford nothing else, and easily dimmed by prosperity. Clerkenwell, along with Holborn, Finsbury, and Shoreditch among others, were manufacturing districts, overcrowded for the same reason, and with no room to grow jobs and businesses were being relocated, as were working people. The expanded underground had expanded opportunities for spacious living in an expanded London, and he wished to avail himself of the new suburbs, coming around from Chingford in the north, through Hendon, Harrow, Hayes, and Hounslow in the west, to Morden and Bexley in the south (if you didn't move up, you moved down)—but Winnie dreamed of nothing more than rooms in the East End. "She parked 'erself right by the Palace gate, she did, chuckin' salt ever'where. If you don't call that barmy, I don't know what's what."

"Where'd she get salt?"

"Damned if I know, but she 'ad a sackful."

"Why's she in 'orspital?"

"She was to be arrested—"

"What for?"

"Fer litterin' an' loiterin'—an' disturbin' the peace."

"But why's she in 'orspital?"

"She was resistin' arrest is what she was doin'—an' she banged 'er 'ead."

"How?"

"I told you. She banged 'er 'ead resistin' arrest. There's nothin' else to tell." He didn't say who the arresting constable had been, nor that Winnie had taunted him, nor that she had fallen during their clumsy tussle, leaping out of his arms like a hooked fish, striking her head because he had held her half in the air by her legs, allowing her head to absorb the greater impact of her weight on the concrete. The sound had been the thwock of a bat striking a ball for a sixer. He had dropped her legs, turned suddenly to lead in his grasp, and she lay on her belly among hillocks of salt seeming barely to breathe.

"For chuckin' salt? Why was she chuckin' salt? Di'n't she say nothin' at all?"

"That's all you need to know. She's in 'orspital now, an' not likely 'ome soon. Do what you want wi' that." The English in India had forced a monopoly on salt, forbidding Indians to manufacture their own, extorting exorbitant taxes, but that seditious bastard, Mr. Gandhi, had picked salt from a beach inciting his followers to pan for salt on beaches the country over. It was perverse, but sixty thousand Indians had been arrested, no one offering resistance, not to beatings with truncheons, not even to death. Worse than perverse, it was madness for a leader to allow his followers to be killed—to encourage them! It wasn't cricket; you couldn't fight madmen. As a man of law himself Harry stood for King and Country, but Winnie had stood against him, extolling Mr. Gandhi as hero and saint at the very gates of the Palace, exhibiting the madness of the Indians. He could have done no less than arrest her. "As God be my witness I did what I 'ad to do. It's all you need to know. Get along with you. Ain't you got nothin' better to do than stare at yer ol' man?"

"I don't understand why she can't come 'ome. I don't understand why she 'as to stay in 'orspital."

"They're watchin' over 'er there. If you gotter know, 'er mum's with 'er."

"Granny Annie?"

"Yuss."

Granny Annie had lived alone in her Chelsea house ever since her fireman husband had been consumed in a blaze. She received a widow's pension, but had family money as well though repudiated for her marriage by the family, the Clive Bunker Tudor Raleighs of the India trade, much as she had repudiated her own daughter in turn for hers. What was the good of making mistakes, she insisted, if your own daughter wouldn't profit from yours? More to the point, her daughter's daughter was not to be punished for the sins of her daughter. Daisy had ever been welcome in her home, and visited when she could on weekends for lunch. She was glad Granny Annie was with her mother, wished she could have been with them herself, but she didn't know the hospital and her father wouldn't tell her.

"When I knew for certain Mum wasn't coming back, I packed everything and went to my granny's."

"It doesn't seem like your mum and dad were much suited for each other."

"They weren't! I see that now. They should never have married. Mum always cared about fairness—you know, the vote, and the poor, and things like that. She was a suffragette, talked her head off about women's enfranchisement and things like that. She thought Mr. Gandhi was a lovely man for doing what he was doing."

"But not your father?"

"He just wanted to get on, you know. He's a policeman, and all he wanted was to do his job, to enforce the law—but me mum …" Daisy shook her head, smiling with pride. "She was all for breaking the law if it was for a higher good—and there's always a higher good—there *al*ways *is!*" She looked at Basil, daring him to contradict her, but he nodded and she continued. "We had a big picture of all the Pankhursts in our sitting-room." She smiled at the memory. "Dad didn't much care for it, I can tell you, but for Mum it was holy—they were like saints. When Emmeline Pankhurst died she said it was such a blessing she had lived to see her life's work accomplished—they won the vote, you know, the same year."

Basil nodded. "The timing was fortunate."

"Yes, it was."

"But it always amazes me when people so different marry. What do you suppose it was brought them together."

She might have told him it had been Armistice Night, but didn't, not wishing him to draw parallels between that night and their own Jubilee night, as if the occasion mattered more than the people. She shrugged. "When Mum died I put everything I could into a bag and left. I didn't have money for the bus, and I walked from Clerkenwell to Chelsea—where my granny lived. I went to a new school—a new life—and after school I got a job in a dress shop. Then I started typing classes—because I really didn't care much for work in the dress shop, but that's where I met Cilla—in the dress shop, I mean. She had bought some things, dresses and … girlie things, if you know what I mean?"

Basil nodded.

"Well, she bought so many things that in the mix of all the parcels and boxes she forgot her own purse—which I found and saved for her. When she knew I had it she wanted to buy me lunch—and we just sort of hit it off, you might say. We thought it might be fun to be in digs together—and we are—and it is—on Eustace Road—in Fulham."

"She seems a very nice girl."

"Oh, she is! She's lovely!"

A whistle and twee came over the loudspeakers as if a giant were tuning a wireless and a hush descended like a cloud on the park. The King was to broadcast a message. Daisy sat up, attention immediately diverted. Basil was no less diverted, but by Daisy. He started to say something but Daisy took his hand to silence him and he said nothing. She no longer even looked at him, and when a voice pierced the snarl and crackle of the airwaves her hand grew tighter on his. The voice was hesitant, humble enough for a bank clerk, and launched without preamble into the heart of the matter.

> *At the close of this memorable day, I must speak to my people everywhere. How can I express what is in my heart?*

Basil looked around. The stillness of the assembly seemed to penetrate even shrubbery, rendering movement sacrilegious. Children sat like dolls, adults like statues. Somewhere behind him someone was crying, more than one someone. For the first time in history a single voice addressed the whole world in one moment—but the King, it was said, was nervous, and a thick cloth covered the table from which he spoke to cushion the pages rustling in his wobbly hand. It was ironic that so unassuming a man as George V owned the voice—a simple man, which made him either charming or stupid depending on your politics. Basil returned Daisy's grip, but for the moment his hand might have been wood. Her gaze was fixed on the twilit sky, attention fully absorbed by the King's message. The King seemed to gain confidence as he spoke, with tones more emphatic, accent of an Edwardian country gentleman, but his voice remained odd, even hoarse, as if sanded by weather.

> *I can only say to you, my very very dear people, that the Queen and I thank you from the depths of our hearts for all the loyalty and, may I say, the love, with*

> which, this day and always, you have surrounded us. I
> dedicate myself anew to your service for all the years
> that may still be given me.

It had been prearranged: as the last cadence of the King died he pressed a button igniting beacons in the countryside. Hills and downs around London and beyond glowed with bonfires and beacons, making a chain from peak to peak from the south of England and Wales to the north of Scotland—as they had glowed with bonfires and beacons in the time of Elizabeth when the Armada had been sighted. That night, from the sky, Britain would have appeared the largest and brightest constellation on earth.

The last reverberations of the address broke into cheers for the King and choruses of "He's a Jolly Good Fellow." Strangers turned to one another with greetings of God Bless the King. Basil turned to Daisy whose eyes shone more brightly for the floodlighting in the park. Trees seemed trimmed with silver, grass a glittering green, and the faces of flowers like those of children past bedtime. "Miss Holiday, are you hungry?"

"Oo, yes, Mr. Ballard, but I'm so comfortable I don't want to get up just yet."

"Who said anything about getting up?" He pulled a brown paper bag from one pocket, a flask from another. "I brought provisions: chutney sandwiches and lemonade."

Daisy clasped hands under her chin in wonder, her mouth a lovely tiny pink round O. She had tasted chutney at the home of Granny Annie's relatives in the India trade. "Oh, you lovely lovely man, you think of everything! Chutney sandwiches, indeed! Wherever did you get chutney sandwiches?"

"I developed a taste when I was in India and packed some for myself this morning."

"India! My goodness! Here you are, been to India and keeping mum, and little old me raving like a hatter about Clerkenwell and Chelsea! What else haven't you told me, Mr. Ballard?"

Basil took sandwiches out of the bag. "I'm afraid they're a bit squashed, not to mention a bit dry, but I think they'll do."

"One doesn't question manna from the gods. What were you doing in India?"

"Oh, I was there on business."

"Ah, doing this and that you mean! You haven't said yet, Mr. Ballard, what it is that you do—or is it nosy of me to ask?"

"Not at all. I'm a writer, you see –"

"Oh, but how wonderful for you! Is that what you meant when you said you did this and that?"

"In part, yes."

"What might I have read of what you've written?"

"More than likely nothing, I'm afraid. I write mainly for newspapers and magazines with very small and specialized circulations."

Daisy was as bright as a child on Christmas morning, munching her sandwich, gulping lemonade. "Mr. Ballard, that is just what I would like to do. I would like to write. I've even taken a course at the London School of Journalism."

"Have you, really? What have you written?"

"Nothing yet, but I have so many ideas."

"Let me see them when you've written them out. Maybe I could help you."

"Oh, Mr. Ballard, that would be lovely! Do you really think you could?"

"I might." By the time they had finished the sandwiches it was eight o'clock. Daisy gathered their papers to deposit in the rubbish bin. When she got back she stretched for a moment and hugged herself. Basil raised his eyebrows. "You must be cold."

"Not cold. Ex*ci*ted!"

"Are you sure you're not cold? You may have my coat if you'd like."

"But what would *you* do then? It wouldn't be right for you to be cold just because I didn't bring a jumper along."

"Well, why don't we share my chair? That should keep us warm."

"Oh, yes, that should. Let's."

Basil reclined in his chair leaving a little room to one side and Daisy squeezed herself slowly under his arm, snuggling her head under his chin, one hand bunched by her cheek, the other spread flat on his chest. She rubbed his chest in a quick to and fro motion. "Are you all right, then, Mr. Ballard? Not cold?"

"Not cold. Never better."

"Me too. It seems the stars have come down to earth. It seems the whole world has turned into a dream, but I'm afraid to shut my eyes because it may all change by the time I open them again—oh, but I said that already, didn't I?"

"Yes."

"Then it must be true, you see, because I had to say it again."

"Yes, it must—and I said before that I would still be here if you wanted me to be."

"I do. Please be here, Mr. Ballard. Please be here when I open my eyes again. Please don't be anywhere else ever again."

Basil laughed. "I will be here, Miss Holiday. When you open your eyes I will still be here."

"Oh, you're too lovely to me, Mr. Ballard."

She shut her eyes. He wasn't surprised she fell asleep and shut his eyes as well though more fitfully, not speaking until she opened her eyes again. "You see, Miss Holiday, I'm still here."

"My goodness, I didn't mean to fall asleep. What time do you make it?"

He jerked his arm to pull the sleeve from his wrist. "I make it a quarter past ten."

She almost jumped out of his arms. "My goodness. You shouldn't have let me sleep, Mr. Ballard. If I don't catch the last train—why … I'll be stranded!"

Basil laughed. "Don't worry, Miss Holiday. I promise not to turn into a pumpkin at midnight. I shall not let you be stranded."

She giggled. "I do feel a bit like Cinderella, and this lovely old London's like a fairyland tonight—but does that mean you'll be disappearing in the morning?"

"As I recall, in the story it was Cinderella who did the disappearing."

"Of course—but I won't—disappear, I mean—but I must be getting home."

"Where do you live?"

"On Eustace Road, I told you. The District Line will take me to Fulham Broadway. It's a five minute walk from there."

"Well, good luck catching the train on a day like this. We'll be lucky if we make it to the station let alone a train—and taxis and buses will be just impossible. It's why I didn't bring my motorcycle."

Daisy wanted to ask about the motorcycle, but remained silent wondering how they might circumvent their problem.

"Why don't we just stay here?"

The park was to be kept open through the night at the order of the King, but she shook her head. "I hate to be a bore, Mr. Ballard, but I'm afraid that's just not on. I have to be working tomorrow."

"Well, then, perhaps we should get started—though I have my doubts."

"I absolutely hate to be a bore, Mr. Ballard, but I would at least like to give it a go."

"Well, then, let's. Let's give it a go."


**They left the park** for the station at Hyde Park Corner. The Palace glowed like a mirage in a desert sun as did London, bathed in lumens, hovering on giant caterpillars of light. The throngs still called incessantly: "We Want George! We Want George! We Want George! We Want George!" They were to remain and the King to make several appearances on the balcony through the night.

The entrance to the station was jammed with people, merry as the people in the park. Basil made his way as best he could, holding tight to Daisy in his wake, stopping finally to look at his watch, turning to Daisy. "It's almost half past eleven. I don't think we stand much of a chance with the train—but I think we can honestly say we gave it a go. The only way, it seems, would be to walk. I'm for it if you are."

## A Googly in the Compound

It was a walk of almost four miles, but Daisy nodded easily. "There doesn't seem to be much else for it—but only if you promise you'll stay at my place when we get there. It doesn't seem fair to pack you off to God knows where after all your trouble."

"I promise."

They walked along Knightsbridge to Brompton Road, down Brompton to Fulham Road, down Fulham to North End Road, off North End Road finally to 5 Eustace Road. Wirelesses blared from windows, people danced in the streets. When the BBC signed off at midnight someone in the Fulham Road with a concertina began to sing "What's the Time When It's Twelve O'Clock." Others along the road seemed to be waiting with mouth organs, barrel organs, accordions. Some of the big houses had bands playing and men in top hats and tails and women with bare arms and backs joined the dancing in the streets as did Basil and Daisy on their way.

By the time they got home it was almost three o'clock. Daisy had long decided to forego work the next day. She had guessed her rooms would be empty, Cilla nursing her sick Bert, but shushed Basil as she drew her latchkey. "It wouldn't do to wake Mrs. Ellery. She's a lovely old thing, our landlady, but I don't know what she would say about a strange man in her house at this time of night." She apologized for the size of the couch in the sitting-room and offered to take the couch herself leaving him her bed, but he refused to chuck her out of her own bed. "Goodnight, Basil."

He smiled, asleep almost immediately. "Goodnight, Daisy."

The next morning found her in a bundle of blankets and sheets on the carpet by the couch, the better to be closer to him he liked to think, her small mouth sporting a smile in sleep.

IT WAS HALF PAST MIDNIGHT on a Saturday, early Sunday morning, when Basil parked his motorcycle in Leicester Square. "Here we are, then."

Daisy loved riding behind him, skirt riding up her thighs, the barrel of his torso secure within the circle of her arms, hands locked proprietarily over the thudding of his heart, soft cheek flush with the hard curve of his back. In his presence breath turned to music in her lungs, the lump of her body to light, her emerald eyes (so he said himself) danced the Charleston—and riding behind him united them like nothing else, ploughing through London like a comet, red hair painting the wind behind them, both of them orphans careening in the arc of the comet.

He was alone no less than herself, no less adrift from his family, for reasons no less provocative: writing was a profession neither respected nor recognized in their circles. Most of all she was amazed that something as big and hard and substantial as himself showed interest in something as slight as herself. She hadn't seen much of him in the year since the Jubilee, he sometimes left London for weeks, but he kept her abreast of his schedules. She wished he would keep her abreast as well of his activities, but was happy enough to ask no more than he chose to divulge. He seemed happy with her occasional company, and she was afraid to lose what little she had by importuning more. Respecting his wishes she was sure he would sooner or later respect hers, but she couldn't have specified her wishes except in the broadest terms. Her yearning spread before her like a chasm: naming it she was afraid she would lose him—but, increasingly, leaving it unnamed she was no less afraid. Their affair, if so it might be termed, remained a courtship, not a consummation. His smiles, kisses, and other indulgences seemed no more than he might offer a child, but he was also flirtatious, daring her to take him in hand as she wished to be taken herself—daring her to share the responsibility for what might happen between them.

A fog hovered masking light and sound, streetlamps appeared suspended like lanterns. He didn't take her hand, but guided her in silence to the end of a long narrow alley. She knew only that they were visiting a club, but the path seemed odd and the entrance odder, a door bearing no identification, appearing to lead to a private more than a public area, opening as it did onto a long dark passage visible only for light filtering around the far corner. The strains of a combo, a woman singing, sounded faintly as they walked toward the light.

Around the corner a woman sat behind a table, her face more caked with makeup than Daisy thought necessary, more grotesque for the harsh light from the lamp beside her. "Yes?"

Basil bent slightly from his waist. "Guests of Rupert Taylor-Rice."

The woman didn't look up. "Names?"

Basil identified himself and Daisy.

The woman entered their names into a ledger, looking up for the first time. "What do you think the King should do?"

"Whatever he damn well pleases."

"Do you really?"

"No, I never really think about it."

Daisy understood a password had been exchanged. The woman nodded, ushering them toward another door with a turn of her head. The sound of the combo was louder, increasingly louder as they passed through the door into a foyer and down a flight of stairs to a large subterranean room. It was too dim, too smoky, to see clearly, but Daisy, feeling conspicuous in her fringed blue party dress barely reaching her knees, square and deep at the neck, imagined heads turning, eyes fastening on her skin like pinpricks. As she grew accustomed to the dark she saw there were more women in the room than men. A few couples danced to the combo: a negro quartet (clarinet, drums, bass, piano) accompanying a tall bald negress singing "Sophisticated Lady." There were negroes as well dancing and circulating among the customers. The other men in the room were older—sleek, successful, each attended by a woman. Tickertape and balloons festooned the room. Adjacent rooms which remained unclear in the dim light seemed similarly festooned. A man with a glass in his hand approached as they found a table. "Bas. Hullo. Are they treating you all right?"

He was shorter than Basil, the same age, cleanshaven, and dressed in a dinner jacket as was Basil under his coat, as were the other men. Basil's eyebrows rose. "Rupert. Well, actually, we just got here."

"Didn't they bring you a bottle yet?"

"No, but I say, we really did—we only *just* got here. Given half a chance, I daresay they will."

"Oh, I'm sure, I'm sure—and who is the enchanting creature beside you?"

She might have been anything but enchanting for all the enthusiasm Rupert mustered. The tips of Basil's moustache extended the wings of his smile. "Daisy Holiday, I'd like you to meet Rupert Taylor-Rice, our host."

She held out her hand. "How do you do, Mr. Taylor-Rice?"

He shook her hand, but seemed not to hear, sipping immediately from his glass, seeming not to talk to her even while addressing her by name. "As you see, Miss Holiday, I am but one host among a sea of hostesses." He swept a wide arc with his arm through the air breathing a sigh which might have launched a thousand ships. "The competition in the West End's nothing to sneeze at, Bas—among the clubs, I mean—numbering now, so they say, in the hundreds. What I need is more guests, if you know what I mean, to keep all these hostesses occupied."

Basil nodded. "Early yet, though, isn't it?"

"Good of you to say, Bas, but it's not. It's late—late enough, anyway."

Daisy understood they were talking about bottle parties. The police had cracked down on nightclubs selling liquor after hours during the Twenties, but lacked authority when no specific laws had been broken, and dedicated clubbers had created the bottle party: as long as organizers were hosts and customers guests, as long as liquor was bought during licensing hours, and as long as entertainment was convened at a private party, the police had all the power of an inebriated lord.

Basil turned to Daisy. "Rupert and I went up to Cambridge together."

Rupert spoke into the floor. "We should have come down together for all the good it's done us—might otherwise have added a couple of years to our lives."

Basil helped Daisy remove her jacket, caught Rupert's look approving her slender bare arms, before pulling a chair for her and seating himself. "I say, Rupe, would you care to join us?"

## A Googly in the Compound

Rupert, sipping again from his glass, seated himself, speaking into his glass. "Don't mind if I do, actually—though just for a bit." A waiter approached with whiskey, soda water, two glasses, and an ice bucket on a tray, but as he set about pouring Rupert waved him away. "Leave it alone, for God's sake, leave it alone. Do stop your hovering. No one's going to run away with your damn tray. We're perfectly capable of doing the needful here."

"Yes, sir. Sorry, sir. Of course, sir." The waiter bowed and left.

Rupert poured. Basil removed a pack of Dunhill's from his pocket, offering a cigarette first to Daisy, then to Rupert. After cigarettes had been lit and glasses filled Rupert spoke again, staring again into his glass. "So, Bas, how was it that you were able to snare this enchanting creature?"

Daisy grinned, but Basil replied with all seriousness. "She gave me a come hither look, and thither I went."

Daisy's mouth dropped to a pink O.

Basil's mouth twitched as he squeezed her elbow. "Well, didn't you, my dear?"

Rupert still stared into his glass. "Well, is someone going to tell me or must I call MI5?"

Daisy recounted their story from Jubilee Day, but Rupert seemed to have lost interest. "I say, did I tell you Shirin and Algy were coming?"

"Yes, you did. Anyone else? What about Goddy and Polly-Wolly?"

Rupert shrugged. "You can never tell with that crowd."

"I thought they needed reservations?"

"They do, of course—only way to make these damn parties function—but that doesn't necessarily mean they'll show."

"I hope they show. I'd like them to meet Daisy." He looked at Daisy, but her mouth had dropped again in an O, her attention arrested by something she had seen beyond his shoulder: a naked man had walked across the doorway to one of the adjacent rooms. "Daisy?"

Daisy took a deep breath, but chose to ignore what she had seen. "Yes?"

"What is it? You seem distracted."

"What? Oh, it's nothing. Sorry. I thought I saw something—but I didn't—I couldn't have."

"What?"

She turned smiling back to Basil. "Nothing. Never mind. Really. Sorry. Don't mind me. What were you saying?"

"Just that I'd like you to meet some friends of mine."

She wanted to meet his friends; it would mean at least that he wasn't ashamed of her; but she was afraid of the impression she might make. "Of course. I'd like to meet them. I *want* to meet them."

"You will—if they show, that is. I make it past one o'clock already."

Rupert shook his head. "They should be here soon, or they're not coming."

"Good old Rupe—eternal pessimist."

"I'm a grown-up, that's all. What were you two children up to before you came here tonight?"

Daisy tapped her cigarette over the ashtray. "We went to the pictures."

"Oh, which?"

"*Modern Times*, Charlie's new one. It was *love*ly! I love everything he does! There was a scene in a department store when he was skating blindfolded"—she clutched Basil's arm, suddenly convulsed with laughter. "Oh, it was hi*lar*ious!"

"I understand it's a silent picture?"

"Yes—but it's a silent *Char*lie picture!"

"Maybe, but talkies're the future. Sound's the big thing now. No one does silents anymore."

Daisy frowned. "Charlie does!"

"Well, yes, but not for long—not if he's to survive. The writing's on the wall, you know."

Daisy tapped more ash into the tray. "Whatever Charlie does is all right with me—and with thousands of others too."

"He didn't do his bit, you know, going off to Hollywood when he was needed right here in his own country—plenty of people offended by that sort of behavior—though he seems to have won back their favor with *Shoulder Arms*."

Daisy continued to frown, tapping ash though there was none left to tap. "Of course, he did. It showed what he really thought of the krauts. It was far more important that he made the pictures, and people understand that now. Just think what it did for morale."

Rupert brushed his hair back with his hand, still looking away. "Ah, Miss Holiday, I am a bad host—a bad host, indeed. I have offended you, and you have been the best guest. Sorry—not my intention, not at all."

"It's all right. I'm not offended."

"Kind of you to say. I like Chaplin, don't misunderstand. In fact, I have an uncle who knew him."

"Do you, really?"

"Yes, he was from Lambeth, you know, Chaplin was—or didn't you know?"

"Actually, yes, I did."

"He was a clog-dancer at the music halls as a boy. That's where he learned his routines. Uncle even remembers him riding on top of the horse-bus with his mother trying to touch the lilac trees."

"Does he, really? Are they still friends?"

Rupert chuckled. "Not bloody likely. It was a long time ago. They're not hardly in the same league anymore—ah, there they are! Shirin! Algy! Over here!"

**DAISY FOLLOWED HIS GAZE** to a couple at the foot of the stairs who appeared as disoriented as she when she had first descended. Both were small, but the woman, barely five feet, made Daisy more comfortable; she had grown just an inch in the year she had known Basil, felt herself still in Cilla's shadow. The man, too, was small. The woman lifted a hand waving a forefinger in response to Rupert; the man guided her by her elbow.

As they approached Daisy saw her features were proportionately small, a long narrow nose like a beak, deep blue eyes, high cheekbones, sleek hair gleaming like the wings of a raven. Daisy barely noticed the man because the woman fixed her with her gaze before she had been introduced. "You have just got to be Daisy Holiday. Am I right?"

Daisy nodded. "Yes."

The woman held out her hand. "Hullo. I am Shirin Saklatvala."

Daisy shook her hand. "Hullo … Shir—sorry?"

"Shirin—just like Sharon, but thinner." She laughed. "That was my daddy's big joke when his friends had trouble with my name. Shirin. I cannot tell you how very pleased I am to make your acquaintance, my dear. Basil has been talking about you so much I said to him finally: When are we going to meet this wonderful Daisy Holiday of yours?"

Rupert, citing responsibilities as host, surrendered his chair to Shirin and tipped an imaginary hat to the table. "I must bid adieu, my friends, for the moment. Duty calls—and calls, and calls, and calls."

Basil grinned. "Adieu, Rupert."

Daisy smiled catching his eye, but remained silent.

Shirin waved him away. "Go, go. Go away, Rupert. If we need you we shall send for you."

Shirin's companion seated himself across from Basil, offering his hand to Daisy. "Algernon Trotteville, at your service."

Daisy shook his hand. "How do you do?"

Basil leaned forward on his elbows. "As you see, Daise, my friends are so anxious to meet you they've introduced themselves—or, as we know them, Alge and Madame Sak."

Daisy's eyes widened. "Oh, I've *heard* about you, haven't I?"

Shirin Saklatvala shook her head. "No, it's my father, Comrade Sak, you are thinking about, Miss Holiday—or may I call you Daisy?"

"Please."

"And you must call me Shirin. Basil tells me you're also a writer?"

"Not really. I've only published two articles—and only with his help."

Basil shook his head. "The only help I provided was direction. I told her who might be interested. She wrote the articles herself."

"What were they about—if you don't mind my asking?"

"Of course not. One was about the Jubilee, where Basil and I met—just an atmospheric piece."

"Oh, yes, so he said—and the other?"

"About how the war affected society, especially women—getting the vote, jobs, that sort of thing—even their clothes."

"How very clever of you to have written a whole article on something like that."

Daisy changed the subject, unable to tell whether Shirin was interested or ironic. "Did you say your father was Comrade Sak?"

"Yes, Shapurji Saklatvala was his name—better known as Comrade Sak."

"Do you mean the communist?" Comrade Sak had represented the district of Battersea South in the House of Commons through most of the Twenties.

"The *on*ly Comrade Sak, my dear—not only a communist, but an Indian to boot."

"Didn't he …" She looked at Basil.

Basil nodded, but said nothing.

Shirin swept the awkwardness away. "Yes, my dear, so he did. Thank you very much for your civility, but it's really not necessary. He died this year, just four days before the King."

Daisy turned again to Shirin. "I *am* sorry."

"Thank you, my dear, but as I said there's really no need to be. You don't know me at all, and most likely you know very little about my father. The tragedy is not just that he died, but that more people don't know him better. When a King dies everyone gets very pious and whatnot no matter how foolish a man he may have been—but when a great man dies, if he happens to be a communist, by and large they don't care a damn."

Basil watched from the corner of his eyes as Daisy's eyes widened again. She and Cilla had lit candles for the King and said a prayer, but she said nothing out of respect for Shirin's dead father.

If Shirin noted her concern, she ignored it. "A foolish man can always be replaced, as we have proven time and time again, if only there are enough foolish people to wish it—and we wished it again this year, didn't we? We now have a beautiful brainless benighted boy on the throne, and should something happen to him we have another, no less brainless, waiting in the wings—and *this* is what we focus on as if there were nothing else in the world demanding our attention. There is a war in Spain, Italy is invading Abyssinia, Hitler is rearming Germany—and what do we talk about? We talk about the King, and what should the King do, should he marry, should he abdicate, should he do this, should he do that. We fiddle like Nero while Rome burns. Why should we care what he does? What business is it of ours? Let him marry, let him abdicate, let him do what he wants—but let us, at least, turn our attention to the things that matter."

The waiter brought more whiskey, more soda water, more glasses for the new guests. Algernon poured. Daisy sat back in her chair, restraining herself from defending the King against Shirin's father, but not without difficulty. She looked at Basil who merely stared into his glass.

Shirin leaned forward. "Ah, I see I have made you uncomfortable. Good! It is only when people are uncomfortable that they begin to think about what is important. Are you a monarchist, my dear?"

Daisy resented Shirin's assumption that she didn't think. "I have never thought of myself as a monarchist—but I am certainly a monarchist more than I am a communist."

"Ah—and why is that?"

"Well, surely the answer is obvious."

"Humor me, my dear. Spell it out for me, please, won't you?"

Daisy looked again at Basil who spoke into his glass. "Don't be afraid to speak your mind, Daise—or Shirin will run over you like a lorry."

Daisy spoke firmly. "Well, I mean because the communists are fanatics—they are worse than fanatics, they are murderers. They murdered the Czar and his family, and looted the palace—and they would do the same anywhere given half a chance. They encourage the worst kind of class warfare. Whatever one thinks of the King, he's clearly not a murderer."

Shirin smiled, still leaning forward. "Oh, really? Do you really think so?"

Daisy felt her resentment thicken. "Of course, I do! What do you mean to say?"

"I will be only too glad to tell you, my dear, but I wonder if you will be as glad to hear what I have to say." Shirin's eyes glistened, seeming paler, almost the color of the sky. "My father was a revolutionary, and was looked upon by the establishment as a danger. In England, revolution has always been despised as something conducted by a disorderly mob, usually in disorderly and shabby countries. War, on the other hand, has always been considered noble and heroic and tragic on a grand scale—but counting the dead and measuring the suffering of the Great War, I cannot help but wonder if a revolution might not perhaps have caused less agony in the long run. Unfortunately, revolution is abhorred by the English. The only revolution in England, which led to the Commonwealth of Cromwell, is always graced by the name of a civil war, giving it the kind of respectability agreeable to the English temperament. Revolutions take place in Russia and South America, not in the neat suburban streets, or even in the decaying slums, of orderly and respectable England."

Daisy leaned back, but Shirin wasn't finished.

"When the troops of the Czar killed hundreds of Russian workers in 1905 in front of the winter Palace no one in England thought twice about it, but when a handful of Russian citizens killed a handful of Russian royals they called it murder. When civilians kill for their rights it's murder, but when armies slaughter hundreds of thousands for no reason other than the pride of their rulers it's war—and not only is it accepted, it's applauded. The more ruthless its practitioners, the more medals and knighthoods and lordships they receive."

Daisy crossed her arms, looking over Shirin's shoulder.

Shirin leaned back finally. "I am sorry. I have overwhelmed you. That was not my intention."

Daisy engaged Shirin's gaze again. Whatever the truth of Shirin's assertions she had no right to lecture her. "You have not overwhelmed me. You have merely bored me."

For a moment Shirin said nothing, then smiled. "Why, Daisy, I think I might get to like you very much after all."

Daisy was surprised: Shirin's smile was devoid of irony, her compliment no less heartfelt than her lecture. Basil too was smiling—the smile of a papa proud of his child's performance.

Algernon smiled as well, speaking softly to Shirin, bringing a measure of restraint to the conversation. "May one ask what your intention was?"

"Oh, what else? Just to get one to think. My father had been the object of a Scotland Yard scrutiny. He was labeled dangerous, he was labeled seditious—and for what? For wanting equality for all instead of the few. The rich are born with their hands in the pockets of the poor, they live off the carcasses of the poor. This has always been the case, and it's no secret. Jane Austen spoke about it in *Mansfield Park*: Sir Thomas's mansion and lifestyle were supported by the slave trade in Antigua. This is clear to all—but unconscionable, it seems, only to a few. My father was of the elite, but fairminded enough to admit his privilege. My mother, on the other hand, was a waitress in Derbyshire when they met, from a large family, the daughter of a quarryman—and my father learned something about inequity firsthand from her. The English can be very smug talking about the rights of the individual in this country—but what about India? what about Ireland? what about our own working class? Do they not have a right to determine their own destinies? Are they not people no different from ourselves? Do they not deserve the same rights and freedoms?" The ancestry explained, if nothing else, Shirin's exotic features, oceanblue eyes, raven hair, but Daisy could think of nothing to say. Shirin surprised her with another smile. "I am sorry. It seems I just cannot help myself, but I really did not mean to unleash a broadside on you."

Daisy shook her head. "You did no such thing—really, you didn't."

Shirin nodded. "That is kind of you to say. It is not your fault, of course, but it *is* most upsetting, don't you agree, when people don't think for themselves? when they simply believe what they are told?"

Daisy found Shirin patronizing, but overlooked the shortcoming, nodding instead. "I can understand why you would feel the way you do about your father—but the King was a good king, and so is our Edward."

"Oh, of course, they are, both of them, good kings—as kings go. As kings go, they are both good kings—and no doubt so is the one cowering in the wings."

The familiar phrase made Daisy look at Basil, but he seemed not to hear, asking Shirin instead to dance, and the two excused themselves from the table. The tall bald negress was singing "If I Could Only Give You the Moon." Daisy felt miserable, wishing Basil had asked her instead, imagining his sympathy lay with Shirin. Algernon pushed a plate of potato crisps toward her which the waiter had brought. His voice was gentle. "She can be rather intense, our Shirin, can't she?"

He was smiling. Distracted by Shirin, Daisy had hardly noticed him, but saw now that he had a thin face, kind eyes. She picked a crisp. "Do you mean to say she's not always like this?"

Algernon laughed. "Well, actually, yes, she is! It's a wonder her friends are not all burned to cinders—but of course we must forgive her. Passion is not to be condemned. There is all too little of it in the world—certainly in support of the worthier causes."

Daisy managed a wan smile. "Yes, of course, I understand. Besides, she has lost her father."

"Yes, certainly, that—and for the moment she has lost even more. Her lover, Goddy Humphreys, sailed for Leningrad just last week, and she feels rather more alone than she has in a long while. She hopes to follow him next year—but a year is a long time as I am sure you can appreciate."

Daisy was relieved to hear Algernon speak so plainly of Shirin's lover and watched Basil and Shirin on the floor with a greater measure of comfort, comforted also by the notion that as short as she was

Shirin was shorter. Basil loomed over her even more than he loomed over herself—but Shirin was also plainly less a child, not for her age (perhaps the same as Cilla's), but her confidence, her willingness to engage a stranger so directly. "I suppose it must be very difficult for her." Her smile was more sanguine, but her brow wrinkled almost immediately. "Leningrad, did you say?"

"Yes, he's a member of the Comintern."

Daisy's eyebrows rose.

"She wanted to go with him, but the authorities gave her the runaround, some rigmarole about her passport. Of course, the main reason—the only reason—is that her dad was among the more famous communists in this country."

"Yes, of course."

"She was very close to her dad, you see, and he was abominably treated by the authorities, and so now is she—and just for being a communist."

Daisy wondered how much she might say, but Algernon appeared sympathetic enough for her to speak with candor. "*Just* for being a communist, but Mr. Trotteville –"

"Please! Call me Algy, and I shall call you Daisy—if that is all right with you?"

"Of course ... Algy." She sighed, looking away, gathering her thoughts. "You *must* understand, I *do* sympathize with her for the death of her father—but he *was*, after all, a *com*munist."

Algernon raised his eyebrows, his tone got sharper. "And what, pray, does that have to do with anything? Why should that qualify him for special observation? Is he not a British citizen the same as you and I? Does he not merit the same treatment?"

Daisy remained silent, understanding only that she had failed to grasp a fundamental point.

Algernon narrowed his eyes. "Daisy, you do know, do you not, that I, too, am a communist?"

Daisy stared.

"Oh, my goodness! Has Basil told you nothing?"

"He hasn't said much—and I haven't asked him."
"What has he told you?"
"He said he was a writer."
"Nothing else?"
Daisy remained silent.
"You *do* know that *he*'s a communist, don't you, my dear?"
"Basil?"
"No other."
She was silent again.
"He said nothing?"
She shook her head.
"Upon my word! We're, all of us, communists—old Rupert, Polly Doodle, Goddy Humphreys, Raymond Rhys-Jones. Most of us went up to Cambridge together. It was where we met."

Daisy looked past him. Basil on the floor appeared suddenly to turn to air and she looked through him as she might through a specter, feeling suddenly more alone than she had felt since her mother had died. Her face shriveled to the size of a pea.

"Oh, my dear, you really mustn't take it so hard. It's nothing. It's not the end of the world. In fact, it might very well be the beginning. What do you think it means to be a communist?"

She shook her head. "I'd rather not talk about it, please."

He stared into her face, but she avoided his gaze, eyes beginning to glisten. "Listen, my dear, if you don't wish to talk about it—why, then, of course, we won't—but let me just ask you something."

She said nothing.

"May I?"

She faced him again. "Yes. Sorry. Of course."

"Let us say you had a nice house, and a certain someone moved into your sitting-room. Wouldn't you want to do something about it?"

"Yes, of course."

"And let us say this certain someone who had moved into your sitting-room refused to be budged, and so did his next generation, and the next, and so on—wouldn't you want to do something about it?"

"Yes, of course."

"Well, then, what the hell do you think we're doing in Ireland?"

Daisy remained silent.

"Not to mention in Africa and India and everywhere else in the world that the sun never sets."

Daisy felt entrapped, but by her ignorance more than Algernon's guile.

"We are like elephants entrenched in the sitting-rooms of the world. Communists, on the other hand, not only do they *not* want to take the world over, but they wish for equity among *all* peoples. They see the world divided *not* into countries, but class structures. For them the world is one, with a few oppressing the rest, and they wish to rectify the imbalance. That is what it means to be a communist. I ask you: What is wrong with that? Is that not a deserving cause?"

Daisy remained silent.

"India gave England millions of pounds for the war effort. Did you know that?"

She shook her head.

"Why do you suppose we never mention it?"

She shook her head again.

"Because India is our vassal; India could do no less; India was *bound* to do no less—but when George V gave a few thousand measly pounds back to the country, which the country had tendered to him in the first place from its own treasury, he was looked upon as a great and generous King—and no one is allowed to forget it. You do know I am not making this up, don't you?"

She didn't know what to think, but didn't think he was telling falsehoods.

"We brag about the freedoms that we extend to our own people, but when Mr. Gandhi wishes the same freedoms for his people we brand him a subversive. I ask you, plain and simple: Is that right?"

Mention of Gandhi gave Daisy her voice back. "I have a deep admiration for Mr. Gandhi. My mother was a great admirer of his."

"Of Mr. Gandhi? Really? He is a great man, isn't he?"

"Yes, he is!"

"But the King found him seditious, didn't he?"

Daisy was quiet again, afraid Algernon meant to trip her again.

Algernon smiled. "Do you know what Mr. Gandhi said when he was asked why he hadn't dressed up for the king?"

Everyone knew what Mr. Gandhi had said. "He said the King had worn enough for the two of them. He said the English wore plus fours, but he was happy enough wearing minus fours."

Algernon sat back grinning. "Aaah, yes, yes, I see you do know Mr. Gandhi—but I must ask you. Does your mother sympathize with Mr. Gandhi's cause?"

"My mother is dead."

"Oh, my dear, I *am* sorry to hear it—but if she was an admirer of Mr. Gandhi, I am sure she would understand very clearly the point I am trying to make—but perhaps continue to make in vain?"

"You mustn't press me, Mr. –"

"Algy."

"Sorry. Algy. As of now I must say I do not know *what* to think."

"Of course, take your time. Rome wasn't built in a day. Think it through. First be absolutely sure of your facts. The authorities, of course, will provide the facts in their favor. It is up to us as individuals to track down the rest. That is all I am trying to do, to give you the facts."

Daisy frowned. "How is it, Mr. ... Algy, that you know these things?"

"Well, of course, the powers that be would never mention these things, but the facts are there for all who are willing to look them up."

Basil and Shirin approached from the floor. Shirin took her seat again across the table from Daisy. "I see Rupert sent us a plate of crisps. I just love crisps, don't you?"

Daisy nodded.

"I simply cannot imagine life without them. I am at a loss to understand how our poor deprived parents managed without them."

Basil took his seat, smiling, but Daisy couldn't bring herself to look at him. She pushed the plate across to Shirin.

"Thank you, my dear. I must say the more I learn about you the more I like you. Basil has been telling me about your mother. It seems she was quite the suffragette. She must have been quite a personality."

Daisy nodded.

"I wish she might have met my father. I think they would have got on like a house on fire."

Daisy said nothing.

"Anyway, I said to Basil we really shouldn't leave you alone with boring old Alge much longer—or you might just leave."

Algernon lifted his glass. "Ha-Ha."

Shirin nudged him playfully. "What I said to Basil was that if he wanted to keep you he should have asked you to dance in the first place instead of a dried-up old dowager like myself, but of course he wanted to give me my comeuppance for taking you to task like I did. He has done so—and he is right. I had no right to plough into you like I did, and I cannot tell you how truly sorry I am."

Daisy was tired of the conversation. "It's all right—it really is. I understand perfectly. Alge has been explaining it to me as well."

"Oh, good old Alge! I knew he was good for something."

"Ha-Ha."

Shirin nudged him again.

Basil looked at Daisy. "Would you like to dance?"

Daisy was out of her seat before she spoke. "Yes—very much."

Shirin spoke brightly. "Toodles, you two!"

Basil led her to the middle of the floor before turning. "Daise, is something the matter?"

"Oh, Basil, I don't know—I don't know what to say, what to think—I just don't know."

"Daise, if this is all a bloody bore for you we can just leave, you know."

"Oh, no, Basil, it's not that, it's not that at all. It's not a bore at all."

"Well, then, what is it? You look like you've just lost your best friend."

"Please, Basil, let's not talk. Let's just dance, please?"

He held her closer. "All right, if that's what you wish."

"It's what I wish." She sighed, collapsing into his bulk, closing her eyes, losing herself in his expanse, relishing the smell of his clothes, the warmth of his body, not following his lead as much as allowing him to guide her any way he wished. The band played a song she hadn't heard:

> *And if I call you darling, darling*
> *It may just be because*
> *I need a rhyme for starling, darling*
> *I need a rhyming clause*

His hands were locked on the small of her back, her arms tight around his waist under the jacket of his suit leaving no space between them, enabling him to guide her with little effort. Her cheek was flush with his chest, his heart beating against her temple. "Daise, it's lovely to hold you like this."

"Mmmm."

"Darling."

It was the first time he had used the word with her. "Oh, Basil!"

Her voice seemed fragile, made of toothpicks. "Darling, what's the matter? Really?"

"Oh, Basil, why didn't you tell me?"

He was silent for a moment. "That I'm a communist, do you mean?"

"Yes!"

"Alge told you, I suppose?"

"Yes!"

"Does it make a difference?"

"I don't know."

"That's why I didn't want to tell you. I was afraid."

"Afraid of what?"

"That it might make a difference."

"You should have told me regardless of the difference it might have made."

"You're right. I'm sorry."

"Oh, Basil, you *should* have! You really *should* have!"

"I know. I'm sorry."

"It wasn't fair to me."

Basil was silent for a moment. "How can I make it up?"

"I don't know."

"Maybe we shouldn't see each other for a while."

"Oh, no, Basil! That's not what I want! That's not it at all! We *must* go on!"

"That's what I hoped you would say."

"Oh, of course, Basil, of course! It's not the long run I'm afraid of. It's the short."

"Do you mean that? Really?"

She hadn't thought about it, but found herself beguiled by her own words. "Yes, of course—at least, I think so. It's just the shock of it all, the not expecting it at all. That's all. I need a little time, but there's no reason for us to stop seeing each other."

"That's what I'd hoped you would say, Daise. That's exactly what I'd hoped you would say."

"Oh, Basil!"

"What, darling!"

She sighed. "Nothing, just … oh, Basil!"

"I know. Maybe it would help you to know something else about me—about my family."

"What?"

"They didn't want me to be a writer."

"I know. You told me. It wasn't respectable."

"Yes, but that wasn't the reason they cut me off. It was for being a communist. They didn't mind my being a writer as much as a communist. You see, my family's rather well off, actually—and, well, to put it in a nutshell, I've sacrificed rather a lot for my beliefs already. I wasn't prepared to give up more."

She said nothing, but tightened her arms around his waist.

"I was afraid you would be like them. I hated to think I might lose you."

"Oh, Basil! You wouldn't have—not if you'd been honest from the beginning."

"And now?"

"I don't know. I need to think, Basil. This is all too much too quickly. I need time."

"Of course."

**The band began to play** "It Don't Mean a Thing (if It Ain't Got That Swing)," and the dancers hopped around suddenly as if the floor glowed with coals, but Basil and Daisy continued to hold each other out of step with the music. A woman's breast escaped from the dress of one of the dancers, but she made no effort to cover it, smiling instead at her partner as she cupped it with both hands. A negro dancer's butterfly hands made sly arabesques appearing continually to lick his partner's hips, arms, and face without touching her in the least—until she flung herself in his arms and he continued his quickstep holding her like a baby. Daisy recalled the naked man she had seen earlier. "Basil?"

"Yes?"

"What goes on in those rooms?" She jerked her head toward one of the doors.

He hesitated before answering. "I understand that's entirely up to the individuals."

His pause gave her pause. "I suppose, I mean—of what nature—I mean, what would be the nature of what goes on in there?"

"Let's just say it's of a private nature."

Daisy's pause was their longest yet. "Can anyone go in there?"

"Yes, I believe so."

"Could we?"

She stared unblinkingly as Basil leaned back to look into her face. "I don't think we should."

Her face remained impervious. "Why not?"

"I don't think it's what you think it is."

"What do you think I think it is?"

"If you need time to think, as you said you did, that's not the place for us."

"Oh, Basil, I need time to think about you as a communist, not as a man. There, I've said it. Now can we go?"

"Daisy!"

"Oh, have I shocked you now?"

"No, it's just that I had no idea you felt that way."

"Basil, I can't say that I believe you—but I'd really rather not talk about it."

"But I think we *do* need to talk about it, Daise. You cannot separate the communist in me from the man so easily. One informs the other, don't you see?"

"Oh, Basil, it's *you* who doesn't see. I *know* what I want—don't *you* see? You can be a communist if you want, and I shall be what I want."

Basil remained silent.

Their steps remained out of rhythm with the combo, but the combo remained an excuse for them to hold each other. Daisy frowned suddenly considering a new possibility. "Is it Shirin?"

"What do you mean?"

"Are you and she ... lovers?"

She felt him stiffen, but again he said nothing.

"You are, aren't you? I can feel it."

"No, we're not. We might have been once, but that was a long time ago. Her lover sailed for Leningrad just last week."

"I know. Alge told me, but I thought ..."

"There's nothing between me and Shirin, Daise, not at all, not anymore. She's a good friend, nothing more. That is not even a consideration."

"Then it must be me."

Basil sighed. "Daisy, you are utterly delightful in many ways—but you're also so very very young—and so utterly unspoiled. I should hate to be the one to disappoint you."

"But why should you disappoint me?"

"Precisely because you're so very young. You have such young and lovely notions about love, but that's not how it is. That's not how it is at all."

Daisy pushed herself away, crossed her arms. "Oh, Basil, you're *re*ally disappointing me now. You're *pa*tronizing me. You're treating me like a little girl to be shown off and tucked in bed after the show's over. If that's how you feel, I want you to take me home."

"Daisy, that's not how I feel."

"It's how you're acting, Basil. I'm sorry, but I want to go home now." She walked off the floor. Reaching their table she put on her jacket managing a smile for Shirin and Algernon. "It's been very nice meeting everyone, but we have to go."

Shirin frowned. "But surely you are not leaving already. The night is young."

Daisy shook her head. "Something has come up. I feel I must leave."

Shirin looked at Basil. "Basil, what have you done?"

Basil could only shake his head, keeping his eyes on the table.

Shirin transferred her attention again to Daisy. "Was it me? It was me, wasn't it? I am the one to blame, am I not? I really am sorry, Daisy. I had no right to talk to you like that."

Daisy shook her head. "No, it's not that, not at all. I'd forgotten that already."

"Well, then, my dear, what *is* it?"

Daisy held Shirin's eyes without a smile. "It's between me and Basil—something personal."

"Oh, well, then, my dear, if it is something personal then you must keep it so. I certainly do not mean to pry, but I do hope we shall at least have the pleasure of your company again sometime?"

Daisy smiled again, looking at Algernon. "It really has been very nice meeting you."

Algernon nodded. "Likewise, a pleasure—perhaps another time?"

Daisy nodded. "Perhaps."

Algernon raised his glass. "Cheerio, then?"

Daisy had reached the stairs. Basil nodded. "It would seem so. Cheerio."

Shirin waved. "Ta-ta."

**THEY CLIMBED THE STAIRS,** negotiating the long dark passage out of the house, out of the alley, in silence. When they reached the motorcycle Basil faced Daisy across the seat. "Daisy, I will take you home—if that is what you want?"

"It is not what I want, Basil, but you leave me no choice."

"What do you mean?"

"All that rubbish about my being so very young, and all my lovely notions about love. Don't you suppose I know that's not how it is? You told me so once yourself."

"I did, did I?"

"Yes. You said that a woman without a past was only half a woman. You said a woman without a past was a woman without a future—or, at least, no more than a conventional future. And you said a conventional woman was a woman who had sacrificed all her rights and prerogatives to her husband. You said she had sacrificed her right to be a woman, agreeing to be a kind of large child for the rest of her life. You said she had no right, then, to complain if her life was boring. Don't you remember?"

"Yes, I do, I said that, I did, but I also said that a woman with a past sometimes comes to a bad end through no fault of her own. It's just the way of society."

"What's the way of society?"

"Well, quite simply that we insist on treating women like children, we punish children for *not* behaving like adults, and we punish women for *not* behaving like children—and this state of affairs will continue as long as there are women who *want* to be treated like children. They *want* men who will take care of them because it's easier than taking care of themselves—and despite what the suffragettes and the labor unions and all the rest have achieved, it remains the dominant way of society."

"Well, I beg your pardon then for not wishing to submit to the dominant way of society. I beg your pardon for saying it doesn't have to be *our* way."

They stared at each other across the motorcycle until Basil finally grinned. "I guess I owe you an apology."

"For what exactly?"

"Treating you like a child."

"You *did*, you know—you *know* you did."

"I did, and I'm sorry—but you *are* just seventeen."

"Basil, you're spoiling it again!"

"Sorry! You're absolutely right!"

Daisy smiled. "You *should* be sorry."

He nodded. "I am. Forgive me?"

She returned his nod. "Apology accepted."

"Well, then, we could either go back to the club, or I could take you home—or we could go to my flat. Whatever you like."

Basil lived in a small flat in a mews off Baker Street. "We could go to your flat."

He grinned. "Not afraid of the big bad bolshie?"

She returned his grin. "What? Of *you*?"

THE NEXT MORNING Basil's bedroom remained dark. Rain sliced the air outside like needles and he got out of bed to shut the window and draw the curtains. Daisy watched with pleasure in the morning-darkness: even routine tasks became exotic performed by a naked man. She followed his course, and when he left her field of vision expected him to rejoin her in bed, but heard him next in the bathroom. She turned in bed, impatient for his return, reviewing the events of the night, wondering how she might appear most appealing when he returned. She lay on her stomach clutching a pillow under the covers—but imagining herself too much a reptile on its egg, turned on her back. She threw the covers from her, but feeling too brazen, too cold, pulled them over her again. By the time Basil emerged she was lost to sight—except for a limp hand, poking from the hill of bedclothes, dangling from the wrist, palm up.

He smiled at her suppressed giggles and tickled her palm. "Is your cave to let?"

Her smiling head emerged from the covers. "To let, and to let, and to let." She raised the sheets, inviting him in, wondering at her appetite, wanting once more to feel his weight, to cling to him like a simian, legs around his waist, arms around his neck, to enjoy his pleasure as much as her own. She reached for his penis, marveling at the growth, limp flabby muscle firming to unyielding bone, marveling at her own power, a slip of a girl able to reduce a man of his bulk to groans and whimpers.

An hour later Basil slipped again from the bed, kissing her forehead. "Tea?"

"Lovely."

"Toast?"

"Mmmm!"

"Scrambled eggs?"

"Mmm-hmmm!"

He caressed her face, pulling on a dressing-gown.

"Oh, don't do that."

"What?"

"No clothes allowed, not even a dressing-gown."

He laughed. "I might get burned otherwise, don't you think?"

"Oh, we can't have that, can we? Clothes, then, if so it must be—but not too many."

The rooms were too cold to wear nothing, and Daisy compromised donning one of Basil's coats for breakfast. It reached almost to her knees and hid her hands in mandarin sleeves, but it was better than wearing her evening clothes again. The kitchen table was narrow, set against a wall, meant for no more than two, three at a pinch. She raised her legs, crossing them in her chair, bundling the folds of the coat into her lap, brushing back the sleeves, brushing back the red hedge of her hair, sipping tea, watching him in his dressing-gown bustling with pots, pans, cups, dishes, glasses. Gown and coat left them with easy access to each other, an access they indulged when proximity allowed. There was a debate on the wireless regarding the abdication of the King, something about Mussolini in Abyssinia. Basil joined her finally, bringing a fresh rack of toast, a bowl of sliced apples, making the table smaller yet, not just for the additional tableware but the bulk of his presence, a smallness translating for Daisy into coziness. He had felt her smile like a butterfly bobbing about the kitchen while preparing breakfast, dimples following like bees, eyes bobbing like puppets to his bustle. "Darling, what *are* you staring at?"

Her eyes widened, apparently startled that he could talk. "Nothing! *You!*"

"What are you thinking?"

"Nothing—just that I feel so ... e*man*cipated—like I really be*long* to you now."

Basil laughed, spearing a slice of apple with a fork. "I'm afraid you can't have it both ways, Daise."

"What do you mean?"

"Well, simply that one can no more be emancipated *and* belong to someone than ... well, than one can be master and servant at the same time to the same person."

"Well, of course—if you put it like that I suppose one can't. What I meant was simply that I'm glad you've ... you've made a woman of me."

"Oh, come now, Daisy. That's silly—girltalk. Only God can make a woman."

Daisy's smile faded. "I thought ... communists didn't believe in God."

"That's an option, I suppose—but, anyway, you're no communist."

"But *you* are."

"Yes?"

"Oh, I don't know. All I meant is ... that is, all I wanted to say is ..."

"Yes?"

"Oh, you're making it so difficult—just that it's lovely to have a lover—lovely to have *you* for a lover."

Basil laughed again. "Thank you, darling, but you'll have plenty of lovers before you're through. I'll just have to be satisfied with being the first."

Her eyes no longer leaped, but she couldn't have said what she had expected. "Do you *want* me to have other lovers?"

"Darling, it's not a matter of what *I* want, is it? It's you that matters, isn't it? I mean, it's not up to me to tell you what to do, is it?"

"But wouldn't you mind?"

"Why should I?"

Daisy frowned, said nothing, forked a morsel of egg and toast to her mouth.

Basil felt her withdraw as if she had left the room. "Oh, darling, of course I would mind—but I wouldn't have the right, don't you see? That's all I meant."

Daisy looked at him again, smiling. "Then it's all right, I suppose—as long as you would mind. I would hate to think you didn't mind."

"Of course, I would mind, darling—but I wouldn't have the right."

*And if I call you darling, darling / It might just be because / I need a rhyme for starling, darling / I need a rhyming clause.* "I understand. I simply didn't understand before, but I do now ... darling." She couldn't have said exactly what she understood except that her relations with Basil were to be different from Cilla's with Bert, but Basil had been clear from the start, warned that she proceeded at her peril, promised her nothing.

Basil sighed, shaking his head again. "Ah, Daisy, I don't know. I've done it now, haven't I? I should have known better, but done's done—and it's done now, isn't it?"

"Done? What's done? What do you mean?"

"I mean I've disappointed you, haven't I—and after everything I said? It's what I wanted to avoid. I tried to tell you last night, but I simply couldn't resist you any further. You were so sweet, and you seemed to understand—but now you'll think I took advantage."

"I don't think that. I don't think you took advantage—at least, no more than I wanted you to."

"Are you sure?"

"Yes, I'm sure. If you'd wanted to take advantage you could have a long time ago."

She spoke with more authority than she felt, unable again to look at Basil though he searched diligently for her eyes. His voice was gentle. "Are you *quite* sure?"

Daisy's hand froze lifting her cup, her tone brimming with warning as she caught his eyes again. "Basil, you're patronizing me again."

He looked away, nodding. "Right. Sorry. It's just that –"

"That I'm so young? Basil!"

He nodded again, and smiled. "Sorry."

She let the moment pass, before returning his smile. "Basil … do men prefer a girl—a woman … of some … experience?"

"Some do."

"Do you?"

Basil seemed to consider her question more seriously than anything she had said that morning. "Yes, I do—but I don't mean just sexual experience."

"What else?"

"Well, what else, indeed? Experience of the world. I could admire a woman for having had some kind of life of her own independent of a man. A woman who has never been tested in the world remains a girl—and the same might be said of a man, that he remains a boy. I prefer someone who thinks things through, man or woman—who doesn't blindly accept the way of the world as the only way, who prefers to find a better way when the standard falls short."

"The way of a communist, do you mean?"

"That is certainly one way."

"Basil, how did you become a communist?"

He raised his eyebrows. "Well, I do think it's rather the obvious choice for anyone who thinks about it—that is, anyone with a conscience. Shall I give you a primer on communism?"

"Please—only because I want to understand why it matters so much to you."

**Basil sighed,** leaning back in his chair. "It's all rather basic, really. You know, of course, that the economic system in England is capitalism—that is, an elite minority benefits from the labor of the working majority—that is to say they own commodities they do nothing to create. What they create is wealth, most of which they keep for themselves, sharing with the workers only as much as they must to keep the workers working, but hardly enough for independence. It's as Shirin said last night: the rich live off the carcasses of the poor."

Daisy frowned. "But the workers *are* independent. They're free to strike, aren't they, if they're unhappy with their conditions—and they *do* strike, don't they?"

"Yes, of course, but they're much too poor to stay on strike for as long as it would take to have the necessary effect. You know, of course, what happened in 1926?"

"The General Strike?"

Basil nodded. "Let me put it another way. Capitalism is an economic system in which the production, ownership, and distribution of commodities is maintained chiefly by private individuals and corporations, whom we call capitalists. Now, capitalists own commodities—but what are commodities if not raw materials yoked with labor? For example, cotton is a raw material, but it needs to be harvested, spun, woven, dyed, and God knows what else by *la*bor before it becomes a commodity—which means the capitalist *owns* the sweat and blood of the laborer, and since the laborer is dependent on the capitalist for his livelihood he becomes little better than a slave—a serf, at best. The genius of Marx was to recognize that the workers of the world could share in the wealth if they organized themselves—and the genius of Lenin and Stalin was to make Marx's dream a reality—and that's it, I suppose, in a nutshell."

Daisy gazed into air.

"Your mother would have appreciated what the communists are trying to do. For the longest time women were to their husbands as workers are to capitalists—I mean, for the longest time women had practically no rights themselves, not to a university education, not to vote, not to property, not to divorce—not even on the grounds of adultery. Your mother's last protest, with the salt, was a protest for the worker, don't you see?"

Daisy remained thoughtful. "I was too young to understand at the time."

"Of course, you were, but that was very likely the source of your father's problems with her. He very likely admired your mother no end, but men don't marry women they admire—at least, by and large, they don't. They marry their maids, someone who will cook and clean and mind the house, mind the little ones, and leave them to the business of men, the business of the world. They want little women who will allow them to be big men, pliant and pliable women, not women who are their equals, not women who will challenge them—but, of course, they get bored with such women and compensate for their boredom with mistresses. They would rather have admirable mistresses than admirable wives. Why do you suppose the suffragettes were so vilified? Not because they were not admirable, which they were, but because they encouraged others to *be* like them, to *think* for themselves. If they had merely behaved like admirable women the men would have admired them, even had affairs with them when they could, but they would not have vilified them—but the suffragettes wanted the same rights for *all* women, including the men's wives, and as far as most men were concerned that simply wouldn't do. Mind, Daisy, I'm not telling you what to believe. I'm only asking you to think for yourself. You do understand the difference, don't you?"

"Yes."

"Believe what you want, but have a firm basis of facts to ground your beliefs. Don't simply parrot the party line—whatever party you choose."

"It would seem I have a lot to think about."

# DAISY'S STORY

THE *STRATHNAVER* was one among a series of cruisers of the Strath class built by the P. & O. during the thirties, modern express liners capable of covering the distance from Southampton to Bombay in less than three weeks. However often Alphonse Fernandes made the voyage back and forth, he didn't think he would tire of the job. The pay was good, the work straightforward, but best of all he got to travel as no one among his peers in Goa, nor in all of India, invoking envy of his situation no less than his prosperity. It helped that he spoke a gentlemanly English, and sported a gentlemanly brawn. It did him good as well to know he was often the subject of admiring if covert glances. He kept himself immaculate, his moustache clipped, white uniform dazzling, hair brushed to appear windswept—and his eye open for passengers inclined to tip generously, more often than not single young women, some of whom knew no better, others whom he pleased with his appearance. Sometimes, seeing the same passengers on the return voyage, he was surprised by the change. India made snobs of Englishwomen—eager as puppies sallying forth and condescending as camels returning. The young woman whose bags he carried might well be one such, apparently beholden to no one, smiling when she addressed him, traveling alone, but he remained impersonal until they arrived at her cabin. "Alone, madam? Madam is traveling alone?"

Daisy smiled. "Yes, madam is traveling alone." The steward seemed solicitous, but disapproving, not unlike a father. Among the first to board, Daisy wanted nothing more than to leave her bags unpacked in her cabin to catch more of the excitement of departure on the pier from one of the upper decks. The cabin was a pokey room with bunkbeds, a porthole by the lower bunk, a closet, a table. He had surprised her, a uniformed Indian with gleaming black hair hovering in a series of crescents over his forehead gliding in waves into a ducktail behind. He was taller than she had expected of an Indian, close on six feet—and handsomer, narrow moustache and high cheekbones bringing to mind a dark Clark Gable—or a dark Basil Ballard. His foreignness alone was charming. He spoke with a lilt, a hint of music—and not perfectly, but she understood him with ease.

There was resignation in Alphonse's tone, grudging admiration. "Madam is very brave."

Daisy laughed. "Yes, madam is very brave indeed."

Alphonse smiled a moment revealing wide rows of sparkling teeth, but grew immediately stern again, teeth disappearing behind thin lips, mouth thinning to a short black line crowned by the moustache. He envied and resented the freedom enjoyed by women such as the passenger, rich young Englishwomen, traveling like men where they pleased, at once courageous and shameless, awakening admiration and resentment, a conflict he had yet to resolve. "Madam thinks I am making a joke, but I am very serious."

Daisy stopped laughing, surprised by a sensitivity so fragile, imagining it had to do with foreignness. She had read that foreigners were different, but not necessarily wrong, and it was the responsibility of the English as their superiors to accommodate them. "I'm sorry. Of course, you are—but madam is not brave at all. She is simply doing what she has to do."

His frown remained. "That is just what I am saying. That is a brave thing to do. How many people do what they have to do? Most people do only what they want to do and leave the rest to others."

Daisy still smiled. "I suppose you are right."

His new smile was again brief, but not without triumph, having wrested the argument from a superior Englishwoman. They were not like Indian women, especially not in their private lives, where again they behaved like men. Their actions by day masked their actions by night, but not from the night staff, some of whom took their advantage where they could, understanding discretion was the key. "Suppose? Nothing doing! I am right—but maybe madam is also right. Maybe it is not so very brave."

Daisy was amused by the quick turnaround, as if having proved his strength he could afford to be magnanimous. She regarded it also as a concession to her own concession and chose to humor him. "Yes, maybe after all you are right. Maybe madam is not so very brave, after all."

"Yes, I am right—and madam is a rich madam, is she not?"

The sudden invasion of her privacy was again surprising, and again she found herself excusing him on the grounds of foreignness: he wasn't English; his curiosity was idle, spurred by a need for conversation more than information—but risking his displeasure she laughed again. "Yes, madam is very rich. That is why she is traveling in the least expensive cabin she could find. That is why she is sharing this tiny space with a perfect stranger. That is why she is carrying everything she owns in three bags."

"Madam is not rich?"

"No, madam is not rich."

"Then how is she traveling so far? It costs a lot, no, to travel so far, even in the cheapest cabin?"

Daisy was surprised she bothered explaining, understood later that she was lonely, had gushed tears the moment she had lost sight of Cilla waving high her pink and white lace handkerchief on the platform as her train had pulled away for Southampton. She was also entirely alone for the first time in her life and making new rules for her new life as she went along. Besides, she was enjoying the unlikely unorthodox conversation. "Madam is not rich, but she has come into some money from her grandmother who has died." She had also sold her winter things, everything she would no longer need, to complement Granny Annie's legacy.

Alphonse's eyebrows dropped at the extremities, rose over the bridge of his nose. "Oh, that is very sad. Someone also has died in my family."

"Who?"

"Someone is always dying. It is very sad."

"Do you mean in your family?"

"Not *just* in my family, in the bigger family—in the family of the world. Anybody, anywhere, who is born, has to die. It is a very sad thing, but true."

He seemed to be struggling to find points in common, but Daisy was losing patience though she maintained her smile. "Yes, well, of course, you're right, but I'm afraid this is getting a bit too philosophical for me."

Alphonse smiled, raising a finger to acknowledge her point. "Philosophy is a great thing, no?"

"Yes, but I'm afraid I don't have the time for it at present. You too must have a lot to do—don't you?"

"Yes, I am very busy, always very busy—especially now, just before we leave."

He made no effort to leave, but showed Daisy the tasseled cord with which he might be summoned. She thanked him, digging into her purse for a tip. He pocketed the tip, touching his forehead in a mock salute, stern again as when they had first met. He might not have left even then, but Daisy held the door and he touched his forehead again, leaving finally without a further word.

She waited long enough only to draw the curtains from the porthole and peer into the water, noting with a thrill the size of the window, the sill wide enough for a girl to curl into (perhaps even a woman her size if she didn't mind a bit of discomfort), the waterline slapping the hull below, screaming gulls gliding by, the vast wild sea beyond. The roundness of the porthole was echoed in the round cabin mirrors, round windows on closet doors, flat round shields for electric lights on the low ceiling, round ashtrays on a round table. She was curious about her cabinmate, but there would be plenty of time later and she wanted to find an upper deck from which to view the departure.

In photographs the decks of ships seemed tiered like wedding cakes, the *Strathnaver* was as white as any such cake, and as Daisy mounted the stairs she imagined dolls planted in the frosting of the topmost tier, herself the bride, Basil the groom. Standing by the railing on deck, prompted perhaps by the three giant stacks behind her soon to chug and propel her away, she lit a cigarette. She pulled out Basil's postcard for the hundredth time, stared at the photograph of the Taj Mahal Hotel in Bombay, and turned it over to read once more:

> *Darling, I won't say much. Explanations can be incriminating, not to say unnecessary and tedious, but*

*some things must be acknowledged. You were right, I was wrong, and I am sorry. One can be blinded, it seems, by zeal as much as by prejudice. It might have been very different, but better by far to bear in mind that it isn't so very bad as it is. As you will see from the postmark, I am in Bombay, and for reasons too numerous and complicated to relate I have chosen to make it my home. I'm afraid we shall never meet again, but I feel I owe you at least this much in the way of an explanation. I know you will have a lovely life, and I am so glad and grateful that you saw fit to share a little bit of it with me.*

Best love,<br>Basil.

The postcard had arrived on the same day as news of Granny Annie's legacy, and she had read the coincidence as a sign. She had also read between the lines, guilt in his gladness and gratitude, as if he might have treated her shamefully. She wanted him to understand that she owed him a measure of gladness and gratitude no less than the debt he appeared to feel. He had sent no return address, but she was sure she would find him. The English in India knew one another, or at least enough other English to help, but the longer she waited the smaller grew her chance of success. There was nothing to hold her in England, Basil had said he liked women of some experience, and surely the experience of tracking him in Bombay would add to her allure. He would be surprised to see her, but not displeased, perhaps even happy. They had been lovers for almost three years, but seen little of each other during that time, owing to his continual travels. She knew little about his destinations and was afraid to ask more, afraid the bump of his political affiliation might become an insurmountable barricade.

Their differences had first rendered her silent, what he said seemed not only rational but fair, but he had also encouraged her to disagree if she wished as long as she disagreed no less rationally, no less fairly.

She had educated herself, and found herself still in disagreement, but no longer silent. The first Russian Revolution, Kerensky's of March 1917, modeled on Marxist tenets, had been welcomed not only by Marxists but socialists and liberals everywhere as the first step toward a truly democratic government; but it had been followed by Lenin's Bolshevik Revolution of November 1917, the October Revolution of the old calendar, and workers freed from the yoke of the Czar by Kerensky's revolution had found themselves yoked again by Lenin's. Instead of losing their chains, as prophesied by Marx, they had merely changed masters. The dictatorship of workers (workers dictating to themselves) was interpreted by Lenin as the dictatorship of workers by a party of revolutionaries.

Despite his iron fist Lenin had been acknowledged the head of the Communist Party the world over though a few managed to keep their own heads. Sylvia Pankhurst, running the British Section of the Communist Party of the Third International, reported to her readers that she had been ordered either to hand over the *Worker's Dreadnought* [her organization's journal] to Party officials, or to stop publication altogether—or, if she were to continue, to put it to whatever use the Party wished under the editorship of whomever the Party chose. Sylvia had refused, explaining that she could have approved so rigid a discipline had they been in the throes of a revolution, but in the weak young evolving Communist movement of England discussion was of paramount importance, and stifling it disastrous. For her pains she had been expelled from the Party.

Daisy's memory of Sylvia Pankhurst was not of her accomplishments but a portrait hung on the sitting-room wall of their Clerkenwell flat by her mother to the great annoyance of her father. In the portrait Sylvia flanked her mother Emmeline, who was flanked on the other side by her other daughter Christabel. Daisy found herself applauding her mother's advocacy as much as Sylvia's courage. Basil had been right to equate her mother with Sylvia, but not with communism—at least, not as expressed by Lenin, and now Stalin under whom Lenin's party of revolutionaries had become

Stalin's party of one, but to her consternation Basil had seemed blind to the merits of Sylvia Pankhurst—and Shirin Saklatvala, or Madame Sak to give her her political name, no less blind, and shriller by far in her denunciations.

Daisy understood Madame Sak's rationale (her father persecuted by the government, tailed by Scotland Yard, his activities restricted), but was hardpressed to find a rationale for Basil. Perhaps he had invested too much of himself to give up the cause easily, perhaps having shared the good days he was too noble not to share the bad, perhaps he felt sympathy with an ideology whose successful practice he felt was close at hand—but perhaps also he simply couldn't admit he was wrong, perhaps he was enough of a chauvinist to imagine Sylvia Pankhurst couldn't be in the right against a man of Lenin's stature, perhaps along with the small band of British Marxists he couldn't help being impressed that they were consorts of the great Lenin, head of not only so vast a power as Russia but communist parties the world over.

Daisy read the words yet again: *You were right, I was wrong, and I am sorry.* What else could it mean? After their last goodbye she had known only that he was going to Moscow with Shirin, nothing more, not even the length of the stay, and that had been more than nine months ago during which time she had received three letters and four postcards from Moscow, none of which had said much more than the postcard she held, not even the letters despite their greater length— but the Moscow trials and purges were no secret, and however the British communists chose to rationalize what was happening it was safe to say no one was happy with the state of affairs. *Explanations can be incriminating.* He might not have felt free to say even that, had the postcard come from Moscow. *Best love,* she read again, her smile wan, before putting the postcard back in her purse, sucking deeply on her cigarette, and leaning on the rail.

The band blared a march by Sousa; porters scurried with trolleys of baggage; voyagers flung streamers and confetti like so many giant colorful webs in the sky linking the ship to the quay with tornadoes of ribbon. On the ground people swirled like an ant colony, boarding in throngs belowdeck. Through the commotion Daisy heard someone calling her. "Madam! Madam!"

She turned. The steward was coming toward her, dark stern handsome face screwed with indignation, black crescents of hair bobbing over his forehead, large bags in his hands, bags across his shoulders, straps making X's across his white brassbuttoned chest. Daisy raised her eyebrows. "Yes?"

"Madam, very sorry to bother you, but please tell these people that I know my job. I know this ship, but they will not believe me. If I say up, they will say down. If I say left, they will say right. Please tell them I know what I am doing."

A small man in a grey suit and homburg stepped around the steward. "My dear lady, I trust this man is not bothering you. He seems not to know his way around at all. In fact, he seems to have got us rather lost, I'm afraid, leading us into the very bowels of the ship. It is perhaps his first day as a bellboy."

Alphonse lowered the bags to the deck with great dignity. "We are not lost. I know exactly where we are." He spoke slowly, narrow black eyes peering from their lids, appealing to Daisy as to a magistrate. "Madam, I am not a bellboy. I am a steward. The ship did not get enough bellboys so they asked the stewards to help. If they will only follow me, I will take them to their cabin."

The man in the grey suit ignored Alphonse, smiled instead at Daisy. "He was leading us directly to the boiler-rooms. Of course, we realized then we would have to puzzle it out ourselves—no telling what he had in mind."

Alphonse looked as well at Daisy, maintaining his dignity. "Madam, I tell you I was taking them directly to their cabin—directly!"

The man had a thin mouth; wisps of wavy blond hair showed in his sideburns creeping from under the homberg; his moustache and eyes were almost too pale for visibility. "I say, this is very rude of me indeed. Do allow me to introduce myself. My name is Bogdan Turpin. We're bound for Bombay, and thence by train for Dehli." He held out his hand.

Daisy shook his hand wondering who he might know in Bombay. "Bogdan, did you say?"

"Somewhat unusual, I know—Polish. I was named after my mother's father."

"I see. I'm Daisy Holiday—very pleased to make your acquaintance."

Bogdan Turpin inclined his head a couple of inches. "Likewise, I'm sure—and this is my mother, Mrs. Flavia Frederica Turpin."

Daisy became aware of a presence looming behind him, a tall woman in a dark skirt reaching her ankles, a dark hat with an ostrich feather, round hornrimmed spectacles. She had a thin face and limbs, but her torso swelled from tiny breasts into a belly like a barrel. She cradled a Pekinese the color of beer in her arms, eyes brown and bulging, one hand like a hat over its head as if to shield it from the sun. On a good day, Daisy would have said, the woman's face resembled that of a horse, on a bad that of an insect. "Come along now, Bogdan. We haven't got all day. What is the holdup?"

"No holdup, Mother, but the bellboy seems to think this lady might be of help finding our cabin."

Alphonse hissed with a sharp intake of breath, making his displeasure known again at being called a bellboy.

Mrs. Turpin was shorter than Alphonse by a couple of inches, but appeared to look down on him from a great height. "Why have you dropped our bags? Pick them up at once!"

"I have not drop them, only stop to see where we are going."

"I say you are to pick them up at once!"

"When we are going I will picking up—but we are only standing."

Daisy was aware at once of the change in the steward's syntax—pidgin English, such as a Mrs. Turpin might expect of a servant class. The switch seemed almost subversive though Mrs. Turpin would never know; even her son seemed not to notice. "If I say you are to pick them up at once, then you must do as I say! I will not have them standing on a dirty deck!"

Alphonse picked up the bags and Mrs. Turpin caught Daisy's eye. "Who is this person, Bogdan?"

Bogdan flushed. "Her name is Daisy Holiday, Mother, and the bellboy seems to think she can find our cabin for us."

Daisy spoke calmly. "No, I haven't the faintest idea where your cabin might be, but I'm sure the steward knows. I can assure you he had no trouble finding mine."

"Yes! I know the cabins, I know the ship, but they will not listen. Madam's room number is three-one-six. Their room number is four-one-two. It is in the same location, only one deck difference, but if I tell them to come one way they go the other way. What to do?"

Mrs. Turpin's eyes glared down at Alphonse from their perch. "Shut up, you silly man, or I shall report you to the captain. You are to do as I say. Do you understand?"

Alphonse's jaw dropped, but he said nothing. Daisy admired his reserve and pitied his situation.

Mrs. Turpin returned her gaze to Daisy, saying nothing for a moment, appraising her in silence, head to foot as if she were livestock, before speaking again. "Charming, just charming. I shall look forward to talking with you on deck sometime, Miss Holiday—or perhaps you will join us some evening for a nice game of Happy Families in the lounge." She paused momentarily, stroking the Pekinese's head, continuing her appraisal of Daisy, awaiting her acquiescence, speaking again when it became clear Daisy meant to say nothing. "You know, my dear, I sailed last year on the *Normandie*. You never saw anything like it. I'm afraid it's rather spoiled us for other ships. Everyone knew his place—most especially the darkies. They just couldn't do enough for us—and it's so important, don't you think, to demand the treatment one knows one deserves. Otherwise, one deserves what one gets."

Daisy, turning slowly impassive, merely nodded. "I do believe if you follow the steward he will take you to your cabin."

Mrs. Turpin nodded slowly, allowing a smile to grace her lower mandible. "I wonder if you might not be right after all. One doesn't need the brains of a radish to be a bellboy, does one? Get along, boy. Take us to our cabin."

Daisy was surprised to see the steward grin. "That is *just* what I trying to do, Mrs. Turpentine."

Mrs. Turpin retracted her smile at once, drawing herself to a greater height yet. "I'll have none of your sauce, do you understand? You can be assured I shall report you to the captain if I have to put up with much more of your cheek."

"But what I say, Mrs. Turpentine? What I say?"

Mrs. Turpin stared unblinkingly at the steward seeming to turn from insect to basilisk. "My name is Turpin. You, on the other hand, are to address me as madam—and nothing else. Is that understood?"

"Yes yes, Mrs. Madam. I am calling you from now on Mrs. Madam only. Nothing else."

Daisy grinned again at his pidgin performance. Mrs. Turpin raised her eyebrows, but otherwise ignored him. "Come along, Bogdan. There is nothing more to keep us here." She turned, seeming to launch herself, a ship in full sail, her rear no less regal, and Bogdan smiled, bidding Daisy goodbye, following in her wake.

Alphonse adjusted the straps of the bags across his shoulders and firmed his grip on the bags in his hands. In a year Daisy might well join the mob of mems like Mrs. Turpin, but for the present she looked ripe and he felt comfortable risking a wink. Daisy flashed him a quick wide spontaneous sympathetic surreptitious smile, aware once more of the narrow Gable moustache, chiseled cheekbones, and crescents of hair hovering over his forehead.

**Daisy didn't meet her cabinmate** until later in the day. When she returned to her cabin she saw another person's things on the lower bunk, a trunk on the floor next to her own, but no sign of the person. The tags on her luggage said Miranda MacNamara followed by a Chelsea address and her destination, somewhere in Aden. There was also a camera on the bed looking expensive and complicated. The thought of a stranger with whom she was to share a cabin was exciting and once she had arranged her own things she left the cabin to explore the ship taping a note to the mirror saying she looked forward to meeting her. When she returned she found Miranda MacNamara had arranged her own things as well only to disappear again taping a note of her own to the mirror below Daisy's saying: *Hullo Daisy, Likewise, Miranda.*

Daisy smiled, left both notes on the mirror as she prepared for dinner in a simple elegant sleeveless blue dress, and was still smiling fifteen minutes later when someone knocked on the door.

"Come in. It's open."

A woman put her head in the door. "Is it Daisy Holiday?"

"Yes."

"Hullo. I'm Miranda MacNamara."

"Oh, come in, come in! At last we meet!"

Miranda smiled coming through the door. "Yes, at last!"

"Didn't they give you your own key?"

Miranda was barely taller than Daisy, wore maroon slacks, a white shirt, a straw hat with a blue band, her hair barely darker than her hat. "Yes, of course, but I didn't want to barge in on you before we'd met." She held out her hand.

Daisy shook her hand. "Oh, I say, thanks."

Miranda's smile was guarded. She stared as if attempting to place her, but said nothing.

"I beg your pardon, but is something the matter?"

"No—but I'd conjured an image of you, and you're not at all like your image."

"Really? How am I different?"

"Oh, much younger—definitely much younger."

"I'm almost twenty, you know."

Miranda's smile broadened. "Ah, young enough to volunteer your age—young enough to say 'almost twenty' instead of 'nineteen.'"

Daisy laughed. "I only said that because you seemed disappointed I was young."

"Not disappointed. Envious. You see, ten years ago, I too would have been 'almost twenty.'"

Daisy laughed again. "I can't wait to be thirty. I hate being young. No one takes you seriously."

"Well, I don't know about that, but I *was* joking. I'm actually glad to say I'm almost thirty—old enough to know better, but young enough still to be foolish."

"And I want to be old enough *not* to be foolish."

Miranda grinned. "You'll have plenty of time *not* to be foolish later. Much better to be as foolish as possible when you're young than to regret never having been foolish at all when you're old."

Daisy laughed. "I'm afraid I don't have to try very hard. It's a gift I seem to have—being foolish, I mean, but I'd much rather not be. I'd much rather know exactly the right thing to say and do all the time. It makes life so much easier, don't you think?"

"Yes, and so much more boring." Miranda still grinned, but her expression sobered as she continued her scrutiny.

Daisy's eyes narrowed. "I say, are you sure nothing's the matter? Are you sure you're all right?"

"I'm sorry, this is very rude of me, I know—but, well, I feel I must say … that is, I do think the steward rather fancies you."

"The *stew*ard?"

"Yes, I really do think so, don't you?"

"I never gave it a thought. I only met him this morning. I can't imagine why you would think so."

"Well, someone else actually helped me with my luggage this morning, but when he saw me—your steward, I mean—he took the liberty of simply waltzing in—and I do mean *waltz*ing in, he seemed in another world. He said I was a very lucky woman indeed because I had the best person in the world to share my cabin."

Daisy raised her eyebrows. "Did he really?" She smiled, shaking her head in puzzlement. "I can hardly believe it. He seemed so stern when I saw him—at least, that's how he appeared to me."

"Well, anyway, I must say I was rather surprised he'd been so very bold as to say anything at all. I mean, he had no idea who I was, or what I might think. I might very well have been one of those burra mems—you know the kind I mean—who might have reported him for taking the liberty. He is, after all, a servant—an *In*dian servant, and you an Englishwoman."

"I never thought about it like that."

"Hmm, well, that explains it, I suppose. I've heard more than one Englishman say India was a paradise for the Englishman until the Englishwoman arrived—and started domesticating and civilizing the whole jingbang lot of them. They laugh about it, of course—the men, I mean—but it makes you wonder, doesn't it? I mean, where there's smoke and all that."

Daisy grinned. "I don't think the steward is the kind to suffer a burra mem lightly. There was a bit of a to-do this morning with a certain Mrs. Turpin, whom he called Mrs. Turpentine—but she deserved it! She was so bossy!"

Miranda grinned. "I think you might fancy him a little yourself, if I may say so."

"I give you my word of honor I have never thought about it, not for one instant."

"Well, then, of course, I believe you—but he is something of a smasher, wouldn't you say, in a dark sort of way?"

"He is rather, isn't he?"

"I always like that sort of bulk in a man. I can't stand small men."

Daisy smiled, thinking of Basil, but said nothing.

"Anyway, he did say something about the altercation with your Mrs. Turpin, but I didn't want to encourage him—at least, not until I knew why he was going on at such length. What exactly happened?"

Daisy told her. "Unfortunately, her cabin's upstairs from ours. We might be seeing more of her than we might wish."

"Ah, well, too bad, I suppose. By the way, you haven't been to India before, have you?"

"No. Have you?"

"Three times since I was almost twenty."

Daisy laughed again. "Really? My goodness! Why not simply stay there?"

"Oh, my dear, it's much too complicated to go into all at once. I'm a photographer as you might have guessed." She pointed to her camera. "My work takes me places I might never otherwise consider."

"Do you mean like Aden?"

"Oh, Aden's a different story, and again very complicated." She shut her eyes, sighing with her thoughts. "I shopped around a bit, you see—shopped myself around, you might say."

"Shopped yourself?"

Miranda smiled. "Not for money, not as you might think, but in a manner of speaking. Let's just say there was a man involved—in fact, more than one—but just one now."

Miranda's smile had turned wistful, her eyes glazed, stirred it seemed by welcome memories. Daisy found herself as envious of the memories as Miranda had seemed of her age. Her own life, lived entirely in a single city, seemed crabbed by contrast, her experience drab, her time with Basil paling before Miranda's cavalier reference to more than one man. "But in Aden—not in India?"

"Well, the geography might have changed, but not the people. You see, Aden was administered by the Government of Bombay—until just a few years ago when it became a separate province under the direct control of the Government of India—but, then again, just a couple of years ago it became a crown colony, and since most of the people I knew were administrators in the Government of Aden they're now practically all in Aden—but enough about me. I was talking about your steward. I had to cut him short finally—told him I needed to freshen up. I could hardly believe he was so bold. Indian servants tend to be rather silent, you know, perhaps because they speak little English—but, of course, stewards are a bit different. I believe English is a requirement of the job. Also, he seemed Goan, very likely educated by Jesuits—very likely finds himself the intellectual equal of his social superiors. I've been in that place myself, you know, acting bold to show you're not timid—instead of actually being bold, I mean—but enough about me. What brings you to India?"

Daisy grinned back. "It's a complicated story. Let's just say there's a man involved."

"Tㅤ HERE YOU ARE! I had hoped I might have had a word with you before the voyage was over, but you always seem to be in such a hurry." Mrs. Flavia Frederica Turpin stood over Daisy in her deckchair, her Pekinese on a leash, son Bogdan behind, her tone suggesting Daisy should long have made herself available, perhaps in her cabin.

To Daisy's relief, and not a little to her surprise, she had not been addressed by the Turpins since the day of departure, though she had nodded when their paths had crossed and the son had smiled and waved, Mrs. Turpin alongside more often than not, peering from her insect face, her insect arms cradling her insect dog. Daisy recalled something she had read: people who didn't like people were often excruciatingly kind to their animals.

On the other hand, to her great delight, she and Miranda had become friends, spending much time together, exchanging stories in full, both in pursuit of men in foreign countries though with one large difference: Miranda's man had invited her. Miranda brought to Daisy's attention the various kinds of people aboard: militarymen, civil servants, business people, all of whom tended to stay within their groups, also families visiting relatives and friends for the winter (in India, an English summer), eligible girls among them called the Fishing Fleet, baiting hooks for eligible men—those still single, turning back the following spring, called Returned Empties.

The voyage had proceeded gaily, but predictably. It wasn't until they reached Port Said that Daisy had noticed a significant difference. They had stopped at Marseilles, but despite the choppiness before entering the Mediterannean, despite passengers the color of seaweed with whom other passengers were privately entertained, the differences had been expected until they had approached Port Said. The heat alone made a palpable difference, blanketing the ship, turning walks into wades. You might have told the difference from the clothing: passengers dressed more skimpily, baring arms and legs, wearing lighter colors, black dinner jackets giving way to white.

Port Said was no longer Europe, but Africa—no longer reality but a motion picture come to life. Those who went ashore were warned about food, water, beverages, pickpockets, warned to stay in large parties since it was otherwise unsafe even for Britishers. Daisy wandered with Miranda and others through a narrow winding bazaar, crowded with barely clothed natives, scrawny vagrant animals, incessant importunate hawkers, making finally what seemed to be everyone's purchase of choice: a sola topi, serving needs both sentimental and practical, providing a souvenir while keeping the sun at bay. Those who remained aboard were entertained by boys diving for pennies, a gully-gully man coming aboard to perform tricks. Hawkers approached in boats throwing ropes up the side of the ship with baskets attached to exchange merchandise for money.

Entering the Red Sea through the Gulf of Suez temperatures continued to rise, but hardly as high as Daisy's fevered imagination sailing with Arabia on her left, Africa her right, one bank or the other in constant sight. Her days had never been so carefree. Her future was a blank slate, but she found herself beguiled by the ennui of her new life and doubly thrilled that Basil might be no less impressed by her worldliness (though her worldliness consisted of nothing so much as the carelessness with which she lazed away her days). She started with a breakfast of fresh rolls, bacon, eggs, ham, kippers, cutlets, and tea—and took a light lunch the better to do justice to dinner: turtle soup, sturgeon, snails, deviled fowl, legs of mutton, shoulders of lamb, roast chicken, nectarines and cream. In between meals her greatest difficulty lay in choosing among the plethora of activities available either as spectator or participant, ranging from golf, squash, and tennis to tugs-of-war, pillow fights, and egg-and-spoon races. There were also shops, patisseries, and the gymnasium to provide only an incomplete list—but the most popular activity was lazing in a deckchair, soaking up the sun, or lazing in the shade, a book in her lap, steward at hand, attentive with tea, coffee, or a clear midmorning soup.

On the morning she was addressed again by Mrs. Turpin, Daisy had been lounging in one of the chairs reading yet again *Pride and Prejudice*, among her favorite novels. To Daisy's dismay, Mrs. Turpin seated herself in an adjacent deckchair. "I must say the service on this wretched ship is not at all what it was on the *Normandie*—not at *all*. Take my word for it. Of course, the *Normandie* was a larger vessel by far, but even so she had more crew members than passengers: thirteen hundred crew to a thousand passengers. I asked the Captain and he couldn't have been more attentive had I been the King himself. Would you believe it?"

Bogdan Turpin said nothing, giving her the smile and wave to which she had become accustomed while pulling up a farther deckchair to join them. According to Alphonse Fernandes, or Al as she and Miranda called the steward, the son did little more than listen to the mother. He gave them the gossip when they returned everyday from breakfast to find him making their beds. The occurrences were too many for coincidence, as if making the beds were his excuse for awaiting their return, continuing Miranda's tease that he fancied Daisy—but Daisy didn't mind, flattered by the attention, Miranda's as much as Al's, though insisting all the while that it might just as easily have been Miranda he fancied. Besides, the more he spoke of the treatment Mrs. Turpin meted the more she was determined to be kind. He also made her laugh. "She says I have got the brain of a radish. Do you know why she says this?" He grinned like a child telling his first joke. "Because a turnip is too much like her own name. Turnip, Turpin? You get my meaning?"

The bulk of his time was spent making the beds of passengers and cleaning their rooms. He was also responsible for any other service they might require and served as well, when required, in the lounges, dining-rooms, smoking rooms, on deck, elsewhere, and everywhere. Daisy smiled absently at her reverie, returning Bogdan's greeting.

"It *is* Miss Holiday, isn't it?"

Daisy marveled that even seated Mrs. Turpin appeared to be staring down her insect nose at her. "What? Oh, I beg your pardon. Yes, of course, it is."

"Well, then, why is it that you cannot answer a simple question?"

"Sorry. Do you mean about the *Normandie*? I thought you meant it rhetorically—but I'm afraid I'm hardly the person to ask. You see, this is my first voyage."

"Well, then, you are perhaps fortunate. You have nothing with which to compare it. I, on the other hand, am accustomed to the very best. I am not joking, my dear, when I speak of the ratio—thirteen hundred crew to a thousand passengers—but on this sorry excuse for a ship it seems they have the same persons doing the jobs of barmen, bellboys, stewards, dogwalkers. I ask you, Miss Holiday, if the same persons are everybody's dogsbodies how can they provide *a*ny kind of service to *a*nyone?"

Daisy closed her book, marking her place with a finger, realizing reading would be hopeless, attempting (since she couldn't escape politely) to guide the conversation. "What's your dog's name?"

The dog stood between their deckchairs, eyes apop like a fish, hair like a mop on spindly legs, so stiff Daisy imagined she could tilt it with a finger, so brittle it might have smashed like china with the fall. Mrs. Turpin turned benevolent eyes on the Pekinese, twisting the mandible of her mouth to an approximation of a smile. "Poor little pet. Her name's Cio-Cio—isn't it, my pet?"

"Cio-Cio?"

"Yes, from the opera. You know it, of course?"

"No, actually, I don't."

"You really should know these things, my dear. It's a sign of breeding, you know. I'm talking about Puccini's divine *Madama Butterfly*—Cio-Cio-San."

"You said 'poor little pet.' Is something the matter with him?"

"With *her*. Cio-Cio-San was a woman."

"Sorry. Is something the matter with *her*?"

"She seems to be blocked, poor dear. That's what's the matter. I shudder to think what they have been feeding her. Of course, it was nothing like this on the *Normandie*—not only that, but she had the best sea legs of any of the dogs. I blame this boat, I do. They know absolutely nothing about anything—certainly not about how to treat their passengers, let alone care for their dogs. One is almost inclined to believe that tomorrow they will leave the navigation to us—not that most of this riffraff would mind. Ever since the fares have been dropped it seems one is as likely to meet a bootblack on board as a baron. Now on the *Normandie* we sailed with Mme. Albert Lebrun." Mrs. Turpin looked at Daisy like a headmistress.

"Do you mean the wife of the French President?"

Mrs. Turpin beamed. "Precisement! I see your case is not entirely hopeless, after all, Miss Holiday." Her mandible expanded into a smile that indicated she had made a joke for Daisy's benefit, not at her expense. "Cartier, the jeweler, sailed on the same voyage—and the Maharajah of Karpurthala."

"I understand Somerset Maugham once sailed on the *Strathnaver*."

"Who?"

"Somerset Maugham—the writer."

"The writer? Well, I can't say that surprises me. It's just the sort of ship for a writer—especially of his sort."

Daisy was having difficulty keeping a straight face. "I understand also that Comrade Sak, the communist MP, also once sailed on the *Strathnaver*."

To Daisy's gratification, Mrs. Turpin's mandible compressed itself again though her eyes seemed still to stare from a great height. "The communist? Well, really, now, Miss Holiday, the less said about such people the better. I seem to recall he's dead now, and all I can say is we're best rid of people of his sort. Good riddance to bad rubbish is what I say. I must say I am surprised you mention him at all."

Bogdan, who had maintained a tolerant smile through the exchange, now leaned forward. "They've actually done all they can for little Cio-Cio."

Mrs. Turpin turned her head from Daisy to stare straight ahead. "I don't see how you can say that, Bogdan. She's still constipated, isn't she?"

"Yes, but Mother, you must admit, they've done a lot." He addressed Daisy, still smiling. "They've actually gone to some rather extraordinary lengths for Cio-Cio. They even fashioned a sham fire-plug to facilitate her flow."

Mrs. Turpin's gaze hardened though she seemed to be staring at nothing. "Yes, but what was the use of that? It didn't get her to squat, or even cock a leg. Now, on the *Normandie* there was never any such problem because they fed her the best food." Mrs. Turpin turned her head again toward Daisy. "On the *Normandie* they had a 24 hour buffet—for the animals as well. Even the kennel had a sun deck."

Daisy removed her finger from her book, inserted the bookmark, shut the book, looked at her watch. "I hope you will not find me too rude, Mrs. Turpin, but I'm afraid it's time for my walk. Isn't it amazing how one gets into such a routine when one is obliged to do absolutely nothing?"

"What? Do you mean this very instant?"

Daisy got up. "I was told that seven times around the promenade is close to a mile, and if I don't get started soon I shall be late for lunch. I find walking the very best exercise, don't you?"

Mrs. Turpin said nothing, staring ahead again, but Bogdan got up with Daisy. "I shall join you if I may, Miss Holiday?"

"Oh, I should hate to put you to the bother of escorting me. I shall be very well on my own, thank you very much."

"Oh, but it's no bother at all, I assure you—and, as you say, a morning constitutional is the very thing. I think I should enjoy it very much indeed."

Daisy's muscles ached from the strain of her smile. "It's really not necessary."

"All the more reason, then, to do it, isn't it, if we do it for the fun of it?"

Daisy sighed. "Well, then, of course, since you insist, I shall be obliged."

Bogdan seemed almost to spring to her side, nodding to his mother. "We shan't be long, Mother."

Mrs. Turpin's face seemed to get longer yet. "Do be sure that you're not, Bogdan. It's almost time for lunch, you know."

Daisy spoke politely. "It was nice making your acquaintance again, Mrs. Turpin."

"We must arrange for a nice game of Happy Families, Miss Holiday. I think I might enjoy that."

"Yes, of course." Daisy turned, showing her own pique in her hurry to leave the deck, ignoring Bogdan rushing in her wake, joining the parade of promenaders as if she were alone, but Bogdan caught up with her easily, matching her stride. "I say, Miss Holiday, I must ask you to forgive my insistence. You see I have a reason for making a pest of myself."

"Oh?"

"It's Mother, you see. She has received a rather terrible shock."

Surprised by the admission Daisy slowed her pace, turning her head to look at Bogdan, holding his eyes. "You don't say? What has happened?"

Bogdan spoke softly, staring at his feet, matching the pace of his talk to the pace of their walk. "Well, for starters, Father died rather suddenly last month."

The second admission surprised her again, bringing her sympathy to the fore. "Oh, Mr. Turpin, I *am* sorry to hear that."

They walked so slowly now they almost stood still, his eyes stayed on his feet, Daisy's on his face. "Thank you, Miss Holiday, but there's more. That was bad enough, of course—but it wasn't the whole story. There was worse to follow."

"Worse than your father's death?"

Bogdan nodded. "I'm afraid so. My father had a mistress, you see, to whom he has bequeathed almost everything." Daisy, embarrassed at the sudden intimate revelation from a stranger, said nothing—but Bogdan seemed empowered, the revelation cementing a bond between them, drawing on her reserves of decency against her will. "We go to meet my elder brother, Barnabas, in Delhi. He's in the ICS."

"The ICS?"

"The Indian Civil Service."

"Was your father also in the Service?"

"No, he was in cotton—other things as well, fabrics and things, but mainly cotton—in Bombay."

"And you?"

Bogdan shook his head slowly, smiling briefly. "Nothing, I'm afraid. I'm good for absolutely nothing, you see—except, of course, looking after Mother. She tried it for a while—living in Bombay, I mean—Father had a fine house on Malabar Hill—but it wasn't her cup of tea. She didn't care for the temperatures, the cookery, the company—and finally she returned to England—Lancashire, actually, her neck of the woods growing up, where she first met Father, and where Father also had many business contacts and did quite nicely for her. She wanted one of us to stay with her, and since Barnabas was bonkers about the ICS—don't ask me why—I was the one to stay. It seemed the best arrangement for all concerned—now, of course, one understands why."

"I'm so sorry."

"No, you mustn't be. I'm the one who's sorry to have burdened you with the problems of strangers. I wouldn't have, you know—except that I didn't want you to think so very ill of Mother. She is accustomed to traveling posh, always first class, never even second—and now she finds herself traveling tourist. You cannot imagine the effect it has on her, at her stage in life. It accounts in no small part for her behavior, you see."

"I see."

"The very first day, for instance, when that bellboy led us to our cabin—he knew what he was doing, of course, but Mother couldn't believe it. She had never traveled tourist before, and was genuinely afraid he was leading us into the bowels of the ship. She doesn't trust the darkies, you know—and not without reason. They might mean well, but ... well, it's not their fault, of course, that they're stupid."

Daisy's cabin was closer to the boiler-rooms by one deck, but she said nothing.

Bogdan allowed himself a smile. "Did you know that it was this very voyage—crossing the Red Sea, I mean—that gave us the word 'posh'?"

"No, I didn't."

"I know it for a fact. POSH stands for 'Port Outward, Starboard Homeward'—referring to the accommodation of VIPs traveling through the Red Sea. On the outgoing journey, you see, the cabins on the port side—that is, facing east—were much cooler for an afternoon nap than the starboard side which absolutely baked the passengers—roasted them till they were swimming in their own gravy, so to speak."

Daisy laughed in spite of herself, finding herself more comfortable with the impersonal turn of the conversation. "That's very interesting, Mr. Turpin. I did not know that."

Mr. Turpin allowed himself his widest grin yet. "Americans sailing eastward, on the other hand, always fight for deckchair positions that are SOPH, 'Starboard Outward, Port Homeward.'"

Daisy grinned. "So they would. They're Americans, aren't they? Already half baked."

Bogdan laughed. "You do understand, then, about Mother? She has always had the best of everything, the very best—but now she finds herself, for the first time in a very long while, a bit short."

Daisy frowned, preferring to talk impersonally. "It must make for a very difficult adjustment."

"Indeed, it does—and at her age! You understand why I wouldn't want you to think ill of her?"

"Of course. There's no need to say any more about it. No one would want anyone to think ill of anyone else—and she is your mother."

"Well, then, it would seem that our little chat has not been in vain."

Bogdan smiled, but Daisy still frowned. She couldn't understand why it mattered to him what she thought of his mother and remained uncomfortable with the confidence, finding his smile sly, his solicitude and sincerity no less, as if he had tricked her good humor from her.

They walked briefly in silence, Bogdan smiling, Daisy frowning, stealing glances at his face, blond wavy hair plastered again under the homburg, moustache like a wraith across his lip, eyes the color of water, skin pale as fishflesh. Once, catching her glance, he turned his smile on her again like a beam. "If you don't mind my asking, Miss Holiday—are you yourself on holiday?"

She laughed politely at a joke she had heard a million times, but turned her head: his unsolicited confidences did not make him privy to hers. "You might say that."

"Are you visiting relatives too?"

"No."

"Friends?"

"Yes—that is, a friend—one friend."

"Really? Might it be anyone I know? We're not total strangers to Bombay, you know—though, of course, it's been a very long while since we were there."

At another time Daisy might have been grateful for the chance of an introduction, but Miranda had given her names of people to contact in Bombay who might in turn introduce her to others, and she found herself mistrusting the Turpins. She didn't doubt his story, but questioned his motive: his help wasn't offered as much as forced, and his continual insistence made him continually resistible. "I very much doubt you would know him, Mr. Turpin. You see, he's only recently arrived in Bombay."

"It's still a possibility, you know—or Barnabas might know him—or he might know someone who might know someone. That's how these things happen in the east, you know. They're hardly as organized as the civilized countries."

"Thank you very much, Mr. Turpin. You have been very helpful, and I am much obliged. I shall keep that in mind." They passed tennis courts, Daisy walking more quickly, both aware his ploy for her confidence had failed. "Do you mind if we walk a little faster? I don't find it much exercise if we simply stroll along."

She found him suddenly a silly man, harmless, ineffective, small in all ways, wishing he had told her nothing, wishing to tell him as little as possible about herself.

Bogdan might have read her mind: his smile slid into his mouth; his mouth turned small, stiff, brittle. "You should be more careful, you know, Miss Holiday, when you travel alone, and particularly when you travel by sea. It only *seems* as if everything is permitted—as if everything might be dared with impunity—because the sea isolates us so."

His reply was not without pique, but the pique of a small man only made Daisy laugh. "Why, Mr. Turpin, I cannot imagine whatever you might mean."

"Only that we are accountable, Miss Holiday, always, and everywhere, for our actions. We are accountable on land for what we might do at sea. The rules may seem to change at sea, but that is the very problem—they only *seem* to change, whereas, in fact, of course, they do nothing of the sort, and we pay dearly for transgressions whatever the circumstances."

"Mr. Turpin, I do not understand you at all. If I did not know better I would say you were threatening me."

"No threat, Miss Holiday, but a caution—for your own good. You seem very young and very impressionable. You do know, I suppose, that no one expects the Raj to last more than another twenty-five years or so. Even my brother Barnabas says so, and he should know being in the ICS—but he's hardly the only one. Everyone says so. They're only in it now for the pensions."

"Mr. Turpin, at the risk of sounding like a complete idiot I must insist I am completely at a loss to understand what you mean."

"It's the reason, Miss Holiday, why people like that bellboy are so arrogant. They know as well as everyone else that their day is coming and they are beginning to take advantage of it already. The bellboy would never have dared to speak to you as he did on our day of departure even a bare five years ago."

"His name is Al, Mr. Turpin—and he's a steward, not a bellboy—and I saw nothing wrong with the way he spoke to me."

"It is of little concern, Miss Holiday, whether he is a bellboy or a steward, and so is his name. If you don't mind my saying so, he speaks rather freely to you, and as your countryman, one who has your best interest at heart, I should remind you that they are not of our kind and we must not let them forget it. Otherwise, they will think themselves as good as us when in fact they're only as good as we let them be—and the closer we get to India the more troublesome such relations become."

"Mr. Turpin, I am surprised—not only by what you say, but that you choose to say it to me. It is of great concern to him, whether he is a bellboy or a steward—and whatever he might be he is a man first, a servant second, and deserves the respect of any man."

"Ah, Miss Holiday, I can see you feel sorry for him, and that is all to your credit, but I can assure you he does very well for a servant. Many of these stewards make more money than the captain himself, more's the pity—in tips, I mean."

"So much the better for the stewards, Mr. Turpin. At least, they earn their living unlike some among us."

Mr. Turpin turned his head. "I am very sorry, Miss Holiday, that you feel that way, but I am not sorry to have warned you. The rest is up to you."

They had made two rounds of the promenade, arriving again at the enclosed deck from which they had started, to observe Alphonse through the French window stumble and spill something on Mrs. Turpin in her deckchair. Bogdan dashed to his mother, Daisy following close behind. Alphonse mumbled something as they arrived and Mrs. Turpin rose, inflating like a balloon, blouse drenched with soup. "Bogdan, thank God, you're back. Did you hear that? Did you hear what this jackanapes called me?"

"It was an accident, Mother. We saw the whole thing. It was an accident."

"It was no accident. He did it on purpose. Did you hear what this wretched nigger called me, Bogdan? He called me a silly bitch. I heard it with my own ears."

Alphonse's eyes were wide and white, his mouth dropped in an O, and he gesticulated wildly, proffering towels. "Nonono, what I say is: I slip on your bitch—see? I slip on your bitch—not silly bitch. Swear to God, that is what I say." It wasn't until he pointed that Daisy became aware of Cio-Cio running circles like a skater pushing with just one leg, yelping the continual tinny arf of a lapdog.

"The insurbordination has gone too far, Bogdan. I shall demand satisfaction from the captain."

LATER THE SAME DAY, Daisy answered a knock on her cabin door to see the purser in the hallway whom she remembered mainly as a handsome man in his forties with a ready smile. "Yes?"

He touched his hat. "Very sorry to bother you, Miss Holiday, but may I come in for a moment?"

Daisy stepped aside. "Of course, Mr. Drummond."

Miranda looked up from the mirror where she was powdering her nose. "Hullo, Mr. Drummond. We were just getting ready for dinner."

"Hullo, Miss MacNamara. Sorry to be a bother. I shan't be long."

Miranda sat on the lower bunk. "No bother, Mr. Drummond. Dinner can wait. We have all the time in the world. Won't you please sit down?"

Daisy offered a seat at the table. The purser sat, hat in lap. "Thank you very much. Let me come directly to the point, Miss Holiday. It seems you were present at an altercation this morning. It would be a great help indeed if you were to recount in your own words exactly what happened."

"Do you mean the altercation with Mrs. Turpin?"

"My very meaning—exactly."

"I'm afraid I only came in at the tail end. I don't know of what help that might be."

"Anything you saw will be of help, Miss Holiday—anything you saw, anything you heard, anything you can remember."

"There's not much to tell. I had been promenading with Mr. Turpin when we saw Al through the door. He stumbled on something—their dog, I believe—and spilled soup on Mrs. Turpin. He gave her some towels to mop up the spill. That's really all there is to it, I'm afraid."

"Miss Holiday, do you remember anything that was said?"

"Well, Mrs. Turpin was quite outraged. She called him a wretched nigger."

"That is helpful, Miss Holiday. Do you remember what, if anything, *he* might have said?"

"Ah! Yes, I do." The drift of the purser's inquiry suddenly became plain. "Mrs. Turpin seemed to think he'd called her a silly bitch, but he insisted he'd said I *slip* on your *bitch*."

"Did you hear what he said yourself?"

Miranda grinned from the bed. "Mr. Drummond, I've had no dealings with that woman myself, but from what Daisy's told me she *does* seem a monster. Calling her a bitch seems almost too kind."

Daisy laughed. "She *is* rather a dragon—not the sort I'd want around if I could help it."

The purser allowed himself a smile. "I'm afraid you may be right—but I need to know what the steward said. She's lodged a complaint against him, you see, which we can't very well ignore—but we need to know as well, of course, if he's actually been insubordinate. We couldn't very well take his word against hers, but if we could corroborate his word it would be a different story. He said I should ask you since you'd been present. Now this is a delicate matter, and you must realize I have come to you in the strictest confidence. It will never get around to Mrs. Turpin that you were the one who was asked, but we may at least then say to her with confidence that the steward's story was corroborated."

"There were others present as well. Why not ask one of them?"

"He was quite adamant, Miss Holiday. He didn't trust the others to tell the truth, only you."

"What would happen if his story weren't corroborated?"

"Well, that's difficult to say. He might very well get the sack. It would depend upon how far Mrs. Turpin was willing to go. She appears to know a number of muckety-mucks in Bombay—as well she might, having a son in the ICS—but if we could resolve the matter with a corroboration right here at sea that might well be the end of the matter. It would save us all a great deal of bother."

Daisy wasn't sure what Alphonse had said; all things considered, Mrs. Turpin's statement had the ring of truth; but she spoke without hesitation. "You can put your fears to rest, Mr. Drummond. I am certain Al told the truth—and I am equally certain that Mrs. Turpin is capable of hearing just what she wishes to hear. In fact, if it suits your purpose, I would have no objection to your making it known to her that I was the one to corroborate his story."

The purser sat up in his chair, his smile almost surprised. "Well, now, Miss Holiday, that is very kind of you, but I assure you that won't be necessary. Your certainty was all I needed, thank you very much—and now, if you will pardon me, I shall not take up any more of your time."

After the purser left Miranda stared at Daisy who spoke defiantly. "She *is* a silly bitch, you know. There's no reason for Al to be given the sack just because she's a silly bitch—she and her weasely son—a more pushy little bugger I never saw."

Miranda put finishing touches to her makeup. "You did the right thing. I would have done the same. Ready?"


**AFTER DAISY AND MIRANDA HAD RETIRED** for the night, a knock sounded again on their door. Miranda, in the lower bunk, stepped to the door in her dressing-gown and asked who it was. Alphonse's voice answered. "Not to worry. Only me."

Miranda waggled Daisy's foot in the top bunk. "It's Al. He says you are not to worry."

Alphonse's hushed whisper came through the door. "Please, one minute only. I want to thank Madame Holiday."

Miranda whispered back. "Madame Holiday says you're very welcome, Al, but we need our sleep. You can thank her properly in the morning."

"Please, for just one minute, can I come in?"

Daisy swung her legs from her bunk, jumped to the floor, and pulled on her dressing-gown. "Oh, let him in. Might as well now that we're awake."

"Now that he's woken us up, you mean."

"Now that he's here."

"Well, all right, all right. Are you presentable?"

"Yes."

Miranda opened the door as Daisy turned on the light.

Alphonse stepped quickly in closing the door behind him, locking eyes with Daisy. "Madam, I am so sorry for disturbing you."

Miranda frowned. "What about me? I've been disturbed too, you know, and not on my own account either."

Alphonse seemed anxious, but Daisy smiled. "It's all right, Al. She's only joking. What did you want to say."

Alphonse turned to Miranda seated now at the table. "Sorry, madam. I am sorry for disturbing you also. I did not mean –"

Miranda nodded. "It's all right, Al. Go on. Have your say."

Alphonse could not have been more solemn facing Daisy again. "Mr. Drummond just told me what you have done. It makes me very happy. Thank you so very very much."

Daisy grinned at his solemnity, amazed at her power. He seemed to have become her charge and she wished to protect him. "Glad I could be of help."

"Mr. Drummond is a very good fellow. He understands how passengers can be, always bothering him in his office. Do you know what he has done?"

The women shook their heads.

Alphonse grinned. "He has a telephone in his office, but not a real telephone. He has a button under the desk. When he presses the button the telephone rings." He laughed out loud. "When passengers come he presses the button. When the telephone rings—do you know what he says?"

The women spoke together. "What?"

Alphonse saluted, snapping his heels. "'At once, captain! At your command!'" He laughed again, grinning unendingly at the two women. "Of course, the passengers leave. When the captain calls no one tells him to wait."

Daisy grinned. "I suppose not."

"What I am saying is Mr. Drummond knows how the passengers are, but he can do nothing if someone complains. That is why I have come to thank you, madam. Thank you so very much."

"You're welcome, Al."

"If you need anything, just pull." He went to the tasseled cord which they had never used. "Anything, anytime—nighttime, daytime. If you are needing something, pull. Without you I would have been sacked, gone, finish, no more." His grin grew wide as a hanger. "Because of you, Mrs. Turnip has to swallow her own turpentine."

Daisy's eyebrows rose. "Actually, Al, there is something you can do."

"Anything! Just say what."

"Al, I know the Turpins are not the best people, but you must be good to them. You must not call them names—not Turnip, not Turpentine, do you understand? She has just lost her husband. You must feel sorry for such people. Do you understand?"

Alphonse lost his grin, shook his head. "With people like her, there is always some excuse—always. It means nothing."

"Nevertheless, Al, you asked if there was something you could do, and this is what I am asking. Do you understand?"

Alphonse didn't reply immediately, apparently mulling what Daisy had said, but smiling shortly. "Because *you* have asked, yes, I will do it—but only because *you* have asked. People like her deserve nothing, but because *you* have asked I will do it."

Daisy smiled, pleased with her accomplishment. "Thank you."

"No. *I* thank *you*."

Miranda got up from the table. "Al, I too would like to ask something if I may?"

"Of course. Just say what. You too have only got to ask."

"Well, then, it's really quite simple. I want to get back to bed. That's all I want. Do you suppose we could manage that?"

"Yesyes, of course, Madame MacNamara. Thank you, Madame Holiday. I will not forget what you have done. Thank you."

When they were alone again Miranda spoke from her bunk. "I knew India was going to change you, but I never imagined it would change you so soon."

"What do you mean?"

"Well, I mean, look at you, making peace between Al and the Turpins—just like Mr. Gandhi with the Hindus and Muslims."

"Oh, shut up!"

Miranda chuckled. "But I was right, wasn't I?"

"About what?"

"I told you he fancied you."

Daisy threw a bolster at Miranda. "You shut up, Miranda MacNamara!"

THE LAST LAP OF THE VOYAGE, crossing the Arabian Sea from Aden to Bombay, took a week. Temperatures rose higher yet, and unlike the passage through the Red Sea there was no land visible, no Arabian or African coastline, nothing for miles around, the monotony of the seascape broken only by infrequent seabirds, flying fish, and the occasional passage of another ship. Daisy had hated to say goodbye to Miranda, waving and smiling like everyone else, calm as the sea on the surface, churning no less underneath, recognizing the body of water in herself, a sea in miniature, swept by tides, swarming with currents, riddled at once by the elation of angels, loneliness of martyrs, resolution of heroes, timidity of rabbits—the schizophrenia of the pioneer.

The days were now intolerably hot, burning her to the color and consistency of a tomato ripe beyond its time, and she preferred to spend her time indoors, taking the deck only after sunset, staying to watch the stars build spires in the sky. Her own insignificance was never more clear than when she watched them ascend, each in its turn, finally the north star, Polaris, shown her by Miranda, hovering on the distant horizon. She realized she had made of Basil her own true north; having nothing to ground her she had let him draw her, giving no thought to what she would do if she didn't find him, trusting fate and faith to guide her. She had enough money for a return passage, living was cheap in India, and she planned to allow at least six months for her search. Once she found Basil the rest would fall in place.

However she managed her internal fears, they seeped into a backdrop of external events beyond her control. No one believed anymore in Mr. Chamberlain's "peace for our time," not even Mr. Chamberlain himself as evidenced by his reinstatement of conscription; increasingly the presumption grew that Munich had been the "total and unmitigated defeat" that Mr. Churchill had recognized from the start; but what one believed other than the inevitability of war was impossible to say. In Aden there had been much talk among passengers and crew about the newest wrinkle, the non-aggression pact between the Soviet Union and Germany, but Daisy kept her thoughts to herself: not only did she not know enough, but even knowing everything there was nothing she could do.

"I say, Miss Holiday?"

Daisy turned from the starry sky, the starlit sea, keeping her hands on the rail. "Yes?"

Corporal Pumphrey, whom she had met playing pingpong, with whom she had dined the night before, stood alongside. He was a small man, inflated in his imagination by his uniform. "I say, Miss Holiday, no hard feelings I hope."

After dinner, strolling along the deck by night, Pumphrey had tried to kiss her. She looked out to sea again. "No feelings at all, Mr. Pumphrey."

She had deliberately omitted his rank despite his uniform. Pumphrey smiled. "That pretty much says it all, I suppose."

"Yes, it does."

"Miss Holiday, surely you realize we must live for the moment—especially at times like these. That's all I was doing, making hay while the sun shone in a manner of speaking, all work and no play and all that—you know what I mean."

It was evidence of bad days ahead: for some, the threat of war provided license for bad behavior. "Believe me, Mr. Pumphrey, I *do* know what you mean, and that is *just* what I was doing—living for the moment. I would not otherwise have dared be so bold."

She had slapped his face hard, and when he had persisted she had slapped him again threatening to scream. Pumphrey's eyes narrowed. "That's all very well, Miss Holiday, to be prim and proper as you please, but it's a transparent hypocrisy when you're prim and proper with some and not with others—if you get my meaning." He raised his eyebrows suggestively.

Daisy's brow wrinkled. "I do not get your meaning—and I do not care to."

"That's very convenient for you, I'm sure, but it's no secret what's going on."

"Mr. Pumphrey, I repeat, I do not know what you are talking about—and I do not care to know. Please leave me alone."

Pumphrey laughed. "Hahah! Garbo speaks! Come, come, Miss Holiday, there's no cause for dramatics, especially when it's no secret whom you're sweet upon."

She knew what he was talking about. The Turpins now looked the other way when their paths crossed. She was sure the purser had said nothing to implicate her, but it wasn't a difficult deduction to make, nor to deduce what stories they might have spread about her. She had been rebuffed starting a conversation with passengers on two occasions before she had understood what might have happened, and had preferred to keep her own company since, but though she knew what he was talking about she didn't wish to give him the satisfaction. "I have no idea whom you are talking about, Mr. Pumphrey, but I do wish you would leave me alone. I shouldn't have to make myself so very clear to a gentleman."

Pumphrey grinned. "That's right, indeed, Miss Holiday. No lady should have to make herself so very clear to a gentleman—but since you have made yourself so very clear, it pretty much gives us an indication of what we are, doesn't it?"

Daisy said nothing, keeping her gaze on the sea.

"You know, Miss Holiday. One can always tell what a man wants by watching what he watches."

"Mr. Pumphrey, I really do not care to hear anything you might have to say to me. I do wish you would leave me alone."

Pumphrey seemed to speak through his teeth, hardly opening his mouth. "Well, then, let me simply call a spade a spade. It's the steward I'm talking about, Miss Holiday, and well you know it. There, I've spelled it out for your ladyship. That makes me something of a gent, doesn't it?"

"I don't know what you mean. If it's the steward you're talking about, then, yes, I was in a position to do him a favor—and I did. That's all."

"Ah, a favor, that's all—but not the kind of favor he'll be wanting, I'm sure. It's a scandal the way he stares at you, Miss Holiday. It's him you should be telling to leave you alone, not me."

Unlike before, returning from breakfast, she no longer found Alphonse making her bed. Instead, her bed was made, her cabin empty, and she missed the occasional conversations, especially with Miranda gone, but made nothing of it. "I have no need to say it to him, Mr. Pumphrey, because he *does* leave me alone. What you choose to make of it is your business, but I would thank you not to make it mine."

"Oh, you would thank me, would you? That's very nice of you, I'm sure, but I'd rather have you thank me for something else."

Daisy was angry with herself for having explained even as little as she had; the man had no right to address her so freely. "I shall ask you just one more time, Mr. Pumphrey, to leave me alone."

"Oh, come now, Miss Holiday! Save your high and mighty ways for someone who cares a damn. I've paid for my passage same as you, and I'll stand where I wish the same as you."

In two days she would be in Bombay. Civility seemed only to encourage Pumphrey. She retreated in silence to the lounge, Pumphrey's laugh coursing in her wake, and settled with the latest *Picture Post* in a red leather clubchair while someone played "Clair de Lune" on the piano.

**DAISY KNEW BEFORE ANSWERING** the knock who stood behind the door. Miranda's departure had left her lonely; the stories circulated by Pumphrey and the Turpins had isolated her further; but she had been alone too long even before that, too long without Basil. She would be in Bombay in two days, and for all she knew it might be the start of no more than a new solitude. It was past eleven o'clock, but whatever the hour she had never been so glad for company, her sole friend he seemed for the moment. "Who is it?"

The response was so long coming she thought he might have left. "Only me, madam … only me."

She opened the door to find him staring at his feet, glistening trails, like the tracks of snails, on his cheeks. "Al, what's happened?"

He continued to stare at his feet. "Please, madam, can I come in—for only one minute?"

"Of course." She let him in, shutting the door behind him, tightening her dressing-gown. She had lit the reading lamp over her bunk to open the door, but left the ceiling lamp unlit imagining too bright a light might inhibit his confidence. "Sit down. Tell me what's the matter."

He sat at the table resting his forehead on his hands. "Madam, a terrible thing has happened."

Daisy joined him at the table, close enough for their knees to touch if she had wished. She had read that Indians looked to the English like children to parents to resolve their problems, in part the reason the English had maintained supremacy so long. She had felt some such responsibility when the purser had paid such heed to her version of events regarding the Turpins and felt again her power over Alphonse despite his advantage in age, size, and gender. She removed his hands from his head, laid them flat on the table, palms down, covering them with her own, a mother comforting a son—or a friend a friend. "What? Tell me."

Claws of thick black hair sheltered his brow; the Gable moustache and cheekbones made him a black sheik on a silver screen; reflections of the reading lamp glinted in each black eye. "It is like you said, madam. Someone is always dying. It is very sad."

"It is sad, yes. Has someone died?"

"My ammy—just like yours."

"Who is your ammy?"

"My grandmother. She died—just like your grandmother. It makes me very sad."

She was glad for the enclosed space, cozier for the dim light, flattered by his confidence. After her stretch of solitude, he seemed a caring friend even talking about himself. "Al, I am sorry to hear that. How did you get the news?"

"In Aden, I have got a friend. He got a letter. They want me to come back soon."

"Who wants you to come back?"

"My family—my mother."

"Is she in Bombay?"

"No, in Dona Paula—in Goa, my home, a fishing village. I grew up in Dona Paula with my ammy, my mother's mother—now dead. As good as my mother she was—to me, she was."

"Where was your mother?"

"Working, in Bombay, sending money home. After my father died, there was nobody else to make money."

"What did she do?"

"She worked for a Parsi family in Bombay, Sanjanas—very rich, very good people. Even now, after she has retired, they send her a pension—very good people."

"A Parsi family?"

"Yes, Parsi. You know Parsis?"

"I had a Parsi friend in London."

"Really? Oh, yes? Sanjanas?"

"No, Saklatvala—Shirin Saklatvala. She had family in Bombay."

"I will bet the Sanjanas know her. All Parsis know all other Parsis. They also have many English friends. They know everybody."

Daisy was silent a moment. "I wonder if they might know my friend."

"You have an English friend in Bombay?"

"Yes, but I don't know where he lives."

"They will know. If they don't, they will know somebody who knows. They know everybody."

"Maybe you could give me their address?"

"Oh yes, of course yes, not a problem. Sanjana House on Cooperage Road in the Fort. They will help you in every way they can—very good people. Say only that I sent you."

Daisy scribbled the information in her notebook alongside names and addresses given her by Miranda. "Thank you, Al. What exactly did your mother do for them?"

"She was Sanjana sahib's ayah—not now, of course, he is all grown up, England-returned, but he was my friend when I was a boy. When I visited my mother sometimes we would play—carom and cricket and monopoly—very good family, Sanjanas, treated my mother very good."

"I think I shall do that. I shall give them a ring. Do you have their telephone number?"

"There is a telephone book. All telephone numbers are in the telephone book. They will help you. You can even stay with them. If you say to them I have sent you, they will ask you to stay with them."

Daisy smiled. "I couldn't impose on them like that—but I shall give them a ring."

"Yes, give them a ring. When you talk to them they will tell you to stay. They will take you everywhere in their motor. How will you travel in Bombay?"

"I really hadn't thought about it—buses and trams, I suppose. I understand they have victorias?"

"Yes, but Sanjanas will take you in their motor. They have a driver. They have many motors. They will give you the motor and the driver to go wherever you want."

Daisy laughed. "A driver's a bit fancy for me, I'm afraid. I'm far more likely to hire a motorcycle myself if necessary than be chauffered around."

Again Alphonse's eyes widened. "You drive a motorcycle?"

"My friend taught me. It was great fun."

"You are very brave."

She laughed. "Yes, madam is very brave."

His eyes flashed. "You do not believe me—but I have always said so, have I not?"

She stopped laughing. "Yes, you have. I am sorry, and thank you for the compliment."

He relaxed again. "How long will you stay in India?"

He called her madam less frequently than before, happily addressing her with a pronoun instead, not in the third person, though never by her Christian name. She had made a game of it, grinning as she spoke. "As long as it takes madam to find madam's friend. If necessary, madam will get a job."

"Madam will work?"

"If madam has to."

"Madam has worked before?"

"Madam has worked all of madam's life."

He smiled finally, understanding she was teasing him. "Madam is a good Christian—like me. In India, there are mostly Hindus and Muslims, and Zoroastrians like Sanjanas—but all of them are heathens, not believing in Jesus Christ. You believe in Jesus, no? English people are all Christians, no?"

He spoke normally again, his grandmother's death no longer in ascendance, and Daisy congratulated herself. "Yes, but how is it that you are a Christian rather than a Hindu or a Muslim?"

"Because I grew up in Goa. In Goa, there are many churches—not like in Bombay. Goa is Portuguese, not English, very different.

You must come sometime. After you have found your friend, you must both come. I will show you Goa. Everywhere there are beautiful churches—and beaches."

"It sounds lovely." Daisy was enjoying her conquest, happy for the camaraderie. "Tell me about Goa. What was it like, growing up there?"

Alphonse spoke readily about his young self, his brother, his sister, growing up in a houseful of pets, among them a mongoose, a squirrel, a pig, a turtle, in addition to commoner animals (cats, dogs, lovebirds); trees abounding (jackfruit, coconut, banana, banyan, mango); cashew groves nearby from which was distilled the local brew, feni.

She listened, entranced by what he said, but no less by herself for her situation, talking through the night with a strange handsome black man, speculating what Basil might make of his new woman of the world, how Miranda would laugh to see her sitting with Alphonse in the night despite her objections to the contrary. She smiled, imagining their responses, caressing Alphonse's hands as he continued to talk.

Alphonse recognized it no longer mattered what he said, only that he said something; she heard his voice, not his words. He had been right, she had been ripe, but he still needed to proceed with caution. He turned his hands to caress hers in turn. "I was feeling so sad, but you have made me better. So much I owe to you. Because of you I still have my job. Otherwise, Mrs. Turpin would have got me the sack—but you are so good, you told me to be good even to her—and I *have* been good to her. I always wish her Good Morning, always say her name properly, never make fun." He grinned. "Very difficult, but I have done it for you."

"Thank you, Al. It was the right thing to do." They continued caressing each other's hands, prompting him to raise hers to his lips, cover them with kisses. She remained still, saying nothing, neither resisting nor encouraging his kisses, recalling suddenly Pumphrey's and Bogdan's warnings, wondering if she had consciously or unconsciously invited his behavior, wondering what she wanted herself.

Sensing her diffidence, Alphonse stopped. To milk the situation he would need to exercise a mix of persuasion and restraint. He looked up suddenly, dropping her hands, sitting back in his chair. "Sorry, madam, sorry. It is not right."

His retreat surprised her as much as his aggression before, but she realized her attraction had begun before they had met, seeking only a situation to reveal itself. The qualms of day receded by night, as did hijinks on the high seas once they were landbound again; she had been accused and convicted of sins that remained uncommitted, if indeed they were sins; the opportunity offered allowed her to perform a kindness while adding to her luster as a woman of the world; and surrounding all her rationales was her loneliness, vast as the sea. None of this was immediately apparent, but later became transparent as air. His withdrawal provided the final impetus. She remained still, but spoke quietly. "It's all right, Al. Nothing to be sorry about."

He took a deep breath, whether of relief or something else she couldn't have said, but as he stared she took his face in both hands, stroking his temples with her thumbs. Getting up, she kissed one cheek, then the other—then, at greater length, his mouth.

Seated in the Sanjana sitting-room, Daisy appeared calmer than she felt, imagining herself mistress of her situation, congratulating herself on managing heat, dust, food, flies, crowds, chaos, stickiness with an aplomb she might have envied in others. A moment of panic overcame her when handing change to a beggar and a sea of frantic spindly arms sprouted around her, palms to the sky, skinny brown fingers scraping her skin with a leathery touch, heads bony as coconuts erupting in a nonsensical clamor for attention. An Englishman had come to her aid shouting them off, tipping his topi to her with a warning: "I wouldn't do that again if I were you. It seems heartless, I know, but if you give money to one of them you'll have the whole damn lot of them on you like leeches." She thanked him and engaged to share a victoria with an Indian gentleman and his wife, both of whom smiled all the way to the Zephyr Hotel on Marine Lines (recommended by Miranda), agreeing with everything she said, answering even questions with a nod and smile, staring as if she were a vision. She congratulated herself on her timing, Britain and France had declared war on Germany the day before she arrived, Britain at eleven in the morning, France at five in the afternoon, and the German submarine U-30 had sunk a British liner, the *Athenia*, the same day.

She had taken an exploratory walk the same evening. Marine Lines ran parallel to railway tracks. Beyond the tracks yawned a massive excavation, land being reclaimed from the sea, a single sweeping roadway, to be called Marine Drive, linking far reaches of the city, so said Mr. Sen, the concierge. He also directed her along Marine lines to Queen's Road, past a round covered bandstand to Sanjana House on Cooperage Road. He offered to call a carriage—but she had chosen to walk to acquaint herself with the city despite his caution that it would take the better part of an hour. He was right about the time, but the route was direct, and she found the house easily, resisting the temptation to introduce herself to the Sanjanas without warning, telephoning instead the next day, saying she was a friend of Alphonse Fernandes who had suggested the Sanjanas might be of help. She had meant to ask about Basil over the telephone, but had been invited to tea, and wishing to establish contacts in Bombay she had accepted.

Arriving for her appointment she had been led by a servant through a hallway to a sitting-room adjoining a verandah overlooking the bandstand, rows of coconut palms, a row of buildings across the Cooperage maidan, the sea visible between the buildings. The sitting-room was large and luxurious: a replica of Michelangelo's *Pieta*, tall as her waist, stood at one end, a replica of Rodin's *Kiss* at the other; statuettes of marble and ivory populated tables and sideboards as did flower arrangements in vases and bowls; impressionist paintings covered the walls; the curtains were a rich heavy burgundy velour, the sofas plush, a paler burgundy than the curtains; showcases along the walls displayed glassware, papiermache, and giltedged volumes titled

# A Googly in the Compound

*Famous Discoveries*, *Fifty Famous Men*, *One Thousand and One Beautiful Things*, and *The Complete Works of William Shakespeare* among many such others; two chandeliers alternated with three fans on the ceiling; a grand piano stood at the far end; a gramophone midway; a grandfather clock by the entrance. The servant, a small bony man, was uniformed in white with brass buttons. He set the closest fan in motion, the closest chandelier alight, and spoke without meeting her eyes. "Please to sit. I will tell seth. He is just coming."

Daisy smiled. "Thank you."

She settled herself in a sofa so deep and plush it almost swallowed her, picking a magazine, *The Illustrated Weekly of India*, the latest edition, but not late enough to have captured the war news, and news of the war rendered all other news extraneous. She leafed through the pages until footsteps drew her attention to the doorway. Looking up she saw a smiling man, not as big as Basil, but beefier, holding out his hand as he approached. "Hullo. Daisy Holiday, I presume?"

Daisy got up to shake his hand. "Yes! How do you do?"

"Very well, thank you. I am Rustom Sanjana. We spoke yesterday on the telephone."

"Oh, yes, Mr. Sanjana, thank you so very much for agreeing to see me. I shall not take up much of your time."

He shrugged, still smiling. "No need to rush on my account. Time I have plenty of."

His voice was reassuring. Daisy allowed herself a deeper breath. "Thank you."

"Now, how about a nice tall glass of nimbu-pani to start things off on the right foot?"

"What's that?"

"Aha! You haven't been in Bombay long, have you? It's lime juice. Would you like to try it?"

"Anything—as long as it's cold."

"Of course." Rustom raised his voice: "Rahul!" When the servant came he ordered nimbu-pani for the bai.

"Won't you have something yourself?"

"Of course, later—with tea, in the dining-room, with the others—my parents and my brother."

"Oh, my goodness! I really didn't mean to put you to any trouble. I have just one simple question to ask. That's all."

Rustom grinned. "No trouble at all. They will be happy to see you—and if I cannot answer your question, maybe one of them will. When I told them you were Aphoos's friend—"

"I'm sorry. What did you call him?"

"Aphoos. It was our name for him, the local name for the Alphonse mangos—anyway, they couldn't understand why I invited you to tea—he is just the son of one of our servants, you know—but when I told them you were English, of course, they understood."

Daisy was beginning to understand the difference it made being English: she had never received such deference in London, such stares in the street, as if she were royalty. "Where are they now?"

"My parents live in the downstairs flat. They run Jilly's Emporium, Indian exports, one of the family businesses. I help out—my only job around here. You may have seen the signs downstairs?"

"Oh, yes, I did."

"I just sent one of the servants to say our guest had arrived. They should be up in a jiffy. My older brother, Sohrab, is a solicitor—but he should also be home soon. He is usually at the office at this time, but when he knew you were coming he said he would take off early."

Daisy was surprised at the fuss. "It really wasn't necessary. I should have asked you on the telephone. You will feel I'm wasting your time now and I will feel perfectly silly."

Rustom laughed. "Not at all. Nothing to feel silly about—but, actually, that was just what Mummy said. What a thing to do, to invite a perfect stranger to tea because *she* wants to ask *you* a question. She will think you have nothing to do—which, actually, isn't far from the truth. I'm fortunate enough not to have to do anything if I don't want to, but after talking to you on the telephone you did not seem like a perfect stranger—and, besides, you know Aphoos. That makes you, at the very least, something less than a perfect stranger—but, anyway, how did you find our good old Aphoos?"

"He was actually quite upset about his ammy."

"Why? What's the matter with his ammy?"

"She died, you know. He got the news in Aden."

"Really? I am so sorry to hear that. He grew up with his ammy. So many stories he told us about his family in Goa—in Dona Paula."

"Yes, he told me stories as well."

"But I must say I am surprised Gracie never wrote to us about it. Gracie is his mother. She was Sohrab's ayah. Lovely woman. I am sure Mummy will want to send her some baksheesh—token of our regret, you know. That's why I am surprised she never wrote."

Rahul returned with a tray holding a tall narrow frosted glass misty with condensation, lime pulp and ice floating within, a straw piercing the surface.

Rustom placed a coaster on a sidetable within Daisy's reach and waited while she took a sip. "How do you like it?"

"Mmmm! Just what the doctor ordered. Cold and sweet."

"Good. So, where are you staying?"

"At the Zephyr Hotel."

"How do you like Bombay so far?"

"Well, I've hardly been here long enough to say—just since Monday, really—but I suppose it's very exotic."

Rustom laughed. "Exotic! Well, yes, of course, for an Englishwoman. For me what was exotic was a strange English voice on the telephone wanting to make an appointment."

Daisy laughed. "I never thought of it like that—but I must say it *has* been rather exciting ever since I left London—just being on my own, I mean."

"Ah, yes, independence is a treasure, I suppose, but I can't say I've had much experience of it. My interests don't require it."

"Your interests?"

"Tell me, Miss Holiday, have you heard about the coelacanth?"

"Sorry? The ... coelacanth? Do you mean that big fish that was in the news a while ago?"

"Yes, the same, you *have* heard about it, that big blue ugly fish, fifty-four inches long, one hundred and twenty-seven pounds, from the Devonian age, more than three hundred million years ago, thought to be extinct. You know about it?"

Daisy's brow wrinkled. "Just what was in the papers. Why?"

"Well, think of it like this. Only one was found though a search has been mounted for others. I mean, just think of that poor fish, it just may have been the last of its kind, trolling the oceans forever, searching for a mate, only to be trawled on the ocean floor. It makes such a beautiful metaphor for loneliness, don't you think?"

"I see what you mean. Very romantic." She smiled, but looked away, brow still wrinkled, wondering what to say when they were interrupted by the sound of the front door being unlatched.

"That will be my parents."

Sohrab appeared with Dolly and Phiroze. Dolly, in a green sleeveless dress, flashed her widest smile. "What a surprise to hear from a friend of Alphonse. I'm Dolly Sanjana. Welcome."

"Thank you, Mrs. Sanjana. It's so very good of you to see me on such short notice."

"Rubbish—and please call me Dolly. No need to be formal. You are among friends."

Phiroze held out his left hand. "And you must call me Phiroze."

"How do you do?" She shook his hand, unable to keep her glance from his floppy right sleeve.

"War injury—from the Great War."

"I'm sorry."

Phiroze smiled. "No need. Ancient history now."

Sohrab held out his hand. "Yes, really and truly—and no need to rehash ancient history. Hullo. I'm Sohrab Sanjana."

Daisy took a breath before shaking his hand. "No, of course not. All I meant was that I have great respect for anyone who did his bit."

Sohrab smiled. "Yes, of course, as do we all. Welcome to our humble abode."

Alphonse had said he was England-returned and Daisy could tell from his accent—and sarcasm. He had a craggier face than his brother, pockmarked on his upper lip and the bridge of his nose. He was shorter than his brother, shorter than his father, but all were taller than her, even Dolly, in a country not known for the height of its population. Daisy returned his smile. "Thank you. This is very kind of you."

Sohrab brushed her gratitude aside with a wave of his hand. "Nonsense! It's not everyday that we have a pretty girl to tea." Daisy felt herself redden, but he turned immediately to his mother allowing no time for embarrassment. "I say, Mummy, I'm starving. Why don't we go straight to the dining-room—that is to say, if everything is ready?"

"Might as well, I suppose—but let me just take a look." She turned to Daisy. "Please excuse me for a minute."

"Of course."

Phiroze smiled as Dolly left the room. "Why don't we sit down. I'm sure it won't be for long, but we might as well sit."

Sohrab locked eyes with Daisy as they sat. "So, how long has our Rustom been boring you with his stories?"

The difference between the brothers, even apart from size, was distinct. Looking from Sohrab to Rustom, Daisy took up the cudgels for Rustom, who seemed to retreat into himself before his brother. Not only had he lost the animation with which he had talked about the coelacanth, but he seemed a smaller man. "It wasn't boring at all. In fact, we were having the most interesting conversation when you came."

Sohrab raised his hand, still staring at Daisy. "Wait! Don't tell me! About the coelacanth—right? That's his favorite subject these days."

Daisy, not wishing to embarrass Rustom further, said nothing—but Rustom confessed. "Yes, we were talking about the coelacanth. It is as Keats said: 'A thing of beauty is a joy forever.' I find the coelacanth a forever fascinating subject."

"Yes, yes, leave it to you to find beauty in that plugugly fish. Really, Rustom!"

Daisy rallied once more to his defense. "But I understand very clearly what your brother means. The coelacanth *is* a very beautiful fish. Its history makes it beautiful, that it's survived so long, seemingly the sole survivor of its race."

Rustom smiled, nodding, but saying nothing.

Sohrab still grinned, staring at Daisy. "I think you mean species rather than race, don't you? One must always resist the sentimental urge to anthropomorphize animals, certainly fish. Bad enough that we subject our children to Mickey Mouses and Porky Pigs—but, ah, yes, who can argue with history?"

Daisy agreed with Sohrab, but was glad to have made Rustom smile and took another sip of nimbu-pani.

Sohrab kept his eyes on her. "If you had come last year the subject would have been astronomy. Anyone unfortunate enough to have a minute with Rustom was subjected to his astronomy lecture. The year before it was evolution. Now it's the coelacanth."

Dolly appeared at the doorway. "If not for astronomy your daddy and I might never have married. If not for astronomy you might never have got here yourself. You should be thanking your lucky stars—no pun intended—that people are interested in more things than Law. Come on now. Tea is ready."

Sohrab continued to speak as they headed for the dining-room. "There is a very strong rationale for Law. It serves an important purpose. I will grant that astronomy is at least not a lot of jiggery-pokery like astrology—but it's just as useless. What's the point of it? Stars in the sky. Very bright, very pretty, very nice—but so what? Now my daddy, he studied Law. He knew what he was doing with his life."

Phiroze touched Daisy's arm to guide her toward the dining-room, speaking as softly as before. "Sohrab's daddy was my brother. Dolly was my sister-in-law before she became my wife. I'm afraid I have no more interest in Law than Rustom—which, I think, is the point Sohrab is trying so very tiresomely to make."

Sohrab laughed. "Painstakingly, perhaps, but not tiresomely. Rustom is my *half*-brother, you see—also my cousin, when you get right down to it."

There was triumph in his laugh that Daisy didn't understand. She bent to return her nimbu-pani to the coaster, but Rustom interceded. "Take it with you, why don't you?"

The dining-room was as luxurious as the sitting-room. The top half of a long dining table which seated twelve had been set: tea, biscuits, pastries, sandwiches, fruit. Dolly sat at the head, Phiroze on her left. Dolly invited Daisy to sit on her right, Rustom next to her, and Sohrab next to Phiroze. Daisy noted there was no cutlery to the right of Phiroze's setting. Tea was poured, plates passed around, Rahul stood in readiness by the door. Dolly turned to Daisy as she poured. "Rustom tells me you only arrived on Monday?"

"Yes, that's right—and you have made me feel right at home right away with your lovely tea."

Rustom smiled. "The pleasure is ours, Miss Holiday. You mustn't think that we have tea like this everyday. Usually, it's a far more desultory affair, each of us taking it whenever and wherever we happen to be—mostly at work downstairs in the Emporium."

Sohrab winked at Daisy. "*If*, that is, you can call what Rustom does work. His motto is: Leave unto others what you would rather not do yourself."

Daisy changed the subject, turning to Rustom. "Please, if I am to call your parents by their first names, you too must call me Daisy."

Rustom smiled, nodding. "I stand corrected ... Daisy—and, as I never cease to tell Sohrab, they also serve who only stand and wait."

Sohrab winked again. "Yes, and if chance will have him king, then chance will crown him without his stir. Those are key words for our Rustom: 'without his stir.'"

Daisy didn't understand the antipathy between the brothers, and might have defended Rustom again, but said nothing. A small woman defending a large man once too often only emasculated the man. Dolly's eyes swept an arc from one son to the other. "All right, you two. Stop behaving like five-year-olds now. Less arguing, more eating."

Rustom passed a plate of cheese sandwiches to Daisy. "Mummy, did you know Aphoos's ammy died?"

"My goodness, no! Where did you hear that?"

Daisy nodded. "He told me himself, less than a week ago. He was very upset."

Rustom shrugged. "There is always the possibility that they haven't had a chance to tell us yet."

Sohrab shook his head. "Not with these people. You can rest assured they will seize the first opportunity to get some baksheesh. They would tell us right away."

Dolly nodded. "Tell us, they would, but not necessarily for the money, not our Gracie." She turned to Daisy. "Anyway, I will find out for myself. In the meantime, I think it would be much more interesting if Daisy told us something about herself. Are you from London proper, my dear, or some other part of England?"

"London proper, born and bred." She hadn't expected to say much about herself, but felt it was the least she could do to repay the Sanjanas' hospitality. She mentioned briefly her Clerkenwell childhood, the death of her mother, her flight from her father to her Chelsea grandmother, journalism class, secretarial job, and the legacy which had prompted her to look for her friend in Bombay since she had no other strong ties in London. She smiled relating her story, saying no more about Basil Ballard than that he had sent a postcard from Bombay and she wanted to surprise him, but she was more transparent than she wished.

Dolly buttered a scone for Phiroze. "Really, Daisy, what a romantic story—and you must be, what, all of twenty years old?"

"I just turned twenty, actually, on the first of the month."

Sohrab chuckled. "A year younger than our Rustom—and what a lot she has got to show for herself already."

Daisy wished he hadn't used her to taunt his brother, but didn't wish to appear rude either to Sohrab by defending Rustom, and was grateful when Phiroze spoke. "He must have been a very good friend for you to have come all the way on the promise of just one postcard."

"He was … he was the best friend I ever had."

Phiroze spoke as much to comfort Dolly as Daisy, knowing how bickering between their sons raised the specter of Kavas. Rustom's violence had long been in check, but Daisy invoked as well the specter of Gillian, and boys vying for the same English girl appeared to be growing into men vying for the same Englishwoman right before their eyes. "Well, then, we must see what we can do about finding him for you. If he is in Bombay we will find him. What is his name?"

"Basil Ballard."

"Ballard? Arre, Phiroze, wouldn't that be our Shirin's husband?"

Phiroze raised his eyebrows. "Yes, it is. I am sure it is. She didn't want to take his name because then people would think she was a song."

Despite the heat Daisy shivered, growing so pale her freckles seemed to turn to goosebumps, her dimples to disappear.

Sohrab slapped the table. "Yes, that is his name, tall fellow. They just got back from their honeymoon—in Simla, if memory serves correctly."

Daisy felt she was choking, a fist forcing itself down her throat.

Rustom spoke beside her, but he might have been in another world. "They are also in the Fort area, very close—with Shirin's family, all the Saklatvalas."

Dolly spoke again. "Daisy, are you all right? You look very pale."

Daisy nodded, looking down. "I'm all right."

Dolly touched her forehead with the back of her hand. "You are very cold. Are you sure you are all right? Have some more tea."

Daisy forced herself to drink more tea, but hardly felt better after she had finished. "I'm sorry. I don't know what's come over me. I must be tireder than I thought."

Dolly's forehead wrinkled with concern. "Yes, yes, it happens. Not to worry. Caught up with the excitement of new things the body bears up perfectly at first—but after a while events catch up. We call it Bombay Surprise. Would you like to lie down?"

Daisy's color returned slowly, but though everyone's eyes were on her she could face no one. "No, really, I'm quite all right. I feel fine. It was just a thing of the moment."

Dolly gripped her arm. "Daisy, I think we may have located your friend. He's married a good friend of ours. They were just in Moscow. It's got to be the same man. Small world, after all, isn't it? Would you like me to give him a ring?"

Daisy managed a smile. "No, please, I'd rather do it myself. I'd like to surprise him. Please don't say anything."

"Of course not. Whatever you say. I'll just copy down the number for you, shall I?"

"Yes, please. Thank you very much."

Daisy didn't stay much longer and refused adamantly to be driven back to her hotel, insisting she was well enough to walk. After she left the Sanjanas looked at one another, Dolly the first to speak. "Well, now, how very extraordinary. What do you make of that?" She looked at Phiroze.

Phiroze shrugged. "Delayed culture shock? Reaction to food, climate, humidity, temperature? Left at the altar? Who can tell? Pretty girl."

Sohrab grinned. "*Very* pretty."

Rustom nodded. "Yes, *very*."

Dolly looked from one son to the other, but need not have worried. True to his word, Rustom gave in to Sohrab in all things. She wished he might show himself in a worldlier light, but realized, not entirely to her regret, that Rustom had chosen to take a backseat not only to Sohrab, but to the world.

T**HE SANJANAS COULD NOT HAVE BEEN MORE KIND,** compensating for the inconveniences of the Pumphreys and Turpins of the world. Her path to India and Bombay and Basil could not have run more smoothly had she planned it, but with Basil married the path disappeared—and thanks to the war the path behind her had disappeared as well. She hated calling Basil in her helpless state, but realizing India was to be her home for an indeterminate length of time she needed to take advantage of her meager resources. She also had no doubt the Sanjanas would get in touch either with her or Basil if she didn't call, and she owed them, if nothing else, the courtesy of taking care of her own business. Steeling herself, she dialed the number, hanging up when answered by a woman's voice, but dialing continually until a male answered. "Hullo."

"Basil?"

"Hullo. Who is this?"

Her throat contracted, suffocating her words, allowing only a series of sobs to escape.

"I say, who *is* this? Please speak up."

She took a deep breath. "It's me—Daisy!"

"Who?"

"*Dai*sy, Basil!"

"Daisy Holiday, as I live and breathe! Goodness gracious!"

"Basil, I can't believe I'm talking to you again."

"Daisy Holiday! Oh, my God!"

"Basil, I have to see you."

"Daisy, my God! Where are you?"

"I'm at the Zephyr Hotel on Marine Lines. I'm in a phone booth in some kind of vestibule."

"In Bombay? How did you get here? How did you find me? How *are* you?"

"Basil, I'm fine—well, actually, I'm a wreck right now, I can feel people staring at the mad English girl bawling her eyes out on the telephone—but I'm *so* happy to be talking to you again. Oh, Basil, I *have* to see you! I *must* see you!"

"Are you alone? Is anyone with you? What are you doing here?"

"It's a long story, Basil. I'd rather not tell you on the telephone. Can't we meet?"

"It will take me twenty minutes to drive to your hotel. Would that give you enough time?"

"I'd be ready in five. I'm ready now. I'll be waiting outside."

"Good. I'll be driving a white Austin coupe."

Basil was five minutes early, Daisy almost late rushing back to her room, drying her face, changing her blouse, then her skirt, then both for a dress, rushing downstairs again still unsatisfied with her ensemble, her room strewn with discarded clothes, rushing through the front door, out of breath again as a white Austin turned into the driveway and a familiar face smiled in the window.

"Hullo, Daisy."

She managed a smile, took a deep breath. "Hullo, Basil."

He got out, unfolding the familiar lanky length, kissed her cheek, led her around the car to the passenger side, and held open the door. "Get in."

She got in, not without chagrin at the sheer professionalism of his greeting, but calmer for the same reason. He was a married man; she had expected no less. "Basil, it's lovely to see you again."

She couldn't keep her eyes from him as he turned the ignition and commandeered the long stick of the gear shaft separating their seats, but he stared at the windshield as if they were on the road already. "It's good to see you too, Daisy."

He appeared changed, his face more wan, more lined, more gaunt, more stern, his body leaner despite the suit. She had imagined they wouldn't be able to stop talking once they met, but found herself swallowing words bubbling in her throat, aware of a difference between them that was new, but unable to define it, and unable to ignore it, recognizing the difference needed to be defined before they could once more be comfortable with each other. She continued to examine his face from the side, wishing she might caress his temple, cheek, mouth. "You seem changed, Basil. You *have* changed. You've lost weight."

Basil kept his eyes on the road, but rewarded her with his first smile. "I got married. I suppose you know."

"Yes. The Sanjanas told me. I had tea with them yesterday. They know the Saklatvalas. I thought I would have the hardest time finding you—but that wasn't a problem at all." Feeling her eyes swell, as they had swollen unexpectedly and intermittently ever since the tea, Daisy turned her head finally from Basil. Finding him had not been the problem—but finding him married had become a Himalayan hurdle, a problem she had dared not imagine, let alone mention.

"Do you mean Phiroze and Dolly Sanjana?"

"Yes, and their sons, Sohrab and Rustom."

"That's funny. They never said a word."

"I asked them not to. I wanted it to be a surprise."

"That it was. You could have knocked me down with a feather."

"But not half the surprise I got when I learned you were married, I'm sure—especially after everything you'd said about marriage. What changed your mind, Basil?"

Basil exhaled a long breathy sigh. "Ohhh, Daise, it *is* rather complicated. Suppose we begin with you. What brought you to Bombay?"

"Oh, Bas, don't you know? Can't you guess?"

"Well, I swear by all the saints! I never took you for one to play games, Daisy Holiday."

"I'm not playing games, Basil. I came for you. I came for you. It was your postcard. I never read anything so cryptic in my life. If anyone's playing games it's you."

"Which postcard do you mean?"

"The last one, in which you said you were in Bombay." She pulled the postcard out of her purse, read out loud: "*Darling, I won't say much. Explanations can be incriminating, not to say unnecessary and tedious, but some things must be acknowledged. You were right, I was wrong, and I am sorry.* Right about what, Basil? And wrong about what? And what were you sorry about? What was I supposed to make of it all? And then to learn you were married! Why didn't you tell me? If I'd known I'd never have come. If you weren't playing games, you might as well have been!"

Her voice had risen as she spoke. Confronting the subject she felt surer of herself, a sureness not lost on Basil. "I'm sorry, Daisy. That was cryptic of me, I suppose, but I wasn't playing games. It *is* rather a complicated story, you see."

"Well, I'm not *stu*pid, Basil. I would have understood. You did the worst possible thing. You aroused my curiosity, you said we would never meet again—*and* you told me where you were! What was I to think?" She read more of the postcard: "*One can be blinded, it seems, by zeal as much as by prejudice. It might have been very different, but better by far to bear in mind that it isn't so very bad as it is.*" She looked up. "Again, Basil, blinded to what. If anyone was blind it was me, not you—and what might have been different? And what wasn't so very bad as it was?" When he remained silent she continued in a softer voice than before. "And then you said the loveliest and the saddest thing all at once: *I know you will have a lovely life, and I am so glad and grateful that you saw fit to share a little bit of it with me. Best love*—and so on and so forth." She was crying again, weeping openly, without fear of discovery. "Oh, Basil, I came for you. I came all the way for you. What a question! There was nothing else in the world I wanted so much as you." She said nothing more for a moment, silent but for the sobs. When Basil remained silent she took a final deep breath and spoke again. "Won't you say something? Won't you say anything at all?"

Basil took a breath himself before speaking, his voice hushed. "Daisy, I had no idea you felt for me so very deeply. I'm very flattered—I can't tell you how much."

"I don't want to flatter you, Basil. I want you to love me."

"Daisy, I can't let you talk like that."

"I know, Basil, I know. I'm sorry. You're married. I'm sorry. I couldn't help myself. But you're right. You're absolutely right. You made no commitment to me. I just feel I've been so very very foolish, such a complete and utter idiot."

"Now you *are* talking nonsense. I *do* owe you an explanation and I would have given it to you before, but it might actually have been dangerous for me to put it in writing. Believe me, I was trying to be careful, not cryptic. I was trying to protect you."

"Protect me? From what?"

"Listen, when I told Shirin you were on the telephone she said I was to bring you back immediately so we could all have a nice long chat over drinks about the old days –"

"Oh, no, Basil—not tonight! I can't! Not tonight! Maybe another time!"

"I was just going to say I can see that wouldn't be such a good idea, after all. I could take you to my club, but everyone knows me there—not that we've got anything to hide, but there'd be too many interruptions. What I have in mind is a club in Colaba, a service club. We could talk at length without being disturbed. Would that be all right? I do owe you, at the very least, an explanation for my behavior."

"I think I would like that."

"I *do* care about you, Daisy. That is not open for discussion. Why do you suppose I wrote that postcard at all? I wouldn't have written if I didn't care. I simply couldn't say more at the time—but I needed to say at least that much to keep you from waiting for me."

Her lungs seemed to expand, air again to be pure, bones light as air, muscles limber as the muscles of an aerialist. She settled herself more comfortably, but said nothing.

Basil faced her for a moment. "That was you then, was it, calling and hanging up today God knows how many times?"

"Oh, Basil, yes, I'm sorry. I couldn't bring myself to talk to anyone else. I didn't want to leave the least hint of who it might be. I'm sorry if I caused any trouble."

Basil grinned. "No trouble at all, except for poor Suzie."

"Who's Suzie?"

"Our maid."

"Your maid?"

"The Saklatvalas are rich, you know—like the Sanjanas. We have maids, bearers, cooks, drivers—more servants than I know what to do with." He laughed. "Some life for a communist."

Her brow furrowed. "Basil, is that why you … why you and Shirin …"

"Don't be silly, Daisy. That was just incidental."

"Sorry, that was *vile* of me. I *am* sorry. I'm just not myself anymore."

"All's forgiven. I owe Shirin my life, you see. The rest developed from there."

Her lungs collapsed again, sank like sandbags, making a bow of her shoulders, wrinkled balloon of her face.

Basil's hand was continually on the horn. He braked for a goat throwing them both forward for a moment. "Sorry about that. I swear it seems everyone owns the roads in Bombay except motorists. Bad enough cows sit like islands in the middle of the road, but people *will* stop to genuflect for the cows before they mind the cars."

Daisy sat up straight again, not wishing to appear a ninny. "It's such a different culture, isn't it? I read up a bit about it before I came, but there's nothing like actually being there."

"When did you arrive?"

"Just last Monday."

"My goodness! In the nick of time!"

She knew he was talking about the war.

He grinned. "Take my word for it. You haven't even begun to notice the difference. I've been in India twice before, but even so I have to pinch myself to be sure I'm awake."

"But I *do* know what you mean. I had the feeling the moment we arrived at Port Said—not India, of course, but a different world—even something as simple as people going barefoot in the streets was an eye-opener."

"You must have been counting your pennies for quite a while to have made the voyage."

She told him quickly about her legacy, the voyage, her introduction to the Sanjanas.

"But how very brave of you to set off like that—at the drop of a hat, so to speak."

She wanted to say again she had done it for him, but didn't. "It didn't feel so very brave. I rather enjoyed it, actually, once I'd made up my mind what I was going to do."

# A Googly in the Compound

By the time they arrived at their destination it had begun to rain again, shafts of silver, thick as spears, raking the earth with tiny explosions at each point of contact. Basil looked at Daisy. "Believe it or not we keep two umbrellas in the Daimler and the Vauxhall, just in case of rain, but the Austin's for my private use and I've got just one in the back. I'm afraid we're going to get a bit wet."

"I don't mind a bit."

"Hold on then. I'll come around for you." He fished the umbrella out of the back, came around the car, and opened the door. "Watch out for the puddles."

She watched her step, sheltered by the black onion dome of the umbrella and his right arm around her like a sheath. "I can see I'm going to have to get some sensible shoes."

"Get chappals, sandals. They're inexpensive and the best thing for this weather. If you'd come in the thick of the monsoon, of course, it would have been a different story."

"Actually, an umbrella was my first purchase after I got here—at the concierge's recommendation, I might add, when I asked what one might do in Bombay. I don't think he quite understood what I meant—but I haven't used it once yet. I must say I find the monsoon's reputation a bit overblown. It's probably rained more in London since I got here."

Basil laughed. "It's petering out now. A London shower's no more than a bit of spit really compared to a Bombay monsoon. The rains come in full force around May—sheets, torrents, cats and dogs—fleets of cats and dogs, you might say—and daily, incessantly, through what might be called the summer months. The roads are impossible then. The drains are so bad the water reaches your knees. Even the flies seem to go mad."

Daisy brushed aside two flies buzzing in her face. "As if they're not mad enough already."

The club was dark: fans spun on long spindles from a high ceiling; potted palms provided an arcaded entrance, wicker furniture and glasstopped tables the ambience; an unobtrusive piano tinkled

"Cathedral in the Pines," a few couples foxtrotted on the floor, British and Indian, men in white dinner jackets and uniform, women in dresses and saris; waiters swept to and fro in white turbans, red cummerbunds. Basil telephoned Shirin to let her know of the change in plans before ordering Scotch for himself, rum and coke for Daisy, plates of tomato sandwiches, chicken patties, mutton samosas, and the yellowest chips Daisy had ever seen. He offered Daisy a cigarette from a packet of Dunhill's which she accepted, recognizing his brand. He lit her cigarette, one for himself, and blew a plume of smoke. "Well, now, where to begin?"

Daisy drew on her cigarette, keeping her eyes on Basil, saying nothing.

"Daisy, I don't mean to be an alarmist, but I must ask you first not to repeat anything I say. I don't know what the consequences might be, or even if there might be consequences at all, but I want your assurance this will go no further."

"Basil, if you're trying to frighten me, you're succeeding. I feel like I'm in an Edgar Wallace or a Fu Manchu already without you talking like that. Whatever do you mean?"

Basil smiled. "Sorry about the melodrama. I'm not trying to frighten you. There's very likely nothing to be frightened about, but it's also perhaps too early to tell. I'm just being cautious. This goes no further, right?"

"If you say so. Of course."

"Good. I suppose then that the beginning for me was at university—my career as a communist. Cambridge was a hotbed for communists—and, well, to mix metaphors for a bit, the hotbed was only the tip of the iceberg—and I'll be a monkey's uncle if it's still not the case. The irony is, of course, as I've learned since, that the theory of communism, which we all applauded, and which I continue to applaud, is rather different from its practice—and this discrepancy between the theory and the practice is a concept which intellectuals appear not to understand at all." He exhaled another plume of smoke. "You, I might add, seemed always to have known that. Compared to the rest of us you were a Solomon. I remember our differences about Sylvia Pankhurst. Well, no two ways about it now: you were right, I was wrong, and I'm sorry. That's what I meant. That's *all* I meant, but I can see how easily you might have misunderstood. I truly am sorry, Daisy."

Daisy dipped a chip in tomato sauce, pursed her lips. "Water under the bridge, Basil. You never forced your beliefs on me—in fact, you encouraged me to challenge you."

"And you did, in a way that I should have challenged myself—my own beliefs. That's the trouble with intellectuals, you see. Once they've got an idea in their heads they can't let it alone—and the brighter the idea the stronger its hold—and communism was, and still is, I believe, the brightest star in the grabbag of governments—but Marxism isn't Leninism, and Leninism isn't Stalinism, and when Stalinism took root the intellectuals defended Stalinism believing they were defending Marxism. They believed, and continue to believe, everything they read and see in *Russia Today* and the *Daily Worker*. They refuse to believe, even now, the vast majority of them, that while Marxism may have been for the masses, Leninism was very much only for those who believed in Lenin—and Stalinism, so it seems, is only for Stalin. Unfortunately, it's the workers who pay the price for the beliefs of the intellectuals. They see things as they are while the intellectuals, with the best of intentions, see only what fits the pattern in their heads—if you have a hammer, every problem becomes a nail—and sometimes the intentions too are not so very good. They'd rather see themselves as saviors than dupes—which, of course, makes them rather easy dupes—certainly easier than the masses for whom they profess to be taking up the cudgels."

Daisy munched on a samosa. "What finally changed your mind?"

Basil stared into his glass. He had defended Stalin's paranoia in the wake of the Kirov assassination of 1934, the series of trials which had commenced in 1936, the executions of Zinoviev, Radek, Piatakov, Tukhachevsky, the gang of generals: seventy percent of those elected to the Central Committee of the Communist Party of the Soviet Union at its Seventeenth Congress in 1934 had been shot by 1938. The party line had been accepted without question in all cases: extreme measures were justified against Trotsky terrorists, traitors, wreckers, and spies; all activities against the Workers' State merited death; the trials and executions were a measure not only of the power but the purity of the Soviet Union. It was only when a friend of his had disappeared that he began to question what might have been happening. "Do you remember Goddy Humphreys?"

"Shirin's lover? I think he was a member of the Comintern?"

"That's the one."

"Whom she followed to Leningrad?"

"Whom we all followed at a later date though for a different reason to Moscow. You see, he became a Soviet citizen—but then he disappeared."

"Disappeared? Do you mean off the face of the earth? But how could that be?"

"Precisely the question we asked ourselves."

"Why didn't you ever tell me about this?"

"I didn't see any point in getting you involved when we hardly knew what was going on ourselves. There was nothing you could have done—and, besides, you weren't even a communist."

"Oh, Basil, I may not have sympathized with your cause, but I could certainly sympathize with you as a friend."

"Well, perhaps I was wrong—but, as you said, water under the bridge. You see, Shirin had a snap that Goddy had sent of himself alongside some of those generals who were executed, and when she stopped hearing from him she wanted at least to find out what had happened. She asked me to go with her—and, as you know, I did. We were quite safe—or so we imagined, because we held British passports."

Daisy's eyes were wide.

"Well, when we got to Moscow we made some inquiries, mainly by showing the snap around, pointing to Goddy, asking if anyone had seen him, but no one seemed to know him—not even his landlady.

Strangely enough, the landlady showed us the same picture in a copy of the *Daily Worker*—but with one difference: Goddy was not in the picture. I mean just what I say: it was exactly the same snap, but without Goddy. He'd been removed from the snap in the picture as he appeared to have been removed from the face of the earth."

Daisy held her rum and coke to her mouth, too engrossed to drink.

"Well, we didn't know what to think. The landlady suggested our own snap might be a fraud."

"She didn't!"

"She certainly did. Worse was to follow. We got home one evening to find our rooms had been ransacked. That snap, other snaps, and our cameras had been taken along with some minor valuables to suggest the motive was burglary—at least, that was what the police insisted—I mean, about the burglary. Not only that, but they were able to retrieve everything—everything, that is, except the snaps."

Daisy's eyes remained wide, her mouth open but silent.

"Worst of all, I had started writing an article which I'd titled 'The Potemkin Pattern.' You know the original Potemkin, of course?"

"Of Potemkin villages fame?"

"Yes—well, the story's apocryphal, but it served my purpose. Just as Potemkin supposedly created dummy villages to provide a false picture of village life for Catherine II, I wanted to show in 'The Potemkin Pattern' that the pictures in the *Daily Worker* among other things were being created to provide a false picture of life in the Soviet Union—which, of course, was tantamount to sedition."

"Did they find the paper?"

"They certainly did. It was their trump. I won't go into all the details, but I was headed for an arrest. The only reason I wasn't arrested immediately was my British citizenship, but a paper of that kind would have branded me a spy, no longer protected by citizenship. I hate to think what might have happened had the NKVD been alerted."

"Oh, my God, Basil!"

"As I said, I have Shirin to thank for my safe return. She was, of course, the daughter of Comrade Sak, Madame Sak in her own right, and she knew people who were very helpful. In the light of what we learned it was too late for Goddy, but not to take any chances we got married. It was easier for her to pull strings for me as her husband. To make a long story short: c'est la vie."

"That was it? That was why you married her? Do you mean to say you're not really married? Do you mean to say you don't love her?"

The questions came unexpectedly, in a flurry, betraying her anxiety, her hope. She fell suddenly silent, but if Basil noticed her embarrassment he was kind enough to fill the silence without hesitation. "That was how it started—but it developed from there. Shirin was in rather a vulnerable state herself over Goddy—and, well, you know how it is: a girl saved by a lifeguard returns to consciousness aware of her heart beating fast, the arms of the lifeguard around her, and associates her heartbeat with the lifeguard rather than a brush with drowning. She imagines she's in love with the man who's rescued her. It was the same with us. We married out of prudence, but the experiences we shared fastened the bond. There were a number of checkpoints at train stations and borders where you might say we held our breaths in unison—and so it grew."

"I see."

"All things considered, we were very fortunate."

"Why did you come to Bombay instead of back to London?"

"It was in the nature of things. There's an Indian Military School in Tashkent where the Indian Communist Party was born in 1920. Lenin had written an open letter of sympathy to all Indians in a nationalist newspaper as soon as he heard about the Amritsar massacre in 1919—General Dyer and all that."

"He never missed an opportunity, did he?"

"It's what made him Lenin, I suppose—and the letter served its purpose. Rebellious souls of all denominations slogged across the Hindu Kush mountains to Termez in Soviet Tadzhikistan where a Red Army band played them aboard a train bound for Tashkent. The rest, as they say, was history. Anyway, as it transpired there were people who had known Shirin's father, some had even met him in Moscow.

If not for them we might have been left languishing somewhere in a cell—or worse."

"Shirin must be very brave."

"That she is—and once we got here we decided to stay. We might leave again yet, but not for a while—not for the foreseeable future anyway, not with the war. I'm now the general manager of a firm manufacturing pills, soap, that sort of thing, just one of many Saklatvala enterprises—and I must say I rather like it. I rather like the humdrum, the routine of the day, the dependability of the income. Strangely enough, this is what my family had wanted for me all along and I gave it all up to become a communist, and now …" He smiled, shrugged.

"Did you ever finish your article?"

"'The Potemkin Pattern'?"

"Yes."

"No, and as far as I'm concerned that's a closed book. There are too many people who helped us who stand to get hurt if they were associated with me now. It's the same with the British Communist Party. They know what's going on, but their hands are tied. They have loved ones in the Soviet Union who would pay the price for their exposés. No, for myself, I'm content to cultivate my own garden, let the dead bury their dead. It's not my concern, if it ever was. You might say we learned our lesson the hard way—Shirin and I—about communism, lovely though the dream might have been."

Daisy gave him a sharp look. "Are you sure?"

Basil grinned. "Sorry. I may not sound it, the dream *is* lovely, but the more distance I develop the clearer it gets: it's just a dream, nothing more. For one thing, the Soviet communists don't seem to realize that what's good for the Soviet Union isn't necessarily what's good for Britain—nor, for that matter, for India or any other country, each of which seems to require its own particular mix of solutions for its own particular mix of problems, but the Soviets seem to have one way of doing things, and anyone who questions their way becomes suspect— round pegs in square holes, you know the sort of thing I mean."

Daisy looked away, pursing her lip.

"For another thing, the British Communist Party denounces the imperialism of Britain, but wants to monopolize the Indian Communist Party. Talk about the pot calling the kettle black. For *yet* another thing, communism absolves the rich of their guilt more than it resolves the problems of the poor—the Cambridge crowd's a perfect example of that sort of thing. In the same vein, the leaders of the Indian Communist Party are comprised mainly of a class of people whose families can afford expensive foreign educations—again, many at Cambridge." He shrugged. "You see, I *have* given it a great deal of thought—and I *have* learned my lesson." He might have said more, but Daisy was gazing into the distance. "Sorry. Enough about me. More to the point, what are you going to do next?"

Daisy stared into her rum and coke. Her voice grew small. "I don't know. Go back, I suppose."

"You can't go back. The seaways are closed—impossible to say for how long."

Daisy looked as if a close friend had died. She had planned to stay until she found Basil, but finding him married she had no plans, no future. Her body seemed to fade as she shook her head, her gaze to lose focus still staring into her rum and coke. She whispered. "I don't know what I'll do."

"I'll tell you what, Daisy. Why don't you stay with us? We have lots of space, plenty of room—really. I know Shirin would love to have you—and I'd love to show you around Bombay. You might as well see a bit of India while you're here. There's plenty to see and do. The difficulty –"

Daisy interrupted, her voice suddenly loud. "No! I don't think I would be comfortable."

"Daisy, you don't have to give me an answer right away. Just think about it. You'd have your own suite of rooms. You wouldn't have to see anyone if you didn't wish it—the house is that big. You could have one of the cars for your needs. You could have that kind of privacy. Just think about it."

"No, Basil, I couldn't."

"Daisy, all I'm asking is you think about it. I would feel better knowing you were all right."

"I'll be all right. Don't you worry about that. I'd just rather do it on my own."

"Daisy, just say you'll think about it. It's the least I can do. I owe you at least that much."

"You owe me nothing, Basil. You promised me nothing, and if I was fool enough to let my imagination get the better of me that's not your fault. You owe me nothing."

"Sorry. Bad choice of words. Of course, I owe you nothing. It's just something I would like to do—for myself more than for you. You'd be doing me a favor."

"Oh, Basil, please, there's no need to be condescending."

Basil was silent.

Daisy spoke with more confidence. "If you owe me anything at all, it's what you would owe anyone—to respect my decision. Give me at least that."

Basil nodded slowly. "Very well, then—but you must also give me this. *If* there is some way—*any* way—that I can be of help, you *must* let me know. Will you give me this?"

"All right, but you must leave it up to me. I think I need to be alone for a while. I need to think about a lot of things—alone. I shall count on you to leave me alone."

"Daisy, I can't promise that. I feel terrible about what's happened. I care about what happens to you. What kind of friend would I be otherwise?"

"It's what I want, Basil. For now it's *all* I want. If there is some way in which you can help I'll let you know. I've said I'll let you know. You must trust me."

"You leave me no choice, Daisy."

She looked away. "Then maybe you know something about how I feel."

THE RAIN THICKENED as they returned, drumming the roof of the Austin, drumming her head, the world a blur for the rain, for the tears she refused to release until she was alone again in her room, against the backdrop of thunder and lightning. She slept hounded by dreams: Basil and Shirin hounded by the NKVD; Basil and Shirin hounded by herself; Basil and Shirin safe, warm, dry, in a canopied bed under satin sheets; she in the compound outside, clawing at a French window, drenched, slouched, shivering, shut out by drapes and walls, hounds baying and snapping at her heels. She woke in the night, hair lank with humidity, sheets and pillows damp with sweat, damp with tears, to the rattling of her window. The black rectangle, drapes left undrawn for the first shafts of daylight, glowed like magnesium as thunderbolts struck the metal core of the earth. Unable to catch sleep in bed she secured the latch on the window to keep it from rattling, watched the sheets and streaks of light, slumping finally into slumber in a nearby chair, waking to a gleaming morning awake itself to the sounds of traffic and trains, the gurgle of pigeons sheltering under the eaves, the nasal caw of passing crows, the mewing of a cat which had been yowling through the night, concluding with the tap of the chaprassi at her door announcing breakfast: her tray of tea and toast.

She roused herself from her chair, crossing the room still strewn with clothes from the night before, passing the unmade bed, barely slept in, to let in the chaprassi with the tray. In the hallway the sweeper on his haunches swept with a long bushy broom drawing crisscross lines of dust on the floor, gathering the lines in a heap, sweeping the heap carefully into a dustpan. Once the chaprassi had gone she seated herself again by the window watching two squirrels chase each other in a tree with wide heartshaped leaves. The window, located on the side of the hotel toward the back, accommodated a narrow vertical strata of footpath, road, rails, road again, reclamation, sea, and sky into her field of vision, but most of all she was conscious of people wading the street, water brown and flooding, itinerant mangy animals, cows, goats, dogs, below her window the bedraggled yowling cat, on the windowsill a red ant lugging a breadcrumb twice its size, and everywhere the buzz and jig of flies, some single, some piggybacked in twos and threes, some huddled and whirling in tiny tornados. From somewhere came the whine of a car ignition helpless to flood into a roar.

The gleaming morning turned gloomy again as zeppelins of clouds loomed overhead, preparing a renewed assault. The rain had never stopped, merely lightened to a mist, and as the morning grew older it seemed to turn to night, curtains drawn across the sky. Someone tapped again at the door, a ganga to make the bed, the chaprassi to take the untouched tray, tea now cold in its kettle-in-a-cosy, butter like paste on the toast. She sat again by the window as they did their jobs, allowing the chaprassi to leave the tray after all, wishing not to hurt his feelings when he said in a loud astonished voice: "Food not good?" He smiled moving table and tray by the window. In the hallway the sweeper now swabbed, still on his haunches, running a damp cloth across the floor, dunking and wringing in a bucket of water.

Alone again she turned motionless again until a line of ants marched into the tray. It was twelve noon, but seemed twilight. Something happened that she didn't entirely understand, but someone slapped her face—hard. She started, jerked her head violently back, heard the slap like a loud clap, raised a hand to a reddening cheek only to realize she had slapped herself to snap herself out of her stupor. She had not moved in almost an hour and entered now into a flurry of activity, brushing the ants from the tray, pouring tea from the kettle, milk into the cold tea, adding sugar, stirring, drinking the sweet cold milky tea, alternating sips with bites of crumbling pasty toast. Unappetizing though the meal was it kept her moving, made her realize she needed to keep moving to keep from swooning into ennui. She tidied the room of her clothes, planning her day: lunch in the downstairs dining-room, shop for sandals, perhaps a good raincoat, perhaps other things, after the rain had lifted, explore the city, explore her options.

The rain didn't lift, but five o'clock found her in the hotel lounge, *Pride and Prejudice* on a corner table beside her, *The Times of India* in her hand, catching up on the war news, attempting to focus on matters not directly related to her, preferring the companionship of the lounge to the solitude of her room—not that there was anyone in the lounge but it was a public area. You were either kind or pompous calling it a lounge depending on whether you were guest or host—more of a waiting room, ceiling dank with mildew, plaster cracking on the walls, pictures of the royal family juxtaposed with pictures of Krishna, Christ, Gandhi, Nehru, and Jinnah among others in a way Daisy found schizophrenic. The rain had confined her physically, but she refused to be confined to her desperate thoughts though the news of the world was hardly less desperate. The Viceroy, Lord Linlithgow, had declared war on Britain's enemies on behalf of India without consulting a single Indian, prompting the resignation of the Congress, its refusal to aid the war effort—but the Muslim League backed the British, strengthening the hand of Mr. Jinnah who wanted a free Muslim state: Pakistan.

Someone entered the lounge whistling a tune, *Daisy, Daisy, Give me your answer true*, and looking up she found a damp smiling Sohrab Sanjana. "Well, well, well, Daisy Holiday, as I live and breathe. There you are, there you are."

He twirled his umbrella, spraying drops in a wheel of water, commas of hair plastered to his forehead, but she couldn't bring herself to return his smile. "Hullo."

He sat in an adjacent couch, pointing his umbrella at *The Times*. "You really mustn't sully your pretty little mind with such tawdry news, Daisy. It doesn't concern you."

"I actually know very little about it. I would like to know more."

"What for? Stuff and nonsense, that's what it is. That Jinnah, for example—he wants a free state, Pakistan he calls it." Sohrab shook his head. "He will never get it, and thank God—a perfect recipe for disaster, that's what it is—but these Congresswallahs are no less stupid. They've all resigned, strengthening Jinnah's hand—and he cares only about what he wants and not a jot about India."

# A Googly in the Compound

"I do actually find it very interesting. I wish I knew more about it. I like developing my own opinions about things."

"If you have questions, ask—ask away, ask to your heart's content. I shall be happy to answer all your questions. Just ask."

Daisy frowned. "Mr. Sanjana –"

He raised a cautionary finger. "No, please—Sohrab. I thought we settled that."

"No, Mr. Sanjana, you must excuse my rudeness, but I must ask you something first."

He shrugged. "I have already said: Ask away."

"Have you come to see me for Basil?"

Sohrab raised his eyebrows, looking past her.

"Please tell me the truth, Mr. Sanjana. I shall know it if you don't."

"Very well, then, since you put it like that, yes, he did give us a ring this morning. He asked us to keep an eye on you. He didn't want to say very much because he said it was personal, but he said the best things about you—and he was anxious about you—but that is not why I am here."

"Why are you here?"

"I meant to see you in any case—whatever Basil might have said or not said."

"What for?"

Sohrab took a deep breath. "You are very direct, Daisy, which is admirable—but it also makes it more difficult—what I want to say."

Daisy said nothing.

Sohrab picked up *Pride and Prejudice*. "Are you reading this?"

"I've read it before—but I'm reading it again."

He grinned. "Well, then, let me put it this way." He opened the book to the first page, read out loud. "'*It is a truth universally acknowledged, that a single man in possession of a good fortune must be in want of a wife.*'" He shut the book, still grinning, looking at her directly. "You see, that is my situation, and I must thank Jane for showing me the way."

Daisy took a deep breath fixing Sohrab with an incredulous stare. "Mr. Sanjana –"

"Please—Sohrab."

"Sorry ... Sohrab—are you—I mean, is this –"

Sohrab still grinned. "A proposal? If you wish it to be, it is. Sorry. I didn't mean it to come out quite so soon—certainly not so suddenly, and not in quite this fashion—but you left me little choice. You were so direct yourself—and I must say I'm not sorry. At least, now you know." He shrugged.

"I was direct, and I appreciate your candor—but we hardly know each other."

"That was why I came. I would like us to get to know each other better. I came to ask you to the cinema tonight. There's a new Gary Cooper picture at the Eros, *Lives of a Bengal Lancer*. We could have dinner afterward. What do you say?"

It seemed a lifetime, but it had been barely a day since she had seen Basil. It was still too early to emerge from the tunnel of her despair, but she smiled not knowing she was smiling.

"There, that's what I want to see, not that long doggy face. When you smile your dimples come out like stars. You should smile more—you should smile all the time."

She continued smiling. "I thought poetry was your brother's province."

"As you can see I just need the right inspiration—but what do you say? Shall we go to the show?"

"I'm afraid I saw that picture in London."

"It doesn't have to be that picture. It can be any picture. There's a Gable picture at the Regal, *Mutiny on the Bounty*. I think *Carefree* is playing at the Metro—Fred Astaire, Ginger Rogers. You have the newspaper there right in front of you. We can easily decide on a picture, but first you must say that you will come."

"Who will be with us."

"Nobody. Just us two."

"Not even your brother?"

"Why do we need him? If we want to get to know each other, what does it have to do with him?"

# A Googly in the Compound

"I just thought he might like to go."

Sohrab shook his head. "He wouldn't be interested. You see, he doesn't much like to *do* anything. These days he cares only about coelacanths." He laughed. "He thinks he's a coelacanth himself looking for a mate—that's all the chance he imagines he has."

"That's so sad."

"Yes, it's sad, but it's his choice—but enough about him. Do we have an agreement for tonight?"

"Yes, all right, I think I would like that—but what about this rain? Won't it be a nuisance?"

Sohrab raised a hand to forestall all further arguments. "Have no fear. I have a good old American car, a Ford. It rides so high it's as good as an elephant for fording any stream."

She rewarded him with her first laugh of the evening.


"You know, Daisy, I almost forgot."

"What?"

"Are you quite sure Aphoos said his ammy was dead?"

"Yes. Why?"

"Well, Mummy sent them some baksheesh with our condolences, and the strange thing is we got it back today with a letter saying Thank you very much, but their ammy is still very much alive and well. Mummy just felt terrible, as you can imagine. She apologized and sent the baksheesh back anyway. You must have been mistaken."

They had mounted the narrow spiral staircase to the upper level of Nanking's for dinner, ordered egg rolls, won ton soup, beef chop suey, sweet and sour pork, chicken fried rice. It was two weeks since Sohrab had first visited her hotel lounge, every day of which they had met for at least a meal, a different restaurant everytime, and twice revisited the cinema, but on weekends they had visited the zoo, Prince of Wales Museum, Hanging Gardens. She had spent time with the family as well, visiting Jilly's Emporium where she had selected an ivory letter-opener for a souvenir which Dolly had insisted she take as a gift. In need of friendship she had been comforted by the gesture, but afraid to select anything else in case it was given to her as well. Dolly, it seemed, couldn't do enough, nor the other Sanjanas, and Daisy was grateful in spite of herself. She shook her head. "It's possible, I suppose, but I'm *quite* sure that was what he said—especially with all his stories about her cookery. I suppose though that he might have been mistaken himself—I mean, in his information."

"It doesn't matter. It was just strange."

"It *is* strange." She frowned, staring past Sohrab.

"Nothing to talk about. I just thought I should mention it."

She continued to frown, staring past Sohrab. "I'm glad you did, but I don't understand it at all."

"Don't worry your pretty little head about it. These Indians are all the same, even the Goans. They don't know if they're coming or going. It might interest you to know that the Hindi word for 'tomorrow' is the same as the word for 'yesterday'—'kal'—and it's the same in Gujarati."

She was aware of his condescension toward her as much as toward Indians, but in the wake of his many kindnesses, the kindnesses of all the Sanjanas, it mattered less. Best of all, they had met friends of the Sanjanas at one of the restaurants, the Chinoys celebrating their seventh wedding anniversary with a quiet dinner, as much in deference to the war as to the weather. When Baji Chinoy, a reporter for the *Indian Express*, had learned she had published articles he had suggested she write human interest stories, "Impressions of Bombay," "Sailing the *Strathnaver*," "A Clash of Cultures," "A Tale of Two Cities," that sort of thing. Ideas had begun to ferment, and she once more to fill with a hope that she might carve a life for herself in Bombay. "Really? How can they know what they mean?"

"From the context."

"Just one of the anomalies of language, I suppose?"

"That's too kind an interpretation. Language *does* say something about the way a people think—sort of a key to the mind, wouldn't you say?"

"Yes, I suppose so, but I don't think it has anything to do with kindness. It may mean simply that 'time' is a more flexible concept in the East than in the West."

"I still say you are being too kind, and I still insist they don't know if they're coming or going, but that's neither here nor there."

"Very funny."

"It was meant to be. If anything, your interpretation is a credit to your broadmindedness."

She narrowed her eyes. "And yours to your narrowmindedness?"

He grinned. "No, my broadmindedness as well for putting up with your broadmindedness—not to mention your little darts always pricking my conscience."

She laughed, glad to see him take her jabs with good humor.

Sohrab leaned forward, elbows on the table. "That's just what I want to hear, Daisy. We *are* getting to know each other, aren't we? Isn't that what you wanted?"

She stopped herself midlaugh, drawing back in her chair, looking away, saying nothing.

"What is it, Daisy? It is what you wanted, isn't it?"

She took a deep breath, still looking away. "I'm afraid you may be getting the wrong idea."

"In what way wrong?"

"I may not be what you think, Sohrab. One can't get to know someone quite so very quickly."

"I know that, and it doesn't matter to me. One can never get to know a person as well as one might wish—but if one gets to know one enough the rest doesn't matter."

"And how does one know what's enough?"

"For me it was enough the day I first saw you. You reminded me of someone I had known in London, Edwina Carbury was her name, but it wasn't meant to be." He shrugged. "For me, that was enough, the resemblance. I felt I had been given a second chance and I want to make the most of it."

She narrowed her eyes. "Sohrab, I'm not what you think."

"Of course not, no one ever is, but it doesn't matter, don't you see? It only matters what I think of you, and what you think of me—then, whatever the reality, if we choose to make a go of it, we will become what we think of each other. They do say, you know, that married couples come to resemble each other after a while. Otherwise, just think: no one would ever get married. All we really need is the initial impulse and the wish to make it work."

"What about love?"

"If we tend to our responsibilities, love will come."

"And what if it doesn't?"

Despite her questions, aggressive and unexpected, the vulnerability of her situation made her easier to approach than Edwina Carbury had ever been; she was lost in his world as he'd been lost in Edwina's; leaving him beneficent, confident, powerful, smiling. "It will. We may have to change our definition of love, but come it will—if we tend to our responsibilities."

"Sohrab, I'm not what you think—I'm even less of what you think than I might be."

He blinked, had a glimmering of what she meant, but chose to be circumspect. "That is a very provocative statement, Daisy. What do you mean?"

"I'm ... I'm not ..."

"Not a virgin? Is that what you're trying to say?"

"I'm afraid so, yes."

It was a subject much in his thoughts since he had met her. He had known modern women during student days in London, modeled on the Mayfair set, the Bloomsbury Group, the putative New Woman, ushered by the war, among them Enid Fitton and Edwina Carbury, but had found himself banned from their inner circle, his own experience restricted to Soho prostitutes. Edwina had been fond of quoting a confounding statistic: the supposedly most moral of eras, the Victorian, had supported the highest number of prostitutes before or since. "Well, now, don't you suppose I knew that? Whatever it was you had with Basil, you don't have to tell me about it. That's the past—and so is my past the past. Let sleeping dogs lie is what I say. You're a modern woman, that's to be expected—and I am a modern man." He shrugged.

"Sohrab, it's more than that. I don't know what I would *do* here."

"Nothing! That's the beauty of it. You wouldn't have to do a thing."

"But I would have to do *some*thing. I would go mad if I did nothing."

"Well, then, you could do whatever you wanted. You could do what you did in London. You could write articles—you know, Baji would help you get them published."

She nodded, but said nothing.

"You could help Mummy and Daddy with Jilly's, you could start your own business. It would be entirely up to you."

Daisy helped herself to more sweet and sour pork, manipulating her chopsticks. "You have given me so much to think about." She sighed, shaking her head. "I don't know what to say."

"You don't have to say a thing. Take your time. Think about it. Take all the time you need." He became quieter the rest of the evening, uncomfortable that there was more to Daisy than he had imagined. A man's misadventures were to be accepted implicitly, part of his maturation, sowing wild oats before marriage—but a woman sowing wild oats was an animal of a different stripe, debased in a way a man could never be—and for him, wellborn, wellbred, wealthy, to marry a woman of that ilk.... She was, of course, English, and that excused much else that might otherwise have been objectionable. In India, for an Indian, it was enough for a girl to be English, not necessarily even pretty, and Daisy was pretty—but she had known another man, perhaps more than one, and he wished to claim at least the same satisfaction before marrying her, imagining himself otherwise less privileged than his predecessors when, as her spouse-in-waiting, he should have been more. His difficulty lay in presenting his case without giving offense.

Driving back to her hotel his silence grew palpable. Daisy guessed the source of his discomfort though nothing had been said. Lodged once more in the driveway she opened the car door, waiting once more for his perfunctory goodnight kiss. "Thank you again, Sohrab. I had a lovely evening."

He didn't look at her, but stared through the windshield. "Daisy, you have always been direct with me. I wonder if you will mind my being direct with you."

"Of course not."

"Well, then, I have already said we should let sleeping dogs lie, and I do mean it, but I can't help thinking about ... about your past, I mean—what it might have meant, what *they* might have meant. I would need to be sure that I meant at least as much to you."

She shut the door again. "How would you be sure?"

"That would be up to you."

"Are you talking about sex? Is that what it would take to reassure you?"

He marveled again at her directness. "Yes, I think that would make all the difference."

Her voice turned sharp. "Why? What do you think it would prove?"

"That you loved me."

"Have I said I loved you?"

"No—perhaps not necessarily that you loved me, but it *would* be an assurance."

"It might be a false assurance."

"It would still be something—a kind of pledge."

"A kind of deposit, you mean—a kind of installment on my purchase—testing the merchandise?"

"Ah, Daisy, you make it sound so sordid."

"How do *you* make it sound?"

Her voice had sharpened and, though he looked at her, she gazed through the windshield. "I'm sorry, Daisy. I've made you angry. That was not my intent. I should never have asked."

"I'm not angry."

"I think you are."

"You're right. I *am* angry, but not at you. I'm angry at myself."

"What for?"

The ugly realization had descended during dinner, settling like gravel in her gut, that Alphonse had staged a performance to win her sympathy, falsified the news of his ammy's death to manipulate her affection, lied to get what he had wanted, manufacturing tears like a faucet. Sohrab wanted no less, but he had drawn the line at lying. "Do you want to come upstairs?"

"Not if it makes you angry."

She was angry not only that Alphonse had lied, but that she realized she could never tell Sohrab about him: it would alter forever the complexion of a friendship upon which she had come to depend. The war had rendered the entire country an island, she was learning again how to swim, and he had proven himself a good teacher. "I told you. That is not what makes me angry."

"Well, then, what?"

He knew about Basil, but appeared to imagine a slew of men in his wake. She couldn't tell him about Alphonse, but sleeping with him could be her way of telling him more about herself, the kind of person she was—as close as she could get to telling him about Alphonse—leaving him to make up his own mind about what he wanted afterward. If, afterward, he decided he didn't want her, it still seemed the fairest decision. "You know, you haven't even kissed me properly yet."

"I didn't want to be presumptuous."

She laughed. He did everything backward: proposed before he propositioned her, and imagined he was presumptuous before even kissing her. She rolled her eyes. "You wouldn't be."

**A MONTH LATER,** awaiting Sohrab again in the lounge, sifting through newspapers and magazines, Daisy felt herself once more mistress of her fate. She couldn't have managed without the Sanjanas, least of all Sohrab, but meeting their friends, even dining with Shirin and Basil on two occasions, she was beginning to establish her independence again, fermenting the ideas Baji Chinoy had forwarded into articles.

Any hope she had entertained of returning to England had long been dashed by continuing news of the war—British forces had begun to land in France; more British ships had been sunk by German submarines; Warsaw had been decimated, Poland divided between Germany and the Soviet Union; the Soviets were demanding a rollback of their common boundary with the Finns—but she seemed in no immediate danger and there was nothing she could do about the news.

She looked forward to evenings with Sohrab who remained thoughtful and attentive, but after the night he had come to her room he had not broached the subject again. Wishing to allay the suspicion of his family he had not even stayed the entire night. Strangely, he had seemed to derive pleasure from her consent more than from sex itself, from what was premarital and illicit more than from the act, remaining for the most part quick, silent, efficient, utilitarian, the deed done in darkness, under covers despite the heat, without subsequent reference to the night. "Hullo. Ready?"

She looked up returning his smile. "Yes."

"Good. Let's go."

She got up, but lost her legs at once. For a moment her eyes caught his, in the next moment the room slid up and away, the threadbare carpet rose to strike her face. Sohrab was immediately beside her, helping her up, first to the sofa, then at her insistence back to her room where he held her head, keeping her hair from her face, while she vomited into the basin.

Later, after she had recovered, they sat in silence in her room. She wanted to believe her bold appetite for curry had finally caught up with her, but suspected a cause more grim. Sohrab suspected the grimmer cause, but knowing nothing about Alphonse found it hardly as grim. She had followed diligently the precepts outlined in Dr. Marie Stopes's manual on birth control given her years ago by Basil, knowing all the while they were fallible. When her breasts had grown tender she had ascribed it to growing pains; when her cycle had changed she had grown concerned; now she knew.

305

# DAY OF THE TIGER: 4
## (September 25, 1945)

SOHRAB WIPED HIS MOUTH with his napkin and slid the napkin through its ring. His thumb still bled from the cut and he sucked it again. Dolly sighed. "Really, Sohrab, I wish you would stop sucking your thumb like a baby and let me apply some mercurochrome. It will only take a minute to dab it with some cottonwool and tape it up."

Sohrab shook his head. "Mummy, that subject is closed." He looked toward the house. "Fakhro!"

Fakhro hurried down the steps and crossed the compound. "Han, sahib?"

"Tell Radha we are ready now for the papaya."

"Han, sahib." Fakhro turned to leave.

"Wait, Fakhro!"

"Han, sahib?"

"What is Victoria doing? Why isn't she up yet?"

Fakhro grinned. "Sleeping, sahib—still sleeping. She like to sleeping all the time. Very lazy girl."

If Sohrab was amused he didn't show it. "Well, wake her up. It's late in the day. She's getting into very bad habits. She is not a princess, after all."

Dolly smiled. "No princess, but a queen—Queen Victoria."

"Very funny. Fakhro, go! Do as I say! Wake up Victoria! Bring her here!"

## A Googly in the Compound

"Sahib, she not like to be wake up. She wake up when she ready. She wake up when she hungry. When she is wake up I will take her food."

Dolly shook her head, amused. "Now she won't wake up. When she was a baby she wouldn't sleep."

They had received Victoria days after her birth (three pounds of blind boneless fluff, just large enough to perch like a glove on the back of one's hand) and set her initially in a wooden crate lined with blankets in Dinyar's room, but her yowling the very first night had kept the family up, bringing her a bottle of formula every three hours and a dry blanket almost as frequently. Daisy had managed the chores the first night, the others cooing and crowding around, but after the second night even Dinyar and Neville wanted their sleep and Victoria was relegated to the care of Patty and Nancy (the ayahs) in their room.

On her eleventh day Victoria had opened amber eyes, on her twelfth wobbled across the floor, on her fifteenth climbed out of her crate, on her twentieth followed Dolly around tugging her sari—but it wasn't until her twenty-fifth day, to the great relief of the ayahs, that she had slept the night through.

Sohrab stared at Dolly, debating whether to ignore her, when two shots rang from beyond the compound. A monolithic howl erupted, shattering into echoes and reverberations to spread like debris through the forest. Squadrons of monkeys scattered and scampered through the treetops like a gale, whooping and hollering, dislodging bark, twigs, and fruit. A terrified voice screamed: "AIYO! AIYO!" The most terrifying sound erupted closest of all, a low moan swelling into a hard, thick, ominous, growl.

The sounds overlapped, following in quick succession, resonating like a single strange instrument, directing everyone's attention toward the gates of the compound. Fakhro spoke almost under his breath. "Rani is wake up now. I will get food ready."

He called her Rani, as did his family, finding it easier than Victoria, not understanding the difference—which, as Dolly said, was a matter of semantics: in living memory there was no queen to match Victoria. Sohrab stopped him as he turned. "First tell Radha to bring the papaya. Then bring Victoria to us. She can eat afterward. What else has she got to do all day?"

Fakhro looked away frowning, but nodded. "Han, sahib."

Running footsteps and a continuous mumble of "aiyo, aiyo" announced Alphonse's return. He slowed to a walk at the compound gate, apparently embarrassed by his flight. "My God, very clever they are, you know, these monkeys. Throwing things, sticks and ... I don't know what else ... kaka, I think. Very dirty they are."

Sohrab didn't smile. "Why are you back already?"

"I shot. You said to shoot. I shot. I came back. What else?"

"One shot you made and came running back like a little boy—like a scaredy-cat."

"Arre, sahib, they were throwing things—and you said not to hurt them. What else to do?"

"Aphoos, don't be silly. When they get scared they jump up and down and of course things are going to fall from the trees. That is all. No one was throwing things at you. No need to get so damn pompous about the whole thing."

"No, sahib! They know! They know who it is!"

"What are you saying? You think this is a personal matter? You think they are going to come after you? You think they have your name and address? You think they are going to call you on the telephone? Man, what are you thinking?"

"They know, sahib. That is all I am saying."

"Well, whatever it is, I want you to go back and let off some more shots. Just one shot is not going to make the message clear. Go on."

"Sahib, I shot two times. Ask anyone. They must have heard."

"Well, then, I want you to go back and shoot two more times. Do you understand? I will be counting. Go on. What are you waiting for?"

"Sahib, I am not going back."

"Why not? I thought you said you had shot monkeys in Goa? Why are you so scared now?"

"I am not scared, but in Goa there were not so many monkeys. Here I am one, they are many."

"You may be one, but you have an automatic—and they are monkeys, for crying out loud—not ... tigers, not cobras—not jackals even, for god's sake."

"Sahib, I am not well. I told you. I came for my health. This is not good for my health."

"You are still a scaredy-cat, Aphoos—still a cowardy custard." Sohrab grinned, enjoying the epithets of their childhood. "Daisybai and Dollybai have both shot at the monkeys before. They don't come running back crying like babies—not like you, a big grown man who has shot monkeys in Goa."

Daisy smoothed the lap of her skirt, speaking loudly enough for Alphonse to hear. "If he's going to be such a coward about it, I'll go. I won't be long."

Dolly raised her eyebrows, as surprised to see Daisy make it a personal matter as Sohrab. "Daisy, first finish your breakfast. Have some papaya. Have more tea."

Radha had brought the bowl of sliced and sugared papaya back, placed it on the table, and disappeared into the house. Sohrab, no less surprised than Dolly to hear Daisy make it a personal matter, grinned, imagining she was making up for her earlier recalcitrance. "See? Daisybai is willing to go. She is not afraid. She is not a scaredy-cat."

Daisy placed a hand on Sohrab's. "It's all right, darling. Some men are cowards. They can't help it. I'll go after breakfast."

She had not spared Alphonse a glance, but watching her his face congealed. He knew she was goading him, but couldn't resist. "I will go." He gripped the gun more firmly. "I am not a coward. I will go. I will show you."

Daisy lifted her hand from Sohrab's as soon as Alphonse disappeared. Sohrab looked at her. "Thanks, Daise."

"Whatever for?"

"Solidarity."

"Oh, you're welcome, I'm sure."

She was nonchalant again as before, and Sohrab turned again to the house. "Fakhro!"

"Han, sahib?"

"Let Victoria out. Bring her here."

"Han, sahib."

The volume of Victoria's moans swelled as Fakhro approached her room. When he unlatched the door she was silent again, coming to the entrance, poking her head out, looking around as if she were gauging the weather. The stripes of her face were black and white, flaring to fluffy mutton chops behind her cheeks, converging to a furry point under her jaw. Along her neck and shoulders white stripes gave way to orange as she ambled into view, appearing longer than her four and a half feet, taller than her two and a half feet, heavier than her hundred and forty pounds. Once fully visible she stopped, yawning to reveal a mouth large enough to engulf a baby's head, jaws and fangs strong enough to crack the leg of a pony. The Sanjanas were momentarily silenced. Daisy was the first to speak, under her breath. "My word! She's a beauty, isn't she?"

Dolly nodded. "Yes, but could be dangerous, don't you think?"

Phiroze shifted in his chair. "Time to put her in the zoo—probably been time for a while already."

Victoria, apparently unaware of her audience, stretched (head to the ground, tail rotating in the air like a periscope) before continuing her stroll across the compound.

Dolly spoke again. "So well she walks, no? Do you remember, Phiroze, how she used to jump around like a puppy dog?"

Phiroze spoke thoughtfully. "She is no puppy dog now."

Sohrab spoke last of all. "That is for a certainty that she is no puppy dog. She was hardly this big even just three months ago when we came with the boys."

Fakhro smiled, standing by. "Growing very big now, sahib—growing very big very fast—my youngest and biggest daughter: Radha, Rekha, Rupma, and Rani."

## A Googly in the Compound

Sohrab was aware of his daughters in a row at the windows, also that Fakhro had closed the door. "Why have you closed the door? She is not dangerous, is she? She has not hurt anyone, has she?"

"No, sahib, but Rani veryvery big now—get hurt just playing."

"Arre, she is still a baby, she is just a big kitty. Bring her here."

"Han, sahib."

"Sohrab, be careful!"

Sohrab grimaced. "Yes, Mummy. Of course, I will be careful. She is not a teddy-bear, I know."

Two shots sounded from the forest and confusion reigned again, the monolithic eruption, a hurricane of monkeys in the trees, but no squawk emerged from Alphonse. All eyes remained on Victoria who stiffened, growling and staring in the direction of the noise. The Sanjanas watched in admiration, not without fear, but as the vault of the forest emptied again Victoria seemed to forget it altogether, as easily diverted by her own tail which next captured her attention. Sohrab smiled again as Victoria's head followed the movement of her tail. "What did I tell you? She may be big, but in her mind she is still a kitty. Her habit is still to act like a baby. She has never learned to hunt. She has no idea of her own power. She might look dangerous, but she wouldn't hurt a fly."

Victoria rose on her hindlegs, attempting to catch a butterfly between her paws, but lost her balance and fell on her side the butterfly bobbing overhead.

Sohrab laughed and Victoria turned her head toward the group, seeming aware of her company for the first time. Her face distended in a smile, as if she were embarrassed, and Sohrab laughed again. "Just look at her, smiling like a big old sheepdog. See? What did I tell you? She may be big, but she's still a baby. Bring her, Fakhro. Bring her here."

"Han, sahib."

"Sohrab, please!"

"Mummy, please yourself! Give me some credit! I am not a complete fool."

The others remained impassive, Phiroze frowned, but no one said another word; Sohrab meant to have his way. Victoria seemed oblivious to Fakhro's approach, but when he touched her shoulder she rubbed herself against his side, purring like a dozen muted trombones. When he walked she continued rubbing herself against him, almost pushing him over. He stopped when he was standing between Sohrab and Daisy. Fakhro scratched her head and neck, brushing her fur in the direction of its nap, playing with her ears, until she turned her head to lick his hand.

Sohrab moved his hand slowly to caress Victoria's neck. "Her fur is getting rougher and rougher—almost as rough as her tongue, like sandpaper. I am sure she could peel the skin of her prey just by licking it." He manipulated Victoria's attention from Fakhro while Daisy stroked the tiger's back and flank. "Go, Fakhro! Bring her food! She will eat it here."

"Han, sahib." Fakhro eased himself away from Victoria and walked back to the house.

Someone spoke, startling the company. "My God, sahib, he will bite you, no?"

Intent on Victoria no one had noticed Alphonse's return, but there was no mistaking his awe, eyes wide and white as golf balls, voice full of air. Sohrab looked up. "First of all, *he* is a *she*—and no, she will not bite. She is our family pet. She has been with us since she was a baby. She will not bite the hand that feeds her. Come here, no? She will let you touch her if you want."

Alphonse shook his head, keeping his distance. "No, sahib, I will stay here. I will keep the gun."

Daisy, also stroking Victoria, glared again at Alphonse, but said nothing.

Dolly noted Daisy's discomfort, but Sohrab remained oblivious. "Come on, Aphoos, show some courage. Victoria will not hurt you. See? We should have just called her Rover." Victoria purred, rolling onto her back beside Sohrab, inviting him to scratch her chest, paws dangling over his hand as he obliged, chuckling knowingly. "See?

## A Googly in the Compound

She is just a big kittycat." Victoria rolled onto her stomach to sit and lap his palm like a saucer of milk. "Not so much, Victoria. You have a very rough tongue—like the back of a hedgehog. You will scrape the skin right off my hand." He tried to remove his hand, but Victoria held it between her paws, her purr rising to a growl. She clamped his hand firmly at the wrist, almost pulling him to the ground, lapping at beads of dark red blood released by her tongue, the pressure of her paws, from the cut reopened on his thumb. Fear enveloped him like a cave of ice. He was afraid to pull his hand away forcibly, afraid she might fight for what she imagined was hers already, afraid for what he might already have lost, a fear which permeated the air, gradually enveloping the other Sanjanas in Sohrab's cave of ice as they became aware of his predicament.

Daisy stopped patting Victoria's side but hesitated otherwise to move, measuring the distance between Victoria and the gun in Alphonse's hand, imagining the possibilities.

# RUSTOM'S STORY
## Burma (1941-1942)

**SOHRAB'S MARRIAGE** to Daisy had been as sudden as it had been unexpected, as had been Daisy's pregnancy and the birth of Dinyar—but so was Rustom's decision to leave Bombay though he spoke as if nothing could have been more normal. "I want to be useful. That's all." They sat around the coffee-table in the sitting-room of Sanjana House, the brothers, their parents, and Daisy cradling Dinyar, her baby of three months.

Sohrab chuckled from his armchair. "You will be most useful if you just go. You don't even have to do anything."

Dolly's eyes flashed a warning at Sohrab, but drooped as she turned again to Rustom sharing a couch with Daisy. "What nonsense! At a time like this the most useful thing you can do is to stay with your family. We all need to stick together as a family. Why does it have to be right now? Why can't you just wait until things have settled down a bit before you try to be useful?"

Rustom knew what she meant. Owing to the war it had been a year like no other and it wasn't over yet. "Mummy, it's just that I've waited too long already. So much is going on in the world, and everyone is doing his bit, but all I have done is wait. I'm tired of waiting."

Sohrab was almost gleeful. "They never serve who only stand and wait."

Dolly turned sharply on her older son. "Sohrab! Shut up!"

## A Googly in the Compound

Daisy had never questioned the rivalry between the brothers and never been so curious as to inquire. She lived too precariously in the glass house of her own duplicities to throw stones, but she was as surprised at Dolly's temper as at Rustom's amiability. "Mummy, no! Sohrab is right. He has always been right on this point. It's just taken me this long to realize it."

"Bravo, Rustom! Better late than never."

Dolly ignored him. "What I don't understand is what has made you realize it now of all times."

"I think I was just waiting for a chance like this without even knowing what I was waiting for."

"To dash off to Ahmednagar of all places? Why Ahmednagar, for God's sake? If you want to be useful, surely you can find some way to be useful in Bombay?"

"Mummy, I'm not saddling up for Siberia or Timbuktu or some other such godforsaken place. Ahmednagar is a morning's train ride from Bombay. You can visit anytime you want."

"But why do you have to go at all? Why can't you do whatever you have to do in Bombay?"

"Mummy, I've already told you."

"Ah, yes, that Bhaskar Banerjee, your good friend."

She spoke ironically. Bhaskar Banerjee was Rustom's college friend whose uncle had come into the inheritance of a building in Ahmednagar on condition that he realize the dream of the donor, a dream shared by the uncle, to open a school. The building had come with some money, but fundraising was a continual task, and knowing the Parsi reputation for philanthropy and enterprise Bhaskar had approached his friend. Rustom had proven generous not only with the Sanjana Charitable Trust, but offered his own services, asking only room and board in return, a room in the school building, board at the school canteen.

Phiroze, next to Dolly in the sofa, squeezed her hand. "Darling, it could be worse, you know."

Dolly turned tired eyes on Phiroze, recognizing herself beaten if he imagined the cause lost. "Of course, it could be worse. Things can always be worse. What does that prove? Nothing. And then to go and live like a mendicant."

Rustom smiled, rising from his couch to sit beside Dolly, putting his arm around her shoulders, kissing the top of her head. "Poor Mummy! Simply cannot understand why anyone would want to live beneath his means."

Dolly shook her head, embarrassed and gratified by his show of affection. She didn't know whether to be relieved or not. Rustom had slid into lethargy for years since Sohrab's cricket injury, and she no longer knew what to make of her younger son. He appeared at times to have succumbed to the melancholia that had affected Kavas—to a lesser degree, but considering their experience she wondered continually if they should have made more of the symptoms. She should indeed have been glad he was showing some initiative. "I do wish someone would explain it to me. Who does he think he is? Gandhi?"

Rustom had been as good as his word to Sohrab, crossing him in nothing, giving in to him in all things, more horrified about his dislocated shoulder than anyone else, clouding himself in shame and penitence, palpably shrinking into his life until Daisy's arrival. Sohrab was right: there she had been, a helpless bit of a thing, a year younger than himself, with so much more to show for her young life than he. "I want to live humbly, Mummy. Think of it as a kind of Ramadan, a spiritual exercise."

"Oh, so now, out of the blue, you're a Mohammadan?"

"No, Mummy, not out of the blue, and not a Mohammadan either. I have wanted to do something for a long time. I just want to give something back. We are so fortunate in everything we have. We throw away more food everyday than many people consume. I just want to do my bit, give something back."

"Oh, so now we should all give up everything we have to live like mendicants."

"No, Mummy, that's *not* what I'm saying. We have to do what's right for us, and this is what is right for me. That's all I'm saying."

Daisy rocked baby Dinyar harder, silent because her loyalties were divided between Dolly and Rustom, grateful to Dolly for her huge generosity in everything, but empathizing with Rustom more than anyone might understand. The Battle of Britain was raging, and grateful as she was for her good fortune, snug in the harbor of the Sanjana home, she wished she might be among her countrymen in their hour of greatest need. She might have said something, but for the falsity of her own position.

"Sir?"

Rustom, seated with Bhaskar, looked up from his lunch of masoor dal with chapatis. The canteen on the ground floor of the King George VI High School for Boys was lined with two long rows of wooden tables and benches. The meals were the simplest, dal with rice and spiced vegetables and chapatis, and once a week meat. He ate from a thali with his fingers. "Yes? Hullo, Pradeep? What is it?"

Pradeep Chandrasekhar was fifteen, a short studious boy in white shorts and shirt. Straight black hair clouded his brow and a diffident expression his face. Behind him stood Vijay Sarkar and Rohit Mittal, both in the same school uniform, both smiling unlike Pradeep who had apparently been elected spokesman. "Sir, may I just say you are the best English teacher we have ever had."

Vijay and Rohit nodded enthusiastically.

"Han, sir, best ever."

"Yes, sir, first best."

Rustom smiled. "Thank you. Very kind of all of you to tell me."

The diffidence disappeared from Pradeep's face. "We are meaning it, sir. We are learning so many things about so many things. Never expected."

Rustom nodded. He taught English, but reveled in sandwiching his many obsessions into his lessons, astronomy, oceanography, icthythiology. He had found a safe harbor for coelacanths and the big dipper, Beethoven and the Battle of the Marne, as he could never have imagined among students who once forewent a game of cricket to hear about Achilles and Hector bounding around the battlements of Troy. He had wanted little more than to be useful, but the affection and appreciation of his students had become an unexpected bonus. "Very glad to hear that, Pradeep—because, you know, it's a two-way street. You might say we have a Mutual Admiration Society."

The boys' smiles touched their ears.

"Yes, sir. Mutual Admiration."

"Yes, sir. Mutual. Most definitely."

The conversation ground to a halt, but the boys remained smiling and Rustom at a loss for words. Bhaskar had watched the proceedings with amusement, understanding Rustom's pride as much as his embarrassment. He was a small man with sharp handsome features, a glorious head of gleaming Brylcreemed hair, and smiled coming to Rustom's rescue. "Okay, now, boys, if you have nothing else to say I think you should let Mr. Sanjana finish his lunch."

The boys nodded, backing away, except Pradeep who dug into his pocket. "One more thing, sir, we are asking. Will you please sign our autograph books?"

Rustom raised his masoor-stained fingers as Raj and Rohit also dug into their pockets. "Let me finish my lunch, okay? Come back in fifteen minutes, okay? I will gladly sign."

The boys backed away again.

"Yes, sir. Of course, sir."

"Fifteen minutes. Yes, sir. We will come back."

Bhaskar looked pitifully at his friend, shaking his head. "All this adulation, and still you are going? Are you quite sure you are not making a mistake?"

Rustom pursed his lips. "Can't be sure. Still thinking about it."

The King George VI High School for Boys on Station Road had opened with thirty-one students and two teachers, but by its fourth year, when Rustom had joined, the complement had mushroomed to two hundred and three students and eighteen teachers. His room was one of a row on the top floor of a two-storey brick building, fronted by a flagstoned portico, embracing a courtyard behind. A narrow bed and desk lined one wall, cupboard and set of shelves the opposite wall, and he shared the bathroom at the end of the corridor outside his room with the boys. His one article of luxury, sent by Dolly, was a carpet covering the middle of the room. Nothing upset him, not even tanks trundling occasionally from the railway station to the military cantonment, not even the ground trembling under his feet. Station road itself was otherwise brilliant, gulmohors blossoming pink and orange in the spring, bougainvillea climbing the walls of the houses. Bhaskar waved a hand in the direction of the boys. "You heard what they said just now, no?"

Rustom nodded.

"My uncle told me once, to get the measure of a man you must talk to his subordinates—teacher and students, sergeant and privates, doctor and nurses, executive and secretaries, master and servants, and so on and so forth. Do you realize what those boys are actually saying about you? They are not just talking about what kind of a teacher you are. They are talking about what kind of a man you are."

"I know, I know, and I'm very grateful—to them, and to you for this opportunity."

Bhaskar had been rolling a ball of rice with his fingers for a minute. His voice descended to a scold. "But still you want to go, join the army, maybe get yourself killed—not even for your country, for a foreign country—not even because your family needs the money, but just because … for what reason? Explain this to me please. I do not understand."

Rustom could not have been happier with his year in the school, he had uncovered depths within himself, talents he had not known he possessed, but his Ramadan had brought him more joy than expiation. The difficulties of the Spartan life had been so ameliorated by his success as a teacher he might as well have stayed in the lap of Sanjana luxury in Bombay. He needed another way, a more significant

Ramadan. "I appreciate what you are saying, Bhaskar, and I appreciate everything you have done for me, but I cannot explain what I do not understand myself. I am a big man. The army needs big men."

Bhaskar's eyes hardened. "With that kind of logic, you are better off talking about coelacanths. Your size only makes you a bigger target, easier for bullets to find you. What are you thinking, man?"

"My father was in the army. That is enough for me."

"Your father lost his arm, man! What are you thinking? Your family will blame me—and with good reason. If you appreciate what I am saying, then listen to what I am saying. Don't go. Stay here."

Rustom shook his head. "They cannot blame you. They can blame only me."

Ahmednagar<br>5-12-1941

My dear Mummy and Daddy,

By the time you receive this letter, I shall be somewhere in Burma. I have enlisted and am now a member of the 12th Frontier Force Regiment of the 46th Infantry Brigade of the 17th Infantry Division of the Indian Army. You will say I have not thought it through and you may be right. Enlisting is my way of thinking it through, but please take it easy. I would not deliberately put myself in harm's way. I am not stupid. It just seems like a natural progression. The 17th Infantry Division was formed just this year right here in Ahmednagar, and we will be taking a train to Madras and shipped to Burma in a rush only to maintain a presence—mainly as a deterrence, to show the Japs that we are not to be caught napping.

I know you will worry, but there is really nothing to worry about. Nobody believes Burma will be attacked at all. The eastern border is protected by Siam which is neutral, and the only other way is by sea. But in order to do that they will have to get past the British at Singapore and Singapore is impregnable. As you may know, on 2 December the HMS Repulse and the HMS Prince of Wales were stationed there. Both battleships have a formidable reputation. There is no way the Japs can get past them.

You may also recall that old ditty from the last war:
Where was I when the war was on?
I can hear a faint voice murmur.
Where was I when the war was on?
In the safest place—in Burma.

We are to be in Burma because whatever the circumstances it is imperative to show that we are prepared. That is all. We have received some training already, but much of our training will take place on board ship and then again in Rangoon where we will be based. You can write to me, of course, at the address on the envelope. I will look forward to hearing from you and trust you will not worry too much.

My one regret is that I will miss the birth of Dinyar's brother—or sister! It really should be a girl this time. We Sanjanas have a dearth of girls in the family. We're good at marrying them, but not at giving them birth. God bless you, Daisy! Boy or girl, I know you're going to have a lovely bouncing baby.

A kiss for little Dinyar from his favorite uncle!
Yours affectionately,
Rustom


"Omigod! Omigod! Omigod! Like father, like son! Omigod! I should have known. I should never have let him go to Ahmednagar. *Take it easy*, he says! What is he thinking? *Stu*pid boy! The *same* thing is happening all over again, *just* like before. Omigod!"

Rustom's letter lay crumpled on the floor. Dolly sat on her bed, head bowed to her knees, beating the bed with her fists, face contorted with fear, wrinkles multiplying by the minute. Phiroze sat in an armchair, understanding Rustom's actions perhaps better than his wife (son of his father that Rustom was, decamping to war as his father had done), but recognizing that nothing he could say or do would make a difference. They had no sooner recognized that Daisy was not to be a bone of contention between their sons than Rustom had breathed new life into their anxiety.

"*It could be worse!* you said. Oh, yes! Oh, yes! It could be worse. How much worse is it going to get now, *han?* Tell me! How much worse is it going to get?"

Phiroze remained still, reaching to comfort her only when she dissolved into loud ugly sobs, shaking as if she had a fever, sitting beside her, holding her tight.

A MAP MAY BE READ like an inkblot. You may see in the map of Burma a genie materializing from a lamp, broad in the head and shoulders, narrowing to a wisp in the waist. You may also see a manta ray, a wraith of rising smoke, or the flared head of a cobra at bay. Rustom saw a monkey on a branch with a long skinny monkey tail half the length of its body, and imagined opportunities to observe the difference that was Burma, experience firsthand what he had known forever from books. He could not have been more mistaken.

Regarding the Japanese he could be certain only that he could be certain of nothing. They continually confounded expectations. No one had expected them to attack America, but they had attacked Pearl Harbor. No one had expected them to get past the *Repulse* and *Prince of Wales* at the British stronghold in Singapore, but they had demolished both battleships. No one had expected them to haul troops and transport to the eastern Burmese border, but they had crossed the border and seized the three British airfields in southernmost Burma, the monkey tail of the country.

From the airfields they had launched the first air strikes on Rangoon at Christmas. Sixty bombers had raided Rangoon's airfield and docks. The city had been defended by the RAF and AVG, each outfitted with just one fighter squadron. Everyone knew the Royal Air Force, but the American Volunteer Group was new, the brainchild of Brigadier-General Chennault. Called the Flying Tigers by the Chinese, they were among the most glamorous units in any war. Dressing in zippered leather jackets and Hawaiian shirts, they painted the noses of their Tomahawks with gaping red mouths and rows of sharp white teeth.

The air raids had continued into the new year, but the RAF and AVG had proven so formidable, losing just two to forty-two enemy aircraft, that the Japanese had restricted their bombers to night flights only—and sad Burmans, mesmerized by the sights, as if the battles were Hollywood extravaganzas, came to watch when they should have been taking cover and died in consequence, crushed or incinerated or blown to pieces, two thousand in the first night, a hundred thousand fleeing the city overnight, Burmans escaping into the jungle, Indians seeking routes to India by land and sea.

Shipped to Rangoon for maneuvers Rustom's brigade had been transported to defend a four-hundred-mile front, to keep the enemy from crossing the rivers, first the Salween, then the Bilin, and finally the Sittang. Bolstered by just two other brigades they had been hopelessly outnumbered, and considering the extent of their training as hopelessly outmatched even had their numbers been even. It was part of a strategy called forward defense, surrendering the line inch by bloody inch, but the title was a misnomer considering it was all backward defense, retreating from one location to the next in the rump of the Burma monkey on their way to their last stand: the bridge across the Sittang. Left undefended, the bridge would provide a welcome mat for the enemy into Rangoon.

The city had been evacuated. Prisons and asylums had loosed convicts and lunatics to join looters and arsonists in the streets.

Police ordered to shoot looters on sight were not above looting themselves. The great houses of the city flamed into the sky like giant lanterns, screams of innocents mingling with shrieks of criminals and crazies. Food, petrol, ammunition, and medical supplies had been backloaded mostly to Mandalay; but surrendering the city would mean surrendering the docks, and surrendering the docks would mean surrendering the only land supply route to China via the Burma Road.

Any residual notions Rustom might have entertained regarding the difference that was Burma had been demolished by the engagement at the Bilin. They had stopped the advance of two Japanese divisions, but it had reduced their retreat to a sorry straggling column of men with red eyes, grey faces, sandpaper beards, matted hair, limbs encrusted with dirt, rags binding their wounds splotched with blood. Their uniforms were torn, khaki shirts striped with sweat, white from dried salt of the day before, black with new perspiration, their divisional insignia hardly distinguishable despite the bright yellow of a bolt of lightning flashing diagonally from bottom to top across a black square. They led mules and donkeys amid ox-drawn carts, but the hot dry climate had emptied their canteens of water, and though they held on to their rifles and bren guns most of their ammo pouches had been emptied at the Bilin. They expected replenishments of troops and supplies from Rangoon at the Sittang, but meanwhile the motor transport (convoys of trucks carrying wounded among other things) kept pace with the oxen, two miles an hour, forbidden by the discipline of the march to speed ahead, hindered no less by lack of dependable wireless communication. From the air the column of thousands, without provost to guide them, resembled a giant meandering centipede so long that head and tail often did not know how the other was doing.

Rustom's section of the column was ankledeep in a chaung, almost to the other side, behind them paddy fields, ahead jungle. A dirt track barely wide enough for two vehicles to pass led into the jungle, when they heard the drone of planes in the distance. Looking into the setting sun above the trees he could distinguish black dots of fighter aircraft and hurried to gain the security of the jungle, as did the entire column breaking ranks to surge forward. The planes arrived with such speed, diving to treetop level, that they seemed to materialize fullblown into sight. Spooked by the noise, animals stiffened and brayed and bellowed as men attempted to push them aside, but Rustom laughed with relief seeing markings of the AVG on the nose of the foremost plane, the grin of a shark, not the red blot of the rising sun. Others, no less joyous, jumped and waved and hollered—as the planes bore down on them, spraying bullets.

Rustom stopped midlaugh, jaw distended, as parallel rows of bullets splashed parallel rifts in the water toward him faster than he could see. Animal transport carrying weapons, wireless, water, and rations vanished into the jungle, lost forever. Men and animals screamed and fell to his left and right. A donkey rose on its hind legs before him, its head seeming to twist through a circle before twisting itself off its neck, blanketing the sky with blood. Rustom was almost crushed by its torso, but dodged in time though it knocked him off his feet. Rising, he charged across the chaung and into the jungle suddenly with the energy of a man rested for days.

They learned later that air reconnaissance had mistakenly reported an enemy column of three hundred vehicles marching to the Sittang and all available aircraft at Rangoon had been ordered to attack, but as Rustom said the dead would have cheered to hear it. No Japanese attack could have been worse for morale. The donkey, taking several bullets for him, had proven a boon more than the AVG. The night came so quickly his clothes remained wet and he shivered, as cold by night as he'd been hot by day.

He was to rise from the rump of Burma to the bowels and through various internal organs to be shot up the gullet and hawked from the mouth back into India, and he was to count himself fortunate. Men were being killed around him with no more consideration than cockroaches. He hadn't known how well off he had been talking about coelacanths at the King George VI High School for Boys.

# RUSTOM'S STORY

**THE SITTANG RIVER FLOWED** north to south from the Shan Plateau, southeast of Mandalay, through the rump of the Burma monkey into the Gulf of Martaban. Its width, where it was bridged, was about a mile, wider when the tide came in, and considerably wider above and below the crossing. The bridge of stone and steel supported a railway, but had been decked to support road transport as well. The field of operations that night comprised six square miles, and from the air the head of the giant meandering centipede appeared to diverge into multiple colonies of ants.

Rustom's was one of three brigades commanded by Major-General J. G. Smyth, heading for the bridge from the southeast. The narrow dusty path they had traveled, which passed for a road, pocked with potholes and bomb craters, had taken the column past a rubber plantation and through jungle infested with monkeys chattering in the trees, but Rustom had long lost interest in the flora and fauna of Burma. They had been bombed continually, by enemy and allied aircraft alike, losing men and animals and transport, not to mention confidence, self-respect, and faith in their commanding officers.

The road converged with a railway at Mokpalin and traveled in parallel until the railway swung west to the bridge and the road northeast through more jungle and rice paddies toward the village of Sittang. Between the bridge and the village the land was marked by Pagoda Hill to the west dominated by a pagoda, and Buddha Hill to the east dominated by an image of Buddha. The column, approaching from the southeast, was so long that even as its head reached the bridge its tail, including Rustom's brigade, remained at Mokpalin, three miles distant, still mired along the jungle path powdered by dust.

Smyth's objective was to get his brigades across the river before the Japanese arrived, but the bridge could be crossed only in single file—and a truck with a wheel wedged between girders had held up the line for more than three hours. He didn't know that his orders to retreat from the Bilin to the Sittang had been intercepted by Lieutenant-General S. Sakurai who had pushed his troops toward the bridge from the northeast even as Smyth pushed his from the southeast. Sakurai had breached a gap between two of Smyth's brigades, commandeering Buddha Hill from which he attempted to commandeer Pagoda Hill. Smyth had formed a bridgehead between the hills to allow his brigades safe access across the bridge, and set sappers to prepare the bridge for demolition in the event they were unable to defend it.

Rustom's brigade, hearing the shooting, deployed for action. Experience had taught them something about Japanese strategy (they attacked in a scorpion formation, brigades branching out from the sides for three-pronged assaults; they doubled behind their adversaries to create roadblocks, cutting off lines of retreat; they feigned surrender only to kill troops accepting the surrender)—but they knew nothing of what was happening at the bridge and remained constantly wary, or as wary as days of watchfulness allowed, asleep on their feet, the sound of mortar and gunfire reduced to white noise.

Ahead of Rustom tramped Ashok Sharma, a camel-driver from Rajasthan, and behind him Narayan Patel, a dairy farmer from Gujarat. They had spoken little, dust so thick it dried their mouths like sand, Rustom divulging no more than that he was a schoolteacher from Ahmednagar, imagining his elite status might estrange him if not worse. The men, divided into squads of five and six, were their own best safeguards against sleep, two on watch while others slept in rotation. They looked forward to crossing the bridge, expecting to be met by trucks on the west bank headed for Rangoon for a period of rest, but the line had been stalled and the uncertainty of waiting through the night was worse than active engagement with the enemy. They didn't know whether to be concerned about the delay or relieved not to have to face another possible Japanese roadblock. Many had given up caring, too exhausted even for fear.

Rustom, on watch, stared across the dirt track. His squad along with all neighboring squads was bivouacked west of the track to impose a semblance of control. By night, the most innocent apparition appeared sinister, a branch became an arm, a twig a bayonet—and the half-moon of the night provided light enough for visibility, but not for certainty. He stared, still as a tree, watching what he imagined was the outline of a peaked cap. Slowly, stealthily, the peaked cap appeared to rise, and something glinted beside the cap providing a glimpse of another peaked cap. He pulled the pin and lobbed a grenade in the direction of the cap, sure of his bowling arm to find its target.

He heard a gasp as loud as a shout, a sound as of animals scurrying through underbrush, followed by the blast of the grenade. The translucent night blazed with light and sound as submachine guns of neighboring squads erupted apparently indiscriminately across the path. The firing continued for a minute before it was silenced by three discharges thundering more loudly than anything they had heard, as if worlds were colliding. The ground shook beneath their feet, the ensuing silence was deathlier than the noise, but on the heels of the silence came cheers from the direction of the bridge. Ashok Sharma's round face turned rounder with astonishment. "Arre, bhagwan! Kya hua? Oh, God! What happened?" Narayan Patel, eyes like white marbles that might have seen a ghost, could only shake his head in wonder staring with other members of the squad in the direction of the cheers, afraid to think what everyone was thinking.

The explosions had sounded at 0530 hours on the morning of 23 February. Dawn revealed a Samurai sword in the dust of the road. Beyond the sword, among torn and mangled and lacerated trees, Rustom saw, amid the carnage of broken bodies, a remarkable sight: one pair of black boots standing upright, as if in a display window, legs to the knees still in the boots, one leg crowned by a peaked cap, the other bloody and bare, like a grotesque couple out for a night on the town. The peaked caps might have been a reconnoitering party, might have been lost, he was never to know. The news, traveling like a fuse down the line, obscured everything else: the bridge had been blown; they had been left to the mercy of the Japanese; he could hear them coming in hordes through the jungle.

**THE MORNING PROVIDED A MASTERPIECE OF MISERY,** confusion, and savagery. Activity everywhere gave the bridge the appearance of a dying mantis, its thorax lacerated, intestines dangling. Of its seven spans two had dropped in the river, one hung badly damaged. Fighter aircraft, British and Japanese, swarmed like prehistoric birds over the riverscape, firing at one another as much as at the ground, adding to the confusion as much as aiding their respective sides. Underneath bobbed hundreds of heads, braving bullets from both banks as they crossed, the west providing cover against the east. Both banks stank, lined with dead and eviscerated fish.

Japanese divisions spread to blockade the British who spread in as wide a perimeter as they could —but at 1430 hours they withdrew to the river, sparing as many as they could to build rafts of bamboo lashed with vines, rifle slings, and whatever else came to hand. The jungle burned, gun ammunition having ignited, but having surrendered the jungle the British were well rid of it. Rustom's brigade, broken into small groups, edging to the river with the others, continued to exchange shots with the enemy as they retreated, swearing as much at the Japanese as at the command that had abandoned them.

The outlook was bad and getting worse when the Japanese chose to withdraw. They may have been as exhausted as the British, they may have wished to look for other access across the river, they may have imagined their task accomplished with the demolition of the bridge, they may have surrendered to the continual superiority of British aircraft. Rustom did not know, Rustom did not care. He was by then on a raft alongside a number of other rafts, racing toward the safety of the west bank, random bullets still zinging through the air. He paddled the raft with one other, three more hanging on to the ramshackle construction as if the river were a bed of flame, all of them villagers, afraid of the water more than bullets because they couldn't swim.

Rustom knew none of them. Toward the end all semblance of order had vanished. Some swam the breadth of the river, some with flotation devices (bamboo, empty cans of petrol, whatever they could find), some without. His left hand had burned as he'd helped lash the raft, but he'd been too overwhelmed to do more than manipulate it so it burned less. One of the men lay on his stomach, gripping the edge of the raft, vomiting into the river. As the raft lurched he slid forward and another one of the men released his own grip on a lashing to grab his legs, but succeeded only in losing his own balance and falling into the river. Rustom thrust his paddle, crudely carved from a branch, into the hands of the remaining man, and jumped after the man overboard.

They were by then more than halfway across. Resurfacing with his rescue, Rustom locked his left elbow under the man's armpit and began stroking with his right arm toward the shore. His left hand burned again, but he was a strong swimmer and used his hand as little as possible. He knew he could make the shore, the wretchedness of the circumstances only spurring his efforts, and a quarter of a mile further, just as he began to flag, his feet found the ground again. Someone stood by to help as he emerged from the river, only to find he had been carrying a corpse. Whether he'd died of a bullet or drowned or something else he never found out.

In that moment he saw in a circle around him Dolly and Phiroze and Sohrab and Daisy holding little Dinyar, their faces grave, calling him home, but they appeared elevated, like phantoms. He could see through them as through gauze, and whether they called him to Bombay or a more celestial destination he couldn't tell. He shivered uncontrollably despite the blistering Burmese sun and collapsed on the bank, grateful for the transport waiting to bear him to safety, realizing only then that his little finger had lost all volition and hung from his hand as limp as the dead fish assailing the air with their stink.

He learned later of the choice faced by Brigadier N. Hugh-Jones. He didn't think his troops could hold the bridge till dawn: if the bridge were to fall the Japanese would have an open road into Rangoon: if the bridge were blown he would abandon two-thirds of his troops: if the Japanese overpowered his troops and took the bridge he would lose troops, bridge, *and* Rangoon. Hugh-Jones chose to blow the bridge but never stopped second-guessing himself. Years later, back in the arms of his mother country, Hugh-Jones walked into the sea.

## A Googly in the Compound

AFTER THE WAR Rustom read exhaustively, every account he could find, but at the time he knew little and understood less. The British strategy appeared no more than a planned retreat, a nightmare of logistics as much as circumstances, backloading supplies north, then farther north, first to Mandalay, then to Myitkyina. As April approached, the hottest month, and the country baked like an open oven, Rustom still shivered, still occasionally hallucinated. Malaria was common in the north, but he had contracted it in the south, and shot full of quinine was ordered rest, his finger immobilized with bandages to allow the fifth metacarpal of his left hand to heal. All the while guns roared, rifles stuttered, and bombs whistled and fell in clusters like nets of pearls gleaming in the sun, wafting to the ground, accelerating at the last minute to slam the earth like a giant hand.

Each side intercepted messages from the other, neither knowing what the other knew. If the Japanese had known what the British knew, they would not have retreated from the bridge; if the British had known what the Japanese knew, they would have come to the bridge sooner. Abandoning the bridge, the Japanese moved north to ferry themselves across the river; the British moved south to reconstitute their surviving units. The Japanese took a fortnight to forward bridging materials to the Sittang, allowing the British time to backload supplies out of Rangoon. Sighting a massive force of the British north of Rangoon, the Japanese called off all roadblocks to march with maximum strength into the city, only to realize the massive force had been the entire British force—by which time it was too late to hem them in—but with Rangoon in their hands the Japanese added supply routes by sea from Malaya to the routes by land through Siam, and the British lost a safe harbor for their planes, leaving the bulk of their squadrons vulnerable. The Japanese could bolster their forces with as many divisions and aircraft as they wished; the British were left with only what they had.

Immobilized by malaria and an immobilized finger, Rustom was moved steadily northward from ambulance to makeshift ambulance, hospital to makeshift hospital, from Pegu to Hlegu to Taukkyan to

Tharrawaddy to Okpo to Prome, as the east-west line of defense of the British moved steadily north and towns were either bombed or otherwise savaged—only to be released after three weeks of hospitalization back to his unit to stagger along with the rest. They had drawn their line at the narrow waist of the country, held in the east by the Chinese at Toungoo and the west by the British at Prome. The road north from Rangoon to Prome had swarmed with refugees like locusts. Towns had been stripped, shops and homes looted, paths laden thick with dust and shit. Through the haze of an early morning Rustom had been halted by a panorama that seemed itself to slow to a halt. An assembly of vultures hovered on huge wings near the ground, rising and falling like the breast of a single beast in a hellish ballet.

When the Chinese lost Toungoo to the Japanese, the line of defense was raised farther north to cover a forty-mile stretch from the Irrawaddy to Taungdwingyi. Neither Rustom nor others in his rank could wrap their tongues around the names of the towns, not that they cared, colorful though they were: wooden houses, thatched roofs, storefronts wreathed with flowers, children in bright clothes strolling down streets alongside creaking ox-carts. The goal was to protect the oilfields of Yenangyuang, and failing that to destroy them. The column marched alongside their horses and mules, boiling under a magnesium sun, sweat caking dust to mud. Without lines of supply, their rations had been reduced to cold dry beef and biscuits like bark fortified with vitamin W (as they called the weevils plaguing their food). As temperatures climbed above a hundred degrees, as skin cracked and lips bled, soldiers pissed on their hands touching fingers to lips and tongues.

They were between villages, the terrain had turned from green and lush to brown and bare. The sun at its zenith left the world shadowless and naked. The man ahead of Rustom seemed to mumble, his throat too dry to be heard. He lurched out of the column, pulled himself back, lurched out again, staggered through a drunken circle before taking his place again, stopped and seemed to slump into himself, unconscious on his feet. Rustom almost bumped into him, but stopped

## A Googly in the Compound

in time to take him out of the line and wedged himself under the man's arm to help him stand. Catching his captain's eye, Rustom pointed to an apparently abandoned hut on the side of the road indicating he would take the man to the shade for a moment to let him regain his senses. The captain nodded.

Behind the windowless hut loomed a sparse and desiccated forest. Rustom approached watchful, left arm around the waist of the man, right holding his rifle steady. He kicked the door so it swung wide, slamming the wall. The room appeared to be a shrine, images of Buddha lining the back. As he stepped across the threshold he heard the familiar roar of aircraft from the south, the sudden alert of the column as it snapped to attention, preparing anti-aircraft batteries, scurrying toward the forest and nullahs for cover. He was too distracted to see a man with a dah lunge at him from a corner of the room until it was too late. The number of Burmese nationalists had risen steadily, propelled as much by Japanese victories against the British as the religion they held in common with the invaders—but these fifth columnists, calling themselves the Burma Independence Army, imagining Japan planned to give them independence, were as likely to comprise dacoits and convicts as patriots. Rustom had just enough time to drop the man he was carrying and thrust the bayonet of his rifle forward. The downward swipe of the dah missed his head by a millimeter, but a volley of shots followed and Rustom dropped senseless to the floor.

**TWO VOICES WITH AMERICAN TWANGS** rose over a bed of groans, but Rustom did not know whether he was dead or alive or dreaming. "I jumped under a culvert, and to my unspeakable disgust someone had been there before me."

"So? There was no one there when you got there, was there?"
"No, but this someone had had diarrhea."
The laugh came in spite of itself, surprised and sudden.
"I'm glad you can laugh about it."
"Sorry. Could've been worse, you know."

"I don't see how."

"It could've been raining."

"Still not funny."

"Sorry. Couldn't help myself."

There was a bustle around him as Rustom opened his eyes to find himself on his back in a bed. Blood pendulumed in his head. The American voices receded, a lighter voice approached. "Hullo, Brai'case! You are awake?"

He turned his eyes toward the voice. A round Burmese face smiled down at him. He had imagined he might be in yet another makeshift hospital, and the broad beams spanning the width of yet another of the great evacuated houses of Burma confirmed his suspicion, but the woman had him wondering again if he was dreaming. "Is there a doctor?"

"Yes, Dr. Sigret."

"Cigarette?"

"Yes, I will get him. He will be happy to see you." She turned to leave.

"Wait."

She turned back, raising faint eyebrows. "Yes, Brai'case?"

He imagined she had baptised him with a Burmese name. "What is your name?"

Her smile returned. "I am Aung Tsai. I will be back soon."

He nodded, aware once more of the groans around him, realizing he wasn't lying on a bed as much as an operating table, as were the others, and shut his eyes again until he heard his name called in a deep voice. "Rustom Sanjana!"

He opened his eyes only to wonder once more if he was dreaming. Beside what passed for his bed stood a naked man in his forties, broadshouldered and brawny, scruffy hair pushed back from a widow's peak, scruffy toothbrush moustache, cigarette clamped between his lips, gazing at him with an open face and smiling eyes. Aung stood smiling behind him. Rustom's voice was barely audible in response. "Yes? Dr. Cigarette?"

The man laughed, removing his cigarette. "Seagrave! Dr. Gordon Seagrave! I know your name from your identity discs, but I don't know what you're doing here. You should be dead by all rights. The Friends found you under a door. Your own medics must have missed you, but here you are now."

"Friends?"

"The Friends Ambulance Unit. We're working with General Stilwell and Chiang Kai-shek. The Friends pick up all the wounded they find—mostly Chinese, since they don't appear to have medics of their own. Very strange, the Chinese—resigned to pain, take suffering for granted, very courageous in battle, but on the other hand they're as resigned to the pain of others. They wait to see what a wounded man will do for himself before they jump to his aid."

Rustom looked cautiously below Seagrave's waist, relieved to see he wore shorts.

Seagrave laughed. "We're quite unorthodox here as you can see. It's too hot for clothes."

Rustom nodded, his mouth twisting in the ghost of a smile. "My head aches."

Seagrave laughed again. "You should be dead. You had a bullet through your brain. Your skull was shattered. I had to pull out my old wastebasket trephine and take out about three square inches of your skull. Your brains were beginning to ooze out even before I cut the dura mater—but I managed to get the bullet. I bet Aung you would die the same night. That was two days ago. You have the strength of your namesake."

Rustom nodded, not understanding most of the words. "Wastebasket?"

"It's the best that we can say about our equipment. We get leftovers from abandoned hospitals and clinics—wastebasket equipment. The Friends salvage what they can and we do the best with what we have—wastebasket surgery. Orthopedic surgery without an x-ray, urological surgery without a cystoscope, surgery without electricity, surgery without cautery—except for the odd soldering iron. Medicine without a laboratory, hospitalization without a hospital." He shrugged. "We do what we can."

"Thank you."

"You're welcome."

Rustom was too tired to keep his eyes open. "I've got to get back to my unit."

Seagrave squeezed his arm. "We'll drive you back to your unit when we can spare the time—we need the space—but I would like to keep you as long as necessary."

"You very lucky, Brai'case. No one else could do like Dr. Sigret. You very lucky."

Rustom's eyes remained shut, but the coin dropped in that moment and his lips twitched in another ghost of a smile as he fell asleep once more. He had been christened Seagrave's braincase.

**AUNG WORRIED ABOUT HER BRAI'CASE.** Everytime the planes passed and they returned from the nullahs, someone had to fetch him. Once found, he allowed himself to be led with the remorse of a child caught playing hooky, but she was afraid of what might happen were he not found, or found by the Burma Independence Army slashing men and women and children alike with dahs for no more than the sin of their presence. Despite the huge intravenous injections of glucose, they continued to wonder why he lived without even the taint of a fever. She saw in the miracle a sign from heaven, he had been touched by a divine hand, but even heaven seemed to need her help to keep him safe. He seemed not to be running away as much as running unaccountably. She had got in the habit of looking for him the moment they headed for the nullahs, but this time he had given her the slip.

She had been on the road for half an hour, stopping frequently to call into the undergrowth on either side—but as shadows grew longer, and the sun withdrew its fingers one by one, and she switched on the electric parabolas of her jeep headlights, she saw him on the side of

## A Googly in the Compound

the road—and, barely yards ahead, she saw a leopard, eyes gleaming in the light from the jeep, as still as Rustom seemed oblivious.

Rustom's thoughts swam in currents, past and present and future in a glutinous mix. He had lived his life like a rich man's wife considering her favored status a direct consequence of her deservedness (when she considered it at all). Daisy's arrival had changed everything, and most particularly Sohrab's comment: *A year younger than our Rustom—and what a lot she has got to show for herself already.* It had triggered the first steps of his independent life, first in Ahmednagar—but then in Burma, and the way forward could not have been murkier. Seagrave was right, he should have been dead—but he should have been dead a dozen times before he had even met Seagrave, and he continued to live, and he couldn't understand why. He was aware of a leopard a few yards ahead, but no more than he was aware of the rock on which he sat, or the jeep rolling up beside him until Aung called urgently. "Brai'case, get in the jeep!"

He got in the jeep. The leopard slipped into the undergrowth. Aung couldn't stop talking, but her words slid past his thoughts like white noise. The more he learned about Seagrave the more he was astonished and inspired—and depressed, considering how he lagged himself. He had seen the doctor at work, often operating on two at once, administering chloroform to one while amputating the gangrenous limb of another. He was the first doctor in a line of Ohioan missionaries to Burma stretching back to the birth of the nineteenth century, and never shirked his responsibilities despite the difficulties of his life. His hospital in Namkham on the Burma-China border had been decimated by the Japanese, but he had picked up the pieces and carried on wherever he could. In Rangoon to secure lend-lease trucks and equipment for his work, he had been subjected with his wife and children to a week of nights in trenches, bombs dropping around them, before sending the family by steamer to Calcutta, but had heard nothing from them since. He had worked for the British until the Americans had joined the fray and requested of General Stilwell himself that he be placed under his command. He suffered from recurring bouts of malaria, days without nights, infected feet, but said nothing about his travails. Rustom got his information mostly from Aung who had been with the doctor from the start, when he'd begun soliciting and training nurses, his reputation made when he'd predicted, a year earlier to the day, the death of a man with tuberculous lungs.

It was nine o'clock when they got back. The Friends had returned with truckloads of casualties from Mandalay laying them on the ground for the doctors to determine the direst cases. The practice was to return them to their units once they were out of immediate danger to make room for others. Rustom would have been returned sooner but for his circumstances: he had been found accidentally; he belonged with the British and Indians in the west, not the Chinese in the east; his unit was considerably farther than the others. The plan had been for the 17th Division to protect the Yenangyaung oilfields, and failing that to destroy them. During his stay with the doctor the fields had been burned to the sky, beanstalks of smoke spiraling toward the clouds, his Division once more scattered and in retreat, the field of operations continually narrowing as the Japanese herded them continually northward from east and west.

Seagrave looked up momentarily from a patient as they alighted from the jeep. "There you are, Aung! Get ready! It's going to be one of those nights."

Rustom took it as a rebuke, and well deserved. There was Captain O'Hara, a picture-perfect American officer of the Dental Corps sent by General Stilwell, under whose hands Rustom had seen a shattered jaw reshaped as simply as a jigsaw. There was Captain Grindlay, graduated from Harvard, trained at the Mayo Clinic, also sent by Stilwell, whom Rustom had seen remove two feet of someone's bowels as if he were tidying a closet. There was Tun Shein, college graduate, elephant catcher, master chef, speaking Burmese, Hindi, and English, winsome as a child and wise as Buddha, who could charm the egg from a chicken while luring the chicken to the knife. There was Dr. Ba Saw, graduate from the medical school of Rangoon University, who had signed up to work without pay if Seagrave would take him

## A Googly in the Compound

as an intern, who read through his books on surgery for the next day's operations whether or not he was to be the surgeon. There were other doctors and missionaries; there were a score of nurses in colorful loongyis; there were the Friends continually unloading casualties; there was Aung already prepared with forceps to extract a bullet from the thigh of a Chinese soldier; and there was Rustom, down in the depths after Seagrave had brought him back from the dead, taking Aung from others who needed her more, adding to everyone's anxieties. He had witnessed the scene before, everyone working as day turned to night and night again to day, and he knew something about procedures if nothing else. He jumped into one of the trucks to help unload remaining casualties. Bill Brough, the Friend manning the truck, looked up. "You don't have to do this, you know. You're a casualty yourself."

"I want to help."

"All right. Be careful. Be gentle."

Rustom nodded, but wondered how the Chinese viewed the Friends. They picked up the bloodiest soldiers as if they were kittens, calling them all George. After the trucks were unloaded and headed back to the front, Rustom sterilized towels and instruments, made and served tea and coffee, and the following evening, after the group had tended a hundred and twenty cases in the span of twenty-four hours, got on his knees to help the nurses scrub the floor with cresol. Seagrave echoed Bill's earlier comment, his face screwed in puzzlement, cigarette twitching between his lips. "You don't have to do this, you know."

Rustom grinned, "I'm enjoying it," but his grin soured as he picked two amputated fingers gingerly from the refuse of plaster of Paris on the floor.

Seagrave laughed. "Think you have a future as a surgeon?"

Rustom pursed his lips. "Maybe."

"There's nothing to it, you know. Once you've applied the chloroform you cut and tie, cut and tie. You debride each case and pack the wound with sulfanilamide powder—and if the damage is extensive you put on a plaster cast. That's all there is to it."

Rustom nodded, grinning again, too happy with his work to be tired, glad to have been useful. "You make it sound so simple."

He stared as if he were sizing up Rustom. "We heard from your unit, you know. You'll be leaving after we've all rested a bit, sometime this evening. I shall be sorry to lose you. I have a soft spot for my brain cases." He laughed. "You've made a brain surgeon out of a country doctor."

Rustom dropped his eyes, losing his grin though he had expected to leave sooner or later. "I shall be sorry to go."

Seagrave nodded, eyes narrowing in thought, but widening almost immediately hearing the sound of a truck. "Dash it all! Bill's back already. I don't believe it."

Rustom looked up again, but Seagrave appeared to have forgotten him, eyes fixed on the truck brought helter-skelter into the compound of the dressing station. Bill Brough seemed to leap from the cab before it had come to a standstill. "The Japs are eight miles away. We have to evacuate immediately."

The company was exhausted, but resembled in a moment a hive. They had evacuated three times since Rustom had joined, and numberless times before, honing their skills so they were ready to leave within the hour, arranging supplies so they could be operating within fifteen minutes of the arrival of casualties. Rustom traveled again with Aung in the driver's seat, keeping his peace until the jeep almost veered off the road. He grabbed the wheel, shouting to Aung who had fallen asleep, keeping his hand on the wheel as they drove on. Ahead Seagrave's truck veered similarly as did the jeep behind them, everyone righting his vehicle in time.

About three in the morning, almost a hundred miles farther north, they came upon a zayat that had seen better days. The joists had sunk on one side, tilting the lodging through thirty degrees; the floor was covered with the shit of rodents and other small animals; the well water was full of alkali and ruined their morning coffee; but for the night they remained oblivious to the discomfort, some sleeping in the cabs of their trucks, some in the seats of their jeeps, some on the filth on the floor as if it were the most softly feathered bed.

## A Googly in the Compound

**R**USTOM HAD RISEN from the rump of the Burma monkey to the mouth. For him the worst was over, he was soon to be expectorated, but he was not to know it yet, especially not amid the horrors he had witnessed and continued to witness, forever to troll his midnight visions: hundreds of thousands set either on the march, on the move, or on the run; soldiers bayonetted to death, hanging from trees, some by their ankles; women raped, throats slit, skirts hiked above their waists; hacked remains of murdered families; charred skeletons of villages; babies in pools of brain porridge; crows drunk on eyeballs of the dead; trees feathered by vultures, watching, waiting.

He had drifted again from Seagrave's corps, wandering alongside a group of refugees so shrouded by flies they might have been dead: pregnant women, babies on their backs; children bloated with hunger, sticks for legs; a mother dead from childbirth lying with the child half-born; a ten-year-old girl, face painted with adult anger, leading two younger boys by the hand; an old man staggering under the weight of two babies carried in buckets under a wooden pole across his shoulder; men on crutches, men with sores, sightless men, a man with a hook for a hand. A vulture ripped into a corpse, its bald head, curved beak, and naked neck perfect for burrowing into carcasses, as inured to the approach of men as they to the presence of vultures, as Rustom too had become. Lost in the wake of the hooked hand, he thought of his father. A war injury was all he had said, all their curiosity had demanded. Some subjects were defiled by an audience. He wondered how much he himself would say if he ever got back.

Someone touched his elbow from behind. "Brai'case, come. Old Man say we have to go."

The nurses nicknamed everyone. Seagrave was "Old Man," O'Hara was "Mr. Bear" for his hairy chest, Grindlay was simply "Uncle," Tun Shein was "Little Uncle," various Friends were "First Love," "Big Brother," "Son-in-Law," General Stilwell was "Granddaddy Joe," Colonel Williams was "Second Daddy," Rustom was "Brai'case" and glad to be part of the group. He nodded, but remained unmoving.

"Brai'case, we have to go. Old Man is waiting. Granddaddy Joe want everyone to come."

Seagrave stayed in touch with Stilwell to learn where they might pick up casualties, but as the Japanese had advanced their paths had converged, the new endgame comprising withdrawal, nothing more. The General had decorated Seagrave with the rank of major of the Medical Corps, and as a major and Rustom's doctor he had ordered Rustom to stay with his group. Rustom's Division was also withdrawing as was everyone, all from different fronts, and Seagrave didn't see that it made a pint of difference from which front Rustom withdrew. Grateful also for Aung's continual watchfulness, Rustom never questioned her, but he knew she had a husband in one of the villages in the Shan States and wondered at her dedication. He turned to go with her. "Aung, why do you do this?"

Aung smiled, puffing her chest. "I am a nurse."

"No, I mean, why do you make me special?"

Her smile broadened. "You are my project, Brai'case. Uncle is Koi's project. Mr. Bear is Esther's project. Brai'case is my project."

The corners of Rustom's mouth twitched. "I am very lucky, Aung, but I also need a project. Will you be my project?"

Aung's round brown face burst with radiance. "Oh, Brai'case, I will be happy to be your project."

**GENERAL JOSEPH WARREN STILWELL** was a long lanky man closing on his sixtieth year. He understood better than most that you accomplished more by projecting confidence whether or not you felt it. Nothing exemplified his strength better than his eyes. Peering through wirerimmed glasses, narrowed with years in the sun, they appeared to see through you, body and soul, but he could not count the number of fingers on a hand held at three feet with his left eye thanks to the explosion of an ammunition dump during the Great War. His right eye wasn't much better and got progressively worse, but if the retreat from Burma were to be a case of the blind leading the blind his followers

# A Googly in the Compound

would be the last to know. His hair grew white at the temples where it was cut close to his head, giving the darker hair in the middle, combed straight back, the appearance of a mohawk, but he was rarely seen without his broadbrimmed khaki hat—which, like everything else about him except his spirit, had seen better days. He wore a light khaki jacket, long khaki pants, heavy army boots. His nose was prominent, his chin resolute, his face lined and leathery.

He had led a convoy of three sedans, a dozen trucks, and a dozen jeeps a hundred and fifty miles or so north from Shwebo, the roads so crowded they'd had to travel much of the time in first and second gear. The group comprised four units and numbered just over a hundred: Americans, British, Seagrave's unit, and Chinese. Their best chance was to head northwest into India, but tens of thousands were heading northwest into India and there was as much danger from the desperation of starving refugees and soldiers as from Japanese.

The crowds had thinned when many British and Indians had turned west, some in the party suggesting they too should turn west, but Stilwell had continued north, transferring loads from sedans to trucks when the terrain had proven too rough for sedans, and from trucks to jeeps when they'd had to ford a stream and sacrifice most of the trucks. They'd had one narrow escape already. Taking two wrong turns they had lost miles when they couldn't afford to lose yards, and having corrected their path they had stopped to confirm their direction and found themselves overlooking a valley of roiling humanity.

At first it resembled nothing so much as a large snake coiling and uncoiling, but grew worse as details came clear: gray-uniformed Chinese dragged a Burman from the cab of his truck, slapped him with a pistol, bloodying his face, breaking his nose, commandeering his truck; blond Britishers struck unarmed families with the butts of their guns for bags of rice; tall gaunt Punjabis with long black beards snatched food from toothpick children; tribespeople looted bodies of the dead; heat waves magnified the disaster like a glass; the smell rose to grip them like a giant hand; someone fired a rifle, someone replied with a tommygun, then came screams, then more gunfire, then silence, first to fall were first to be trampled, women and children the fairest game of all.

They had hurried back to their convoy to find families of skeletons, grey with dust, holloweyed and leatherskinned, foul with shit and blood and flies, beyond the shame of their nakedness, crawling and rising from the ground, cracked cups and broken bowls in outstretched hands, babies sucking from dry dugs, children picking grains of rice from piles of shit. Stilwell had walked into the midst toward his jeep, shouting his concern out loud. "Hold it! Don't give them anything or we'll be mobbed! Crank up and get moving and don't stop for anything!" They had started engines, honked horns, and hurried away.

He had conferred later with his officers, many of whom suggested taking the shortest route in the shortest span of time, turning west immediately. He had continued to differ, choosing a more difficult route, heading farther north, making for a longer journey, but reasoning that time lost by the longer route would be compensated by lack of interference from the multitudes who would also run interference for them with the Japanese, and the farther north they were the more certainly they would avoid trouble—but the General soon realized they would have to jettison even their jeeps. There were too many rocks, roots, and high ridges, too many twists and too many stream crossings with banks too steep. They reached a monastery with a bungalow attached, gulmohors and other flame trees illuminating the grove, and the General called a halt to gather the group in a clearing.

His voice was hoarse with dust and exhaustion, his brow damp and gleaming with perspiration, his shoulder slung with a Thompson machinegun. "Everyone, form a circle around me—Americans over there, Seagrave and nurses to my right, British to my left, Chinese here, everyone else over there—and quickly. We don't have time to waste."

He stood himself in the center of the circle, smoking and chewing gum, cigarette in an amber holder, as they took their places, shading eyes from the sun, sweatstains showing in armpits and backs.

## A Googly in the Compound

"First of all, there's been a rumor that we Americans are going to take the jeeps and the food in the night and desert everybody else." He glared around the circle. "That is ri*dic*ulous! We are *all* in this together, and we will get out of it together, but I insist on discipline. If there is anyone who will not accept my orders without question, now is the time to speak up. You can go your own way with a week's rations." He looked around again, checking one face after another. "Anyone?"

No one moved, no one spoke.

"Good! This means everyone will do exactly what I say, when and as I say it. Next, about food, all food will be pooled. If you have any stashed away, now is the time to turn it in. If I find anyone has held anything back I'll run him out of the party and let him shift for himself. Is that clear?"

Heads nodded, a murmur of assent spread around him.

"Good! Keep your weapons, keep your ammunition, you may need it. Keep your cigarettes. But throw away your heavy baggage, your bedrolls. Keep only what you can carry yourselves. Those of you with extra clothing and shoes, share what you've got. I expect the strong to help the others. We will march to Maingkaing, we will build or buy or rent rafts to take us along the Uyu River to Homalin, then cross the Chindwin and then the mountains to Imphal in India. That's a hundred and forty miles we'll be covering, about fourteen miles a day, through some pretty rough country, but we've got to keep moving. We can expect reinforcements at Homalin, and I'll take it easy to begin, to break everyone in, but time is not on our side. If the Japanese don't catch up with us, the monsoon will. It's almost time, and if we get caught the river will flood its banks, and the mountains will be impossible. We have food, but we may be reduced to half rations if we don't find more along the way. By the time we get out of here, many of you will hate my guts—but I'll tell you one thing." He looked around again at the circle, defying them to contradict him. "You will *all* get out."

His lips were tightly pressed. What his poor eyesight showed only he could have said, but doctors, nurses, officers, men, were all comforted imagining he knew them by sight if not by name.

"Tonight we will eat, we will throw away our extra baggage, we will hire coolies from the village to carry our provisions, and we will send out our last radio message so they will be prepared for us when we get to Homalin. Tomorrow we march with the dawn."

The nurses set the best example, throwing away everything but a change of clothes, keeping one blanket for every three nurses, ditto mosquito nets, sighing as they divested themselves of their belongings with longing glances, giggling as they arrayed the lower branches of trees and thorn bushes with bright reds, greens, blues, yellows, and pinks—skirts, sweaters, bodices, loongyis, and brassieres of cotton and silk and satin by the dozen—bundling what they kept in towels and sheets. One of the men, joining in the spirit of the game, wrapped himself in a green loongyi and pranced on the grass as if he were on a runway in Paris, setting everyone laughing.

Seagrave advised the nurses each to maintain a first aid kit with quantities of quinine for malaria and emytine for dysentery among other medicines and pills. The men discarded less imagining they could carry more, filling the grounds with pants, coats, shoes, underwear, notebooks, empty bottles of whisky, many emptied on the spot. The Chinese stood by, discarding nothing because they had nothing to discard, picking through the items left by the others that might help them on the journey, primarily shoes in preparation for rough roads. The place was beginning to look like a rummage sale. The girls picked among the shoes as well because their straw sandals were not built to last, but the men's shoes were too large by far. They also donned sola topis too large for them falling over their ears.

Dinner was at five, rice with corned beef and tea. Stilwell stood last in line, but had no sooner sat on the grass than a skinny shorthaired mongrel scampered to his side, tongue lolling, tail wagging. The General grinned. "I suppose you'll be wanting some chow too, hey, boy?"

The dog sat patiently, neither losing sight of the plate nor intruding on the General's space.

"Well, what's one more? Come on, boy. Here you go."

## A Googly in the Compound

The face of General Tseng, the Chinese officer sitting nearby, screwed into disapproval. They had little enough food, Stilwell should know better than to feed a dog, but even if Stilwell saw despite his blunted vision he ignored him. He had served three tours of duty in China between the wars, living in the country for more than half a dozen years with his family in a Chinese house with Chinese furnishings and objets d'art. One of his five children had been born in Peking, another in Tientsin. He spoke the language, understood the customs, had seen the carcasses of dogs hung for sale in the marketplace, but it made no difference. Tseng was currently under American command, and that was the bottom line.

"That's my dog, sir. James. I'd like to join you too, sir, if you'll have me."

A tall gaunt man with a face like a hawk stepped forward wearing khakis and a sola topi.

"My name is Breedom Case, sir. I've been a missionary here for years, sir. I speak Burmese, I know the dialects, I know the pathways and the trails. I could be of use, sir, if you'll allow me."

Stilwell nodded and held out his hand. "I could use a good interpreter. Glad to have you. Get yourself some chow."

Case had barely nodded thanks when everyone's attention was drawn to a tinkling of bells, and looking up they saw a mule train driven by two Chinese men in large round conical straw hats.

Stilwell grasped the possibilities immediately. "General Tseng! I want those mules, all of them! Get your men to round them up! Immediately!"

General Tseng was thickset with more poundage per cubic inch than a wrestler, but moved like an armadillo, shouting to his men in Chinese to get the mules. The muleteers skedaddled back up the trail they had just descended, hats twirling like tops to the ground in their wake, but returned to satisfy their curiosity, scratching their shaved heads.

The circumstances fit like a tongue and groove. The muleteers were on their way to India to pick up merchandise. Stilwell asked no questions about the merchandise which he guessed was opium, but offered instead to pay substantially for the hire of the mules, optimizing the profit for the train and offering Stilwell a safety net. If they ran out of food he could buy the mules, tough and chewy though they might be. He smiled, lighter in his step than in a long while. "That's our first stroke of luck."

Later in the evening they radioed their last message to HQ in Delhi:

> HEADING FOR HOMALIN AND IMPHAL WITH PARTY OF OVER ONE HUNDRED. INCLUDE HQ GROUP SEAGRAVE'S UNIT BRITISH CHINESE OTHERS. WE ARE ON FOOT FIFTY MILES WEST OF INDAW. WE ARE ARMED HAVE FOOD AND MAP. SHOULD REACH MAINGKAING IN THREE DAYS RAFT DOWN UYU RIVER TO HOMALIN CROSS CHINDWIN AND HIKE OVER MOUNTAINS TO IMPHAL. ALERT BRITISH TO SEND FOOD AND COOLIES AND MEDICINE TO HOMALIN. TENS OF THOUSANDS OF REFUGEES AND TROOPS HEADED FOR INDIA ON TRAILS FROM SITTAUNG TO HUKAWNG VALLEY. URGENT REPEAT URGENT TO STOCK TRAILS WITH FOOD AND MEDICINES SOON AS POSSIBLE. SEND POLICE AND DOCTORS. URGENT OR THOUSANDS WILL DIE. CATASTROPHE POSSIBLE. WE DEPART EARLY MORNING. THIS IS OUR LAST MESSAGE REPEAT OUR LAST MESSAGE. CHEERIO. STILWELL.

The radio, weighing two hundred pounds, was decisively smashed, until it lay a carapace of wires and bulbs, codes and files burned to ash. The General and his officers settled for the night in the bungalow, the others spread themselves in the monastery to which it was attached. Mosquitoes were so thick they hovered in clouds, whining and spitting like electric discharges. The sounds of the forest were easily audible—trumpeting elephants, screaming monkeys, the growl of a tiger—but above everything rose a choir of women's voices in harmony singing "Onward Christian Soldiers," girded by a deeper bass voice. Seagrave, the missionary, was leading his nurses in prayer

# A Googly in the Compound

and song. The General sighed, his face widened in a smile, and the lines on his forehead seemed momentarily to disappear.

**THE NEXT MORNING** they set off as the General had ordered at five o'clock. Reveille had sounded at three-thirty, followed by morning ablutions, quick breakfast of rice and tea, and loading the mules for the march. Coolies from the village, shirts hanging over loongyis, dahs hanging from fiber belts, rags around their heads, blowing smoke from pipes and cheroots, bore down on their loads, securing ropes around the baggage to be lifted by poles. Water, drawn from a well, had been boiled or decontaminated with iodine and stored in canteens. Stilwell led, tommygun in hand, setting the regulation pace, planning five-minutes rest every hour, Breedom Case behind him, James at his heels, followed first by the Americans, then the British, then Seagrave's unit, the Chinese bringing up the rear.

The narrow jungle trail descended shortly to a stream. The General looked over his shoulder at Breedom Case who nodded, saying nothing, scooping James from the ground, and Stilwell maintained his stride from land to water as if there were no difference. Ferns crowded the banks of the water corridor, lianas climbed the sheer rock walls, blossoms of pink and blue and lavender lined the galleries, white orchids shed petals on the water, songbirds provided a soundtrack, monkeys swung overhead, sunlight filtered through the green canopy casting a shimmer on the water. The stream was a foot deep and the laughter of the nurses provided the illusion they were on a picnic, but at midmorning the water deepened, the trees thinned, the sun glared, water reflected the blinding glare, sand sucked each footstep, heat beat them like a hammer, and the first of the casualties succumbed. Colonel George Holcombe stumbled, turned white, and fell. Another colonel, Robert Williams, Stilwell's medical officer, dragged him to the side, held a rag soaked in ammonia under his nose, lightened his load by a ground sheet, two water canteens, and a pistol, and splashed forward to the General to say the man couldn't go any farther. Stilwell replied without stopping. "He's got to. This column can't stop. Bring him along when you can."

Holcombe was only the first, followed shortly by a major-general, a lieutenant, another colonel, and a major, all Americans. Seagrave, coming forward to help, overheard the General grumble to his medical officer. "Dammit, Bob, you and I can take it, and we're older than any of them. Why *can't* they take it? If I was their age I'd be ashamed. We've got to average fourteen miles a day. We haven't made five yet and it's almost eleven o'clock. Christ, they're a poor lot!"

Forty-five years of age, suffering from sores on his feet, Seagrave gritted his teeth. The nurses dressed his sores several times a day, but there had never been time for them to heal. Discharges from the wounds of casualties in his makeshift operating chambers had kept his shoes wet and his sores dirty since the beginning of the year, but he found his feet hurt less when he set them down squarely on as smooth a surface as he could find.

It wasn't quite noon when they reached a narrow stretch of beach and Stilwell called a halt. Brambles and bushes lined the embankment. The column emerged from the stream to crumple on the bank recovering its breath. Seagrave worried in particular about one of his nurses: Than Shwe. He had opened her abdomen for an appendicitis less than a year ago to discover her peritoneal cavity full of tuberculosis and her appendix hard against the horn of her uterus. One of the Friends was pulling her and her pack on an air mattress. A second mattress was inflated to pull one of the colonels. Rustom, owning nothing, not even a rifle, carried Aung's pack and volunteered to pull the second mattress. Stilwell took off pants and shirt and sat in the stream to bathe. Others followed his example as much to cleanse themselves as escape battalions of ants and other bugs. Aung dug a small hole in the sand, lined it with leaves, and when water seeped through as through a filter helped Rustom fill canteens for their group.

A couple of hours later, shadows growing longer in the canyons, packs reduced to ten pounds by order of the General, replenished with more rice, the last of the corned beef, and tea, the company resumed its

## A Googly in the Compound

journey. Some of the men had cut the arms and legs from their clothing to stay cool, only to find themselves more vulnerable to mosquitoes and leeches. Stilwell maintained his earlier pace, stragglers fell behind to be picked up by a unit the General assigned for the purpose. The nurses, livelier than everyone, splashing water, holding up their loongyis, charming as children, perked everyone's spirits, chanting as they marched.

> We will follow General Stilwell when he comes.
> We will follow General Stilwell when he comes.
> We will follow General Stilwell,
> We will follow General Stilwell,
> We will follow General Stilwell when he comes.

Stilwell grinned. "I thought we'd have to gear ourselves to their pace, but they're showing us a thing or two about marching."

With nightfall they encamped, Seagrave led his nurses in prayer in Burmese, two hours later Rustom and Aung and two Friends arrived pulling the colonel and Than Shwe on the mattresses. The other nurses had stayed up to welcome them with tea while the rest of the company slept.

**THE NEXT TWO DAYS** were much the same, but the company appeared to grow into its marching shoes though the water was deeper, reaching their knees. Everyone was repeatedly dosed with quinine, blistered feet were taped and bandaged, monkeys continued to scold and scream, General Tseng managed to purchase eggs and chickens from a village along the way so the company had a teaspoon of scrambled egg with breakfast and slivers of chicken with rice for lunch, and Stilwell continued to show himself a canny steward of the company. On the first day, when a squadron of nine Japanese bombers flew overhead in V formation, he reassured them that they could not have been spotted because they had taken cover in good time, the river no more than a guide for the squadron. On the second day, when a bull elephant appeared in a clearing beside their trail, a brass bell around its neck marking it for a rogue, he called all rifles to his side as the company hiked past to safety behind them, explaining later that rifles could kill the beast, but machineguns would only prick its hide, heightening its rage.

No less to his credit, Stilwell showed no patience for sneaks, and revealed shortly why he was called "Vinegar" Joe by his men. Checking the bags, finding a huge bedroll, he read the name of the owner, ordered the roll to be spread out on the beach, and redfaced and sputtering gathered the company. "I want everyone to see how little one of you thinks of everyone else. I won't mention his name because the commotion would slow the column, but I want you to think about how petty, how selfish, how smallminded some of us can be in the most dire circumstances. I ordered all personal belongings discarded except what you could carry, I later ordered all packs further reduced to ten pounds, but this man has twice disobeyed my orders. This bedroll was slipped in with the kitchen loads and rations in the dark. There are some in our company who have collapsed because they are not well enough to carry their own packs, because the mules and coolies are overloaded—because *this man's bedroll* took up so much space, because *this man* couldn't bear to part with this"—Stilwell lifted a blanket with a stick as if it were verminous—"and this"—a shirt—"and this"—a towel. There were more blankets and shirts and towels, also sheets, shoes, two complete uniforms, underwear, ties, socks.

"I'll take care of this when we get to India, but when we take off in a few minutes, all of this"—he waved the stick around the items—"all of this stays here, and I hope the owner is properly ashamed."

The General was shaking with rage, so much so that his hat quivered, eliciting a comment from one of the men. "Jeez! Even his hat looks mad!"

The company was subdued as they prepared once more for the march, Rustom looking for Aung's pack which he still carried, when he heard her scream followed by a louder animal scream. She wasn't far, standing at the line where the beach met the forest, facing a monkey snarling and baring its teeth. He ran at once to shield her from the monkey, but by the time he reached them the monkey had leapt into a tree and she was laughing. "I not afraid, but he surprise me! He come from nowhere!"

They had drawn the attention of the entire camp. The General approached them, smiling. "What's your name, soldier?"

"Rustom Sanjana, sir."

The General nodded, still smiling. "Good man. Good work."

Rustom dropped his head. "The monkey wouldn't have done anything, sir. They're harmless."

The General nodded again, still smiling. "I know."

Aung hugged Rustom. "I am his project!"

The General raised his eyebrows, Rustom explained, and the General nodded again. "That's a great idea. Everyone in the military should have such a project."

Seagrave was standing by, also grinning. "Everyone in the world."

The General turned, tipping his hat to Seagrave.

The company set off in a lighter mood once more, nurses as indomitable as ever, singing as they brought up the line.

Singing ai yi yippee yippee yi,
Singing ai yi yippee yippee yi,
Singing ai yi yippee yippee,
Ai yi yippee yippee,
Ai yi yippee yippee yi.

RUSTOM STOOD AT THE FRONT of the 80-foot raft in the first sneeze of the monsoon and sank the heavy bamboo pole into the bottom of the river. Bamboo poles also formed the deck of the raft, twenty lashed in a row, two more crosswise underneath, but water seeped up between the poles, lashings came undone, and the construction needed continual refurbishing. He pushed the pole in at just the right angle, and as the raft advanced hurried aft to raise the pole and sink it into the riverbed again. It was their second night on the water, and despite his little finger continually wrapped and rewrapped by Aung, the newness of the exercise, and the toll on his muscles, he had developed a rhythm, his eye as much on the water as on the fireflies of flashlights on the rafts ahead. Kevin, one of the Friends, manned the other side of the raft, sharing the two-hour shift, and Robin, yet another, sat in front with a flashlight, attempting to steer them clear of logjams and branches along the way, but they often had to call everyone overboard to unsnag the raft and set it in the right direction again.

They had arrived after three days, on schedule, at Maingkaing. With its temple and pagoda, the village was a hub of civilization, but they had found only half the rafts they needed. The rest had been taken by other parties, some of which they had seen along the trail, picking grains and weeds and berries from the forest to mix with a handkerchief of rice, skimpy meals for scrawny refugees, most of whom would die in the forest. Stilwell had been obliged to send half their company by land: the mule train, the Chinese guard, and a handful of American officers. They planned to meet again in Homalin. He had set sail with a flotilla of thirteen rafts, an advance guard to ensure the Japanese had not reached Homalin, followed by four groups of three rafts lashed to one another: the flagship bearing the General, foodship bearing cooks and coolies, hospitalship bearing Seagrave's unit, and rearguard bearing the British.

Rustom's regard for the General had mounted daily. Whatever the challenge, he had proven himself equal—or blessed. When their coolies had deserted, convinced the squadron of Japanese bombers overhead meant Japanese awaited them around the corner, he had found a village to supply more. When the drone of a bomber had assaulted their ears, appearing from out of the sun on their first day on the river (nurses screaming, men praying), it had opened its bomb bay to release burlap bags of corned beef, graham crackers, sardines, milk, and cigarettes, on a nearby sandbank, kindling hope that they had not been forgotten. The General had led the way, bounding from his raft, in shorts and hat, hipdeep in water, to secure the bags. The beef tins, cracking open on contact, had been consumed immediately to prevent spoilage, allowing for once for full bellies all around.

## A Googly in the Compound

Rustom's regard had mounted no less for the nurses. While the last of the rafts were being lashed together, they had undertaken to build shelters of bamboo and thatch to buttress them against sun and rain. The General had grinned. "You mean you're doing all this on your own steam?"

Koi had shaken her head. "Oh, no, sir! No steam, sir! We know how. You don't. So we do it."

At the first rest stop they had rushed into the jungle reappearing with edible roots, vegetables, and berries for Tun Shein to work his magic, producing a curried rice with the mix. Seagrave was all smiles despite the worsening sores on his feet. "I think I could eat anything if it was seasoned by Tun Shein."

Best of all, young though the nurses were, giggling like girls more than women, with flat chests and streamlined torsos, they were tireless, never without a smile, never without a song, bringing everyone tea, binding everyone's feet, never minding themselves, coy and flirtatious and chaste all at once. Too small to be effective polers, they spent their days on the raft sleeping, swimming, and securing lashings that came undone. Barely five feet and a hundred pounds each, they were livelier than the men, but small and girlish as they were Rustom found them worldlier than himself. As nurses, they were more familiar with the male body than he with the female (or, for that matter, with his own), and Seagrave had educated him further.

Burmese was the umbrella under which many tribes fell, but only one was intrinsically Burmese. The rest were Karen, Kachin, Shan, and Taungthu, each with habits and histories of its own. Kachin children, for instance, were introduced to sex from the age of ten. Families were expected to be as hospitable with food to travelers as with their daughters. A pregnant girl was more desirable because she had proven herself fertile. The more "husbands" a woman had the more attractive she was presumed. These customs had been wiped out with the advent of missionaries in the nineteenth century, but sex was hardly the great closeted subject it was with the British and Indians even in the twentieth. They hardly cared if loongyis strapped under their armpits slipped occasionally, and were more comfortable with the naked British than the naked British with them though their long communion had gone a long way toward shedding everyone's inhibitions.

In Rustom's Bombay they would have been invisible, no more than servants—but, seeing them meet their challenges as well as Stilwell met his, Rustom found them admirable and attractive in ways that his clubbing friends could never be and would never understand. His affection for Aung would have been impossible in Bombay, and he wondered what might have developed had she not been married, but laughed immediately imagining how the Sanjanas would react if he were to take her for a wife.

A spring rain had fallen on the first night of the voyage. Sounds of the jungle, traveling farther on water, more loudly by night, had erupted with twice the ferocity of their treks by day, but on the second night of the voyage the rain poured as thick as soup, and jungle noises—hooting owls, scolding monkeys, screaming panthers—were drowned by the drumming of rain on the river. Lightning brushed the sky and thunder beat the earth. They were on the last of the hospitalship group of three, linked to the middle raft by just one bamboo, Robin attempting to secure another as they floundered ahead. Rustom was astonished to hear anything above the downpour, but Kevin on the other side of the raft howled more loudly than the biggest monkey.

"GOD*DAM*MIT! *RUSTOM!*"

"*WHAT?*"

"I *CAN'T REACH* THE *BOT*TOM!"

"*ME NEI*THER!"

The two forward rafts got away, Robin falling into the water in a lastditch attempt to secure the lashing. The raft was at the mercy of the current, but the current itself was at the mercy of a whirlpool. They were spinning in circles in blackness. Seagrave came on deck. "ALL HANDS OVERBOARD!" When they hit snags they couldn't sail past, they jumped in the water to paddle the raft with their feet, lining up on both sides, pushing from behind, each member of the company with a "project" of his own to ensure everyone was accounted for at all times. Rustom and Aung kept each other in sight as did the others who had lined up their own "projects." Than Shwe stayed aboard at all times, astonishing everyone just by keeping up.

They had developed a routine, each knew his place and moved without being told, but they were soaked through before they entered the water, flashlights losing power, and rain spattering the river with the rapidity of machinegun bullets. It took them twenty minutes to find their rhythm; it took them two hours to inch the raft past the whirlpool. They found themselves completely turned around, but the current pulled them in the right direction and they were glad enough to let it do their work. It mattered less that they were going backward than that they were going in the right direction.

The raft took its own course for the next couple of hours during which they caught up with the forward rafts of the hospitalship, visible again for the zigzag of flashlights, and as dawn pinked the eastern sky and rain softened to a drizzle they could see mountains to the west. Over the mountains lay India. Seagrave shut his eyes, drawing a deep breath, thinking of the long trek still ahead, and of his torn and festering feet.

They caught up with the other rafts in Homalin at three in the afternoon, surprised to find the company glum. The dropped burlap bags of food had rekindled everyone's hope that their radio message had been received, that they could expect rice, meat, medicine, mules, ponies, coolies—boats—in Homalin, but they found only an official saying the British Commissioner, who had received a message for Stilwell, had taken off on the only steam launch out of town. No one believed he would be back.

Stilwell's crew had not survived the voyage as well as Seagrave's though they had arrived sooner. Two of the officers had soiled their pants and appeared so pale they seemed hardly able to clean themselves. Two others smelled as if they had vomited on themselves. Stilwell himself seemed yellower, malarial despite the quinine with which all dosed themselves.

# RUSTOM'S STORY

The town was deserted in anticipation of the Japanese. Those who stayed either had no place to go or were too listless from poverty to leave and waited in dread, resigned to their fate. The shops were almost empty, food was scarce—but Tun Shein, bright and gay despite the ordeal, charmed even the desolated villagers into producing cigarettes, batteries, shoes, and most importantly four ponies.

The mule train with the Chinese arrived and Stilwell sent them ahead to cross the Chindwin, charging Tseng to get boats at gunpoint if necessary. They waited the rest of the day, still hoping for reinforcements, tending the sick, taping and bandaging feet. Stilwell conducted an arms inspection in anticipation of a confrontation with the Japanese, finding to his disgust too many weapons out of commission: rifles too filthy to be fired, breeches spotted with rust, muzzles fouled with mud and dirt, slings broken or cracked. Outraged, he had ordered all weapons cleaned and oiled.

They spent the night in a nearby monastery, pushing past four angry priests into the principal shrine, a vaulted hall decked with multiple rows of lifesize Buddhas, each lit by the flame of its own oil lamp. The main altar heralded a giant Buddha draped in satin and silk gleaming before a coal brazier. The company gazed, mouths agape, but only momentarily, before slumping to the stone floor, guns clattering to the ground, asleep the moment they shut their eyes—all except the General, pondering their next day: whether they would find boats; whether finding boats they would cross before the Japanese arrived; whether outrunning the Japanese they would outrun the monsoon; whether outrunning the monsoon the sick would keep up; whether, underscoring everything, they would have enough food.

**IT WAS A SAD, SORE, SORRY TROOP** that stumbled from the monastery the next morning following a meager breakfast of oatmeal and tea across two and a half miles of forest, to emerge on the beach before the Chindwin, doctors and nurses, officers and privates, coolies and cooks and Friends, British and Indians and Burmese and Americans. More than a hundred pairs of eyes gazed across the river, many hundreds of yards in width, to a narrow beach. Forests cloaked the Naga Hills, the easternmost foothills of the Himalayas, their tips lost in fog and clouds, seven thousand feet at their lowest. The longer they waited, the sooner the Japanese would appear, and the river presented their most dangerous hurdle yet, vulnerable to gunboats around the corner as they crossed—but they had neither boats to cross the river nor hope to cross the hills ahead. Too many had rested too many hopes on reaching Homalin safely, too sick, footsore, travelweary, and disappointed to imagine the road ahead.

Rustom had heard talk among the men of striking out on their own so they wouldn't be burdened with the weak. The General himself looked older for the day in Homalin with no plan but to keep on going until they could go no farther. The river and mountains appeared to reduce him to the old man that he was. He had lost weight as had they all, some beginning to show skeletons. Despite quantities of quinine, his skin still held its malarial pallor as he gazed across the river, chewing his cigarette holder.

Whatever the men said, Rustom was determined to stay the General's course, and what happened next only confirmed his faith. Half a mile downriver, around the bend, as if Stilwell had willed them, came five dugout canoes and a larger boat, setting everyone yelling and jumping, nurses laughing and screaming, men waving topis, James no less crazy, rolling on the ground, skipping from one wild bunch to the next, wagging his tail so vigorously the tail seemed to wag the dog. Stilwell had to calm them for fear of scaring away the boats before Breedom Case, speaking the dialect, could cup his hands over his mouth and lure the boats ashore with sums of money.

The General lined the company in six queues for the boats, canoes taking six at a time, the larger boat nine. A few trips back and forth ferried everyone and everything across, including the four ponies led through the water. Stilwell was last but one. In their flurry they had left James behind, head cocked to one side, tail barely sweeping the sand, until Stilwell turned the boat around to pick him up and the tail once more wagged the dog—but reaching the other side, hiking inland until they were out of sight of the river, waiting for General Tseng and his men to approach with the mule train, realizing they might have escaped the Japanese only to fall prey to the mountains, they might as well have stayed on the wrong side of the river for all the excitement they showed. When bombers droned overhead they showed not even fear. The jungle provided all the cover they needed, but they needed more than cover.

The midday meal, the only meal of the day, was rice and cheese. At two in the afternoon, stomachs still growling, feet barely patched, they began the long hike into India. The trail through the jungle followed a shallow gradient to begin, but got much steeper within a couple of hours. Stilwell used a bamboo to help him along and others followed his example, all perspiring as if they walked under direct sunlight. The teak trees, over a hundred feet tall, provided leafy canopies, but bamboo thickets reflected heat, focusing it like a glass, and thick and winding roots grabbed at their feet.

Rustom followed Aung, who panted audibly, but like all the nurses never complained. Seagrave, riding behind, sharing a pony with Than Shwe, hating to get special treatment despite his pusridden feet, had wondered how he would get through the mountains, feet throbbing even as he rode. He had walked to the Chindwin with the others, and would have continued walking if not for the express command of Colonel Williams, Stilwell's medical officer. "A doctor shouldn't tell another doctor what to do, Seagrave, but you're just too damn dedicated for your own good." Seagrave, conceding the point, had gratefully and graciously accepted Than Shwe's invitation to share her pony.

The complaints grew stronger as the day grew long, men more than women falling to the ground, supposedly on their last legs, and when the trail dipped into a ravine Stilwell called a halt. They were in a clearing beside a stream which poured into a pool. It was earlier than he might have stopped for the night, but the company appeared to need time to find its climbing legs as it had taken time to find first its marching legs and then its rafting legs, but he was firm regarding rations for the night. They were served only tea.

To Rustom's surprise, with the threat of the Japanese behind him, he was becoming aware of his surroundings again, stronger in his mind even as his body deteriorated than when he had marched through the rump of Burma. Their path was strewn with damp leaves and red and yellow flowers. Thick braided lianas dangled from heights of fifty feet, and banana leaves, six feet by three, allowed them to waterproof their things. He had seen hornbills, snipe, teal, birds he couldn't recognize, hares and otters, the ubiquitous monkeys audible even when invisible, rekindling his interest in things other than the war. The underbrush rustled with toads and lizards and other amphibious things, Stilwell had pulled a green leech eight inches long from his leg as if it were a length of string, setting the example again for the others. Despite the setbacks and the apparent hopelessness of their situation Rustom's faith remained strong in Stilwell, and beyond Stilwell in his own good fortune. He also had Aung, without whose attention he might have faded into apathy and worse.

Seagrave had bathed his sores in the icy water, and feeling his malarial chill come on again he had rolled himself in a blanket when the General walked by. "What's the matter, Seagrave? Got a fever?"

"No, sir. I got wet and felt a little cold. Just warming up."

"How are your feet?"

"Better, sir."

"You are lying."

"Yes, sir."

The General laughed, walking away. The unfolding scene could not have been more sylvan, the company cavorting in the pool, Chinese in green uniforms, nurses shedding colorful loongyis, festooning their hair with pink and white flowers, Americans and British in khakis, some men down to their shorts, some to nothing, bathing, shaving, soaking their feet. Rustom kept his shorts, kept his eyes on Aung laughing and splashing with other nurses, with no more concern than children on a swingset. A sudden unexpected burst of thunder raised a communal wail, from none louder than the nurses, but to their pleasure and amazement they found themselves in the eye of the storm, rain pouring all around leaving them dry in Eden, raising their spirits enough to set them singing again, Seagrave leading them in a rendition of "There's a Church in the Valley" before branching into other songs.

**THE PATH GOT STEEPER** the next day, and steeper again. They had risen from their blankets, curled on carpets of leaves, and breakfasted on the last portions of rice, groaning as they prepared for the day's march, but Rustom's faith had deepened. Despite cases of malaria, dysentery, swollen ankles, and bloody feet they had suffered no fatalities though every successive part of the journey had proven more perilous than the last. They had rafted down the Uyu River imagining it would prove easier on their feet, only to find water more treacherous than earth. They had arrived in Homalin with expectations of food and rest, only to find themselves deceived. They had crossed the Chindwin ahead of the Japanese, only to find the hills more impenetrable.

They would not have got even as far as they had without the General's bullwhip on the column, his adherence to the calendar, and his eye on Imphal even as he took one day at a time. They had about a week of the most difficult trails ahead and no more than two days of rations, but there had been talk of killing the mules if necessary for food and Rustom marshaled his mental forces even as his physical flagged. He shivered continually, hot or cold, but taking quinine he was comforted that he had done all he could. He could do nothing regarding his growing weakness except push on as if all were well, and with Aung by his side he did just that.

A fog blanketed the ground as if a cloud had descended and the carpet of leaves squelched with dew under their feet. The path seemed to turn perpendicular, the ground to glue, and legs to rubber,

## A Googly in the Compound

but Stilwell didn't falter, and the marchers pressed hands on knees to keep up. For all their complaints, for all the talk of deserting the column, no one faulted Stilwell. They admired him for asking no more of anyone than he would of himself, for sleeping on the ground like everyone else, for standing last in foodlines, for pushing them with his example more than his authority, for treating officers and enlisted men alike. Rustom grinned, catching an unexpected exchange between the General and one of the other generals. "What's the matter? You're holding up the column."

"Can't help it. It's the pace, the altitude. We should rest more. The Japs are no longer on our tail."

"Dammit! You know we've got other things to worry about than the goddam Japs. Are you sick?"

"No, sir. Just my legs. I'm winded."

"You'll have to do better. You're a general. You have to set an example."

"Sorry, sir. I can't help it."

"Dammit all to hell! You've *got* to help it! I *mean* it!"

Even so, coming upon another ravine, Stilwell called a halt. Cold water bubbled from a brook into a pool and splashed over rocks and ferns down the side of the hill. They consumed the last of their sardines, sweetened tea, and sat in the spray from the waterfall pouring out of the brook. Below them the Chindwin shone like a ribbon, fully a day's climb away, but seeming no farther than a stone's throw. The trill of the whistle called them once more to their feet, many to be dragged upright to wakefulness.

The fog lifted, but clouds got darker, and sunlight turned violet before disappearing altogether. The storm came with a thunderclap, pelting them with raindrops the size and speed of bullets, before coalescing and falling as if an ocean were pouring from the sky. Coolies slipped and fell dropping what food they had left, mules brayed gathering in groups to resist the march, nurses shivered and whimpered even as they forged ahead, strong men buffeted by the wind lost their balance.

Rustom climbed the path, treading blindly, visibility reduced to a few feet, thumping his bamboo with each step of his right foot, recalling what Seagrave had said about the monsoon: *We don't measure the rainfall in inches, but in feet.* It fell no less heavily in Bombay, but in Bombay he was never far from shelter. Aung had wanted to take her pack from him, but he insisted on carrying it piggybacked on his own. He couldn't have said whether he slipped or whether his knee had buckled, but he found himself on his back, unable to get up, lashed by the deluge and weighed down by the packs. He groaned, sensing an unwelcome warmth fill his pants, an unwelcome stink rise to his nose despite the beating rain.

Stilwell clamped his hat on his head, never letting up the pace, striding with his bamboo and staring down the lightning before coming suddenly to a full stop, staring like mad pegleg Ahab on the deck of the *Pequod*. He had come upon a clearing with a dozen huts surrounded by a crowd of naked men. The officer behind him whispered. "I don't believe it. Are you seeing what I'm seeing?"

"I can't tell. My glasses are fogged up." The men stayed where they were as he advanced, neither saying anything nor taking cover. Stilwell shook his head, speaking almost to himself. "My God, I hope they're not refugees. That'd cook our goose for sure."

He moved toward the open door of the closest hut with the first members of the column to be met in the doorway by a tall blond smiling Englishman, arms akimbo. For a moment everyone was speechless, Breedom Case the first to break the silence. "This is General Stilwell. His party is coming up behind us."

The Englishman nodded, smiling as if his face might split. "Yes, I know. I was sent to meet you. You have reached Kawlum."

Stilwell spoke with narrowed eyes, wiping his glasses on his wet shirt. "Who the hell are you?"

"I'm Tim Sharpe, sir, President of the Manipur Durbar, sent by General Wood. He's in command of supply in Assam. I've been on the trail from Imphal for five days. Come in from the rain, sir."

Stilwell nodded, stepping into the hut. "Any Americans with you?"

"No, sir, but I have five hundred coolies, food, cigarettes, even whisky and rum on the way—some here already. A doctor with medical supplies is one day behind and hundreds of pack ponies. Your messages and recommendations all got through, sir. My instructions are to guide you to Imphal and help in any way I can."

"How did you know which way I'd come?"

"There are four routes, sir. I called Delhi to find out what kind of man you were. They said you were very intelligent. This is the most intelligent route you could have taken. There was a note in one of the burlap bags we dropped, but maybe you missed it."

Stilwell nodded, seeming to deflate as if he no longer needed to appear larger than life. The rain gave way to a rainbow as if they were in a movie. A soundtrack of swelling strings with a fanfare of brass would not have been out of place. Down the path Rustom lay pantless on the ground, Aung beside him washing the shit and blood of dysentery from his legs. For dinner the company had fresh barbecued pork served over rice, as much as they wanted. The nurses talked about all the ice cream they would eat when they got to Calcutta, all the movies they would see. James groaned with pleasure, gnawing on bones. Rustom subsisted on nothing more than a warm broth, but couldn't stop smiling, grateful once more for what he could only account as a divine hand in the proceedings.

They still had five days of hiking ahead, but relative to what they had endured it was a cakewalk. They needed to carry not even a matchbox, not even to walk if they preferred to ride as Rustom did the rest of the way, Aung walking alongside. Stilwell led the muddy column emerging from the jungle into Imphal on 19 May, hat still clamped on his head, amber cigarette holder in his mouth. They had been marching since 7 May. A British Officer in the government station at Imphal greeted him with a question. "How many did you lose on the march?"

Stilwell seemed to smile through every wrinkle on his face. "Not a one! Not a single one!"

A MONTH LATER Rustom was back in Bombay, darker from the sun, skin more parched, down from two hundred pounds to 136, resembling a wraith of his former self. Daisy said reverently that he looked like Gandhi. Sohrab smirked, saying nothing. Rustom said nothing about what had happened and was relieved not to be pressed. Sohrab was curious, but Dolly told him to sit on his curiosity. Rustom would speak when he wished, and not at all if he did not wish.

Rustom was grateful for Dolly's thoughtfulness, wondering what his father might have told her about his own war experience, but returning courtesy for courtesy he asked no questions himself and said nothing more than that he was glad to be back. He wrote to Aung, who wrote back to her "Brai'case," setting Sohrab's tongue wagging again until Dolly told him to shut up. She had stayed in Calcutta with the other nurses, well cared for until she might return home with the others. He recognized they had little in common aside from their astonishing experience, but wrote back to say she would be treated like a princess should she ever visit Bombay, but never heard back.

He followed the war as much as he could through newspapers, newsreels, books, enjoying Stilwell's response at a press conference to statements by the British regarding his "glorious retreat," his "heroic, voluntary withdrawal." The censor in New Delhi had tried to block the statement, but in vain. Rustom had clipped the statement and put it in his wallet:

> IN THE FIRST PLACE, NO MILITARY COMMANDER IN HISTORY EVER MADE A *VOLUNTARY* WITHDRAWAL. AND THERE'S NO SUCH THING AS A *GLORIOUS* RETREAT. ALL RETREATS ARE AS IGNOMINIOUS AS HELL. I CLAIM WE GOT A HELL OF A LICKING. WE GOT RUN OUT OF BURMA, AND IT'S HUMILIATING AS HELL. I THINK WE OUGHT TO FIND OUT WHAT CAUSED IT, GO BACK, AND RETAKE BURMA. THAT'S ALL, GENTLEMEN. GOOD NIGHT.

Rustom grinned, hating the hypocrisies spouted by newspapers and PR machines as much as Stilwell, and saluting the General for speaking his mind.

He recognized also the great fortune that had separated him from his Division. The 17th also found its way to safety in Tamu, southeast of Imphal, but with many more casualties. He had found himself instead first with Seagrave's unit, and then Stilwell's, managing always to stay a step ahead of the enemy. A detachment of the Japanese cavalry had ridden into Homalin just thirty-six hours after they had left. They would never get an exact accounting, not even after the war was over, but a general reckoning had the British losing almost 13,500 men (including Indians and Burmans), the Chinese as many as 40,000, the Japanese less than 5,000.

The following year Dr. Gordon Stifler Seagrave published his autobiography, *Burma Surgeon*, emphasizing his roots, his work, and including his walkout with Stilwell. The year after, Stilwell was back in the theater among the Allies, taking Burma back from the Japanese. Rustom collected books, memoirs, articles, pictures, everything he could find about the war, and reading Seagrave's book, learning the stories of the nurses he had known, he received the first glimmer of what he might want to do with the rest of his life.

He had resumed his clubbing, many commenting how little, aside from his appearance, his experience had changed him, he accepting their comments with grace, saying nothing, knowing they could never understand. He was sometimes oblivious, blanking out in the middle of conversations, once disappearing without knowing where he had been. His left hand had healed, he had been examined by a neurosurgeon, but whatever needed to be done Seagrave had done. The rest was in God's hands. The conflagration, when it came, took him by surprise as much as Dolly who was the first to find him.

He had settled in the den with tea and jam tarts to read yet another story about refugees. Eleven-year-old Colin McPhedran and his thirteen-year-old brother, Robert, were turned away from a Dakota meant to fly refugees from Burma. His mother and sixteen-year-old sister, Ethel, got off the plane to join them, his mother lifting a child holding its arms out to someone into the hatchway. As the plane headed for the runway it was strafed and bombed by two Japanese planes. There was nothing the McPhedrans could do but watch in horror as people fell from the flaming Dakota.

The family of four set off planning to walk to safety among thousands with the same plan, passing hundreds dying from exhaustion and hunger along the way. The farther they walked the greater grew the numbers of the dead until one morning the mother could not get up. Robert, pulling on her arms, was too weak to lift her. She gave her rings to Ethel saying they must go on and get help. Colin would have stayed with his mother, willingly died with her, but she whispered to him words he would never forget. *The world is full of good people. I know you will find them and be well cared for. Son, you must walk on. Don't look back.*

Reading the words, Rustom's throat filled, his shoulders shook, his breath came in short quick gasps, but his eyes remained dry. He read on to find the children had huddled together for a night to find Robert dead the next morning. Brother and sister moved on for a bit, but lay down shortly in the mud, too comfortable and warm even to think of food or water, and shut their eyes. Colin woke later in a refugee camp to learn he and his sister had been rescued, but she had died since. He had started the journey weighing 124 pounds. He now weighed fifty.

When the tears started Rustom couldn't stop them. He cried as if his own mother had died, he cried as if crying were breathing, as if he cried for the world. He cried for two days, asleep and awake. Dolly held him, stayed with him, saying nothing, giving him her presence, her closeness. Rustom understood, though not until much later, that she had been this way before.

Then came the death of Hitler on the third anniversary of the day Stilwell began his walkout. Then came Hiroshima, then Nagasaki, then the annual pilgrimage of the Sanjanas to Navsari.

# A Googly in the Compound

THE RETURN OF RUSTOM provided the biggest blessing of the war for the Sanjanas, more than the birth of Neville since Neville had never been given up for lost, even for Daisy for whom Neville provided finally a solid tie with the Sanjanas unlike the elastic tie through Dinyar. She wheeled a pram into the lift from their flat in Sanjana House. Neville, now a year and a half, lay in the pram; Dinyar, a year older, toddled alongside, squeezing beside his mother in the confined space. She remained closelipped and smiling about the difference between her sons, Dinyar darker than Neville, but otherwise more European, less round in his face, eyes, and cheeks, bearing the stamp of his heritage: Goan, not Parsi; more Portuguese and English than Indian.

Most mothers left the morning constitutional of their children to the ayahs, but Daisy liked it for herself as much as the time alone with the boys. It also allowed Patty and Nancy time for chores unhampered. During the time of her pregnancies she had let herself be pampered, honeymooning in Kashmir, holidaying in hillstations, balmier resorts along the coasts, sometimes with Sohrab, other times with various combinations of the others. She had found the rhythm of her life; everything was ancillary to motherhood; other mothers let ayahs take the children on their daily outing, but nothing satisfied her more than her walk through the Oval maidan, wheeling Neville, Dinyar by her side or in her arms.

The months leading to Neville's birth had included the worst of times. Germany, in bed with the Soviet Union (Fatherland and Mother Country), had slithered through the continent, a serpent gobbling Poland, Czechoslovakia, Denmark, Norway, Holland, Belgium, parts of France, rising on its belly, raising its head to spit poison across the channel at England. Italy had fused with the German serpent (fat with Yugoslavia), and trained its venom on Greece. The throes of the thrashing bodies had ravaged countries in the Middle East and Africa unleashing neverending rivers of refugees into the ruin of the world until the serpent, swollen with pride, had slithered back to sink its fangs into the jugular of its late bedmate.

# RUSTOM'S STORY

In the east had risen the Japanese sun, red as blood, a twin juggernaut to the German in the west, slamming the British against the eastern gates of India, daring even to knick the hand of Uncle Sam. In India the British had made more hollow promises of freedom to ensure the loyalty of the colony, but Mr. Gandhi, imagining the Japanese interested only in the British, had based his Quit India movement on a simple equation—no British, no Japanese—and Mr. Bose, imagining a British defeat would spell freedom for India, intrigued for a German victory. Mr. Churchill, signing the Atlantic Charter guaranteeing the right of all people to choose their own form of government, stated bluntly that it did not apply to India—and while Daisy couldn't agree with Mr. Churchill, much as she admired him, neither could she disagree, not as a loyal Briton, not in her country's hour of distress.

She might have had no worries about the war, but Rustom had surprised everyone, joining the 17th Indian Division, swanning off to Burma, saying nothing to anyone until it was too late to stop him. Her personal worries were a thing apart: Basil was married; Alphonse had abused her; the war had stranded her in India—pregnant. Sohrab had proposed; she had accepted. He treated her well and she was determined to make him a good wife. If they minded their responsibilities love would come; if it didn't they would change their definition of love; so Sohrab had said, and so she had done, changed her definition of love, shifting its focus to her sons.

Pregnancy confirmed, they had married six days later, a small civil ceremony, befitting matters during the war, Sohrab convinced the child was his, Daisy exercising her privilege as a Briton to keep a stiff upper lip. Dinyar was born the following June, the day Italy declared war on England and France, a striking baby for the contrast of colors: light brown hair for which the Sanjanas credited Daisy; also for the green eyes though Phiroze and Dolly credited Kavas no less; but only Daisy credited the chocolate skin to Alphonse, only Daisy understood the compounded nature of the lie she continued to live, only Daisy breathed a sigh of relief after the birth of Neville the following June, the month Germany invaded the Soviet Union, a paler baby with darker hair and freckles. The freckles were soon to die, but never to be forgotten, continually flashed in photographs to visitors. Her tie to the Sanjanas through Dinyar was spurious, but her tie through Neville impeccable.

It was a slow lift, but her time was limitless. Arriving on the ground floor she slid the inner wooden latticed grill back on its castors followed by the outer metal grill, too intent on maneuvering the pram to notice the person in the lobby until he spoke. "Madam?"

She looked up. It was Alphonse showing rows of teeth. She felt enveloped in sheets of ice and gripped firmly the handle of the pram to keep her hands from shaking. "What are you doing here?"

His smile vanished. "Very sad thing has happened, madam. My mother. Dead. I feel so sad."

She knew about Gracie's death, but found herself unsympathetic, raising her chin, pursing her mouth. "Just like when your ammy died?"

Alphonse's eyes widened. "But my ammy is still alive."

Daisy kept silent, preferring not to squabble over who had lied.

Alphonse smiled again. "I have come for baksheesh. Dollybai said to come."

She had known about the baksheesh as well, but Dolly had said she would send it in the post; she would otherwise have been warier of his reappearance; but again she didn't want to squabble. She tried to keep herself and the pram between Alphonse and Dinyar. As he stepped toward the pram, presumably to see the baby, she wheeled it suddenly forward. "You are in my way. Please get out."

He looked up, the smile vanishing into a hard line, eyes narrowing to slits, recognizing the dependable transformation, unspoiled girl to burra memsahib, once his friend, now too good for him—but he got out of her way. She continued to wheel the pram, keeping Dinyar out of his sight as far as possible, rocking the pram carefully down the four steps to the street, turning into the hot sun, away from the doorway, lifting Dinyar in her arms, hurrying across the road to the far side of the bandstand, out of sight of Sanjana House. She was still shaking when she reached it and sat on the steps leaning against one of the supports, afraid he would still be there when she returned, wanting to give him time to leave and herself time to recover. Ten minutes later she heard his voice again behind her. "Madam?"

She refused to turn. Dinyar was playing with blocks in the bandstand. Her hands were shaking again, but she gripped them into fists. "What do you want?"

Alphonse came into view, smiling before her. "He is my son, no? That boy is my son, no?"

"Rubbish! I was married almost as soon as I came, in October. He was born in August."

Alphonse's grin spread into a chortle. "Lies, madam. I know it is lies. He was born in June. I know. Dollybai wrote to my mother when he was born. I know. Even then I thought he might be my son."

No servant would dare call her a liar, not in India, not with such confidence, not unless he were sure of himself, sure of his target. Daisy felt herself tighten, shrivel, sink. "If you thought so then, why didn't you do something then?"

"What could I do? He was here. I was there. What could I do?"

"Alphonse, what do you want?"

"I want to see my boy. I am here now. I want to see my boy."

"He is *not* your boy."

"He is my boy." Alphonse grinned again, more widely than before. "He is a blackie—just like me. If I did not see him I would not know, but I see him and I know. He is my boy."

"He is the boy of whoever looks after him. He is the boy of whoever feeds him and clothes him. He is not your boy."

Alponse opened his palms skyward in mock appeal, smiling his triumph. "I lost my job, you know. Wartime, no steward needed—no steward, no baksheesh." He shrugged as if there were nothing more to say.

Daisy knew he had lost his job, but she also knew his sister's husband in Dona Paula ran a lucrative liquor business, she knew his brother managed a pig farm, she knew his difficulty was boredom more than money, she knew Dolly had enlarged Gracie's pension to compensate vicissitudes imposed by the war, she knew Dolly's baksheesh to compensate Gracie's death would be generous. She also knew no such arguments would make a difference to Alphonse. She repeated herself. "He is the boy of whoever looks after him. He is not your boy."

Alphonse frowned, surprised she had ignored his argument. "If I knew I would have done something—but if I didn't know what could I do? Why are you angry? What have I done?"

"You lied to me. You lied to me about your ammy."

Alphonse's grin turned sly. His eyes narrowed again. He flicked his tongue over his upper lip. "If I not lie, you not fuck me, no? But you like that I fuck you, no?"

He was being twice insolent, for what he said as much as for how he had said it, pidgin English pigeonholing her with Mrs. Turpin. She felt as threatened as if he had pulled a knife. Dinyar had stopped playing, sat watching the man standing a yard from where his mother sat. Neville started crying in the pram. There was no one else in the bandstand, but they were plainly visible from the street. She moved quickly, rising to her feet, covering the distance between them, slapping his face hard, in a single sweeping movement.

Alphonse stepped back, raising his hand to his cheek, glaring again through narrow eyes, nodding. "It is true what everybody is saying. All English memsahibs are the same. All are thinking they are maharanis in India."

Daisy took Neville out of the pram to calm him. Dinyar came to her, clutching her skirt. "I don't care what you think. I don't care what you say. I only want you to go away. I don't ever want to see you again. You are not welcome here. Do you understand?"

Alphonse grinned. "But why I should go? Just because maharani has spoken? He is my boy, no?"

"He is *not* your boy. I have told you. He is the boy of whoever looks after him."

"And I have also told you: If I not know, what I could do? Let us go see Dollybai. She is very good. Let us ask her what I could do. She will tell you same thing. Let us go. Then you will see."

He taunted her with the manner of his speech as much as his smile. Her slap had encouraged him, told him he was important. She should have ignored him. She rocked Neville in her arms, avoiding his eyes. "Dollybai is very busy. I will not bother her with something so silly."

"Then you only tell me. What I should do?"

"I have told you already. Go away and never come back. There is nothing for you here."

He waggled his head in figures of eight, unendingly confident, knowing his power. "He is my boy. That is something. Who are you to say such things to me? Why I should go just because you say? Why I should have nothing? He is my boy. I should also get something."

"What do you want?"

"What you will give?"

"I have a hundred rupees in the flat."

Alphonse laughed. "Hundred rupees is nothing for Sanjanas, hundred rupees is spit for Sanjanas."

"How much then?"

"One thousand rupees."

"I will give you five hundred."

"One thousand—has to be one thousand. Then I will go. Then I will not come back."

"I don't have a thousand rupees in the flat."

"You can send me, in the post."

She refused to look at him, spoke quietly. "I will do that. I will send it in the post. You will have it in a fortnight. Now go! Get out!"

He glared, debating for a moment whether to leave, nodding finally. "I am going, madam, but only because you were once upon a time good to me. Now you think like a burra memsahib, but you are not even a chhota memsahib. Do not forget where you are coming from. In England you were what? Shopgirl? Seamstress? Waitress? No better than myself."

She didn't look up, didn't say a word.

"Do not think I do not know what is going on, Madame Daisy Holiday Sanjana Turpentine. You marry Sohrab seth because he is rich. He marry you because you are English. I know how it is, I know."

Still she looked down, remained silent. Explanations would have been hopeless; worse, humiliating. Alphonse spat on the ground, a large red blob of betel by her feet, before he turned and left.

**DAISY'S FRIENDSHIP CIRCLE** met for lunch every Tuesday at the Willingdon Club, activities including talks, debates, guest lecturers, poetry readings, gramophone concerts. The atmosphere had grown proportionately more gay with the continual improvement of the war news: Russians blunting the German advance at Moscow, billowing around the Sixth Army at Stalingrad, boxing and bagging soldiers on the Volga; Mussolini dead, swinging, desecrated; British winning the Battles of Britain and the Atlantic; allies swarming along the Normandy coast, sweeping German rubble from France; British entering Brussels, taking Antwerp, recapturing Rangoon; Hitler entombed, incinerated, blasted in his bunker; Americans bombing Hiroshima, bombing Nagasaki.

For the subject of her talk, Daisy had chosen to revisit the article she had liked best of the few she had published: the effect of the Great War on women, their mores, rights, clothing, attitudes, adding a postscript speculating on the effect of the war now winding to a close. The fight for independence remained strong in India, but hardly dimmed the optimism following first VE day and then VJ. Even the specter of Alphonse had begun to wither; she had sent him the thousand rupees the same week against her better judgment, knowing she had not seen the last of him, and after three years of looking over her shoulder was beginning to hope he meant to uphold his end of the bargain—but waiting at the entrance to Sanjana House for Vinod, their driver, to bring the Humber around, rehearsing her talk to herself, she found her hope pricked like a balloon as she saw him striding toward her and realized he had been waiting for her to show. He grinned. "Hullo, Madam."

Her hands shook as before and she clenched them again into fists. "What do you want?"

"Arre, madam, what? Not even saying hullo to your old friend?"

"I thought we had an understanding."

"Yesyes, we are still having. I only want a little bit talking with you."

She wondered how she had ever trusted him. The exaggerated pidgin only deepened his duplicity, the guile of adopting guilelessness, revealing the Hyde within the Jekyll, the creature within the lagoon. He was proving himself no less a monster, but she understood also from his speech that he now equated her with Mrs. Turpin. "I don't want to talk to you. I said I never wanted to see you again."

"That is just what I am wanting to talk about—only a small talk."

"I do not want to talk to you, not even a small talk. We have nothing to say to each other."

"But maybe, yes, we are having? Things are not that much changed, no?"

"I'm afraid I have no time at all. I'm just waiting for the car. Please go away."

His smile was sly. "If not now, then after you are coming back?"

"Afterward I have to pack. We are going to Navsari tomorrow. We will be gone for a week." It was time for the annual family pilgrimage, in memory of Kavas Sanjana's death.

Alphonse sighed. "Arre, madam, what-all you are talking? In this much time I could have said already what I want. You want I should go to Dollybai instead?"

"What do you want?"

"Same thing."

"What?"

"Ten thousand rupees."

Dolly's eyes glazed. She had debated the wisdom of submitting to blackmail three years ago, but she had easily advanced the thousand rupees, and could as easily advance ten thousand, but those would be just the first cracks in the dam. Recognizing finally the vastness of the Sanjana fortune she knew he would return with a sledgehammer. "What nonsense! You must be mad."

"Who is mad we will see—you or me or Dollybai."

"Ten thousand rupees is out of the question. Besides, we both know you are a liar."

"How I am a liar?"

"You lied about your ammy. You lied about not coming back."

"That was before. Now is different."

"How is it different? How do I know you will not come back even if I do give you the money?"

"I am giving you my hundred percent guaranty. On ten thousand rupees I can live until I am old."

"Well, then, let me say simply that I do not believe you. I refuse to give you any more money. I shouldn't have given you any money at all. It was a mistake, but I am not going to repeat it."

"Then I will go to Dollybai."

"It will be no good for you to go to Dollybai. She will not give you any money either. You may cause trouble for me, but it will do you no good. In the end, I will be all right, and you will not get anything out of it."

"You think so? We will see."

"Indeed, we will. If you want to wait around while we are in Navsari that is up to you, but I have made up my mind. I refuse to let you bully me anymore."

His mouth dropped for a moment before he repeated himself. "I will go to Dollybai."

"Do what you want. I don't care. Here is the car."

She stepped forward, but he grabbed her arm. "Madam, think what you are saying. If you are giving me trouble, I can also give you trouble. If I ask Dollybai she will let me come to Navsari."

Daisy stopped, eyes narrowed, offering no resistance, speaking in a soft cold voice. "How dare you touch me! Let go my arm!"

He let go her arm, but laughed. "Now I am not to touch you—but before …" He nodded his head, showing he understood how it was. "I will come to Navsari. Wait and see. Dollybai will let me come."

Daisy said nothing, getting into the Humber, but could think of nothing else during the meeting of the Friendship Circle. Her stomach was a rock coming home, and when she learned Dolly had agreed to let Alphonse join them she felt the rest of her body turn to stone. Dolly had been surprised: if he wanted a change for his health as he said she could think of no place better than Goa, but had not given his request a second thought. He could sleep in the storage room, and there were plenty of ways he could make himself useful. Daisy felt sick enough to consider staying in Bombay, but realized it would only delay the inevitable and whatever the outcome she wanted everything settled.

## DAY OF THE TIGER: 5
### (September 25, 1945)

VICTORIA SAT COMFORTABLY, Sohrab's hand her plaything and prey, seemingly unaware of the rest of his body, licking blood from the cut. Sohrab's breath slowed almost to a halt, his body cold and white as one already dead except for beads of sweat trickling from his brow, eyes blinking rapidly as butterfly wings, his face old as an Indian sage, skin sagging on the bones, lips tucked over toothless gums. He tried to speak, but could barely breathe.

The temperature seemed to have fallen in the compound, freezing the tableau motionless. Phiroze was first to move, rising from his chair, motioning others to get into the house, motioning Alphonse to bring the gun closer.

Rustom, Daisy, and Dolly rose from their chairs and began to move toward the house with Phiroze, careful not to be sudden, eyes darting between Victoria and Alphonse; Fakhro latched his family into the kitchen and stood by the back door, ready to slam it shut as soon as everyone was inside; but Alphonse froze. Phiroze spoke calmly. "Come closer. You must not miss."

Alphonse held the gun ready, but shook his head, eyes white and round, voice soft and trembling. "If I shoot, tiger will kill me first."

"Shoot straight and tiger will die. Miss, and she will kill us all. Gun is wonky. Come closer."

Alphonse shook his head again. "It will know I have shot. It will kill me."

## A Googly in the Compound

Phiroze pushed Dolly toward the house, but she refused to leave him. Rustom and Daisy had been closest to the house, but they stopped moving as well, waiting to see what Alphonse would do. Daisy's voice was soft. "Give me the gun. I'm not scared."

She stood to his left behind Victoria. His mouth twisted, his voice gaining strength despite the sweat breaking in a tide down his forehead and he pointed the rifle as if to threaten her. "Of course not. Madam is never scared."

Victoria raised her head to yawn and looked around, purring and content, forgetting the hand she was nursing. Sohrab might then successfully have removed his hand, but he was paralyzed.

Phiroze raised his voice infinitesimally. "Alphonse, are you crazy? What are you thinking?"

Sweat descended like a curtain across Alphonse's brow, but he kept Daisy in his sights. "Ask her. She knows."

Phiroze looked at Daisy who kept her gaze on Alphonse, her voice hard. "He wants money."

"Alphonse, money is not a question. Just do as I say."

"Ten thousand rupees I want."

"Twenty thousand if you aim straight."

Alphonse nodded, training the gun again on Victoria.

"Come closer or everyone will be killed. Put the gun right up to her head."

Alphonse came within six feet of Victoria, face blurry with sweat, pointing the muzzle at her head.

"Closer. Then she will die right away. And you will get twenty thousand rupees."

Alphonse took another step and aimed the gun again.

"Closer. Put the gun to her head."

Alphonse shook his head. "I am shooting now."

Daisy shook her head. "The gun is shaking. You are afraid. You will miss. Let me do it."

Alphonse looked up suddenly, face in a grimace, eyes catching hers like hooks. He said nothing, but took two more steps. He was close enough to touch Victoria when he steadied the gun, took aim again, and fired.

In the wake of the blast there was once more the howling of monkeys, the screeching of fowl in the forest, but in the compound there was only a wide white silence, the sentient stillness of cemeteries awaiting the advent of ghosts, followed by an awful vibration riding the air, sweeping the grounds like a grating, atomizing all it swept, the savage roar of the tribe of tiger, Victoria erupting in an orange flame as if the ground were a bed of lava. Sohrab was jerked from his chair, flung in the air, and flopped in the tall grass like a puppet. Alphonse screamed, dropping the gun, rushing past Daisy toward the house, but fell before reaching the stairs, and Victoria descended upon him.

Daisy dashed for the gun, but holding it seemed hypnotized by the cyclonic whirl of dust and grass, flesh and fleece, the hopeless match of tooth and nail against fang and claw. Alphonse's screams seemed pitched impossibly high, above even Victoria's roars. Consciously or not, she saw providence in the turn of events and shook herself back into motion, shooting continually, clicking the trigger even after she had emptied the magazine, stopping only when she realized the cyclone was past. Fate had bowled her a googly and she had batted it for a sixer.

A new sound swam to the fore from the house, the long keening siren wail of a woman, Laxmi kneeling before her shrine, a pantheon of manyheaded manyarmed gods and goddesses. Daisy screamed, catching sight of Sohrab's disembodied hand; her legs buckled and she fell; without its thumb, it appeared like a white peeled bloodstained orchid, ribbons of pink flesh trimming jagged wedges of bone against a damp dark patch of ground.

# PHIROZE'S STORY
## Mesopotamia (1914-1916)

DAISY WALKED PAST THE BANDSTAND, Dinyar and Neville on either side, five and four, returning from their morning walk. The retreat of the war had ushered the advance of modern India, but the shape of modern India shifted with the wind. Jinnah's call for Pakistan, sounded at the beginning of the war, had been amplified, however unconsciously, by Gandhi's QUIT INDIA movement. Gandhi surmised that the British had drawn the Japanese to India's eastern gate, and the departure of the British would spell the departure of the Japanese, but creating greater headaches for the British he had driven them into Jinnah's welcoming arms, and toward the jeering slogan of his Muslim League: DIVIDE AND QUIT.

She didn't know what it meant, Churchill deposed, Attlee instated, but her place in India seemed increasingly precarious. Many of the Bombay English had either left or made plans to return to England, and she felt increasingly abandoned and homesick. The details of Indian independence remained murky, but the fact was no longer disputed. She could see it in the face of the man on the street, in his smile, milk teeth turning to fangs, the confidence of the young pup yapping at the old lion too tired to blink.

"Madam!"

She turned her head, trembling suddenly in the grip of a current from the past, crossing her arms to control her shaking hands, to confront a young Indian man she had passed a moment ago heading

# A Googly in the Compound

in the opposite direction, one of the nationalists, all in white from his dhoti to his Nehru cap, chin in the air, eyes of a headmaster, at once haughty and familiar. The day had opened brightly, but chose that moment to become overcast. "Yes, what is it?"

The man smiled, as delighted to be acknowledged as he seemed determined to abuse the acknowledgment. He waggled his finger between Dinyar and Neville. "Those are your children? Both?"

"Yes?"

"Excuse me, please, but they are having different fathers, are they not?"

Daisy had lived long enough in India to recognize that so very rude a question to English ears might well be asked in a spirit of friendship by an Indian, and as easily answered with a nod and a smile as a word, but what passed for idle curiosity from a fellow passenger in a train or a bus, or some other such conveyance that made friends of strangers, seemed more sinister from a man on the street. Under normal circumstances she would have shaken her head, "No," and moved on, but her circumstances had long ceased to be normal. "Who do you think you are to ask me such a question?"

She turned, uncrossed her arms, and walked on, holding her hands out to the boys, but he shouted after her. "Who am I? That is not the question. Who are you? That is the question. This is my country. Your days are numbered. English is finish. Only thing for you to do is Quit India."

He was right, and he knew it, or he would not have addressed her so boldly. He knew what was his, and knew he was about to get it. It was Britain for the British and India for the Indians, but ironically it was Britain that had taught India about nationhood, it was Britain that had built railways to unify India as India had never been unified, it was Britain that had built universities where Indians had learned about human rights from the works of Bentham and Mill. She wasn't so stupid as to imagine the English were boy scouts, they never did anything that wasn't in their interest, but in that they were like everyone else. She had one of the boys in each hand, but couldn't resist a final sally over her shoulder, mocking the man's pidgin. "Not quite. English is not quite finish."

She was exhilarated and frightened by her own behavior, she should never have allowed herself to be drawn into a shouting match, not in front of the boys—and wondered if, like the rest of the British, she had overstayed her welcome. King and Country was in her blood and bones; the Sanjanas, except for Neville, only in her skin. If a stranger had seen so clearly the difference between her sons, others had to have seen as clearly though no one had said a word, not to her face, and her need for absolution ballooned as her deceptions continued to loom. She was bound to the family by Neville—but, with the war over, not necessarily in Bombay.

Dolly continually explained Dinyar's darker skin saying the Dalals were darker than the Sanjanas and focusing on the Sanjana legacy, Dinyar's eyes green as Kavas's—ignoring Daisy's eyes, no less green. They had been married on 28 October, 1939, and Dinyar born on 10 June the following year. No one questioned the short gestation, not out loud, war changed priorities and proprieties; Sohrab had winked, hinting they might have usurped the privileges of the marital bed; but she was sure many speculated about what might have happened, counting back months and weeks and days; and seeing Alphonse again, her discomfort in his presence, her continual silence about their shipboard friendship, a similarity in the twist of Alphonse's ears and Dinyar's, they might easily make the jigsaw whole.

Returning home she relinquished the boys to Patty and Nancy. They were to spend the day with friends in Colaba. Sohrab had left, saying nothing about his destination. Aside from medical attention he had preferred to be left alone in the two months since their return from Navsari, erupting like a madman at whoever invaded his solitude, and she preferred to give him his way in all things. Two broken ribs had healed, but the doctor explained that his hand would remain a phantom presence; it would be a while before the gulf disappeared between what he felt and what he saw.

## A Googly in the Compound

**DAISY'S FEAR OF MODERN INDIA** wasn't idle. No matter the accommodation, no one was satisfied, neither Indians nor British. British soldiers were dissatisfied because they had enlisted for the war and wanted nothing more now than a discharge. Hindus were dissatisfied because Pakistan was to become a reality, a thorn in both sides of the country. Muslims were dissatisfied because a third of Indian Muslims lived as minorities among the Hindu population, and the creation of Pakistan would render them overnight aliens and foreigners in their homeland.

On Monday, 18 February, 1946, the dissatisfactions spilled into the streets of Bombay. Sailors of the Royal Indian Navy refused to obey orders protesting inequalities between the food and pay of Indians and British. Slogans appeared on the bulkheads: QUIT INDIA! REVOLT NOW! KILL THE WHITE BASTARDS! Guns were mounted and prepared to open fire. Sailors flooded the streets, glutted the byways, and filled up the public buildings, hoisting Congress flags, tearing down Union Jacks, civilians supporting sailors. Three were killed, many injured, until troops were called to quell the disorder, and RAF Mosquitoes grazed the city, threatening fire.

The boys had rushed to the windows at every roar to catch glimpses of the Mosquitoes, but Daisy had been more concerned about Sohrab, returning from lunch at the club, only to learn he had acquitted himself with distinction when the Humber had been halted by a mob. Vinod had stopped, unable to plough through the flood of rioters, faces had pressed themselves against the windows, rebels had clambered onto the bonnet—but Sohrab, wild with indignation, had forced open the door, stepped out of the car, and brandished the stump of his arm, claiming to have lost his hand in the service, and they had been allowed to pass, Vinod full of admiration for his master's ingenuity.

Caught in her conflict of loyalties, Daisy read the papers and listened unendingly to the wireless, looking to the news for direction. Her best course appeared to be to leave Bombay with Dinyar, no more a Sanjana than herself, and no one's responsibility but her own since Alphonse's death—but that would mean sacrificing her darling Neville. She could not have been more uneasy ascending the lift. The millstone of her deception long grown too heavy. She took such tentative steps toward the dining-room that Dolly and Phiroze didn't notice her until she spoke. "Dolly, Phiroze, good morning!"

Both looked up from Sunday breakfast, sipping tea, newspapers spread before them. Daisy remained in the doorway. The hesitation in her voice spurred Dolly to a warmer welcome. "Daisy? Come, come. Sit, sit. Have some tea."

Phiroze smiled. "Good morning, Daisy."

Daisy found it difficult to smile and joined them at the table, eyes downcast. "Thank you."

Dolly called Rahul for another cup and poured the tea. Phiroze closed his newspaper, recognizing Daisy's discomfort in the way she had tiptoed to the table, speaking calmly. "You just missed Rustom. He just left for the Gymkhana."

The new year had begun a new life for Rustom. He had gained admission to the University of Edinburgh to study medicine, determined to be a surgeon following in Seagrave's footsteps, and immersed himself in a flurry of activity, studying, researching, and filling out forms amid his usual activities. Daisy knew his routine and had waited for him to leave, listening for the descending lift, watching his car drive away. "I know. I wanted to talk to you in private—both of you."

Dolly lowered her cup to its saucer as if she had anticipated Daisy's request. "Of course, my dear. Shall we take the tea things to the den? We will have more privacy."

Daisy knew she meant from the servants who understood bits and pieces of English. "Yes, I think that would be best." She remained still, watching Dolly as she summoned Rahul again to bring the tea things to the den. "You don't seem very surprised, neither of you."

Dolly exchanged glances with Phiroze. "We're not. We have been expecting it for some time now—at least, since we came back from Navsari. It has to do with Alphonse, doesn't it?"

# A Googly in the Compound

Daisy realized she had been more transparent than she had realized. "How did you guess?"

"From the moment I told you he was coming to Navsari I knew something was wrong."

"Why didn't you say something?"

"At the time there was nothing to say—and so much has happened since then that we didn't want to rush you. There were more important things to take care of." Daisy pursed her lips, looking away, but Dolly shook her head. "Don't be alarmed, my dear. We are all in your debt now, but something is still the matter, isn't it?"

Daisy nodded.

Dolly's brow wrinkled. "Where is Sohrab?"

"He went to the club. I don't know when he'll be back."

They moved to the den closing the door behind them, Daisy and Dolly in a loveseat, Phiroze in a clubchair to Daisy's right, teatray on the coffee-table. Daisy told her story, leaving out nothing, sipping tea. Dolly and Phiroze listened in silence. When she was finished they remained silent, appearing still to absorb what she had said.

Daisy stared from Dolly to Phiroze and back, uncertain what to expect. "That's it. That's the whole story. Now you know. Dinyar is not your grandson."

Still they said nothing.

"I didn't say anything before because I didn't know what else to do. Now, with the war over, I think the best thing would be for me to go back to London."

Dolly exchanged a glance with Phiroze before she spoke. "What will you do in London?"

"I don't know, but I'm sure to find something. I could be a secretary again. I could write articles. You wouldn't have to worry about me."

"And what about the boys?"

"I have thought about this a lot." She swallowed. "I shall take Dinyar with me since he is not your grandson … but Neville …" Daisy had told her story without emotion, but now she slowed, swallowing again, seeming to draw words against her will. "I shall take him with me"—she spoke quickly, voice in splinters, "or leave him with you, just as you wish." Her cup rattled in the saucer in her hand. She set it down on the table, knotted her hands in fists on her knees, clenched her eyes shut, rocking in her seat, breathing in gasps and spasms.

Dolly smiled, immediately taking Daisy's hands in her own. "What nonsense, Daisy. Dinyar is our grandson every bit as much as Neville."

Phiroze spoke softly as always, also smiling. "Of course. Nothing to worry about on that score, Daisy. What you do is up to you, but you will always have a place with us—and so will Dinyar and Neville. You seem to be forgetting one very important detail."

Daisy was gratified, but bewildered, by their smiles. She had expected consternation, she would have accepted condemnation, but smiles she didn't understand. "What?"

"You have saved all of our lives."

Daisy shook her head. "If I hadn't gone for the gun Dolly would have."

Dolly squeezed Daisy's hands. "But you were the one, my dear, you were the one. I merely stood by. We all merely stood by."

"But that, even about that I feel terrible. You see, I wasn't … I wasn't just aiming for Victoria. I was aiming … I wanted … I wanted Alphonse dead. I had thought … all night long, I had thought … how I might somehow—I had the most terrible thoughts."

Daisy shook her head again, eyes shut, fists clenched, rocking more violently than before. Dolly let go Daisy's hands, put her arms around her shoulders, rocking with her. "Oh, my dear, my very sweet dear. We had no idea, no idea at all, but it's all right, it's all right now."

Daisy continued to rock. "I can't bear to think I killed him. I can't bear it."

Dolly stroked her as she continued to rock with her. "You are right, my dear. Some things cannot be borne, but they *must*—as you *must*, and as you *will*, bear this. We will help you."

"But I can't! I feel so guilty. I just *can't!*"

"You will. You have already taken the first step. You have told us everything."

Phiroze nodded. "Daisy, you mustn't blame yourself about Alphonse. He was finished. Once Victoria got hold of him he was finished. Nothing you could have done that Victoria didn't do better—and even if you *did* shoot him, so what? We have to take care of our own—and you have proven yourself one of our own many times over. Alphonse got what he deserved. If anything, I am more responsible for his death than you."

Daisy kept her eyes shut, continuing to rock, but shaking her head.

Phiroze nodded more vigorously. "Yes, yes, of course, I am. Who told him to get closer? Who told him to hold the gun to Victoria's head? Who kept pressing him forward? I knew the gun was wonky. I knew if the shot went wild Victoria would go for the closest person. Alphonse only made it worse for himself by running. He drew Victoria to himself by running away—*just as I had hoped.*"

The amplitude and violence of Daisy's rocking decreased.

Phiroze's eyes were narrow and hard. "We *have* to take care of our own, Daisy—or who is going to? It was the only thing. You did what you had to do and so did we. You were being loyal to your own kind. No need to beat yourself up about it now."

Daisy spoke with greater self-possession. "You are very kind, both of you—but I just can't see it that way. I will always feel I have brought disgrace on the family—and you've done nothing to deserve it. No, I really think the best thing would be for me to leave as soon as I have made preparations. I should have left long ago, but I think I waited this long to be sure Sohrab was all right, but he doesn't need me anymore, and I'm not sure an independent India would be the best thing for me and Dinyar."

Dolly looked at her husband, but said nothing.

Phiroze spoke thoughtfully. "Daisy, what is the hurry? I think you may be overwrought for the moment—and understandably so—but in two or three months you will feel differently. Why not give yourself a little more time?"

Daisy shook her head. "In two or three months I will be in London. The longer I wait the harder it gets, and I've thought about this a lot already. I don't feel I belong. You are too kind, both of you, and I don't deserve it. The longer I wait the more time I waste—the more I waste everyone's time. I just want to get on with it. I'm so very sorry to have disappointed you so very badly—after everything you've done for me. I hope, in two or three months, you will not think too badly of me."

Phiroze remained thoughtful, pursing his lips as he spoke. "I do not think badly of you at all—quite the contrary—and I know it will be the same in two or three months—*and* I know I also speak for Dolly—but, since you feel so very strongly about it, I will ask you only to give us a day. Say nothing to anyone about your plans for a day. I would like to talk things over with Dolly, and then let us meet again here tomorrow. Will that be all right with you?"

Daisy's eyebrows rose. "Of course!"

**DAISY DIDN'T UNDERSTAND** the difference a day would make, but she could do no less than give them the time they wished. The next day found them once more in the den, once more with the tea things, Phiroze holding a large envelope, yellow with age, cracked along the edges, which he placed on the arm of the clubchair as Dolly poured for them all. She was smiling, bewildering Daisy still further. "My dear Daisy, have we got a story for you!"

Daisy said nothing, pouring milk, spooning sugar.

Phiroze seconded Dolly's mood. "No one knows, not even Sohrab and Rustom. You will be the first—a measure of our trust. I think the time is ripe—in fact, I think it will do us *all* a heap of good."

Daisy was bewildered, but relieved at how little her story appeared to have affected them. Regret she would have understood, even recriminations, but they seemed glad instead for the opportunity to tell their own story, whatever it was.

Dolly's smile grew in strength. "Don't be surprised, Daisy. It is not a story we ever meant to tell anyone, but we've talked it over and the time is ripe. As you know, I married Kavas first, but Phiroze was my first love—actually, my only love, always."

She squeezed Daisy's knee, asking her patience while she gave her husband a long sweet gaze. Phiroze said nothing, but seemed to glow.

Daisy sipped her tea. "If I may ask, why didn't you marry Phiroze from the beginning?"

"He made me very angry. That's why." She related the story of their courtship, Phiroze inserting details. "He wrote me the sweetest letters for a whole year. I thought for sure he was going to propose, but when we met again he was planning to go to Australia! Without me! To see the southern sky! Where was his head? What was he thinking? What was I supposed to do while he was gallivanting around Australia? I was so hurt—and then Kavas proposed. He gave me the attention I wanted from Phiroze. With hindsight I can see I married Kavas out of spite, but at the time I didn't know any better. I was only fourteen."

"Fourteen! My goodness!"

Dolly shrugged. "It's how things were done—still, in many places. A girl went to school until she was ready for marriage. She wasn't good for anything else—but, in any case, it didn't seem to make a jot of difference to Phiroze."

Daisy looked at Phiroze who shrugged. "I was stupid. I was young. I thought the older brother should marry first. I never imagined he would marry Dolly. I never imagined she would want to marry him. I never even thought of proposing because I assumed Dolly knew how I felt. I assumed she knew we would marry. I was angry myself when I found out she had accepted Kavas—in fact, I was so angry I did the stupidest thing. I joined the army."

"That was actually when I knew, in my heart I knew, that it was Phiroze I wanted—but I kept telling myself that the sensible thing was to marry Kavas. It was, in any case, already too late. The marriage plans were like heavy machinery. I couldn't stop it by myself—and Phiroze was gone, and I had no idea how he felt anyway. He gave me no indication, he made no promise, he said nothing—"

Phiroze smiled, shaking his head. "Arre, still, after all these years, you are making excuses? Really? I said nothing?"

Dolly's eyes flashed. "I was so completely confused, so helpless. If you had just said 'Marry me' it would have been enough. Instead, what did you do? Joined the army! Went off to Mesopotamia! Like it was a jaunt or something! To fight Turks! Big brave man!"

Phiroze said nothing, but couldn't stop smiling.

Dolly turned her attention again to Daisy. "I should have been suspicious from the start, that the Sanjanas never objected to a Dalal—especially not for their Kavas, pearl of the family, green eyes, tall white fellow, England-returned, and all that. We Parsis are crazy for green eyes. It is almost a virtue."

"Not just almost."

"The trouble was, of course, his disorder. He had been to the best doctors, got the best advice. Not to worry, they said, nothing serious. Just don't let him get too excited and he will be all right. No one talked about it, but everyone knew—and if I was just a Dalal I had other attributes in my favor."

Daisy's brow wrinkled at the mention of the disorder, but she said nothing.

"We have many words for it now, and everyday we are having more: mania, melancholia, depression, schizophrenia, manic-depressive." She shrugged. "I had no idea what it all meant, but it seemed everybody was making a big fuss about nothing. He was irritable, they said. He lost his temper. If that was all, it didn't seem very serious. Everybody loses his temper. Very mild form, they said, so I didn't worry. My own daddy died in an asylum, and compared to him Kavas was a Greek god. Why should I complain?"

"I didn't know that about your father."

"I will tell you about it another time if you want—but, again, about Kavas. One day he seemed to disappear. No one knew where he was until I found him under our bed, very quietly drawing pictures—very childish pictures, you know—and speaking like a child, asking for his mummy."

Daisy was now listening intently.

"Of course, his mummy was long dead, but he refused to come out if he couldn't be with his mummy. Finally, I said I would be his mummy, and then he came out. I knew the story, you see, about his mummy. He had told me himself before we married, how she had a heart attack while he was kissing her goodnight. Before that his disorder had been very mild, barely even noticeable, but afterward it became a problem. I didn't understand until I read something by Virginia Woolf. I forget now exactly what she said—something about endless nights, not ending at twelve o'clock, but going into thirteen, fourteen, twenty-five, forty-seven, sixty-four—long tunnel of night without morning. Nothing to prevent such nights, she said. I felt so sorry for him—but what could I do? What could anyone do?"

Daisy still frowned. "How does one get such a disorder?"

"It is genetic. That is why I have always been so worried about Sohrab. He is Kavas's son, as you know, as he never stops telling everyone. Rustom, as you know, is Phiroze's son—and, my God, when he went off to Burma—ohmiGod, I should have seen it coming. It was the same story all over again."

"But if Kavas had it, and if it's genetic, then why not …"

Phiroze nodded. "Of course, I might have it in a minimal form as well. No telling what triggers the mechanism, but so far at least I have been fortunate—even with all the Mespot trouble, even losing my arm, I seem to have pulled through. Knock on wood." He rapped the table.

"Mespot?"

Dolly also rapped the table—for attention. "In a minute. First, let me finish. I was going to say we were so focused on Sohrab that we completely ignored Rustom—and then about the time he was six he surprised us. He was almost as big as Sohrab, even three years younger, and he attacked him without any provocation, any time of the day—with such fury, you wouldn't believe it—saying things like 'Bang, you're dead' and 'Rustom killed Sohrab,' for absolutely no reason that we could see." She stopped, drawing a deep breath. "It's what I had always been afraid of. As you just said, if it's genetic, and if Kavas had it, then why not Phiroze? And if it passed Phiroze by for some reason, why not Sohrab or Rustom? When he attacked Sohrab I went crazy myself. We took him to Dr. Porus Dadabhoy, the son of the fellow who had treated Kavas, also a psychiatrist, and he said there were new methods that were now available, but not in Bombay. He had colleagues in Vienna who would help, so I told Phiroze to take him to Vienna—but when they started talking about electric shocks and all that I said No. We are not going to do that to Rustom. It is not a subject about which doctors know very much even today, and I wasn't going to let them make a guineapig out of our Rustom. I told Phiroze to bring him back home."

"I didn't know that—that you had taken Rustom to Vienna."

Phiroze shrugged. "We were only there three or four weeks, and it is ancient history now. No point rehashing the past."

"Anyway, by the time I realized the severity of Kavas's problem Sohrab had been born. So many times I found him crying in our bedroom—Kavas, I mean. He said he wasn't good enough for me, he said he had stolen me from Phiroze—which, of course, he had, but what could I say? We had a long chat and I convinced him that I loved him, only him—ever since Phiroze had the bee in his bonnet to go to Australia there had been no one else, and for a while it seemed to work—and then …" She looked at Phiroze.

"Then I came back from Mespot—what they called the campaign in Mesopotamia. It was a complete absolute mess."

"We were in Navsari at the time and he showed up without saying anything to anyone, not even telephoning. I was in shock, just from seeing him—and then his arm was missing."

"I couldn't wait to see her. She was all I had thought about for so long, ever since my release—even before that. I didn't want to wait until they came back to Bombay."

"But he never said a word, not one word. Everybody had so many questions, but he said nothing—not one thing about what had happened, hardly even smiled. Just kept looking at me—looking and looking. At no one else he looked, not at his daddy, not at his brother, not at any of our guests and visitors, not even at his nephew—Sohrab was then not even one year old, and I was holding him in my arms as he was looking at me. Even before I noticed his arm was missing I noticed his eyes. Smaller, they were, like marbles, like they had been pushed back into his head—his whole head was smaller, like a skull, his hair was cut so short. He looked like the ghost of himself. You know how Rustom looked after he came back. It was the same with Phiroze."

Daisy looked at Phiroze who could not have been more at ease, composed and attentive.

"One more week we stayed in Navsari—and he did nothing but eat and sleep and look at me. Everytime I saw him he was looking at me. In every other way he was different, but in this one way he was the Phiroze I remembered—actually, he was the Phiroze I remembered multiplied by one hundred and one, so intense he seemed. If it had been anyone else I would have been scared—but he was Phiroze, *my* Phiroze, finally back. I was married, I had a baby son, but all I could think was that he was alive, he had come back, and that was a lot, that was a lovely thing. We could do nothing, of course—didn't even think about doing anything—but it was enough that he was back. His presence was enough."

Dolly spoke more slowly, almost reluctantly. Phiroze gave her a questioning look, tapping the fraying envelope on the armrest, raising his head in question.

Dolly shook her head. "About Mespot you can tell her, but I will finish it off. I want to tell the last part of the story." She turned to Daisy. "For the whole week he said nothing. First no one wanted to leave him alone. Then, on the day before we were to return, everybody had gone for their evening walk. Usually, we were gone about two hours, taking snacks and drinks, sitting and eating in the open, coming back when it was dark. On that last evening I myself did not go. I had to pack for Kavas and myself. Sohrab, of course, I kept with me also, sleeping in his little cot."

Phiroze leaned forward. "Let me."

Dolly leaned back in the sofa. "All right."

Phiroze looked at Daisy. "I may have said nothing, but there was so much I wanted to say—but only to Dolly. I didn't want to talk about it as if it were some great adventure story. I didn't care about the others, but I wanted Dolly to know—so when I knew she wasn't going I also excused myself. I think I said I was tired or something. Everyone was so solicitous about my return I could have said I was going to see the King and they would have said Yes, of course, of course, take as long as you like."

Dolly smiled. "Really, he could have said that—anything he could have said."

"There was no one in the house except me and Dolly—and Sohrab, but he was just a baby. The servants were also there, but in their hut, outside. You know where it is."

Daisy nodded.

"As soon as they were gone I went to Dolly's room—the same bedroom you and Sohrab take when we are in Navsari." He took a sip of tea. "There is a window, as you know, looking from the bedroom into the hallway. For whatever reason, I couldn't bring myself to say anything. Instead, I placed a chair silently by the window in the hallway and sat watching Dolly packing."

Dolly touched Daisy's arm. "And all the time I thought he was sleeping in his room. Such a shock I got, I can tell you, when I saw him, just sitting there, looking at me from the window."

Phiroze shook his head. "I just didn't know how to approach her. I didn't know what to say."

"*He* didn't know what to say, and *I* didn't know what to say. Finally I said, 'What is the matter?' and he just shook his head, wouldn't say a word, not a word, not even then, but there was a look on his face I will never forget—like a prisoner looking out of a window, with that starved look. Of course, the window was really there, and it is barred as you know—which only made him look that much more like a prisoner. Finally, again, I said, 'Is there something you want to tell me?' This time he nodded and I called him into the room, put away everything I was doing, and I said, 'Tell me what has happened. I want to know everything that has happened.' Sohrab, I must say, was being a very good baby through all this—just kept on sleeping and sleeping."

Phiroze raised the envelope in his hand and Dolly nodded, surrendering the floor. "It is a very old story now, the Mespot campaign—of course, that is not what it was called then." He smiled at Daisy. "I think it might be best if I gave you a little background."

Daisy smiled: Phiroze was always thorough, always courteous.

"You see, the Tigris and Euphrates rivers meet at Qurna, a hundred and some miles inland from the Persian Gulf, and their confluence, known as the Shatt-al-Arab waterway, flows into the Gulf near Abadan. Our objective was to secure the fuel supply for the Royal Navy, most of which came from the Abadan oilfields—and that was *it*. That was the whole ball of wax. A convoy sailed from Bombay to garrison Abadan in October of 1914—and that, they did. Had we been content simply to meet our objective, there would have been no Mespot—but instead the Government of India argued that we should dislodge the Turkish garrison at Basra, about seventy-five miles inland. Otherwise, we would have been looking constantly over our shoulders from Abadan to Basra for the Turks." He shrugged. "And that was where we came in, the Sixth Poona Division, to dislodge the Turkish garrison at Basra."

Phiroze opened the frayed envelope with his practiced left hand, extracting a black and white photograph the size of a postcard wrapped in cellophane and passed it to Daisy. "This snap is my prize possession, some of the fellows in my platoon. It was taken before we left Bombay by someone who came to see us off."

The photograph was grainy, browning with age, ten turbaned men in uniform, grouped around a gun battery, brandishing rifles and smiles. Daisy shook her head. "They look so jolly for men going off to war. If not for their uniforms and artillery I would have thought they were off on a picnic."

"Well, remember, we thought of war as a chance to redeem ourselves—reap good fellowship, build character, that sort of thing. We were always joking, calling one another Sinbad—he was from Basra, you know, and here we were, sailing for Basra, maybe to be carried off by a roc, maybe to find the elephant graveyard. In any case, no one expected the war to last beyond December."

Daisy nodded, staring at the photograph; she had heard stories of men going to war. "Right—except for that fellow there, with the sour puss. He must have known what was going to happen."

Phiroze laughed. "That's me."

Daisy held the photograph close. "Oh, I say, Phiroze, I *am* sorry. I would never have guessed—not with that turban."

Phiroze grinned. "Part of the uniform, but I do have a sour puss, don't I—but I wasn't thinking about the war. I was thinking about Dolly marrying my brother. In those early days I could think about nothing else. Afterward, it became a different story. Afterward, I could think about nothing except how to get back alive." He tapped the photograph. "These men, I owe them my life—especially this fellow, Rajan Sarkar, our corporal."

Daisy looked where he pointed, to a man with a round face, rounder for its grin.

"I would even go so far as to say my sour puss helped. Rajan, sterling fellow that he was, tried to cheer me up on our way to the Gulf, telling me the war was going to be over soon, everything was going to be all right—you know, the usual things—and I told him it wasn't the war. I told him I had joined the army because I *wanted* to die, I told him the girl I loved was marrying someone else, and that turned the tide in my favor. I became a romantic figure for the men, and once they knew they could not have been more sympathetic—and then, when Rajan told them I was a Sanjana, they could not have been more solicitous. You see, they were not well-to-do, none of them. Some, like Rajan, were career soldiers, but many were just laborers looking to make money for their families. The Sanjana name didn't mean much to them, but Rajan explained that I was rich, and if they took care of me then I would take care of them and their families after the war was over. It became our standard joke, but when push came to shove it was a joke that saved my life. I'm no fighter, there were times I was just paralyzed with fear, but one or other of them was always looking out for me. The ugly irony is that I was the only one who wanted to die—and I was the only one who survived."

Daisy's mouth opened, but she said nothing, releasing her breath in a sigh, pursing her lips.

"They saw I was different from the start. I kept to myself, I was a Parsi—my speech, mannerisms, education, complexion, everything was different. Rajan called me their token Angrez. I took it as a compliment—not to be counted as an Angrez, but to be accepted by them—for the generosity with which they accepted someone whose life had been so much more privileged than theirs." He grinned. "It helped that I was given the status of a pagul for what I was doing—and I suppose a romantic is a kind of madman, certainly taking it to the extreme that I had. Anyway, to get back to the campaign ..."

Daisy continued to study the photograph, and he continued his story.

"The trouble from the very beginning was transport. There were no roads. We advanced along the river and along the banks, more than twelve thousand fighting men, four thousand dhobis and cooks and servants, two thousand mules and ponies and camels, not to mention sloops and steamers and barges and gunboats and God knows what else—and I've said nothing about the cavalry. It was a slog. We waded ankledeep in mud through temperatures of a hundred and twenty degrees, mosquitoes big as pingpong balls, the ground alive with sandflies. Somehow we made it—but some of us were luckier than others.

"It was raining on the day we advanced on Basra, raindrops heavy as bees, the air itself heavy with water—impossible to aim, barely possible even to walk. It was the artillery that gave us the edge, but even after we had the Turks on the run we couldn't follow them. The ground was too muddy, certainly for the cavalry—but something happened again that day to consolidate my image as a pagul."

Daisy looked at Dolly who sat like a statue, almost unblinking, staring into space.

"I never knew what it was—a mine, grenades, mortar fire, something else—but there was an explosion, maybe more than one, just a couple of yards from us. I remember flying through the air, nothing more. When I regained consciousness I was all right, but the men around me—Ashok and Avinash Ghate, Tickery Timblo, Gopal Sachdev, Raju Mahadev, Maxim D'Mello, Joseph Mazumdar—" He stopped talking, throat constricting, jaw trembling, but gritting his teeth, clenching his fist, he continued. "Sorry ... I haven't talked about this in a while."

Daisy squeezed his hand.

He returned the squeeze. "It is all decades ago now, but all those men—they were all ... killed." He wondered how much he might say without soiling his memory of the men, recalling the ground squelching with blood, steam rising like wraiths from bodies, bones peering from sacks of skin, screams of men and animals lacing the explosions, the battlefield a yawning graveyard, the devil's operating chamber, nightmare landscapes stretching to the horizon. "War has a way of making men superstitious. What was very likely a coincidence acquired the aura of a miracle. I didn't know what to think myself, but couldn't help wondering if they had absorbed my portion of the blast—consciously or unconsciously, if they had died so I might live. What had started as something of a joke was acquiring an iron reality. In any event, Basra became ours in November of 1914, too easily for our own good."

"*Too* easily?"

Phiroze sighed. "It gave us a false sense of security. Next, forty miles upriver from Basra, was Qurna, the reputed site of the Garden of Eden. They called the strategy Forward Defense: just as we had needed to capture Basra to secure Abadan, we would need to capture Qurna to secure Basra; and since the capture of Basra had been a cakewalk, we went on to capture Qurna—and, again, unfortunately, we were easily victorious. December of 1914 we captured Qurna, losing just three hundred men to fifteen hundred Turks. It was like that all the way, almost up to Baghdad. In order to secure Qurna we took Amara, another hundred meandering miles up the Tigris; and in order to secure Amara we took Kut, yet another hundred and some miles upriver from Amara; and we did it all without too many casualties—but our line of communication with the Gulf thinned to the snapping point."

He sighed again, collecting his thoughts. "Then there were the floods. Every spring the snow melts on the Zagreb Mountains, swelling the rivers, flooding the plains—very likely a similar flood inspired the story of Noah. We spent that whole spring in Qurna, almost four months, consolidating our gains, strengthening our lines of communication with the Gulf. Any kind of advance would have been impossible in all that water."

He stopped momentarily, sighing again. "When we began the advance again it was on two fronts. We entered Kut by water and by land. I was on a gunboat between Bharat Bandukvala and Harsha Malhotra. We had the advantage, of course, since we were attacking their flank as well by land—but at one point Bharat Bandukvala stood up, almost as if he were presenting a target. Sure enough, he attracted a fusillade of bullets, but seemed too dazed to understand what was happening. He got shot in the shoulder before I pulled him down to safety, and I got shot myself in the bargain, two bullets, my hand and my wrist—not serious, and as it turned out later a blessing in disguise, but Harsha was furious. Was I trying to get myself killed? Was all their trouble to be for nothing? Had they made it their business to ensure my safety just so I could die a hero?

"I was so surprised. They truly believed they had put themselves in harm's way for my sake—and, of course, I could not be so ungrateful as to disagree. They needed something to die for—and I became their cause, for what I could do for their families. They were villagefolk at heart, sentimental and straightforward, with simple answers to complex questions—but I came to wonder myself if they might not after all be right, if I had simply been too obtuse, too egotistical, to see the service they had rendered." He shrugged. "One thing was for sure: what had begun as a joke was a joke no longer. My wellbeing during the war had come to mean the wellbeing of their families after the war. Harsha made it quite plain, I owed them my life, nothing less—and I had no right to be so careless."

Dolly pushed his cup forward and Phiroze sipped before resuming his story. "Next was Ctesiphon, just twenty miles south of Baghdad, where our advance was finally checked, but I didn't go." He milked his sleeve. "My hand, you see—bandaged, but temporarily useless. I stayed in Kut for the duration of the twenty and some days that the troops were gone. They were exhausted when they set out, and returned in a rout. We had been outnumbered two to one. We had won against worse odds before, but the Turks at Ctesiphon were better prepared, with extensive deployments of mines and artillery, camouflaged trenches on either side of the river. Instead of scattering as before, they regrouped—*and* they had reinforcements, newly victorious and battle-hardened troops from Gallipoli, not to mention supplies from Baghdad in their backyard whereas our line of communication now stretched almost four hundred miles to Basra." He shrugged. "We lost hundreds on the flight back to Kut, not to mention dozens of ships."

Phiroze sipped again from his cup. "That was the beginning of the end. Hindsight showed that General Townshend who commanded our troops made one bad decision after another. The Turks at Ctesiphon were about to retreat, but he retreated first. He did not expect the Turks to follow, but follow they did. Choosing to retreat he should have retreated all the way to Basra, but he chose to hold off the Turks at Kut. Instead, the Turks held him, circling the town, cutting off lines of communication. He insisted on immediate relief, giving the British time to organize only small rescue efforts, all of which were defeated, instead of a larger force which might have prevailed. Townshend was responsible for almost sixteen thousand men, including noncoms— but he also maintained many of the residents in Kut, feeding them in an effort to win their allegiance, only to learn later they had buried vast stores of grain which might have saved the garrison. Townshend hadn't even bothered to look."

Phiroze pursed his lips, recalling the makeshift hospital, inmates of cork and wire and cardboard, eyes peering from tunnels, concave cheeks and torsos, dying of cholera, typhus, and scurvy through lack of supplies, continually incontinent and starving, Indians accustomed to strict vegetarian diets reduced to eating horseflesh and muleflesh, even cats and dogs toward the end. They would have been better off starving, but instead had been given opium pills to blank out the hunger. He shook his head again. "The bottom line was we had overextended ourselves. The tide had turned. The siege began on fifth December and lasted five months. To top it off it was winter again, temperatures dropped from one hundred and twenty degrees to just twenty degrees. Then, something happened, another miracle, just for me."

He took a deep breath. "You see, up to now, whatever the men said, whatever I said to them, however much I appreciated their regard, I had attributed my continuing safety to providence more than their protection. Chance had provided me with a romantic story and coincidence had fueled the myth. In the heat of battle it is every man for himself, but something happened to render all my doubts finally irrelevant—thanks to Rajan Sarkar, the corporal in that snap."

Daisy looked again at the photograph, at the round face rounder for its grin.

"It was on Christmas Eve, the Turks attacked our makeshift fort, and Rajan … at one point … he simply threw himself at me. I didn't understand, I hadn't seen the shell whistling its way toward …" Phiroze was once more speechless. Rajan had thrown him on his back and spreadeagled himself to cover him like a second skin—before growing suddenly weightless. His back had ripped open releasing fluids coagulating around Phiroze, encasing him in a gelatinous mold. He had tried to hold Rajan close, tried to hug him, but he had hugged bones, a ribcage clawing his chest, a skull like a lover's head lolling over his shoulder. The smell of shit was overpowering, but in that moment of sacrifice everything pertaining to Rajan became sacred, and he had breathed the odor as if to make it part of himself, wallowing in the clay that had once been his friend.

Phiroze swallowed, but still could not speak. Daisy squeezed his hand again, gripping and rubbing his arm, seeming to understand what he couldn't put into words. "My God, Phiroze, I'm so sorry. I'm so glad … I'm so grateful you're still here."

He shook his head, eyes glistening, speaking again though his voice still trembled. "*I* am the one who is sorry. All this happened so long ago, more than thirty years—and here I am, an old soldier, blubbering like a baby."

Dolly shook her head. "We never forget, how can we, what those men did—and we kept our word. We started a trust for some of the men after Phiroze got back, from which the families still get a monthly stipend. What we spend in a week they can live on for a year."

Phiroze said nothing immediately. The blast that had eviscerated Rajan had, again miraculously, barely touched him. "Then, in April, again, the floods, Noah's floods. The rivers swelled, the whole plain between them was underwater. Six o'clock one morning they came, black as oil, in a deluge like a dam had burst, like a wall rushing toward us. In the trenches we were immersed to our necks in seconds. As someone said: Kut Khuttum—Hindi for 'finished'—as perhaps you know?"

Daisy nodded.

"Finally, on the twenty-ninth of April, after we had destroyed our arms and ammunition, Townshend surrendered. Ten thousand combatants went into captivity, the highest number up to that time that the British had ever surrendered—and this was a particular blow to British prestige, coming on the heels of Gallipoli."

He shrugged. "Less than a year later Kut was back in British hands, so was Baghdad—just like Burma—but for us it was too late. We were to be marched to Anatolia for internment, all ten thousand of us." He shook his head again. "We were like matchstick men—be*fore* the march." He recalled rows of skeletons, clavicles and breastbones protruding like fleurs-de-lis, like crucifices embedded in their chests. "The march began on sixth May. We reached Baghdad on the eighteenth."

He paused, wondering how much to say. "Easily the worst part of the campaign. At least, before, we could fire back at the Turks, we could run for cover. Now we were at their mercy, no shade, the barest provisions. Those who lagged were whipped, kicked, beaten with sticks, clubbed with rifle butts, gagged with sand in their mouths. Some of the men—God knows what it was, but their mouths hung open in a rictus, dripping a green ooze, flies buzzing in and out, crawling on their lips—and the men too oblivious even to brush them aside. Many of them, their feet were bleeding. They had either bartered their boots for food or had them stolen in the night—or simply taken from them."

He had slept at night in a fetal position, wrapped around boots tied to his wrist, careful not to attract attention. He had been in better shape than many of the men, fortunate not to have endured the miserable fight and flight from Ctesiphon—and not above eating horseflesh. He had sustained wounds other than to his hand, shrapnel which to this day stiffened his legs when the temperature dropped, but hardly deserving mention in the larger scheme of events. Someone had watched over him, and he was glad enough simply to credit the men. "I was lucky. I had incurred very few permanent injuries—my feet were blistered, but I still had my boots. I was exhausted, but so were we all. I had a bit of a fever, but so did everyone—how could you not in that sun. Even my hand seemed to be doing all right except for a smell, like rotten meat, from bubbles of gas, bluish green bubbles of gas in my arm. By the time we got to Baghdad I realized it was gangrenous, I knew I was going to lose either my arm or my life, but that was also when I had my best luck since I had joined the army."

Dolly interjected, smiling. "Mr. Brissell."

Phiroze nodded. "Mr. Brissell, the American Consul at Baghdad, was an old family friend. He had been our guest for dinner in Bombay. Of course, he didn't recognize me, but I made myself known, and it was fortunate that I did. The Turks had been paid and he had been authorized to send five hundred men to hospital and back to Basra.

Thanks to him, I was one of the five hundred. Of the ten thousand, four thousand died on the march—not to put too fine a point on it, but they might as well have been murdered for the way they were treated. Townshend was also interned, but in luxury on an island near Constantinople. In fact, he was treated so well he spoke glowingly of his captors, not endearing himself to his men about whose experience he must have known. All this, of course, is only the gist—but perhaps enough for now. I have talked altogether too much."

Phiroze didn't like talking about Kut, wishing neither to trivialize nor dramatize the experience, nor trusting himself to do justice to the men. Dolly understood his discomfort and turned to Daisy. "Mespot is no big secret, it was in all the newspapers, but what happened afterward we have told no one."

Daisy nodded, saying nothing.

"Believe me, Daisy, we have discussed the matter thoroughly. There is no one else in the world we would trust with our secret—but maybe it will help to put to rest some of your doubts about not belonging with us."

Again Daisy said nothing.

Dolly took a deep breath. "Actually, not much more to tell. After Phiroze finished his story you cannot imagine how I felt. All my fault, it was, that he had joined the army, that he had lost his arm—and all because he loved me, and I loved him, and we were too stupid to acknowledge it. Oh, my God, my dear Daisy, I cannot even begin to tell you all the things I was feeling. We were suddenly hugging each other, and kissing each other, and telling each other how much we loved each other, laughing and crying at the same time. I was so happy, and at the same time so much in conflict—and then, I swear, I heard the click of the trigger first, and then the bang. Kavas had come back from the walk alone. He had told everyone he had a headache or something, but I knew better. He had sensed something, whatever it was between me and Phiroze. He had known ever since Phiroze returned. Then I saw him, just for an instant, through the window, sitting in the same chair I had just seen Phiroze—the muzzle of the rifle was in his mouth. His head just disappeared into a geyser. I can still hear the sound, not the shot so much but the splashing afterward—like water spattered on mud, so innocuous it was. How much he had seen, how much he had heard, who knows, who cares. It was the end—end of everything, it seemed."

Dolly's face turned to stone, her voice a monotone. "The shot alone would not have brought the servants running, we might only have been shooting at the monkeys or something—but Fakhro told me afterward I would not stop screaming, I and baby Sohrab. I have no memory of anything, and Fakhro was himself then just a boy, but he said that was what had brought them all running—double screaming, me and the baby. Phiroze, on the other hand, was sitting on the bed, saying nothing, he might have been unconscious except that he was sitting. The next day, I found a piece of brain or something still in the soapdish in the basin in the hallway and began screaming all over again. Phiroze became even more silent than before, said nothing for days, even after we got back to Bombay.

"We never told anyone. If anyone asked, it was an accident. No one knew. Maybe he was cleaning the rifle, maybe he dropped it, maybe God knows what else, and of course no one asked questions. Afterward, when Phiroze began to talk again, he said we should tell people what had happened, out of respect for Kavas, take our punishment, but I said No." She shook her head violently. "This was our chance finally for happiness. We would have been fools to waste Kavas's sacrifice. The rest you know. We got married and lived happily ever after."

Phiroze was no less stony than Dolly. "My Lady Macbeth! *Screw your courage to the sticking-place*, she said, and she was right. After what had happened all we had was each other. Without each other we were as good as lost—might as well have followed Kavas there and then. What would have been the point of saying anything? We would have been the only ones to suffer."

Dolly looked like a parade that had passed. "But guilt there was—so much guilt. How could we get married after what had happened—and, still, what else could we do?" She shook her head.

Phiroze's tone echoed Dolly's. "Daisy, we are not saying your guilt is the same, nothing like that—but we overcame, and you will too. We did what we had to do. We were his legacy. We had to become the best people we knew how to be. Maybe knowing this will help you."

Staring at her, suddenly silent, they seemed to want vindication, even absolution for soiling a memory perhaps best left unresurrected. Daisy had remained silent through the confession, perhaps encouraging the perception that she disapproved, and they stared like sphinxes, eyes of stone, awaiting her judgment—but knowing their secret she could penetrate their eyes, peer to the rough root of their lives, glorious as a star for what they had endured, what they had sacrificed for their happiness, what they had made of themselves.

She recalled her own brief shining moments with Basil, the memory aglow within forever despite the outcome. The trick was to make it glow through the shell that seemed since to have encrusted her, made her no less a sphinx—to bring the memory to bear on everything she did, make it the hammer to break through the sphinx. To do other than Dolly and Phiroze had done would have been an immeasurable ingratitude, an offence against God—no less an offence for her to condemn them, or to stay herself in the skin of the sphinx. She spoke firmly. "In your place, I hope I would have done exactly the same thing. I hope I would have had your courage."

For a long moment no one said a word. Dolly's eyes glistened. She was the first to speak. "Of course you would, my dear. You are the daughter of my heart. We cannot choose our children, but you I have chosen." She looked at Phiroze. "We have both chosen."

Phiroze's voice trembled. "Anything you want, my dear, you have only to ask."

Daisy's eyes glistened no less than Dolly's and she raised her handkerchief to her face. "We *are* a bunch of crybabies, aren't we?"

Dolly smiled, wiping her eyes. "I think you might say we have earned the right."

Daisy took a deep breath. "The question is whether and when to tell Sohrab—about Alphonse and Dinyar." There was another question, perhaps deeper and more profound, what she would tell Dinyar himself about his father, but she would deal with that question when Dinyar was older.

"That is up to you. That is your business, no one else's. Any help we can give, you have only to ask." Dolly couldn't stop smiling. She had wrapped herself so long in guilt that relief had turned the ground under her feet to air. She recalled Santayana, *those who couldn't remember the past were condemned to repeat it*—but Phiroze had countered with Heraclitus, *you couldn't step into the same river twice*. Considering all the wars that had been waged to end all wars, the one thing to be learned from history was that nothing was learned from history. History was no more dependable than astrology in predicting the future. All repetitions were repetitions with variations, and variations made important differences. Sohrab honored his father's memory like no other, often slighting Phiroze in the process, but in losing his hand he more closely resembled Phiroze than even Rustom. Her smile widened as a second irony crystallized. "There is a kind of poetic justice about this, you know. Sohrab goes to such pains to let everyone know that Phiroze is his stepfather and Rustom his stepbrother—and now here he is, himself a stepfather."

Daisy pursed her lips: not only a stepfather, but the stepfather of his servant's son. "That's actually my fear, that he will recognize Dinyar now only as a son who is no longer a son—persona non grata, in a manner of speaking. He is *not*, after all, his son."

Dolly was quick to respond. "Through no fault of Dinyar's."

"But no fault either of Sohrab's—my fault, entirely my fault."

"My dear, you are at once too arrogant and too hard on yourself. You saved his life. All debts are paid where that is concerned." Another irony suggested itself to Dolly about which she said nothing: her mother had been killed by a servant—and a servant had died so her son might live. She had flashed back more frequently in recent days to the murder of her mother, the photograph of her father ripped in eighths and sixteenths, felt herself witness to the pulse, the heartbeat and flow of the universe, the clockwork of gods in their glory, balancing events through space and time, the moving finger moving on, dominoes clack-clack-clack-clack-clacking.

Daisy's lips remained pursed. Outside the world went its worldly way, crows among the palms, kites crisscrossing the sky, horses clipclopping along Cooperage Road drawing carriages amid motorists and pedestrians, boys at cricket in the maidan, girls jumping rope in the bandstand where a uniformed band would play in the afternoon around which children would ride ponies in the evening—but in the room the moment congealed to a point of clarity. She nodded. "Thank you, Dolly—and Phiroze. I know what I have to do next."

Dolly smiled, squeezing Phiroze's hand. "That is a lot."

# AFTERWORD

My grandmother, who lived in Navsari, was a great storyteller. She was also one of the models for Dolly Sanjana. My brother and I grew up in Bombay, but paid her annual visits, much like the Sanjana brothers. Before going to sleep the three of us would lie together in her wide four-poster bed, mosquito netting pulled close, my grandmother in the middle, and she would launch into tales from the Ramayana, Mahabharata, Shah-Nama, Arabian Nights, Hans Christian Anderson, and Brothers Grimm—or she would make up stories. She knew how to stretch a tale, how to conclude with a cliffhanger, much like Scheherazade even without the threat of the sword of Damocles.

One of her stories was of a shikari who had bagged a maneater and brought home an orphaned cub to raise as a pet. The story ran much as it does in *A Googly in the Compound*. The shikari wakes from sleep to find the grown cub licking a cut on his hand. When he attempts to remove his hand the cub growls and the shikari realizes it may pounce, even maul or kill him if he gets too proprietary about his hand—and calls his servant to shoot the cub without further ado.

The story stayed with me, becoming gnarled and tangled with time. The hunter developed into a solicitor and his family, the family developed a history, the servant developed a grudge, and I provided him with an opportunity to feed his grudge. I cannot say how many of my decisions were conscious and how many unconscious, but I started with my grandmother's story of the shikari, I added a woman to complicate the issue between the servant and the master, I made her English to highlight the differences.

The individual stories fell neatly into place once I had the long central scene settled. New episodes swam continually into the narrative as I turned to research the elements with which I was

## A Googly in the Compound

unfamiliar: astronomy, coelacanths, the Kut campaign, London between the wars, the communist party in India, the Silver Jubilee of George V, and so on until the pattern became clear.

I named Dolly's sons Sohrab and Rustom, taking off from the legendary story from the Shah-Nama and planning to develop a rivalry between them to parallel the rivalry between Kavas and Phiroze, but that aspect of the story remained mute when the novel was first published under the title, *Servant, Master, Mistress*. It bothered me that Rustom did not have much of a story of his own in that edition, but I let it go because I had run out of storylines and rationalized that his story might well be that he was too effete to have his own story—until a friend of my mother told me a story about her father who had been a doctor in Rangoon at the time of the Japanese invasion. She and her family were sent by boat hugging the shore to Chittagong. In Chittagong they boarded a train followed by a ferry across the Brahmaputra and another train to her father's brother's home in Calcutta. They might otherwise have taken the boat directly to Calcutta from Rangoon across the Bay of Bengal, but the Bay was then lousy with German submarines.

Her father was held back by the British to help fight epidemics during their retreat, but left to find his own way finally out of the country. He was stopped by four British tommies along the way who commandeered his jeep and left him to negotiate a journey of about 900 miles from Rangoon to Calcutta on his own.

Astonishingly, he found his way to Calcutta amid tens of thousands of refugees who died, some of whom I attempted to imagine for the novel—but he arrived at his brother's flat more dead than alive to have the door slammed in his face by his sister-in-law, too scared by his appearance to recognize him.

# AFTERWORD

That story had a happy ending. Ironically, he came across his jeep again during his journey, the four tommies still in their seats, throats slit from ear to ear—but more to my purpose the story lit my imagination again. I saw Rustom in Burma and began researching the campaign. Learning that the 17th Indian Division had been formed in Ahmednagar, I realized that would be Rustom's point of entry, and coming across Seagrave's memoir and Stilwell's diary I realized he would join them on their walkout. His new story also allowed me to circumvent a bit of melodrama I had invented in the original manuscript—about which, the less said the better.

The story about Colin McPhedran (page 368), which unleashes Rustom's floodburst after his return from Burma, had a similar effect on me if not quite so intensely. Rustom would be glad to know that Colin McPhedran went on as his mother had prophesied to meet many good people in the world. He also wrote a memoir about the exodus titled, *White Butterflies*, and died peacefully on June 3, 2010 though he branded himself to the end of his days, despite husbandhood and fatherhood, despite a wide circle of friends, despite great worldly success, a refugee.

On a superficial level this is a colonial novel and colonialism may seem outdated in a postcolonial world—but on a more profound level colonialism provides the clothing for themes of race and class, master and servant, cause and effect as ineluctably as postcolonialism. These are themes longerlasting than their clothing, longerlasting than either colonialism or postcolonialism. Colonialism is with us today, illustrated among other things by the unrepresentative incarceration of Blacks and Hispanics in the US, healthcare and tax systems unabashedly favoring the wealthy, bankers and brokers exonerated of grand larceny, and presidents of manslaughter in the name of war against countries helpless to assert their rights.

# A Googly in the Compound

Sohrab's meditation on marriage (page 166), another pervasive theme, is exemplified by many of the couplings in the book, most glaringly perhaps that of a nonfictional couple: Comrade Sak (the communist Indian member of the British Parliament) and his wife (a quarryman's daughter and Derbyshire waitress). The novel illustrates that mutual differences may bring disparate couples together, and mutual dependencies may keep them together, but only mutual affection makes the togetherness worthwhile. Dolly and Phiroze provide the best example, also Basil and Shirin though their story is peripheral—and Guy and Lavinia though they provide a contrary example. There is also hope for Daisy and Sohrab, despite their differences, depending on how Sohrab receives news of his son's parentage—and, taking the analogy to its apotheosis, for others willing to adjust to the cross of their particular circumstances.

# GLOSSARY

Acouri: *eggs scrambled and spiced*
Angrez: *English*
Arre: *Oh, ah (an exclamation)*
Arre baap re: *Oh, my God!*
Attchha: *okay*
Baba log: *little people, children*
Babu: *uneducated person*
Bageecha: *garden, park*
Bai: *madam*
Bailo: *sissy*
Baksheesh: *tip, wage*
Bandar: *monkey*
Banduk: *gun*
Bapavaji: *paternal grandfather*
Bas: *enough*
Bawa: *colloquial for Parsi*
Behenchot: *sister-fucker*
Bhel: *snack of grams and cereals with sweet and spicy sauces*
Bor: *a kind of date*
Bundobast: *arrangement*
Burfi: *a kind of sweet*
Burra: *big*

Carom: *a game for two or four players, played on a square wooden board with pockets at each corner, into which round black and white coins are struck*
Chaddi: *underpants*
Chapati: *wheat flatbread*
Chappals: *sandals*
Chaprasi: *peon, menial worker*
Chatai: *cane mat easily rolled and stored for board games to be played on the floor, or to sleep on*
Chaung: *creek*
Chhota: *small*
Choli: *blouse worn with a sari*
Dah: *long knife or sword with a gently curving single-edged blade*
Dal: *lentils*
Ganga: *washerwoman, but the word is flexible enough to encompass a cook as easily as a woman working on a construction site*
Garbar: *noise, disturbance*

## A Googly in the Compound

Ghati: *unmannerly lower-class person*
Gulmohor: *tree with red and orange flowers in spring*
Han: *yes (the "n" is silent, but nasal)*
Hanuman: *monkey god who accompanied Ram and Laxman to rescue Sita from Ravana*
Harami: *bastard*
Jaldi: *quickly*
Jalebi: *sweet which looks like an orange pretzel with a hard casing and soft center*
Jhinga: *shrimp*
Jiddi: *obstinate*
Khuttum: *finished, the end*
Lal dava: *red medicine, Mercurochrome*
Madarchot: *mother-fucker*
Maha Yogi: *great yogi*
Maidan: *cross between a park and meadow*
Mali: *gardener*
Mamra: *puffed rice*

Memsahib: *madam*
Mithai: *sweet*
Mohollah: *neighborhood*
Mota Bajar: *big market*
Naryal: *coconut*
Naryalpani: *coconut water*
Nimbu: *lime*
Nimbupani: *lime water*
Nullah: *ravine, dry riverbed*
Pagul: *madman*
Penda: *a kind of sweet*
Sahib: *sir*
Salo: *swine*
Sambhar: *a kind of deer*
Seth: *sir*
Sev: *crisp gram flour noodles*
Sev-ganthia: *deepfried snacks from chickpea flour*
Swaraj: *independence, self-rule*
Talao: *pool, well, pond*
Thali: *metal dish to eat from*
Toddy: *fermented drink made from the sap of palm trees*
Wadi: *neighborhood, alley*
Zayat: *rest house*

Boman Desai was bound for a career in market analysis when a chance encounter with Sir Edmund Hillary, his first hero, turned him back to writing. He had his first break when an elegant elderly woman submitted half a dozen of his stories for publication to *Debonair* (in Mumbai)—all of which were published, but the woman vanished and her identity remains a mystery to this day. His second break came when another elegant elderly woman, Diana Athill, published his first novel, *The Memory of Elephants*. Desai is best known for that novel, published subsequently by the University of Chicago Press and for TRIO, *a Novel Biography of the Schumanns and Brahms* which was awarded the Kirkus star and listed among their Best Books of 2016. The book was subsequently transcribed into an opera, *Clar*a, and may now be seen on youtube. Desai has published other novels, won about a dozen awards, and taught fiction at Truman College and Roosevelt University (both in Chicago), and the University of Southern Maine. He is also a musician and composer, with among other things a symphony and piano concerto to his credit (though yet to find performances). You may learn more about him at bomandesai.com. He may be reached at boman@core.com.

Printed in Great Britain
by Amazon